PARANORMAL HUNTERS EPISODE 1

BLACK WITCH
magic

MILA NICKS

This is a work of fiction. Names, characters, places, and incidents either are the product of the author's imagination or are used fictitiously. Any resemblance to actual persons, living or dead, events, or locales is entirely coincidental.

First paperback edition October 2020

To all the bookish girls out there…

PROLOGUE

HALLOWEEN 1976

Lightning flashed on the horizon, illuminating the dead-end street. The earsplitting crack of thunder soon followed, so loud the road vibrated underneath Aurora Langston's bumbling, dented-in Datsun. The rain fell at a bullet's pace, fast and hard, blurring shapes in the car windows. The windshield wipers whooshed back and forth to keep up, wiping away the droplets only for new ones to plunk down.

Aurora pulled over to the curb in front of 1221 Gifford Lane and turned off the engine. 1221 was dark. The gothic home towered over its neighbors, a landmark of sorts. Compared to the mild-mannered Cape Cods, the house looked downright obscene. Its hunter-green shade stood out against the purpled sky, offset by earthy-brown trimming. The many stained-glass windows and panels of carved stone didn't help. But probably most unforgettable was the home's tower, the turret rising high like a watchful eye over Brimrock.

Trick-or-treaters in clown and ghost costumes floated by as Aurora got out of the Datsun and glared at 1221 Gifford.

Their childish giggles faded away, replaced only by the trickle of heavy downpour. The lights might have been off, but she knew they were inside. Aurora unscrewed her jaw and then grit her teeth. Her feathered, honey-colored hair lost its volume within seconds, pelted by endless raindrops, but she didn't care. She shook her bangs out of her face and crossed the empty road.

The doorknob wouldn't budge. A ball of red light glowed above her palm and she directed its heat onto the brass handle. It melted within seconds and prompted a smirk out of her. The shadows inside swallowed her up. She wasn't fazed wandering into the darkness. She drifted up the staircase onto the second floor and turned down the hall that led to the room she sought. Her footsteps were soundless, her presence itself as unseen as any ghost. The last door at the end of the hall stood out among the others. The moment she had been waiting for was so close yet still another sneaking second away.

Their snores were soft and unsuspecting. Two heaps in the bed curled into each other. For a long while, she stood at the foot of the bed and stared, dripping a pool of rainwater onto the carpet. The betrayal burned her lungs. It spliced right through her and broke her heart into pieces. She went from hot tears pricking her eyes to anger flushing her skin to a cold grin spreading on her lips.

She had given up years, spent so long imagining a future where they were together—her own happy ending at last. She had played nice, played fair. She had trusted and believed. And now she was left foolish. The brutal slap in the face of it had her seeing red. What John didn't count on was that she wasn't what he believed her to be. She was no regular woman. She wasn't going quietly without a fight. Without the revenge she deserved.

He half stirred with a snort and then rolled over onto his side. The smaller heap remained still, mostly silent but fast asleep. The perfect opening for her to do what she had been dreaming of since she discovered the ugly truth. Coming up on his side of the bed, she slanted her head sideways for a closer look at him and his dopey face. His expression was blank, no discernible emotion arranged on his features. No guilt. No regret. No care at all for what he'd done.

Lightning blinked in then out on the night sky. For one millisecond it highlighted the bedroom before disappearing and darkness won out. The thunder rumbled louder, sounding closer than it had even when cruising in her Datsun. Neither of them woke up or so much as moved in bed. If anything, the stormy elements aided their sleep.

It was exactly the right time.

Aurora's honey-colored hair whitened and thinned into scraggly strands. Her once smooth skin creased with deep wrinkles, her cheeks hollowing. Her youth melted away for her haggish features hidden underneath. Last and most disconcertingly, she unhinged her jaw. It widened like a snake, stretching in gruesome fashion. A black hole on her face, she was ready to feed.

Her hands found John's mouth and she forced his lips apart, prying them open. He sputtered and his body twisted, but she pinched his nose to keep him from breathing. She bent low and inhaled deeply. John flailed in resistance. His attempts were futile as her pull was too strong. She was a vacuum, suctioning the wisps of pale golden glisters that emitted from his mouth. The energy was as delicious as she had imagined.

The more she drained, the more he lost the fight in him. The less his body struggled. The bulgier his now-open eyes grew. The color erased from his skin and he stared up at her in frozen horror. Second to second the life left him and he turned as cold as ice. She swallowed the energy she harvested, the tiny golden glisters candy to a being like her.

The mattress creaked and in the dark, the heap next to John snapped upright. Luna Blackstone woke with a frightened gasp, startled by the scene. The crystal necklace around her neck glowed like a night-light, illuminating her face. Aurora stood up straighter and growled, throwing out both hands and blasting a ball of fiery red light at her nemesis. Luna anticipated her move. She waved her arm and sent the table lamp to come whizzing between them. Aurora's blast shattered the ceramic lamp and shards flew everywhere.

Luna spun in the air, flying out of bed amid billowing blankets and sheets. A second growl vibrated in Aurora's throat as she hinged her jaw again and shot another blast of red light in Luna's direction. Again Luna was a step ahead. Her hands moved so fast they were shadowed blurs. She sent furniture flying across the room. First a barreling table and then a chair, which Aurora narrowly avoided.

The table she scorched. As Aurora rushed forward, Luna hurried back. Her necklace was still aglow, brighter as time passed. They played a game of cat and mouse. Luna was on the defense, Aurora on the offense, firing off jet after jet of red light. Smoke filled the room with a thick haze among the already deep shadows, holes burned into the wall.

"You're going to regret this, Aurora!" Luna yelled breathlessly. "Look what you've done to John."

"Did he not deserve it? Do you not?"

Aurora shot more dark red magic in Luna's direction, but the lunar witch maneuvered out of the way. She had created a force field of sorts around her, a sparkling bubble that proved impenetrable. Aurora was not to be deterred, eyes beady and mouth open for a maniacal laugh.

"You may think you're more powerful than me, but you're a stupid woman!" she shrieked. Her wet hair swung as she whipped up her arms like a fanatical composer conducting an invisible symphony. From her coat pockets, she had withdrawn a thick stub of chalk. "You can hide behind that bubble all you like. You'll still be cursed!"

Doubt flickered over Luna's face. "You're insane."

"You'll never escape the wrath of a scorned woman! You or your family," Aurora told her. The magic chalk acted of its own accord, drawing a large circle on the floor. "I've put a hex on you, Luna. 'Til your dying day, you're doomed. You'll live in misery like you deserve, and so shall the other Black-stone witches."

"Aurora—"

"There's no undoing what I've done!" She shrieked in hideous laughter, head tossed back and face twisted in ugly bitterness.

The powdered chalk finished drawing the circle of its own accord. The ground beneath their feet began to quake. Wind stormed into the room, banging the window open and torpedoing inside. The lone candle on the mantel lost its flame and any knickknacks in the room tipped over and chinked onto the floor. The quakes in the ground deepened, rocking the house itself. The white-chalked circle glowed, a field of red sparks forming around Aurora.

She lost the whites of her eyes, the balls and irises going black. She raised her arms higher toward the dark energy swirling around her. The hundreds of bloodred sparks multiplied into thousands, energy surging, bending, breaking objects in the room at their will. A vase on the end table smashed and the fire pokers liquified in their holders. Luna backed against the wall, protected only by the thin lunar shield she had conjured.

When Aurora spoke the incantation, it was in an echoing, sinister voice more magnified than her usual. "Luna Blackstone, for so long as you wander this earth, may you and all witches with your bloodline be doomed to an existence of misery. May you be trapped forevermore within the borders of Brimrock, forced to live your days in despair and loneliness. May you weep 'til your dying day for the suffering you have caused and repent by suffering in equal measure. You and every Blackstone witch after you until the cost of your sin has been paid."

The white-chalked circle opened up into a widening black hole. More bloodred sparks emitted as the house rocked and creaked on its very foundation. Aurora lifted from the ground and spun in the air, emboldened by the dark magic seeping into her veins. For a stretch of seconds everything became a dizzy blur of rushing wind, quaking earth, and blinding magic. From the corner Luna looked on with a horrified expression. The spell spread like a virus, piercing the walls of 1221 Gifford, layering over its borders, and most satisfyingly, burning through Luna's protective force field.

Everything went dark. The wind ceased. The magic sparks injected themselves into the reality of the newly cast spell. Aurora dropped out of the air and smacked into the floor. The white-chalked circle lost its glow and the candle earned back its flame. In the shocked silence, bullet-sized raindrops pelted against the bedroom window, more thunder roaring.

The whites returned to Aurora's eyes and she sat up. Looking over at a stunned Luna, she released the witchiest cackle ever heard by human ear.

"I truly hope it was worth it."

CHAPTER ONE

PRESENT DAY

"**Y**ou hear that?"

Aiden glanced up and quirked a brow at his best friend Eddie's question. The paranormal investigators stood in the middle of a dark, dank hallway, long ago abandoned, clutching their prized spirit box. The time was half past midnight and the cameras were rolling. The night's ghostly shenanigans were just getting started.

If Aiden had his way, filming would have wrapped a long time ago. Unfortunately, in the urban legend, ghost-hunting business, daylight was considered boring. Nighttime was when all of the magic happened. He should have been used to the late nights by now. *Should* being the key word.

A deep yawn hit Aiden and reminded him that he wasn't and probably never would be. If given the choice between a warm bed and great book and an abandoned house haunted by a scorned, brokenhearted woman, he would choose option A every time.

"It sounded like it was coming from over there," said Eddie. He turned to face their cameraman Dale and met the watchful eye of the camera lens, speaking directly to the viewers who would later watch on YouTV. "Many past residents claim to hear Macy Bibbman's cries up and down the halls. She's rumored to wander the house in search of her lover. Let's go say what's up!"

"*Or* we could say night night and head home," sighed Aiden under his breath. He followed anyway. It was his job to shadow Eddie and make offhanded remarks that dripped with sarcasm. He was the skeptic. Eddie was the believer. The fans loved that about them. *Paranormal Hunters* wouldn't have been half as entertaining without their butting ideologies.

The two trekked down the shadow-heavy hallway with the white glow of their flashlights paving the path ahead. The all-encompassing darkness left them blind otherwise, a black wall no matter the direction. The century-old floorboards creaked. More than once the wood bent under his lean one-eighty-pound body. He aimed the flashlight at the ground for any gaps.

Eddie trudged on without hesitancy, his stockier build producing louder groans from the weak wood. He stopped and called out to the spirit of Macy Bibbman. "Hey, Mace, you there? Why don't you come out and say hi? Let's chat. We can talk about how your lover left you for his mistress. Who would've guessed there were side chicks in 1847?"

"I'm sure that's exactly what they called them back in the olden days." Aiden delivered his one-liner in true O'Hare fashion, sounding as dry and aloof as Dad. Like father, like son.

They continued until the end of the hall, turning a corner to find another dead end. The scents of grime and gore floated in the air and created a putrid superstench. Aiden pinched the bridge of his nose. Eddie's face screwed up as if he had sucked on a lemon. The partners had no choice but to head through the last doorway left. Aiden ducked his head to avoid a low-hanging beam, but Eddie breezed inside without issue.

The camera caught the second they both stepped into a giant sheet of cobwebs. They fought off the clingy fabric sticking to their skin, Eddie releasing a scream into the night. His pitch rose, sure to garner laughs from the audience, but he didn't care. His back hit the wall as he flailed his arms.

Aiden snickered. "You okay over there, Ed? Sounds like that arachnophobia is kicking in."

"Shut up, shut up. I think I swallowed a mama spider and her eighty-three babies," coughed Eddie. He wiped his mouth on his sleeve.

Dale the cameraman panned closer, giving viewers a clear shot of Eddie's retching. Another bit that would entertain the YouTV watchers at home.

Aiden addressed the dusty, shoebox-sized room. "Macy, did you see that? Your pal Eddie is swallowing spiders for you! It's only fair you reveal yourself if you're here. Come out and say hello."

The spirit box crackled in his hands, lighting up brighter than a Christmas tree in the dark. Eddie and Dale crowded closer. The crackling doubled in volume. The frenzied static noise turned painful, penetrating their eardrums. Even Aiden lost whatever smart-aleck retort he had lined up. The sound was drilling a hole in his cranium. He tried shaking off its effects.

A powerful wind blasted the glass doors of the window open. The temperature dropped as the cold gust swept through the room, its soughing background noise for the crackling spirit box. Aiden held it up higher, his palms glowing pale blue. The static was so loud now that the low whine was almost missed. It was soft, part-whimper, part-sigh, definitely female.

"Did you hear that, America? Clear audio evidence of a specter!" Eddie exclaimed, instantly excitable. He bounced forward, searching for the source. He stopped at the window and eyed the glass doors hanging loose on their hinges. "That was Macy reaching out to us."

"*Or* a gust of wind." Aiden blinked dryly.

"That was no gust of wind!"

"So the more reasonable explanation is that there's the ghost of a 200-year-old woman trying to communicate with us? Is that what you're saying?"

"Well…it sounded like…the noises weren't just…shut up, Aiden!"

Eddie snatched the spirit box from Aiden and paced the length of the small room. The flashlight in his other hand lit up the sparse furnishings. The iron bed frame sat rusting in the corner and the full-length mirror against the opposite wall was cracked and spotted. Next to it was a propped-open wardrobe with moth-eaten fashions from over a century ago.

The wind had gone nowhere, circling the room, tousling hair and chilling spines. Aiden glanced at the camera and searched for a crumb of sarcasm. His mind had gone perplexingly blank and he had yet to recover. The sudden cold, the intense noise made it difficult to think.

"Macy!" Eddie called over the frenzied racket. "Show us yourself!"

The wind answered with another fierce howl. Eddie spun around the room with his flashlight and spirit box. He lost his footing and tripped, falling backward onto the dirty floorboards. Aiden sighed and went to help him up. Eddie locked on to his arm, but then screamed at the top of his lungs. A rat darted across the floor, scurrying by his head.

"Will you calm down—?" Aiden started.

The lone light bulb overhead flicked on and chased away

the deep shadows. The wind seemed to vanish as did the crackling from the spirit box. They squinted against the sudden bright light. Even Dale struggled to adjust, lowering the camera. The security guard stood in the doorway with his finger on the light switch.

"It's go time, fellas. Your filming permit's up." He pointed at the watch strained around his thick wrist. He spoke in the same authoritative, false sense of importance tone he had earlier when unlocking the gates to the Bibbman residence. Hooking his thumbs through the belt loops of his pants two sizes too tight, he escorted them out of the room. "I can't have y'all wandering around here after midnight."

"But Macy was *so* close."

"You're gonna have to be so close to Macy another night," he mocked. He walked them up to the front and tugged open the gates to let them pass onto the other side. "You ain't have to go home. You just ain't gonna be here. I'm off duty. See ya."

Aiden and Eddie exchanged looks as the tall iron gates clanged shut. Dale hovered between them, uncertain what they wanted to do next. Eddie looked up and down the silent street and admitted defeat with a low sigh.

"Fine, we'll call it. At least we got decent footage. It's enough for us to edit into a full episode. Viewers are gonna be happy."

"I'm sure your high-pitched wail will impress them very much," teased Aiden. He shook the keys to their van and started across the street. "Who's driving?"

"Toss 'em here," said Dale. "We still stopping at that burger joint on our way back to the hotel?"

The three men headed for the vintage Dodge Caravan they had affectionately dubbed Ghost. The name seemed appropriate given it was the main mode of transportation when filming *Paranormal Hunters*. Ghost had stuck with them through thick and thin, their wheels as they traveled cross-country filming.

They filed into the van and buckled up. With their headlights on and the heat blowing, they bid farewell to the Bibbman residence. If he was honest, Aiden wasn't sorry to see it go.

————

"I've never met anybody who hates Christmas."

"I never said I hate Christmas," said Aiden, sucking on the straw to his soda cup. "I said I'm not a fan."

Eddie's light brown eyes clouded with disbelief. "Who says that? Nobody!"

"Aiden O'Hare does," offered Dale. He was more interested in the greasy double cheeseburger in his hands. It disappeared with each bite as he listened to the best friends squabble, offering only the occasional input.

"That's what makes it crazy." Eddie shook his head at Aiden and swirled his already-soggy French fry in more ketchup. "You're the only person on the planet who can legit say he's meh about Christmas. Some people out there—yeah, they hate it. But they usually have a reason. You? You're just indifferent. For no real reason."

"Who says it's for no reason?" Aiden asked. He sat alone on his side of the booth, cutting glances at his watch. The three of them had driven to the first burger joint they found that was still open at one in the morning. Eddie and Dale were fine sitting there all night. He had other things in mind. Like bedtime reading. And his bed itself...

"Cool, so there *are* reasons. Which are?"

"I told you, I think it's pointless."

"Ain't nothing wrong with celebrating with friends and family," chimed in Dale. Rather than grab his napkin to wipe the Thousand Island sauce on his chin, he used his shirt. "Plus there's all the food."

"Exactly! You love food! Maybe more than we do."

Aiden's smirk was subtle. "Why do you sound like a prosecutor presenting his case in a court of law?"

"Are you honestly gonna pretend like you don't? Look at your tray and look at ours. Your food's gone. You inhaled that shit."

"Like a Hoover." Dale added the *vroom* sound for optimal effect. "And still ain't got an ounce of fat on you. Meanwhile, I've got this gut."

"Yeah, but Dale...to be fair, last time you ran a mile, it was 1983 and hair metal was still a thing." Eddie's joke earned him a ripple of chuckles from the other two.

"Fellas, blame it on the fast metabolism. Anyway, are we headed out anytime soon?" Aiden raised his brows at them. The fluorescent lighting caught in the tiny hairs and highlighted the natural reddish tones in his eyebrows. His entire family was known for it. The reddish-brown hair on their heads was an O'Hare staple. "I'd like to get some sleep before we hit the road tomorrow."

"You say that like you drive," said Eddie.

"I drive plenty of times. You don't like me to because then I put on my podcasts."

"Nobody wants to listen to an etymology podcast for six hours. *Nobody*."

"Speak for yourself." Aiden got up from the booth and followed the other two to the trash. They dumped the scraps of food and stacked their trays. "Besides, I need some incentive for the torture that's about to be the next two weeks."

"Poor you. Spending Christmas in a nice, cozy Massachusetts town. You've met my aunt Priscilla before. She's practically going to make the holiday nothing but food, gifts, and cheer."

"Food good. Gifts and cheer bad."

"Again, only you would say that. Only you'd call cheer bad."

"And gifts," supplied Dale.

"You know," said Eddie as they pushed open the glass doors and entered the breezy night, "you can stop acting like you're on an audition for the *How the Grinch Stole Christmas* reboot. It's okay to enjoy yourself this Christmas."

"Eddie, I'm grateful your family has invited me to stay with you for the holidays, but you know why I agreed. It wasn't because of a cheery, hunky-dory Christmas in Brim-rock. Otherwise I'd be spending Christmas like I always do—going for a hike with Ruby and catching up on some reading."

"Can we at least suspend the Luna Blackstone talk 'til after we open presents?"

"You celebrate Christmas," said Aiden. "I'll research background info on the case."

Eddie sighed, sliding into the driver's seat this time. "Suit yourself, Grinch. But be warned. Aunt Priscilla has an ugly Christmas sweater with your name on it."

———

The rest of the night consisted of Aiden carrying out his bedtime routine. He removed his contacts and replaced them with his glasses. His eyes ached from hours of long filming. Next he tackled his wardrobe. He lined up his shoes in the closet and hung up his coat. He folded his shirt and pants—even if they were going in the laundry bag. His methodical routine carried on in the bathroom with his grooming and shower. Twenty minutes later, he emerged in a T-shirt and sweats, rid of his thickening stubble, smelling of what the aftershave described as *alpine fresh.*

His nights were for his books and research. He clicked on the bedside table lamp and powered on his laptop. If he was going to spend the next two weeks in Brimrock, Massachusetts, he was going in prepared. The more info he gathered, the easier it would be to form a game plan for his investigation. Christmas wasn't going to stop him from working on the show. Episode fifty needed to be special.

He typed "Luna Blackstone Brimrock" into the search engine. The results were a mixed bag, a quarter irrelevant and another quarter dead links. The few decent ones were websites that looked straight out of 1995. He scrolled through the two-dimensional graphics and text reminiscent of Microsoft Word art and pulled up the page on Luna Blackstone. The backstory earned a quiet laugh out of him.

"Though Luna disappeared in 1976, to this day, residents in Brimrock are shaken by the evil witch," he read aloud to no one. "It's believed that Luna wanders the streets and haunts residents. No proof exists showing Luna is responsible for the strange proclivities in town, but many believe the witch's spirit is still out for revenge. She is survived by her granddaughter, who refused comment when we reached out."

Aiden tore off his glasses and pinched the bridge of his nose.

Of course there was no solid evidence. He chuckled again and closed his laptop. Maybe he didn't have the patience to parse through crackpot paranormal theories after all. Better to do so after a full night's rest and some coffee.

"Lots of coffee," he muttered, fluffing his pillow. The

lights were the next thing to go, commencing darkness. "I'm really going to enjoy proving this one wrong."

———

The drive to Brimrock was a day of gas station pitstops, hot dogs with chili cheese and onions, and Eddie's cringe-inducing carpool tunes. Aiden pressed his forehead against the cool glass of Ghost's passenger-side window and groaned. Eddie acted out his lifelong dream of being a rapper, gripping the steering wheel and botching the lyrics to the latest Billboard chart topper.

"Are my ears bleeding yet?" Aiden asked when they pulled over for another pitstop.

Eddie popped open the gas tank and unscrewed the cap. "You swear your boring NPR is any better."

"How about silence?"

"How about Skittles? Grab me a pack!"

Aiden waved him off as he headed for the gas station convenience store. They were only an hour outside of Brimrock and that last sixty minutes couldn't go by fast enough. He stalked the aisles and loaded up on sugar and salt. Both were perfect distractions for the remaining miles. At the register he put twenty on pump seven, withdrawing a crisp bill from his wallet.

The middle-aged clerk flashed her crooked teeth, hair a burnt and brittle orange, and bagged up his items. "Never seen you before. You visiting from somewhere?"

He nodded. "I am. Here on a work trip."

Eddie was right. He was the Grinch incarnate. Only he would describe visiting Eddie and his family during the holidays as a *work trip*.

The clerk handed over his plastic bag of snacks. "Well, it's a whole week early, but Merry Christmas."

Before Aiden could reluctantly cave to social convention and wish her a Merry Christmas in return, his gaze drifted toward the left. On the rack beside the counter were postcards. The word *Brimrock* jumped out on many of them. Some seasonal with mistletoe and reindeer featured on the front. Others with more neutral graphics like an overhead shot of the town. But it was the novelty collection that most held his attention. Luna Blackstone–themed postcards. He picked up one with the dark silhouette of a witch cackling against an illustrated full moon.

"Those are half off," said the clerk nosily. "They're left-over from our special spooktastic Halloween collection. Buy one, get a second for fifty cents."

"Mind adding this to my total?" Aiden plucked two from the rack and slid them across the counter.

"No problem."

"And, uh, Merry Christmas," he said in goodbye.

Eddie waited for him in the van. He tore into the bag of Skittles Aiden tossed his way. Aiden clicked his seat belt into place and pulled out one of the postcards, studying the Halloween-inspired illustration. The postcard was obviously tongue in cheek, but even still, it showed how infamous Luna Blackstone must have been. Maybe the 1995-esque conspiracy website undersold her.

"Almost there," Eddie announced.

Aiden looked up from the postcard and then glanced out the window. Nothing but trees and snow surrounded them, the sky itself a steel gray. The mood was less festive Christmas and more witchy dread than anything. He stuffed the postcard into the breast pocket of his shirt and said, "I can hardly wait."

CHAPTER TWO

Tonight, Selene Blackstone had a blind date. Today, she was spending her shift at the Brimrock town library thinking up excuses not to go. She nudged her book cart down the J–K fiction aisle with a groan vibrating in her throat, wondering why she let her best friend, Noelle, talk her into this type of silly thing.

When it came to matters of the heart, it was pointless to even bother. The blind date would end like all other dates she went on: after a long night of awkward silences and intense study of restaurant menus, she would go her way. He would go his. They would never speak again. Nights at home gorging on fatty snacks and binge-watching *Project Runway* were more productive.

Selene's cart squeaked to a halt in front of Stephen King's massive selection of books. She glanced over her shoulder. Not a soul anywhere in the vicinity. Exactly what she was hoping for. She waved her hand and the stacks of books levitated off the cart. They floated across the aisle, sorting themselves onto the shelves in neat order. The last book wedged itself into the only open space left.

Just like that an hour's worth of work was done in seconds. Selene smirked and dusted her hands off on her ribbed cardigan as if she had labored long and hard at the tedious work. Nobody would be the wiser.

"Finished with that cart already?" Miriam Hofstetter breathed on her horn-rimmed glasses and wiped them off on her fuzzy cat sweater. The fiftysomething woman slipped the glasses back onto her face and gestured toward the next cart in line, this one loaded with even more books than the first. "Here's the L–Ms. Do those."

Selene clamped her mouth shut, holding in the frustration on her tongue. "Sure. I'll get right on that."

"I'm not finished," snapped Miriam. She pursed her thin lips and waited for a tick of silence to go by. "Then I need you to wipe down this place. We've got dusty little bunnies hopping around everywhere. It's unsightly."

"Okay." Selene moved to go, but again Miriam wasn't done.

"Ger and I are taking a long lunch today. You'll be down to thirty by the time we get back."

Selene grit her teeth and said nothing. Any words would come out with biting sass and she couldn't afford to get fired. Miriam eyed her closely, her thin Russian-red lips spreading. Her smile, as cruel as it was, only revealed she had a smudge of lipstick on her teeth. Selene relished in that discovery. Small victories.

"I hope your weirdo friend isn't going to come around," said Miriam. Her nasal voice pitched higher. "Just because I'm out at lunch doesn't mean I *don't* have eyes watching."

In the L–M aisle, Selene shoved books onto the shelf, mumbling under her breath. It might have been the harder way to sort books, but she was too mad for her cheats. Something about snatching books off the cart and ramming them between other books was therapeutic. Considering the sound restrictions in the library, it was the only real way to expel pent-up frustration.

Miriam lorded over the library like a fuzzy-sweatered, horn-rimmed-glasses-wearing, lipstick-on-teeth queen. Miserable and widowed with children long flown from the nest, the library was Miriam's life. She also saw it as an opportunity to exert power over her least favorite person in town. If there was one motto Miriam lived by, it was keep your friends close but your enemies closer. The cruel head librarian had hired Selene for a reason.

It wasn't like Selene wasn't used to cold shoulders. She had spent her whole life on the receiving end of snotty stares and pearl clutching. It was par for the course when you were a rumored witch in a town terrified of your deceased grandmother.

The thing was, the rumor was true. At least half of it. Selene *was* a witch. But she wasn't a bad one. She wasn't evil and she didn't eat children for breakfast. She also didn't worship Satan—or anyone for that matter. Her telekinetic-like abilities were by birth, strengthened by the nightly moon. She was blind without her glasses and could barely make it a block without tripping over her own two feet. She was *harmless*.

A kitten and its little claws were more dangerous.

"Selene, I thought that was you." A friendly smile flashed across Officer Adam Gustin's face. He was still in uniform, holding a history book on World War II in his gangly arms. One of the library's most regular patrons, he usually sought book recommendations from Selene. Most times he seemed oblivious to how Selene felt about it, as she wasn't the biggest fan of authority figures in town, but he asked anyway.

"I was hoping you can help me find a book on President Eisenhower. I've looked everywhere."

Her expression was blank as she gave a reluctant nod, straightening her bold-framed glasses. "Sure, follow me."

She led him to the section he was in search of and he reached the top shelf with ease thanks to his tall and lanky frame. "I must've walked right by it. You're the most helpful librarian here. Thanks, Selene."

Selene merely gave a short nod. Officer Gustin might've seemed unassuming and friendlier than most authority figures in town. That didn't mean she was fooled. She hadn't been born yesterday and knew all too well the target she had on her back. At her first opening, she retreated back to the aisle she had been in, picking up where she left off with her book returns cart.

"When are you on break?"

Noelle Banks popped onto the scene practically out of thin air. Her best friend appeared dressed to make a fashion statement rather than keep warm in the cold. She defied convention in a long-sleeved crop top that spelled "Black Girl Magic" on the front and thermal leggings in a neon green, zigzag, arrow pattern. As if in last minute thought of the winter snow, she tossed a scarf around her neck and threw a beanie over her pixie-length crop of curls.

Selene turned to face her. "No time for a real lunch today. Miriam told me thirty. Which means twenty."

"Where is she now?"

"At lunch with Gerri. She won't be back for a while."

"So take a break," said Noelle with a hapless shrug.

"Are you kidding? Miriam made sure to tell me the hills have eyes." Selene sighed heavily, grabbing the next book off the cart. "I'm not going to chance it. It's not like I have the best luck."

Rather than argue, Noelle changed the subject, popping her chewing gum. "We should start prepping for Yule. We need to mix things up. We always do the same thing on Winter Solstice."

"I like our little party at your house."

"You mean where it's just me, you, and Bibi?"

"Best coven ever," said Selene with a tinge of sarcasm.

"Careful or the nonwitches'll hear you. What are you wearing tonight?"

"Now you know I haven't planned an outfit." Selene slid a book between Laidlaw and Laine. A part of her still searched for an excuse to cancel. No outfit might have been trivial, but it was valid enough.

"Don't worry about the outfit. We'll figure it out."

Selene groaned. "Noe."

"Selly," Noelle countered. "You've seen pics of Peter on InstaPixel. You know I don't even like men like that, but Peter's fine as hell. I wouldn't set you up with him if he wasn't."

"We're not compatible."

"How do you know?"

"Because he's Daniel Cleaver and I'm Bridget Jones!" Selene held on to another book and glared at Noelle from behind her thick glasses.

Noelle stared at her with a blank face. "I don't know who those people are. Anyway, point is, Peter deserves a shot. I already told you how I know him from university."

"And that's supposed to mean something?"

"We need to list the reasons. You're downplaying this too much. One," said Noelle, holding up a lone finger, "free meal. Not just any burger shack. Peter's using that investment banker money to take you to the Mulberry."

"I'm fine eating a ham sandwich at home."

"Two," said Noelle, ignoring her, two fingers now up, "have I mentioned he's fine as hell?"

"He was okay in an over-the-top, chiseled Greek god sort of way." Selene kept her expression level so not to give away the fact that Peter was indeed fine as hell with his beefy arms, California surfer hair, and dimpled, Colgate smile.

"Three," Noelle continued, louder than ever, "it'll get you out of the house! Selly, you never go anywhere or do anything!"

"Doing things is overrated. Next."

Noelle dropped her three fingers and put her hands to her waist. "Girl, if you don't get your ass to that blind date tonight, I'm gonna drag you my—"

"I'll go," interrupted Selene. "But only because I already said I would—*and* I'm all out of ham."

"That's what I'm talking about. I'll call you later. We can go over your outfit."

Before Selene could protest, Noelle was gone. She disappeared as quickly as she had arrived. Selene rolled her eyes and picked up the next few books to file. She would be polite on her date with chiseled, Greek god Peter, but it didn't mean anything. Her reality was immutable and always would be. She was a Blackstone and Blackstones were cursed.

———

Brimrock was a quaint, historic town months away from celebrating its 288th birthday. Selene strolled among the redbrick buildings and gas lantern lampposts on her walk home. Tiny snowflakes drifted in whatever direction the wind carried them, backdropped by the white-crowned mountains hundreds of miles away. She plugged her hands deeper into her peacoat and plunged onward, her cheeks numbing.

Each of her twenty-six years had been spent in this town. She could sleepwalk through and still find her way. For however many years she lived, she would be stuck here. Another unfortunate part of being a Blackstone. No matter what she did—how many reverse spells she cast or magicked rabbit feet she carried—she couldn't leave the town. She, like Mom and Grandma Luna before her, was confined within its borders for life.

Gifford Lane was a dead end, but it was the end of the road for her. She wandered by modest Cape Cod after modest Cape Cod and admired the cheery Christmas decorations festooned on the front lawns and perched on the slanted gray roofs. At the end of the block was 1221, the house nobody in Brimrock dared trespass. The three-story gothic architectural masterpiece rumored to be haunted: 1221 Gifford was *home*.

It might've intimidated others with its large, protruding bay windows and castle-like tower on the third floor, deep hunter-green shade and intricate stone panels considered ominous, but for Selene, everything about the home was perfection. As empty as the house was these days, it didn't matter. The house represented the Blackstone family and always would.

Funnily enough, there wasn't much spooky about the house. Nothing evil in her family. It was nothing but witch stereotypes, most of which had never applied to anyone in the Blackstone family, herself included.

Selene preferred dogs over cats. She owned no pointy hats. Her favorite color was pink, not black. She didn't melt when splashed with water, though she was mildly allergic to the sun. She had replaced her broomstick with a robotic floor sweeper and her skin wasn't really green. It was brown—a warm-toned brown as rich as amber. Honestly, she watched witches in TV shows and movies and laughed at the frivolous depictions.

But she liked to think of it as all in good fun. Most of the time.

The day's stack of mail awaited her on the bottom porch stair. The mailman, Mr. Higgley, hated walking it up to the letterbox in the door. Instead he stayed safely on the sidewalk and tossed any letters and packages at the porch. Better not to risk an encounter with Luna's ghost. Rumor about town was that she sometimes wandered the garden out front. Selene didn't care about others thinking the house was haunted so long as she still got her mail.

Warmth from the brass heaters radiated in the hall when Selene entered. She shrugged off her coat and stepped out of her boots, sorting through the pile of mail. Too many sheets of sales paper and utility bills later, she came to the last envelope. It was a strange off-color white, like rotten eggnog, and, pressing her fingers against it, lumpy to the touch. So much for it *finally* being the Hogwarts acceptance letter she'd been waiting on since she was eleven.

The name and address on the back were hers. The sender none other than Uncle Zee. Selene frowned. Uncle Zee *never* sent letters. Definitely not lumpy ones in weird egg-colored envelopes. She tore into it as Yukie barreled down the hall with her tongue dangling from the side of her mouth. The Yorkshire terrier's paws slid to a clumsy but excitable stop and she rose on hind legs for Selene's attention.

"Don't look at me like that, Yukie," said Selene with torn envelope in hand. "I was at work. Look, I got a letter from Zee."

Yukie shadowed her down the hall lined with old oil paintings and peeling, charcoal-gray, damask wallpaper. Many would consider the furnishings dusty and dated, but

Selene joked it was cobweb chic. Right down to the chain-link chandeliers overhead and the worn area rugs beneath her feet, the home hadn't been refurbished in years. Each item was a Blackstone relic of the past and Selene wouldn't have it any other way.

The kitchen lights blinked on for her and the far-left cabinet sprang open. Yukie's bag of dog food floated midair and stopped above her ceramic bowl on the floor in the corner, tipping onto its side to pour her kibble. Selene multi-tasked, reading the letter but also summoning Yukie's water bowl. That she sent to the faucet, which twisted on and streamed fresh water.

"Dinner is served," she said to the pooch once both bowls were replenished.

Yukie was fast on them, munching on the turkey-flavored kibble bites. Selene scanned the letter and noticed the envelope still felt lumpy. She turned it over and a bunched silver necklace fell onto the palm of her hand. Like most other things in the Blackstone family, it looked about a million years old, the silver slightly tarnished and discolored.

But it was still beautiful—or had been in its heyday. The pendant dangling on the end was large and crystalline. When it caught in the light, it shone and changed color, one moment clear and another pale pink and then again sky blue. Selene studied the necklace with interest and then referred back to the letter.

Selene,

Sincerest apologies it's been so long. You know I like to be on the move, never staying in any one place for too long—that's much too boring. But I figure after all these years it's time to slow down and take a breather. All this extra time on my hands finally gave me the chance to look through some old boxes. It's no surprise many were full of Luna's and Estelle's things. It'd cost too much to send everything, but here's a little something something just for you. It used to be Luna's and she passed it to Estelle. Doesn't it seem right for it to be given to you now? Stay safe and always take care.

Zee

Uncle Zee was always a mystery to her. He visited from time to time when she was younger, but stopped altogether when Mom passed away. Being the son of Luna, he was fortunate enough not to have any magical ability and could come and go as he pleased. His address on the envelope was in Brooklyn, New York, a place Selene had only read about in books or seen on the TV screen. She'd kill to try a slice of that infamous New York pizza pie…

Selene pocketed the letter and necklace and turned back to Yukie. She had swallowed every last bite of kibble and drank so much water it sloshed out of the bowl. Selene smirked and plucked Yukie off the floor, holding the eight-pound dog in her arms.

"You are the world's smallest garbage disposal," she teased. She laughed as Yukie's head tilted sideways as if attempting to understand the joke. "C'mon, let's go upstairs. Time to get all fancy and dressed up so that I can spend the night miserable on a date."

———

Selene opened the door to her closet and inhaled a deep, shuddering breath. The clothes hanging from the rack were more practical, less fashion. She had a whole corner devoted to varying tones of black denim and her wool sweater collection was second to none. Here and there she had a twill skirt or button-up blouse for the rare occasion she craved variety. Then there were her shoes—the pair of fur-trimmed boots she wore when it snowed and the Oxford flats she slipped on when the sun was out. Noelle said the ladies on *The Golden Girls* had better fashion tastes, but Selene saw no reason to switch up her style.

Her gut instinct was to grab more of the same. There was no use in wearing anything special when the blind date was doomed from the start. The Mulberry was the classiest restaurant in town, but it seemed useless to put in any effort when Peter and she would never go out again. Who would care if she tossed on another patchwork sweater and acid washed jeans?

It was like Noelle read her mind from halfway across town. She video called at that exact moment. Selene rolled her eyes before she answered.

"You didn't think I was gonna forget, did you?"

"You never do—not where my dating life's concerned. But I'm glad you called. I almost just put on another pair of jeans."

Noelle's eyes twinkled, framed by her thick false lashes. "We're gonna have you looking *fine* tonight. Guaranteed. Give me a tour of the closet."

Selene waved her fingers and her phone drifted on its own toward the racks. The camera hovered over each article of clothing for Noelle's viewing pleasure. Noelle provided commentary when necessary. Almost all of the items were immediate nays. The one yay was from a studded leather jacket tucked away in the bowels of her closet. Selene snatched the phone out of midair and turned it around to herself.

"Noe, that's *your* jacket, remember? You left it here last time you slept over."

"I thought that looked too cute to be in your closet." Noelle snorted out a laugh and then caught herself half a second too late. "Errr, I mean…we can build an outfit around that. It's a real statement piece!"

"I'm *not* wearing a studded leather jacket," said Selene, brows raised. "Too Fonz from *Happy Days*."

"You're right. Not your style. Okay, can I look at the back of the closet again? What was that LBD on the last hanger?"

"LBD?"

"Little black dress. That could work!"

Selene waved her fingers and the black A-line frock jumped off the hanger and hung midair in front of the phone's camera. Noelle hummed her approval.

"You'd look so cute in that! Add some heels and it's perfect!"

"No dresses. You know I hate showing my thighs."

"*Selly*," said Noelle in exasperation, "you will slay in that dress, do you understand me?"

"It's supposed to snow tonight."

"So wear some tights. Take your coat. You'll be fine."

Selene hung up and took another look at the black frock. She still remembered the afternoon she had bought it. She had been shopping at the mall with Noelle, half-heartedly pursuing the racks. The black polyester dress flared slightly at the skirt but hugged the bust to create a flattering shape. She had modeled it in the mirror and couldn't resist its 20% off price point. She hadn't worn it since, leaving it buried in the closet to collect dust.

Sliding it on that evening, the dress fit just right, giving her an immediate confidence boost. Selene hurried to the floor-length mirror across her bedroom. Maybe Noelle was right. The dress looked great on her. A certifiable slayage indeed.

Yukie yipped from where she lay perched in her sheepskin dog bed. Selene laughed. "I'm going to take that as you agreeing. But I definitely need tights."

Five minutes later, she returned to the mirror in thick cobalt-blue tights and ankle booties. It still wasn't what most would call fashion forward, but it was comfortable and she looked presentable enough.

"Makeup and hair," she muttered to no one.

Selene glanced around her room. The rest of it was a mess. For all of the magical ability she possessed, she usually forgot to use her powers to clean the place up. It was a lot easier to leave everything cluttered. From her two big bookshelves overstuffed with books to the bed with a thousand and one mismatched throw pillows, it was a headache trying to find anything. She couldn't remember where she left her little travel-size case of makeup.

Her desk was probably the worst offender. In one corner was her black cast-iron cauldron. In another corner was an assortment of melted candles. Books were strewn in between, including her spell book and her beloved copy of *Pride and Prejudice*, of which she was rereading for the thirteenth time. Even her desk chair was a victim; she had slung a cardigan over the top.

On the verge of casting a locator spell, she spotted her makeup case on the windowsill. How it got there, she had no clue, but she had no more time to waste. Peter said he'd meet her at the Mulberry at six and it was already five. If there was one thing she hated, it was being late.

Selene scurried to the bathroom sink. It took her eight minutes to slap together a makeup look that was amateur at best. She dabbed on lip gloss, swiped her waterproof mascara wand along her lashes, and blended a bit of concealer on blemishes. Her head of curls she left framing her face. She spritzed some soft lilac-scented perfume and then coughed as she accidentally caught a mouthful.

Halfway out of the bathroom, she remembered the necklace Uncle Zee had sent her. Earlier she had no intention of doing anything with it except stashing it away in a drawer somewhere, but maybe some jewelry for her date night outfit would give an extra pop. More slayage. Could there ever be too much?

Selene buckled the clasp behind her neck and checked the end result in the mirror. A faint tremor of excitement strummed through her. For a split second, she considered the possibility that tonight would be different. Tonight she would go out with Peter and actually enjoy herself. The blind date wasn't doomed and could be the start of something promising. The fantasy bubble burst as her eyes fell on her phone and she saw the time.

"How am I so late?" she shrieked, running downstairs. Coat swathed over her arm and keys in hand, she called goodbye to Yukie and slammed the door shut.

———

The evening was darker and windier by the time she emerged from the house. On normal occasions she didn't mind traveling by foot, but she was already running late. She brought up the URide app on her phone and submitted a request. The fifteen-minute wait time flashed across her screen. She groaned and glanced around the empty street.

She should've known better. It was days before Christmas. Half of the town probably had relatives flying in. URide drivers probably had their hands full ferrying them to and from the airport. She retreated inside, taking up post in the bay window to watch for her car. When fifteen minutes came and went, she checked the app and saw he was still miles away. Sighing, she weighed her options. If she canceled right now it would be understandable...wouldn't it?

Peter was undeniably handsome; he'd sit in the bar section at the Mulberry and pick up another woman with ease.

Her phone vibrated in her hand and she glanced down. A new notification popped up on her screen, informing her she'd been assigned a new ride share. Car number 34892 would be here in sixty seconds. She perked up and jumped off the bay's window seat.

"Bye, Yukie—for real this time!" she shouted, locking up.

"Over here!"

Selene was halfway down the front path when she saw the man. He was on the sidewalk's edge in a tan overcoat, his arm high in the air, flagging down the car on the street. The car with the yellow checkered URide logo—*her* URide car. Her mouth dropped open in instant horror and she rushed over as fast as she could given the snow.

"Excuse me," she snapped, "that's *my* ride share!"

"Doubtful. I've flagged him down first."

"That's not how this works. I ordered the car on the app."

"And you think I didn't?" he asked back with lifted brows. The manner in which he posed the question confused Selene. His tone was dry but also half-amused, making it impossible to tell if he was serious or if it was all sarcasm.

Selene didn't care to find out. She refused to give up the ride share that was hers. On tiptoe, she stretched her arm higher into the air. He was a foot taller than her, so it didn't have much of an effect, but she only stretched more, snatching every inch she could. He stood back and watched with an expression that was again hard to read. He was either impressed or irritated.

The URide car slowed to a stop in front of the curb. The driver rolled down the window and they launched into explanations at once. Selene ranted about the car being hers. The man thanked the driver for showing up when needed. The driver blinked back at them, unsure how to respond.

"Hop in…?" He trailed off.

"Thank you," said Selene, reaching for the door handle.

The man in the tan overcoat held out his arm to block her. "Look, you're in a rush. I get that, but I've been waiting on this ride share. I'm meeting someone and I *can't* be late."

"So that means I'm supposed to be late? I've been waiting longer than you!"

"There's no such thing as a participation trophy for a ride share," he said. He turned to the window and spoke directly to the driver. "Thanks for showing up. There seems to be some confusion, but this is the car I've reserved."

"Confirmation number 34892?" the driver read off.

"Yes!" Selene and the man answered in unison.

Their heads snapped to the side for a glare at each other. Both held up their phones and showed off the identical confirmation number.

"This must be some sort of glitch with the app," said the man. "I'm headed to 690 Charleston Lane."

Selene scoffed. "That's exactly where I'm headed. The Mulberry Steakhouse. You're not… You can't be…"

She scanned the man up and down, head to toe all seventy-five or so inches of him, ending on his face. It was dark out and the streetlights only lit so much, but he *couldn't* be Peter. Sure, they were both white males clearly in their late twenties. But similarities ended there. For one, this man was leaner than Peter, who was beefy judging off of the photos. Secondly, the lamppost illuminated the guy enough that his reddish strands were impossible to miss. Peter was a blond. Lastly, Peter was hunkier, more of a pretty boy, Hollywood actor type looks-wise. This guy, whoever he was with his strong, downslope nose, ever-changing hazel eyes, and clefted chin, was more of a cute guy at the coffee shop down the block. Strange that they were headed to the exact same restaurant.

The man spoke and snapped Selene from her thoughts. He popped the back passenger door open and stepped aside. It was a second before she realized what he was doing. He was holding the door for her.

"Well, if we're headed to the same place, I guess it's settled," he said, waiting on her to slide in first. "Looks like this URide is *OurRide*."

CHAPTER THREE

Aiden hated awkward silences. Awkward silences called for useless chitchat. The small talk that Aiden dreaded. He would rather sit alone and soak up his solitude than engage with strangers. Stuck in the back seat of the ride share, he was forced to do just that. He sat beside the woman whose name he didn't know, the middle seat empty between them, and he stared out the window, racking his brain.

What was the proper etiquette for shared rides? Was he supposed to ask her about the weather? Crack a joke about their circumstance? Busy himself with his phone?

He decided on the latter, digging into his coat pocket and pulling out his phone for distractive purposes. A full minute passed before he realized he wanted nothing to do with the dozen plus social media notifications piled up on his accounts. Normally, he tackled those with a clear head over coffee in the morning. Doing so now was out of his usual routine.

He considered texting Eddie, but what use would that be? Eddie was at the Mulberry with his family. They were waiting on him. Texting Eddie and letting him know what happened would interrupt their dinner plans and cause unnecessary hassle. The more sensible option was for him to stay in the URide and be late. Even if it killed him a little on the inside.

It was all Ghost's fault. While the vintage Dodge Caravan had gotten them from Macy Bibbman's home in Oklahoma to the Myers residence in Brimrock, Massachusetts, it had clunked out when he needed Ghost most. He and Eddie had settled in at Eddie's aunt's house, lugging their suitcases upstairs and unpacking in their rooms, but the festive, cheerful home quickly grew claustrophobic. Eddie decided to spend the afternoon with his family. Aiden decided he'd take Ghost for a ride around town.

His stops included Balford's Books, the indie bookshop in the town shopping square, but also one he planned on keeping to himself. He had searched the address for the supposed haunted house Luna Blackstone once lived in. It was far too soon to explore the premises. He only wanted to drive by and scope out what exactly made 1221 Gifford Lane terrifying to residents in Brimrock.

And then Ghost broke down. He was half a block off from the house when the engine juddered, slowing into a full stop in the middle of the street. He twisted the key in the ignition to more groans from the engine. Popping the hood and checking out the engine was no help. He wasn't a car guy, knowing next to nothing about repair. The realization had washed over him and he cussed under his breath. He had told Eddie they should've opted in for the roadside assistance on their insurance policy.

Enter the curly-haired woman with thick glasses and blue tights. He had waited for twenty minutes on his URide car only to be reassigned a new one last second. Number 34892 turned onto the block and his mood soared, chasing away any grumpiness. He waved his arms in the air to draw attention to himself, paranoid the car would overlook him. The curly-haired woman in thick glasses and blue tights darted onto the scene out of nowhere, so fast he didn't even see where she came from. But he couldn't let her have his ride share. Car 34892 was *his*.

Aiden cut a furtive glance in the woman's direction. Like him, she seemed to struggle with their current predicament. She kept her eyes glued onto the car window and stared at the snow-smattered streets. He hadn't meant to watch her, but as he hit the eight second mark, it dawned on him that he probably came across as a creepy weirdo. Nobody wanted to be a creepy weirdo. Least of all him. He quickly looked away.

The URide car braked for a red light and the driver peered at him through the rearview mirror. "So how do you two lovebirds know each other?"

Aiden and the woman sputtered for an answer. The woman came up with one first. "We don't know each other. We're just headed to the same place. Didn't you hear us arguing over who gets the ride share?"

The driver shrugged, indifference on his mustached, doughy face. "I figured you were in a lovers' quarrel."

Everyone dropped the subject. Aiden felt relief pool in his stomach and was grateful he didn't have to explain that they weren't in fact lovers. He didn't even know the woman's name. He knew nothing about her except she was stubborn and probably thought he was an inconsiderate jackass.

And that she smelled nice. Whatever fragrance or shampoo she wore, it permeated the closed space of the URide. He inhaled the scent in secret, its sweet and floral notes reminiscent of lilac and something else he couldn't exactly place. Nevertheless, he enjoyed the smell much more than the cheap pine air freshener that otherwise stunk up the car.

He chanced another peek at the woman. The heavy shadows engulfed the URide, making it difficult to get a good look. She wore bold-framed glasses with lenses so thick she must have been blind without them. Her hair was a dizzying fluff of curls, tight and tiny little coils that looked soft to the touch. She was dressed conservatively, wearing a black dress and those bright cobalt-blue tights. But she was also practical, keeping warm with a peacoat and scarf for when braving the winter cold. He wasn't the type of guy who scoped out women off the street, but he couldn't deny the obvious. She was *very* cute.

"Are you looking at something?"

The sudden question stopped his heart. He flinched as if shocked by electricity and then hurried to explain. "Yes... actually, no. Errr, I was just—"

"You don't want to share the URide. I got it," she said tersely. Her eyes returned to the window. "But hasn't anyone ever taught you it's rude to stare?"

"I must've skipped that lesson in school." He cringed at his own brand of O'Hare sarcasm. The compulsion was innate, jumping out of him whenever possible. He shoved it aside, shuffled fingers through his reddish-brown hair, and tried again. "Look, I'm sorry for staring. I wasn't doing it because we're sharing the URide. It was me being nosy."

"Are you normally this nosy with strangers?"

Aiden never got the chance to answer the woman. The URide car swerved hard to the left side of the street, the loud pop of rubber bursting and then slapping tarmac paining their ears. The driver flicked on his hazard lights and pulled over to the side of the road. Aiden already knew what the problem was before he even said anything. What were the chances of two car mishaps in one evening?

"Flat tire," said the driver, opening his car door. He got out to investigate. "Stay put, folks. We've got a delay."

"Great, just what I need when I'm already late," muttered the woman under her breath. She folded her arms and sunk lower in her seat.

"The URide app is saying there's a thirty-minute wait for another car," said Aiden. He logged off the phone app and stared out the window at the street sign. "How far from the Mulberry are we?"

The woman seemed to forget she hated him. She sat up and checked the same street sign. "We're three blocks away."

"It's stopped flurrying. It might be worth the walk."

She said nothing, in silent deliberation over his suggestion.

Aiden opened his door. "Well, good luck with the flat. I'm going to take my chances in this unprecedented arctic blizzard and walk the three blocks."

Still, she said nothing as he got out of the car. He bid the URide driver farewell and then steeped his hands into his pockets for warmth. He set off down the slushy sidewalks and made it about five steps before the woman's voice called after him. He stopped to turn around.

"You might be right," she conceded, her fluffy curls flapping in the winter wind. She bypassed him on the sidewalk with strides surprisingly long given her height. "The Mulberry's a straight shot down this street. It'll be quicker to walk."

———

For the second time that night, Aiden and the woman were stuck in each other's company. At first they walked out of sync with each other. The woman stayed a full pace ahead of him, though with each passing second that speed proved unattainable for her shorter legs. After a block they skipped any pretense and she fell into step with him. His hatred for small talk aside, he figured there was no way around it now.

"Dinner at the Mulberry," he said, tone low and nonchalant. "I hear the food's great."

She shrugged. "It's one of the nicer restaurants in town. You're not from here, are you?"

"Visiting."

"Family?"

"A friend and his family."

"That explains a lot," she said mysteriously. The evening's temperature must've dipped, because their breath began to produce puffs of frost. "I don't know everyone in town, but I can tell you're not from around here."

"Is that a bad thing?"

"I'd say it's a good thing. At least you have a life outside of Brimrock."

Aiden's brows pushed together. The woman sounded cryptic and he wished he understood what she meant. A small part of him was curious about her, but he also didn't want to steer into nosy territory again. He searched his limited catalogue of casual conversation with strangers and decided on a topic change.

"Who are you meeting at the Mulberry?"

"I'm...I'm meeting a date—a blind date."

"Sounds like an interesting evening." He was lying, saying the first thing that popped into his head. In actuality, his stomach clenched at that revelation. He hadn't considered the possibility she was on a date tonight. He had no clue why that mattered. With a block and a half remaining, they would soon part ways inside the doors of the Mulberry, probably never to talk again.

"I didn't want to, but here I am—walking in the snow at night to meet some guy I don't know," said the woman. She folded her arms as another gust of cold hit them. "Last time I let my friend talk me into something stupid like this."

"Your friend does that too, eh? The friend I'm visiting here in Brimrock never stops involving me in his antics."

"Sounds like your friend and my friend should be friends," she quipped.

Aiden's laugh surprised even himself. He wasn't a laugh-out-loud type of guy. He usually gave a quick chuckle if he found something funny and even then, it was a composed one. His laugh at the woman's comment was uncontrolled and abrupt. He caught himself midway through and cleared his throat.

"If I'm honest, I'm not exactly looking forward to the next two weeks." He looked up at the lampposts they passed and noted the festive red bows wrapped around the poles. "I don't think I've ever spent Christmas in a town so obsessed with velvet."

She laughed this time. "Welcome to Christmas in Brimrock. There's plenty more where that came from."

"Wait, wait, let me guess: candy canes."

"Brimrock staple."

"Snowmen?"

She rolled her eyes at him. "Do you see how much it snows here? *Of course* there's snowmen—whole snow families. Don't forget snow angels. Just everything and anything in the realm of snow."

"Caroling?"

"If you need any earplug recommendations, let me know."

Aiden was grinning. Actually grinning. He didn't feel it at

first because his face was numb from the cold, but he was *grinning* from ear to ear. Each clever reply the woman gave was a shot of energy to his system. It turned into a high for him as they traded one-liners. He wanted more, jonesing for another hit, testing the waters.

"If this were a live adaption of *The Christmas Carol*, and I were cast as Scrooge, you would tell me, wouldn't you?"

"That depends," she said in consideration. "Which Ghost of Christmas am I?"

Aiden never got the chance to answer. They slowed up, their gazes landing on the red-brick building with wide windows showing off a full house inside. The sign in embossed gold letters gleamed even on the night street, spelling the restaurant's name in capitalized letters: THE MULBERRY.

Aiden dropped his eyes to the woman beside him. "We're here."

———

The Mulberry was an American steakhouse with atmospheric lighting and woodsy decor. The insides reminded Aiden of a wine cellar, its layout a deep sprawl of heavy mahogany furniture and displays of pricey art and even pricier wine. The hostess greeted them at the front, wearing a smile so broad it looked painful.

He mentioned Eddie and the Myerses and she knew exactly where to take him. He gave a half-hearted nod to the woman whose name he didn't know, but who he had spent the better part of the last hour with, and followed the hostess. The faces of Eddie and the Myerses lit up as soon as they saw him.

Eddie rose from his seat to welcome him into the fold.

His aunt Priscilla got to him first. A short and stubby woman, she scurried around the table to greet him with a big, nurturing hug. The others watched on, caught between a smile and a laugh. Aiden did his best to humor Mrs. Myers, her head of wavy chestnut hair tickling his chin. She pulled back slightly and smiled up at him, skin a pasty white tinged with pink from emotion.

"Sweetie, I was about to send Eddie and Jake to look for you! We thought you were lost. I was telling everyone that I knew you shouldn't have taken that van to go exploring," she crooned, her grip on him tighter than a spider monkey. "Brimrock can be a confusing place and you shouldn't be wandering around alone."

"Priscilla, he's a grown man, not a little boy," chimed in the patriarch of the family, Eddie's uncle Jake. He looked like an older Eddie, with light brown skin, salt-and-pepper hair, and kind eyes. "Aiden is perfectly capable of driving around Brimrock on his own. I'm sure he has his reasons for running a little late. It's no big deal."

"Did you go into the town square?" Mrs. Myers pushed. "I was out and about a bit ago running some very important errands. I didn't see you around—"

"*Priscilla*," Mr. Myers repeated more sternly. "Your soup is getting cold."

"I hope you don't mind that we ordered appetizers without you." Mrs. Myers sniffled and resumed her seat.

Aiden took his. "Not at all. I'm the one who's late. I was hoping you didn't wait on me."

The others at the table seemed content minding their business. Eddie merely smirked at him. His teenage cousin Camilla fiddled with her phone, shooting off text after text, her meal untouched. Last but not least was Rory, the oldest of the Myers cousins. She unfolded her cloth dinner napkin and placed it neatly in her lap, the calm in which she did so strangely forced.

Aiden couldn't help comparing how this family dinner differed from any sit-downs at the O'Hares'. Their dinners were usually crowded around a wobbly table in the kitchen with less fancy silverware and more cold retorts. His stomach roiled with unexpected nerves.

Eddie sensed this and elbowed him. "What took you so long anyway? Let me guess, you were at Balford's Books."

"I lost track of time."

"At least you read," said Mr. Myers, tucking his cloth napkin into the neckline of his wool sweater. "The last time Eddie read a book it was Dr. Seuss."

The table erupted in laughter, including Eddie. Aiden was the only one who hesitated, joining the Myers family after a second went by. He couldn't explain why the familial occasion evoked a twitchy sense of nerves out of him, but he hoped for it to go away soon. He couldn't spend the next couple of weeks like this.

"We're happy to have you, Eddie, and even happier you brought Aiden along," said Mr. Myers eventually. His kind eyes shone as he smiled from beneath his shag of a mustache. "This Christmas is going to be a special one with all of us together."

"And we'll ring in the new year and leave behind the bad!" Mrs. Myers added with a nod. She elbowed Rory on her right side, her mouth a proud smile. "Rory will be moving on to bigger and better things. Won't you, Rory?"

Rory seemed reluctant to answer. She offered a nod and an embarrassed mumble.

Aiden glanced at Eddie and Eddie leaned closer to fill him in. "Rory's boyfriend dumped her. Aunt Priscilla's just trying to make her feel better."

The toast, though awkward in its beginnings, soon turned into merry laughter. The family split off into side conversations over their glasses of wine. Aiden scanned his surroundings. Elsewhere around the Mulberry, tables jammed with patrons elbow to elbow dined over their bloody steaks and garlic mashed potatoes. The dozens of voices buzzed louder than a beehive to his ears, a sound that exhausted him. Large crowds were his least favorite.

The sea of faces in the steakhouse meant nothing until he picked out the special one in the crowd. His eyes landed on the curly-haired woman with the thick glasses and blue tights. She was seated at a table for two at the front, but she was alone. He couldn't help watching from afar as she studied the menu with a pinched brow. Under better lighting, he was right about his earlier impression. She was definitely cute. Her features were soft and curved, a round nose and round cheeks paired with pouty lips and warm brown skin. His gaze dipped to beneath the table and he put two and two together. She wasn't concerned with the menu. She was nervous, her foot tapping and knee bouncing. Was it because she was alone? Had her blind date stood her up?

Aiden failed to notice Eddie speaking to him. He jerked in his chair and blinked out of his trance. Eddie prattled on about a phone call with Paulina, the executive producer for their show. He was saying something about filming their next episode in the New Year.

"She asked if we could start before, but I told her it's the holidays," said Eddie, spooning his cream of mushroom soup. "It can wait 'til after, you know? Paulina's always trying to boss everybody."

"Right…" Aiden humored, trailing off and saying nothing else.

The waiter arrived with their main courses. For the next

half hour he and the Myerses dined over prime-cut steaks and wine ripened by tannins. Occasionally, whenever the urge struck him, he tossed a look in the woman's direction, checking to see if she was still alone.

She was. She texted on her phone, fingers moving at a furious speed.

Aiden didn't know why he kept checking on her. Why it mattered to him that she was sitting alone, apparently stood up. He intentionally kept his circle small and rarely gave strangers a second thought. Yet here he was pondering about some woman he shared a car ride with. His interest was inexplicable but also inescapable.

Before he grasped what he was doing, Aiden rose out of his chair. Half of the Myerses didn't notice, too deep in their delicious meal and avid chatter. Both Eddie and Mrs. Myers questioned him, but he muttered something about the restrooms and abandoned the table. He cut across the steakhouse and its dozens of crowded tables, heading for the one where the woman sat alone. She looked up at the last second, the surprise clear from the lift of her brows and slight part of her lips.

"How's the date going?"

She gestured to the empty chair across the table. "As you can see, it's going great. I'm out with the Invisible Man."

He almost grinned. "Was that an H. G. Wells reference?"

"The seat's empty, isn't it?"

Intrigued more than ever, he said, "I noticed. Are you headed home soon?"

"I'm waiting for my bill. They *actually* charge you for a glass of water."

"How about the free bread. Is it really free?"

"I'll find out when the bill comes."

"Did you try to text or call him?"

"No answer," she said, sighing. "It's probably for the best. I'm not feeling too great anyway."

Already acting off of an unusual pluck of courage, Aiden figured he would keep going. He dropped into the empty seat across from her and said, "Is there anything I can do? The hostess is around here somewhere. She can call you a taxi or ride share."

"I've been trying to flag her down for a while, but she's ignoring me. No surprise there," the woman explained. She showed him her phone screen. "I tried the URide app too, but it's booked for the next hour."

"You finish the not-free water and I'll grab the hostess."

"Why are you helping me?"

He hung halfway out of the chair and considered his answer. "Because it seems like it hasn't been a great night for you."

"And? You don't even know my name."

"Easy fix. I'm Aiden," he said, extending his hand for a shake. "You're…?"

"Selene."

"Nice to meet you, Selene. Excuse me a second, I'll get the hostess." Aiden enjoyed the visible shock on her face as he rose to his feet. She gaped at him like his skin had tinged a tangerine orange. He assumed her surprise was from how forward he was. Little did she know it was a rarity for him.

Aiden spotted the hostess on the opposite end of the dining room in talks with what looked like her replacement for the coming shift. He moved to cross the room, stopping at the sound of his name. Eddie had gotten up from his table with the rest of the Myerses, though it seemed Mrs. Myers and Rory were now missing. He slipped his arm around Aiden's neck and pulled him aside for a quick detour.

"What are you doing?"

"I'm going to speak to the hostess. Where did your aunt and cousin go?"

"Rory was a little upset and left early. That made Aunt Priscilla upset and I think she's trying to bring her back," Eddie answered. "But that still doesn't answer my question."

"Unless I'm developing early onset dementia, I'm pretty sure I told you I'm going to speak to the hostess."

"Why?"

Aiden shrugged off Eddie's arm, confused by the line of questioning. "Why does it matter?"

"I saw you stop at the table over there."

"I went over for a few seconds. I'm still lost why you're bringing it up. Do you know her?" Aiden asked. The possibility hit him at once, sinking like a stone in a river. He should've pieced together the connection from the get-go. Brimrock wasn't the biggest town; it stood to reason Eddie would know Selene. His throat dried at the thought, turning his voice hoarse. "Of course you do. Which crazy ex from high school is she? The one who left twenty voice messages on your phone or the one who slashed your tires?"

"She's not my ex, but I do know her. So does everyone else in town."

"Is that supposed to be a clue?"

Eddie smacked his palm to his face. "I'll spell it out for you since you don't know who she is. That's Selene Blackstone. Granddaughter of Luna Blackstone. *The* Luna Blackstone."

CHAPTER FOUR

Yukie's tiny yip woke Selene from a deep sleep. She lay on her stomach, face burrowed into her pillow, still dressed in last night's date outfit. Lifting her head up, she squinted around the room, vision blurry from more than grogginess. Without her glasses, the candles and lamp on her bedside table looked like floating blobs. She found her glasses between the sheets and slid them back onto her face. Her bedroom came into focus. So did the time.

It glowed 8:38 a.m. back at her.

"Oh, crap!"

Selene scrambled out of bed but didn't get far. Her foot caught on the blanket, forcing her off balance, yanking her toward the floor. She shoved away the blanket with an impatient kick of her foot and half crawled, half ran for the bathroom. Yukie yipped again, trotting in her wake.

She was late. More than late. She was *screwed*. Miriam, like many in town, had it out for her. Being late for work, even once, meant the real chance she might be fired. A deeper tremor of panic rocked Selene at that possibility. She couldn't let that happen. She had twenty minutes to pull off a miracle.

Three times she botched her magic. She summoned the shampoo instead of the body wash. She waved her fingers and dialed the water to cold, not hot. She sent her toothbrush flying toward the toothbrush holder, but misjudged and dropped it into the toilet.

"I'll worry about that later," she muttered as the toothbrush plunked into the bowl and water splashed onto the seat.

She threw on the first thing she found in the closet—a loose pair of boyfriend jeans and a wrinkled V-neck T-shirt she soon discovered had a hole. Both would have to do for the day. She would keep her coat on and hope no one noticed.

Emerging from the closet, she was at least relieved her things had done as requested. They had started packing themselves. Her leather book bag hovered in the air as her wallet dropped inside followed by her phone. She went to the mirror and groaned at her reflection. Her once lively coils were flat and matted on the left side, their volume long gone. She scanned her messy room and spotted a knitted beret underneath her bed.

Her book bag flew toward her waiting arm, sliding up onto her shoulder, and she set off at a light sprint down the hall. Yukie again trailed behind as though in hopes she'd get to come along.

"Sorry, Yukes, you have to stay put. I'll see you later."

Selene stopped on the sidewalk outside and glanced at the time on her phone. She had six minutes left. Short of searching her spell book for a spell to stop time, she was going to be late. But maybe if she were only a few minutes late, Miriam wouldn't be too hard on her...

She brought up the URide app with hope ballooning in her chest. It quickly burst into nothing as the wait time flashed across her screen and told her it'd be twenty-five minutes. With no choice left but to hightail it like her life depended on it, she gripped the straps of her leather book bag and then sped off.

Today was brighter than yesterday. The sun peeked out from a cluster of clouds and the snow melted into slush, the pine trees turning green again. She almost slipped twice on the sidewalk's slick surface, but regained balance at the last second. It was times like these she wished she could pull a Mary Poppins and travel to work by magic flying umbrella.

Selene jogged the six and a half blocks, growing angrier with herself for each step. Last night was a blank after the Mulberry. She had walked through the front door and kicked off her boots. The humiliation of being stood up still stung as a fresh wound, making her want nothing more than to bury her face in her pillow and go to bed. She had found her way to the kitchen for a glass of water, the cool liquid soothing her dry throat. By the kitchen sink, she had turned her gaze on the garden window. Through the multi-dimensional glass, the moon hung half-full and silver, glowing in all of its lunar beauty. The thought of an impromptu lunar ritual entered her mind and then…

Nothing. The moment cut out. She woke hours later to Yukie's impatient yelping. She was late and all hell was about to break loose.

Selene bounded up the stone steps of the library, breathless and clammy even in the winter cold. She checked the time before crossing the threshold. It could've been worse. She was only half an hour late.

"You're thirty-two minutes late," Miriam groused. Today she wore a feathery, loud pink sweater that looked fresh off an ostrich. She lifted her leg and kicked the book returns cart with her clunky orthopedic shoe. It wheeled over toward Selene. "Sort those. They're outta order. Then file them. Can you do that on time or is this going to be an ongoing problem?"

"I'll have them done in fifteen minutes." Selene left out how she would do it—a wrist flick here and a wrist flick there —but Miriam didn't need to know that part. She wheeled the cart out from behind the giant L-shaped librarian's desk, its squeak harsh on her sensitive ears. Her throbbing headache had gone nowhere, a constant ache on her temples.

She wasn't big on over-the-counter medicine and she hadn't had the time to pick up any even if she wanted. Plus, she had *Noelle*.

"So I messed up."

Selene jumped, dropping the book in hand. She had thought she was safely alone in the W–Z aisle. She should've known better than to assume Noelle would go a day without stopping by the library. Her best friend wore an apologetic smile that looked more like a cringe, paired with a faux leopard print coat.

"We're not going to talk about last night right now," hissed Selene, pressing a finger to her lips. "I was already late. I'm past the point of caring why your boy Peter stood me up."

"I lit his ass up on InstaPixel. Tagged him and everything. Wanna see the post?"

"No!" Selene caught herself, clamping her mouth shut. If she was any louder, she would draw Miriam's attention. Every noise in the near-empty library sounded five times louder than it actually was. "Do you see me right now? The wrinkled T-shirt I grabbed from the hamper? The matted curls I didn't bother to wrap overnight, so I just shoved under this beanie? I'm having a rough morning."

Noelle appraised her look from head to toe and reached out to tuck a loose, frizzy curl behind Selene's ear. "You do look like a hot mess. I thought you were going for something new—'just hopped outta bed and threw on the first thing I could find chic'. I've seen hipsters that look worse."

"That's a backhanded compliment if I've ever heard one."

"Okay, I get it. You're having a bad day. How can I help?"

"I feel like crap," Selene moaned. Her posture slackened as for the first time since she got out of bed she acknowledged the throbbing aches coursing through her body. "I have a headache, I'm groggy, and my whole body feels like it's been mowed down by a garbage truck."

"I got you, boo. Give me an hour. I'll whip you up something herbal."

Selene smiled with gratitude. "Thanks, Noe."

"Then I'm taking you out for dinner to make up for last night."

"It's okay, I'd rather be in bed. I'm going straight home after work."

"Then I'll bring dinner to you. Be back with a little something something to make you feel better."

Noelle disappeared from the aisle a second later, slinking off as quietly as she'd arrived. Selene had no doubt she would return with an herbal remedy of some sort to help her feel better. Like her, Noelle was a witch. The strange similarity had been what formed their friendship. Though their brand of magic differed, with Noelle's power derived from Mother Nature herself, they both understood each other.

After Selene sorted the book returns cart, she headed to the back room to check in with Miriam. She didn't want to risk pissing her off twice in one day. Miriam had clearly hired her for gossip purposes. Outside of the library and her ugly knitted sweaters, Miriam's biggest pastime was gossiping to any open ear.

Selene overheard Miriam and the others chatting in the back room. She stopped outside the door and ducked out of sight, choosing to eavesdrop first.

"Strange times we're living in," said the other librarian, Gerri. She had a permanent smoker's voice and the lines in her face to match. "I keep telling everybody to be on the lookout for evil forces. The devil never stops his work."

"Ger, I love you, but shut up," snapped another woman. Named Libby Samson, she was Miriam's good friend, allowed to spend hours lazing around the library as company. "They'll probably find the guy who did it and then you'll be ranting about your next crackpot theory by next week."

"Who says it was a guy?" Gerri asked. "You saw the news report. It said unidentified assailant, no physical description as of yet."

"Ladies, keep it civil, please," interjected Miriam. "If I wanted to listen to people talk over each other I'd turn on one of those awful political shows."

Gerri's sigh was loud and heavy. "Peter's always been a nice young man. I belong to the same book club as his mother, Cecile—she must be *distraught*."

Selene almost choked on air. She held back her cough by biting on her closed fist. Her mind was blank as she tried to process what she was overhearing.

"Have you spoken to his mother?"

"I left her a voice message with my condolences this morning."

"Who would do such a thing?" Miriam asked with a cluck of her tongue.

"We should know soon enough if the police have their way."

"And they will. They'll catch him."

"That'll be too little too late. I'm about done with bad things happening in Brimrock," ranted Gerri. "It seems like every few years we're dealing with something. And then you've got that girl working here, Miriam. She creeps me out every dang day."

Selene's glasses slid down the bridge of her nose. She didn't bother pushing them up. Her heart had started to hammer so loudly against her chest she questioned if they could hear. She should've walked away as the conversation turned to her. Nothing good was going to be said. The old biddies loved gossiping about her. Yet, she couldn't bring her feet to move, an inexplicable flush breaking out across her skin.

"Somebody in town had to hire her. Besides, she keeps me entertained."

"You mean she gives you fodder to yap about to us," sneered Libby.

"That's exactly it. The girl's odd just like her mother."

"Forget her mother," said Gerri. "She's odd just like that grandmother."

A beat of silence passed over the three women as if they didn't dare go on. Luna's memory lived on that infamously.

Selene had had enough. She wasn't going to stand by and let them drag Luna through the mud. Her hands curled around the handle to her cart and she barged into the room. Her sudden appearance startled the women. They flinched and hurried to cover their tracks, changing the subject to the weather. Though none of them said a word to her as she hauled the cart across the room, she could feel their furtive glances her way.

They were wondering if she'd heard them. Selene smirked to herself. She wanted to keep them guessing.

"Done with that cart?" Miriam finally asked. She rose out

of her chair with her hands on her generous hips. "I've got another few carts you can do."

"I think I'll take my break," said Selene defiantly. The move was unlike her, but she couldn't back down now. Her earlier headache throbbed harder than ever, her skin growing warmer. She was hot and it was their fault. They had triggered something inside of her. "I'll be back."

"A break when you were half an hour late," mumbled Gerri in the background. She shared an amused glance with Libby and sipped more of her tea. "Sure sounds like a cozy work setup."

Selene couldn't resist. She was wrong for it, and she knew it.

But Gerri was the last straw. Her snide side commentary earned a little payback. Arms limp at her sides, Selene gave the subtlest flick of her wrist. The mug in Gerri's hand slipped out of her grasp, spilling tea down her front and shattering on the ground. All three women jumped in alarm. Gerri shrieked, blouse now stained a pale brown.

"What in the world, stupid cheap mug!" Gerri reached for a napkin and began dabbing at her wet blouse.

Miriam and Libby watched their friend in confused silence. Selene didn't want to stick around. She parked the book cart where it belonged with the others and strode for the door.

"Break time!" she called from over her shoulder, riding the adrenaline-inducing wave of defiance every step of the way.

———

"Crazy," said Noelle in a hushed tone. She sat with Selene in the courtyard outside the library. As promised, she had returned with an herbal remedy she whipped up from her garden. "So Peter's in the hospital. And here I was cussing him out all morning."

"I looked it up online and they say he was attacked inside his apartment."

"I know I wished bad karma on him for being a fuckboy, but this isn't what I had in mind."

"Your words, not mine." Selene brought the flask to her lips and swallowed another mouthful of Noelle's potion. The brew tasted sharp and bitter, but the ache in her temples had lessened considerably in the last few minutes. "Anyway, the news reports say they're not sure when he'll wake up. I feel bad for him."

"I do too. I might go see him. Wanna come?"

Selene scrunched up her face. "You're not serious, are you? I don't know the guy!"

"That might be kinda awkward," Noelle admitted. "'Hey, remember me? You ghosted me before you were attacked by some psycho. Ring a bell?'"

"What time is it? I don't want to go back, but Lord Voldemort—I mean, Miriam is waiting." Selene checked the time on her phone and groaned. The past twenty-five minutes had sped by faster than she hoped.

"You've been extra spicy today. I like this you," said Noelle, giggling. "You need to get ghosted more often."

"Noe."

"Kidding! Anyway, let me go before Lord Voldy comes out here looking for a duel," Noelle said, rising from the bench. "I'll text you later about dinner."

Selene started to answer Noelle, reminding her she wasn't up for dinner tonight, but she gave up midway through. Noelle was already gone and she didn't care enough to raise her voice. She chugged the last of the herbal potion and screwed the lid back onto the flask.

When she returned to the L-shaped desk, she found four
carts overflowing with books. Miriam's special present for
her was the definition of passive aggressive. Selene bit down
on her jaw and took the slight in stride. She wasn't going to
let them rile her up two times in one day.

She wasn't an angry person, rarely the type to lose her
temper. Certainly not on a day she was in the wrong, showing
up half an hour late to work. She had little ground to stand on
being pissed at Miriam other than she was a cruel gossiper.
Could she blame the older librarian? She knew what she was
getting herself into working for her...

The rest of the afternoon passed with little interaction
with anyone but the books. A couple of times Selene helped
visitors locate the books of their choice. At another point she
helped a frustrated teenager fix the printer in the computer
lab. She was happy for the seclusion, sticking to the deep
bowels of the library with the carts of books Miriam had left
for her. Instead of magicking the books on the shelves, she
actually stocked them by hand.

The longer she took, the longer she avoided Miriam and
the others. Selene was in the references section shoving bulky
dictionaries onto the shelves when a familiar timbre spoke
her name. She looked up and discovered she was no longer
alone.

"I didn't know you worked here," said Aiden, hands
stowed in his pockets.

"What are you doing in the library?"

"You mean to tell me this isn't the post office? Second
time today I've done that. The search continues."

Selene rolled her eyes. "Do you ever drop the sarcasm?
You know what I meant. Take a look around the place. It's
basically empty. Not many people want to come to the library
on a Tuesday afternoon."

"I'm not many people," Aiden answered, shrugging. "I was going a little stir-crazy at my friend's family's house, so I decided to check out the town. Turns out I end up at a bookstore or library every time."

At first she said nothing, picking up another book to slide onto the shelf. She had no clue what Aiden was doing striking up a conversation with her, but she couldn't exactly say she minded either. Last night started out with Aiden aggravating her, only to soon be impartial to him. He came across prickly and hardheaded and she could tell he wasn't the biggest people person. But his sense of humor and wit also called to her.

"What are you reading?" she heard herself ask before she registered the question on her mind.

"Haven't decided," he said. He leaned against the bookcase and his lips quirked into a soft grin. "I'm in the mood for something off the wall. Maybe an action adventure type of book with something nutty like dinosaurs or giant snakes. Any recs?"

Selene sensed the sarcasm, but the temptation to play into his humor was irresistible. She grabbed his arm and tugged him along, leaving the book returns cart behind. He hardly protested, his long and lean frame following dutifully, as though she possessed the power to make him. They stopped in the fiction A–C aisle and she unloaded a frayed paperback into his hands.

"Just what you wanted," she said with a satisfied smirk.

Aiden turned the book over in his large palms and read the title out loud, "*Jurassic Park*."

"The one and only."

"This is your book recommendation?"

"I handed you the book, didn't I?"

"Have you even read it?"

"Yes," she answered smartly. "Twice. And I've seen all of the movies. Even *Jurassic Park III*. I'm not proud."

Aiden chuckled, an uncertain pause stretching on afterward. He cleared his throat and looked away. The humor faded from his features, his brow furrowing as a deep line, clefted chin tightening. He seemed to be in his head about something, holding the copy of *Jurassic Park* as though it weighed more than it did.

Selene's gaze dipped and watched his long fingers rake over the book's spine, nice and slow. Her breathing stalled and unfettered heat flushed over her skin. She couldn't look away as Aiden flicked through the paperback and then smoothed over the cover with his large palm, handling the book like a familiar friend. The heat warmed up and the urge to fan herself set in. For one ridiculous moment she wondered if a bookgasm was really a thing...

Noelle was right. She *was* extra spicy today.

He surprised her when he held *Jurassic Park* in one hand and ruffled through his carefully combed, reddish-brown strands with the other, gaze trained on her. "Listen, I don't normally do this, but...but would you like to get coffee? Sometime. Anytime. You know, if you happen to be free. *Sometime.*"

He smiled. She smiled back, sensing his was out of relief. His was a nice addition to his face, giving a curve to his linear features. She suspected it wasn't seen often.

"Sometime," Selene repeated, "like tomorrow?"

"Sometime like tomorrow sounds like the right kind of sometime."

"Noon?"

"Noon is also a time."

Selene's smile touched her eyes. "The Magic Bean is the best coffee shop in town. My best friend's aunt owns it."

"The Magic Bean it is," he said and then he laughed. Again out of clear relief. He *was* cute. Especially when humor split up his straight face. "Don't worry, I won't stand you up like the Invisible Man."

"Already an improvement from last night."

"I'll try to keep the trend going. We can talk about the finer points of *Jurassic Park*." Aiden ended their exchange there, saying goodbye with a quick wink.

Selene stood still until he was gone and she was alone in the aisle. Then she bent over, hands on her kneecaps, and released a short, giddy laugh. She had no clue what was funny, or even why she had agreed to meet Aiden for coffee, but tomorrow excited her. Her stomach rocked with thousands of little nervous butterflies fluttering uncontrollably.

Today had started off terribly with her waking up late for work, and she might've been stood up last night by Peter, but things were on the up and up. Aiden was interesting and the fact that he had asked her out was an added bonus. Even for a cursed witch doomed for a miserable existence in Brimrock, she couldn't help smiling like a fool. Dare she look forward to tomorrow?

CHAPTER FIVE

"Rockin' Around the Christmas Tree" boomed from the stereo for the fifth time that night. The dinner party guests livened up just as much as they had the first time, bobbing along to the Christmas classic with brash confidence only brought on by alcohol. More often than not they were off beat, but that didn't stop them from swaying and spinning, spilling the drinks in their red plastic cups. Aiden backed into a corner of the room and tried fighting off the secondhand embarrassment washing over him.

He sipped from his glass of scotch on the rocks and contemplated if anyone would notice him slinking off. He had grit his teeth and bore the minutiae of the Christmas dinner party Mrs. Myers put together for the neighborhood. He had played nice seated between Miriam Hofstetter and Libby Samson as they gossiped about scandals in town, including some involving guests at the party. Twice he offered to trade seats with them, but they declined, smiling at him and switching topics to what a fine-looking man he was. Why was a handsome man like him single?

And he wanted to take his scotch to the head right then and there.

When the dinner block of the night was finished, everyone crowded into the den and mingled over drinks. Mrs. Myers boasted about her "Christmas Jams" playlist and dialed the stereo volume to full blast. He had been stuck weaving through the passel of tipsy party guests ever since.

"Sweetie, is everything alright?" Mrs. Myers asked, swooping in unseen from his left. She descended on him like a mother bird checking her precious eggs in the nest, fussing over him wherever possible. She picked a piece of lint off his rich, indigo blue sweater and shoved a napkin loaded with sugar cookies into his free hand. "I've noticed you've been quiet all night. It isn't too many people for you, is it? I forgot how shy you are."

The tips of his ears colored red and he shook his head. "Uh, no…I'm fine. Just sitting back and watching."

"No need to be afraid to mingle! Nobody here bites," she simpered. Her tone sweetened up as she picked another fleck of lint from the wool of his sweater. He wondered if she had had one too many spiked eggnogs. "Rory is feeling a bit uncomfortable tonight too. Do you mind keeping her company?"

"Mrs. Myers, I don't think—"

"Auntie Priscilla," she corrected. Her sweet smile spread, rounding her already-plump rosy cheeks. "Anyone who is a good friend of Eddie's is family of mine."

Unsure what to say to that, Aiden remained silent. He glanced into the crowd and spotted Rory on the opposite end. She *was* his party twin. Probably the only other person in the house not currently rocking to "Run Rudolph Run." Instead she hovered by the drinks table with red eyes and a heavy frown, absentmindedly running her fingers through her wavy chestnut locks. She was hatching an escape plan just like him.

"Why is she so upset again? I tried asking earlier, but Eddie shushed me."

Mrs. Myers sighed. Her smile disappeared as motherly concern set in. "Unfortunately, it's been a rough few weeks for Rory. First she and Peter broke up and then she found out he was already dating again. And now the attack. *Such* a tragedy."

That last bit seized Aiden's attention. He had read up on the breaking news earlier that morning. Peter Feinberg had been found collapsed and shriveled up inside his apartment, the front door hanging ajar. The news report stated he was in a coma the doctors had yet to diagnose the cause of. The police investigation was underway, though it didn't seem promising with no witnesses and no signs of a break-in. Not even a single fingerprint or footprint to work off of. The ordeal wasn't a first in Brimrock…

"I'll head over and see if she's okay," Aiden volunteered.

A beam filled out Mrs. Myers's round face again. "You are a godsend, Aiden! I'm sure she'd appreciate a shoulder to cry on right now, especially from a guy as handsome as you."

He waited until Mr. and Mrs. Jorgensen from next door interrupted for a chat with Mrs. Myers before he wandered off. He had little to no interest in being a shoulder to cry on for Rory, but he knew an investigative lead when he came across one. What it could lead to, he wasn't sure. It could have been a dead end or it could have been another connection for his investigation into Luna Blackstone and the strange happenings around town.

Earlier that day he had worked up the courage to approach Selene Blackstone. From their first encounter bickering over the URide to their stroll in the snow to the

Mulberry, she intrigued him. Even before Eddie told him who she was. But to know she was *the* granddaughter he had hoped to work with for his investigation was the smooth layer of buttercream frosting on the red velvet cake. Their coffee date was hopefully the beginning of his deep dive for the Luna Blackstone episode. It didn't hurt if he had the opportunity to be around a cute, smart girl at the same time.

Aiden shook off thoughts of Selene and sidled up to Rory. If he wanted intel on what happened with Peter, he should probably focus.

"Great music," he said. He took up his post at the drinks table and feigned interest in the gaggle of tipsy dancers. "I can't wait for that sixth round of 'Rockin' Around the Christmas Tree.'"

She missed his sarcasm, the point of her nose pink as she sniffled. "Not me. I'm ready for bed. Every time I try and head up, my mom sucks me into a conversation with the neighbors. I'm sick of hearing about the Jorgensens' cat."

"Suzy, right? I heard about her dragging dead birds into the house." His attempt to engage fell flat as Rory half rolled her eyes and turned away from him. He must have come across as just as nosy and intrusive as her mother and the other party guests. He adjusted his approach with a husky clearing of his throat. "I heard about what happened with Peter. That…that sounds terrible. If you want to talk about it, I'm here."

"Why would I want to talk to *you* about it?" she snapped. She slammed down her drink, its contents sloshing over the sides and onto the table. "You're Eddie's friend. I don't know you."

He fumbled, trying to clarify. "Well, no, but what I meant —if you need a shoulder to cry on—"

"A shoulder to cry on? Are you *hitting* on me?" Rory

made a sound of disgust and then stormed off, her long, wavy, chestnut hair swinging behind her like a cape.

Aiden's jaw had dropped open; he was speechless and confused. He hadn't expected his attempt to gather intel from Rory would be too successful, but he hadn't expected to crash and burn so quickly either. He replayed everything he had said and searched for what was offensive. This was exactly why he preferred an evening with his books and research over a Christmas dinner party.

"You couldn't pretend for one evening, could you?" Eddie strolled over with his own drink in hand, grinning wide. He was tipsy already, on his third Jack and Coke. Unlike Aiden, he had relished in the chance to socialize with the dinner guests. Many of them were people he had known since childhood. "The party's not that bad, is it? The grub was good."

"The food was amazing. Best part. But this…" Aiden scanned the room, watching as the guests in their ugly Christmas sweaters and Santa hats exploded in laughter. He sipped from his scotch to wash down the residual shock from his encounter with Rory. "This isn't my thing."

"Everybody and their mom can see that. You don't exactly hide it well."

"I tried to talk to your cousin Rory, but she wasn't exactly thrilled."

Eddie groaned and said, "You're the last person who should be chatting with Rory. She's extra sensitive right now —the Peter thing has hit her pretty hard."

"Your aunt told me to keep her company."

"My aunt loves playing matchmaker," Eddie said with another swallow of his drink. "She's been trying to patch things up between me and Margot all evening."

"I saw. She seems into you."

"Still. After all these years." A proud grin broadened on his face.

"High school relationships work out in the real world all the time." Aiden wasn't able to resist the cynicism. He only caught it after his quip. He steered the conversation elsewhere, figuring he had had enough love talk. "I've been researching the history around Luna Blackstone and the town. We have a lot of content for our fiftieth episode."

"The last thing I wanna talk about at a party is work stuff," Eddie said, his eyes drifting to Margot from afar. "What happened to leaving it 'til *after* the holidays?"

"I never agreed to that stipulation. That was you."

"Paulina gave us our deadline. We have plenty of time. Relax and enjoy the holidays, Aiden. It won't kill you."

"And do what? Throw on an ugly Christmas sweater and drunk dance to 'Santa Claus is Coming to Town'? No thanks."

"Suit yourself. I'm choosing to soak up the time off. Matter of fact, I'm about to head over and ask Margot if she'd like to get some fresh air now." Eddie drained the last of his Jack and Coke and ditched the cup on the drinks table. The party crowd swallowed him up in seconds.

Aiden's chance to disappear finally arrived. He double-checked Mrs. Myers was off giggling with Miriam Hofstetter and then he executed his great escape. He tiptoed out the room and flew up the stairs, breathing deep relief when he closed the door to his guest bedroom. Mission accomplished.

————

The next morning Aiden woke with the coffee date on his mind. The Myers household was quiet enough for him to hear his own heartbeat as he crept to the bathroom in the hall for a hot shower and quick shave. Mr. and Mrs. Myers probably wouldn't be up for another couple of hours. The dinner party had still been going when midnight rolled around and he clapped shut his book and turned off his bedside lamp. The downstairs likely resembled hurricane wreckage with how sloppy guests were getting, partying to the twelfth rendition of "All I Want for Christmas is You."

Aiden stopped on the bottom stair already dressed and ready to go, a jolt of shock pinging him. The hall was as neat and tidy as before the party. He explored the ground floor, ducking his head into other rooms as he passed them by. The first floor half bathroom gleamed. The den looked immaculate with its towering Christmas tree lit up and the furniture stylishly arranged around the room. Last night he, Eddie, and Mr. Myers had pushed each piece against the wall to make room for guests. The dining room also showed no signs a raucous party had taken place less than twelve hours ago. The mahogany wood was polished and chairs tucked neatly in place. Had a magical fairy maid fluttered through the home and righted the mess in their sleep?

Now *that* was a potential subject to explore for their fifty-first episode…

"Sweetie, what are you doing up so early?" Mrs. Myers asked into the loud silence, appearing suddenly from around the corner in the kitchen. She had a gingham apron tied about her front, her wavy chestnut brown hair pushed out of her face by a matching headband. She held a carrier stocked with household cleaners, hands covered in rubber gloves that reached her elbows. "It's barely a minute past eight. You should be sound asleep. We're not taking family pictures 'til one."

"Family pictures?"

"Didn't Eddie tell you? It's a Christmas tradition. Every year we take holiday-themed family photos."

"Oh, but I'm not—I don't need to be included—"

"*Of course* you do," she interrupted. She set down the carrier full of cleaning products and tugged off her rubber gloves, putting a nurturing hand on his back. He was more than a head taller than her, making it awkward, but she guided him to the breakfast table anyway. "I don't need to tell you to wear something nice, because you already look great. Very presentable."

"Mrs. Myers—err, I mean, Aunt Priscilla, I don't think I feel comfortable being a part of the family photos," he said. He sidestepped to the right, out of her reach. "But I'm grateful you're inviting me. It's nice of you."

"Our family is very big on Christmas. When Jake and I adopted the girls, we made a pact to give them the kind of upbringing we never got to have. Now I get to finally make family a big thing on Christmas," she explained. "And Eddie —we as good as raised him too once Jake's brother passed. Christmas is the perfect time for togetherness."

"We were never too big on it in my household. I'm not a fan."

"It's never too late to start. Sit down, I was about to whip up some blueberry pancakes. I shape them like Christmas trees and dust them with sugar to look like snow."

"Thanks, but I actually have to take Ghost to the auto shop. We need to get him fixed before we leave town and then I'm meeting up with a friend. But, uh, good luck on those holiday pictures."

Aiden could feel Mrs. Myers's heart break as he turned to go. The joyful expression on her face faded and she sucked in a small but audible breath. He didn't stop or glance over his shoulder, afraid if he did he would be guilted into staying.

Ghost needed to be fixed and he wanted to sip coffee with Selene. Anything else would have to wait.

———

Brimrock was the cozy New England town seen on TV. The downtown square was a collection of historic buildings and gas lantern posts lining the street. Thick forests of trees surrounded the area, centuries old and caked with last night's snowfall. The morning cold hung in the air so thick frost glazed over shop windows and fire hydrants. Judging by the gray sky, the sun wasn't making an appearance today.

Aiden dropped Ghost off at the auto shop and spent the rest of the morning exploring Brimrock on foot. He swung by Balford's Books again and perused its aisles, in the back of his mind thinking about Selene at the library. When he noticed her hidden away in the references section, unloading her cart of book returns, his heart had jumped. He had inhaled a breath of excitement and fought off the sudden invasion of nerves. He blanked on the last time a woman had evoked this type of a reaction of him, and at only a distance…

The coffee date was an opening for his investigation. The fiftieth episode covering Luna Blackstone was most important. He couldn't lose track of his goal regardless how much Selene interested him. He repeated that thought over and over again as he approached the Magic Bean. He was early— twenty minutes early to be exact. Enough time to admire the menu and decor.

The tiny coffee shop certainly stood out from the others on the street. Its brick walls were painted an emerald green, the sign hanging on the front a giant coffee bean wearing an oversized witch's hat. In the window was a kitschy Christmas display. A miniature tinsel Christmas tree was perched with gaudy baubles and knickknacks like rabbit's feet hanging from its branches. A dozen different tea lights lit up the display and a giant stuffed black cat, tail curled into a question mark, rose on its paws.

He entered to more tea lights and tinsel. On the inside, the shop was crammed even with a few customers, the furniture an assortment of patched armchairs and wobbly tables. Against the walls were shelves bending under the weight of potted plants, stacks of books, and more tea lights. He bumped into the corner of a table, pain shooting up his thigh, and maneuvered the rest of his way to the front counter on a limp.

The barista on shift matched the eccentric style of the coffee shop. She had a short crop of curls pinned down by silver snake clips, her nails also a glittery silver. She wore corduroy overalls with one strap dangling free and the brightest shade of fuchsia lipstick he had ever seen. He walked up and gave a nod as a hello, but she merely heaved a sigh as though the idea of another customer was bothersome.

"Your order?"

"Oh, I'll take a black coffee. Three sugar packets on the side."

"Size?"

"Large."

She punched his order into the cash register and said, "That'll be $4.30."

"Right." Aiden fished into his pocket for his wallet and withdrew a five. The woman snatched the bill out of his hand and popped the cash register drawer open. His eyes dropped to her name tag and he almost said her name aloud. *Noelle.*

His coffee was ready in less than two minutes. He thanked a second barista behind the counter and turned to choose a table. He was setting down his coffee as the bell above the front door chimed and he looked up. Selene walked through dressed in a peacoat and her usual thick glasses, her curls pinned up in that intentionally messy type of bun women did. His face relaxed into a smile, but then he realized her attention was on someone else.

"Selly!" shouted the woman behind the counter. "What're you doing here?"

"Coffee date."

Aiden's nerves kicked in sudden and strong like they had yesterday at the library; he had approached Selene with his strategy for the show but wound up a nervous wreck. He shut out thoughts about yesterday and leveled his heart rate with an inhale. Selene interested him as a person, and sure he thought she was attractive in a smart, cute librarian sort of way, but that was the end of it. For the dozenth time, he reminded himself not to lose focus on the investigation. No matter how cute she looked with her tight curls and bold framed glasses.

As if Selene and her friend Noelle figured it out at the same time, both sets of eyes fell on him. The women glanced his way from across the coffee shop and Aiden hesitated before giving a slight wave. His skin betrayed him and tinged a pink that revealed his nerves. To his surprise, Selene's lips spread into a smile.

Let their coffee date begin.

CHAPTER SIX

"You're early," said Selene, stopping at Aiden's table.

"I can say the same about you. Fifteen minutes early." Aiden raised his brows and pointed at the time on his watch.

She shrugged off her coat and dropped into the seat across from his. "I don't like being late."

"Does anyone?"

"You haven't met my best friend, Noelle."

"Actually, I have. Barista?"

"Barista."

"I can tell she loves her job," Aiden said, his eyes drifting to the front of the coffee shop.

Selene followed him, peeking over her shoulder. Noelle was at the counter unabashedly rolling her eyes at Gerri Halsey. Her fellow librarian berated Noelle for the wrong coffee order. An automatic snicker slipped out before Selene could hold it back. She played it off by clearing her throat and sitting up straight.

"Not a fan of whoever that is?"

"More like she's not a fan of me," said Selene. "Coworkers."

"How about I get you something to drink and then you can tell me about this evil coworker who's not a fan? Coffee? Hot chocolate? Hot tea? What's your coffee shop poison?"

"A latte with soy milk and two pumps of hazelnut, please."

"Be right back."

Selene sat back and watched Aiden go. She blinked three times and questioned if she were dreaming. She never went out on spontaneous dates. Mostly because guys never asked her out on them. Definitely not guys like Aiden—witty, intelligent, cute guys who had an affinity for books and specialized in quips. Only minutes into their coffee date and Aiden had already surpassed half the men she had been out with.

The bar really *was* low.

She snuck a peek at him over at the front counter and then dug into her leather book bag. A quick mirror check couldn't hurt. Just to make sure she wasn't pulling a Miriam with lipstick smudged on her teeth. She flashed her teeth at her compact mirror, ensuring they were perfectly pearly white. One less thing to worry about.

The longer Aiden took to make it back, the more nerves wormed around inside her stomach. She breathed in and out and tried not to focus on the increasing pressure. If their coffee date was already off to a good start, that only meant it would have to continue on that trajectory. Otherwise she'd bear the sinking disappointment that always came whenever she had a shred of hope. Any time she believed even for a split second that this time could be different. The solution was to stay out of her head and enjoy the moment for what it was.

No thoughts on the curse. No pessimism about her bad luck. No hope inevitably setting her up for failure.

If only her nerves would scram…

"One hazelnut latte," said Aiden from behind. He clutched her latte in one hand and a plate of fresh croissants in the other. Their buttery aroma immediately inspired stomach growls. "The baked goods in the glass case were calling my name. Hope you like croissants."

Selene smiled. "The croissants at the Magic Bean are the best in town."

"Interesting name for a coffee shop."

"Noelle's aunt Bibi owns it."

"I'm surprised you don't work here."

"If Noelle and Bibi had their way, I would," she replied. She blew on her latte to cool it off and then took a small sip. "I love my job at the library. Except my boss. And my coworkers—including the one you just saw."

"Why don't you get along?"

She swallowed tightly and half shrugged. She hated lying. "Age difference."

"That makes sense. Different generations sometimes don't mesh."

"It's fine, though. The books make it worth it."

"I'd work in a bookshop if I could."

"What do you do?"

Now in the hot seat, Aiden hesitated, wiping crumbs from the croissant on his napkin. "I guess you can say I'm a…a freelance writer."

"A writer? You?"

"I don't seem like the type?"

"Not at all," Selene said with an unabashed laugh. "I peg you for an accountant. Maybe an engineer. Definitely *not* a freelance writer."

"Well, I am. Why else would I have such an interest in books?"

She studied him over the rim of her latte cup, processing this new information. The flutters in her stomach grew more insistent, pouring out in nervous ticks. Her knee bouncing or foot tapping, or even combing her teeth over her bottom lip. She breathed deeply and pressed on as though the nerves ceased to exist.

"I could tell you weren't from around here."

"How so?"

Selene allowed a small, playful smirk. "You just seem…different."

"I could say the same about you," he flirted back. He reached across the table and gave her hand a quick squeeze.

Her heart rocketed up into her throat. She choked on it, coughing as her brain went haywire. In its frenzied state, she lost control of her magic and sent the plate of croissants careening off the table. The porcelain plate shattered into pieces against the nearby wall and the half-eaten croissants spun into the air before flopping to the ground.

For a long second, it seemed like nobody inside the Magic Bean moved a muscle. At the front counter, Noelle and her latest customer Mr. Higgley cut themselves off midconversation. Aiden glanced from Selene to the wall then the floor and back up at her again. Selene sat frozen with her mouth stretched so wide and open her jaw started to ache.

When she racked her brain for an explanation, nothing came up. She was screwed. *So* screwed.

"Uh," Aiden muttered, "what was that?"

"The heater's on full blast," said Noelle out of nowhere. She sprang up on their table with a dustpan and broom, rushing to sweep up the mess. "It's really powerful. Sometimes too powerful. Your table's positioned exactly in front of the vent."

Aiden looked up at the vent Noelle spoke of. His brow was lined, suspicion bleeding onto his features, but slowly, he gave a nod. "I guess it is…isn't it?"

"Sorry about that," apologized Noelle, holding up the dustpan of broken plate chunks and crumby croissants. "I should've warned you. Give me a sec and I'll grab you new croissants. Fresh out the oven."

Aiden waited until Noelle bustled through the flapping door leading into the coffee shop's kitchen before he leaned closer. He whispered as if paranoid Noelle would overhear, "Did you feel a blast of heat? I didn't notice anything. The plate seemed to fly off the table on its own…"

Selene placated his suspicion with a soft, harmless smile. "That's weird. I felt the blast of heat. Maybe you were too busy drinking your coffee. You didn't notice. Anyway, tell me more about your freelance work. It sounds interesting."

The pivot in conversation worked. Aiden spoke about his experience as a freelance writer and she asked enough questions to distract him. Noelle delivered a new plate of fresh croissants, pausing for a second long, narrowed-eyed look at Selene. Their coffee date continued with the talk shifting onto the holiday season. Aiden told her about the Myerses' Christmas dinner party, detailing the gaffes he'd made.

"The food was great, but everything else I could do without. Mrs. Fraser kept trying to set me up with her niece Sharon. She started off telling me what a nice girl she is—and then threw in that she's had some trouble with the law. She's a kleptomaniac."

"I've heard about her," said Selene with an easy laugh. "She's gotten caught shoplifting at the U Save a couple of times."

"What was I supposed to say to that? I ended up escaping to the laundry room."

"Good strategy."

"My friend's aunt wasn't much better. She was trying to pawn her daughter off on me. She's the ex-girlfriend of the guy who was attacked—Peter Feinberg."

Selene stopped midbite of her croissant, the mention of Peter catching her off guard. She hadn't given him much thought since the night he ghosted her at the Mulberry. She wasn't sure what to think about him. Guilt took anchor whenever she fixated on it for longer than a few seconds. While she sat disgruntled at the candlelit table at the Mulberry, cussing his name and the day he was born, he was likely off being attacked by...*someone*. How could she not feel at least partially responsible?

Aiden hardly noticed. He went on about the dinner party. "Apparently, the Myerses have a couple of holiday dinner parties. Last night's was the opener. There's another one this Saturday."

She held her breath. This was it, the segue into asking for date number two. His hazel eyes shone like earthy stones caught in the morning light and she brightened up in her seat. Today *was* different after all.

"Up for a second round?" Aiden asked.

The hope swelling popped and her face fell. "Oh. Right. Sure. Another would be great."

Selene hung her head and admonished herself in his absence. She had to stop doing that. Jumping to conclusions was not only embarrassing but it was the worst thing to do on a first date. If their coffee outing could be counted as one. Maybe Aiden wanted to be friends. She knew better than to compare the fiction in books to reality.

"Round two, here we go," said Aiden, resuming his seat.

He let a slow grin work at spreading his lips. "I forgot to tell you I've been reading your book recommendation."

"*Jurassic Park*? How do you like it?"

"I have to give it to you. I wasn't the biggest fan of the movies, but you were right. Crichton writes a great story."

"I told you so."

"Normally, people don't say 'I told you so' after someone tells them they're right."

"I'm not normal," she quipped before she could stop herself. She was buzzing off the sudden discussion of books. The one topic she could talk about for hours without worry. "I love a good adventure book and *Jurassic Park* has everything you'd want in that kind of story."

"You know what you're talking about."

"There's nothing like reading about that hero—or heroine —going on this amazing quest."

Aiden's features curved, curiosity forming on them. "Reading about it is great, but experiencing it firsthand is worthwhile too."

"I'm sure. I mean I…I wouldn't know."

"Why?"

"I just…I can't. Brimrock's my home." She shifted in her seat and began picking at the lid of her latte cup.

"You can book a trip somewhere. Leave for a week or two. I do it all the time. It's a nice breather."

"I'll think about it," she said dismissively. She began gathering her things, sliding her book bag over her shoulder. "It's time for me to get back to work."

"I forgot not everyone's a lazy freelancer like me," he teased with a slow grin. Like yesterday, she couldn't help noticing how well it fit his face. The curl of his lips offset his angular features, from his strong-bridged nose to his square jaw nicely. He rummaged in his back pocket and produced his phone. "Feel free to turn me down and shatter my ego, but I was hoping to get your number."

From behind her bold-framed glasses, her eyes widened. He wanted her number. He wanted to keep in touch. She softened, emitting a quick laugh. "Sure. I had a great time. Sorry, you caught me off guard. I live in my head sometimes."

"I thought about living in mine, but the rent's too high."

Selene smirked at the response she had learned was *so* Aiden. The dry, tongue-in-cheek humor was right up her alley. He was right up her alley. For the first time in her life, it truly seemed like her bad luck was waning. The curse was lifting. She had met her match.

———

"I shouldn't have eaten that cheese Danish. Now my stomach's acting a fool," said Aunt Bibi with a hand to her belly. Her wire-rim glasses hung low on her nose and her lavender-gray hair framed her face in soft, short curls. She sighed in resignation and then crossed the room to dim the lights. The coffeeshop had closed for the day moments ago and it was now time for locking up. "Thank the powers that be you two girls are here to help with cleanup."

"Whatever you need, Bibi," said Selene. She waved her hand and the chairs in the room rose up and stacked themselves onto the tables.

Noelle tore her eyes away from her phone. "What was that, Auntie?"

"Girl, if you don't pry those eyes from that phone, I'll do it for you. Don't try me," warned Aunt Bibi. Her slippers scratched against the oak tiling for every move she made. "One of these days you girls are gonna realize real life doesn't happen in those phones—or in those books."

Selene cracked a slight smile. The last part was directed to her. The lecture was par the course for Aunt Bibi, who liked to school them on life. Neither of them objected. Bibi's wisdom had proved to be helpful more often than not.

"It happens out there," said Aunt Bibi. Her hand shot to her stomach again as it gurgled. "Except when you have a case of the bubble guts. Then it happens in you-know-where."

Selene and Noelle laughed as Bibi's head tilted in the direction of the coffeeshop restrooms. The sixtysomething woman threw in the towel against her upset stomach and excused herself. Both watched her go, unable to resist the amusement curling their lips.

"Or except when there's a psycho in town out to attack you," Noelle finished once Bibi shut the restroom door. She held up her phone for Selene to see. "I was reading up on the latest with Peter's attack. It looks like doctors are baffled."

"How can they be baffled? Can't they diagnose whatever's wrong with him?"

Noelle shrugged, eyes falling to the light of her phone. "Guess not. They're saying it's like he's been drained of his energy—they're saying it might be an extreme case of dehydration."

"Dehydration?" Selene repeated, the skepticism thick in her normally soft voice. "That doesn't make any sense. We *know* he was attacked. What did the attacker do? Steal the water from his body?"

"Don't know. Just telling you what I read. They're saying the attacker somehow knocked him unconscious. But it looks like they're saying the dehydration is just a preexisting thing that's making his condition worse," Noelle recited from the text on her phone.

Selene leaned against the front counter, frowning. "I mean I'm no medical expert, so if that's what they think it is…"

The diagnosis didn't sit right with her, but she dropped the subject. She had no medical knowledge to argue with doctors. If they believed Peter's comatose state was a culmination of factors, who was she to argue? Her gut instinct didn't override medical professionals.

"Did you go visit him?" Selene asked.

Before Noelle could answer Selene's question, the flush of a toilet echoed from the bathroom. They ignored it and pressed on.

"I think I'm gonna send him and his family a card and flowers. Seems less awkward, you know? After I cussed him out."

"Probably, yeah."

"So," said Noelle with a growing Cheshire grin, "you had a little coffee date you didn't tell me about. I'm offended."

"Don't be. It was kinda spur-of-the-moment."

"You're welcome I saved your ass. What were you doing sending that plate crashing against the wall?"

"Nervous reflex! You know how I can't control my magic when I get too emotional."

"That's the problem with you lunar witches," teased Noelle. "You can't be sane and levelheaded like us green witches."

Selene raised her brows, skepticism on full display. "Since when are green witches sane and levelheaded? Have you met you?"

"Girl, that's beside the point. You can't go firing dinnerware at the walls. You know how everybody in town already thinks you're nutty."

"This is true."

"You do seem to have a lot in common. I'll give you props on that."

"*Finally*," sighed Selene.

"He looks familiar. He's not from Brimrock, right?"

"Nope, he lives in Arizona now. Grew up in New York."

Noelle said nothing, but Selene understood what the heavy brow look on her face meant. She was thinking, combing the recesses of her mind for whatever it was she wanted to say. Selene waited with a patience practiced over time. Her best friend was good at connecting dots, and the dots she was on the cusp of lining up were big. Selene could tell.

"I've seen him somewhere," Noelle muttered. She swiped her finger across her phone, unlocking the passcode protected screen, and hurried to bring up her web browser. "I can't remember where, but I've seen that guy before."

"He's a freelance writer. His best friend is Eddie Myers." Selene offered the tidbits of info in hopes it would jog Noelle's memory.

From the wrinkle in Noelle's brow as her gaze raked over her phone, Selene sensed something was up. Noelle was on the fast track to solving whatever puzzle she had been presented with. She scrolled through a long list of what looked like videos and then gasped.

Selene inched closer. "What is it?"

"Oh, crap. Selly," Noelle breathed. Her eyes, framed by a layer of false lashes, looked up at Selene. "I know who he is."

"Are you going to tell me? Why are you looking up YouTV videos?" Selene refused to wait a second longer. She rushed behind the coffeeshop counter to join Noelle at her side for a peek at whatever was on her phone.

"He's a cohost on *Paranormal Hunters*," Noelle said, holding the phone out. "Him and his friend Eddie. They travel the country investigating urban legends and paranormal stuff. I'm subscribed to their channel. I've seen a few of their episodes. I knew I knew him from somewhere."

Selene's breath hitched in her chest. She stared blankly at the screen as the episode on Noelle's phone began to play. Aiden and Eddie waved at the camera and launched into an introduction chock-full of witty banter. Her eyes bulged until they couldn't widen any further, and her lack of breathing ushered in a dizziness that made the room sway.

In this episode, he and Eddie were on a hunt for the Skinner, an infamous urban legend about a man who hitchhiked and skinned his victims alive. Selene watched as the two beckoned to the camera—and the viewers at home—to follow them toward their caravan. They hopped into the driver and passenger seats on the empty desert highway and hilarity ensued. Eddie was terrified. Aiden cracked well-timed, sarcastic jokes. The episode had over forty thousand likes on YouTV…

Aiden was a paranormal investigator. He hosted a semifamous show online. He spent his time looking into strange occurrences and phenomena. Oddball things that were both mystery and myth. Things like Luna. Things like *her*.

The revelation uprooted her entire perception of him. She blinked at Noelle's phone screen and digested the truth for what it was. The hurtful, awful reality that he wasn't who he said he was—that he was a man out to investigate another urban legend. He was using her.

Selene swallowed against the golf-ball-sized lump in her throat. She shoved down the hurt feelings, reminding herself that she was foolish to think of Aiden as anything different. How could she have been so naive when time and time again she was proven wrong?

She was a Blackstone. She was a witch. She was doomed to retrace the same miserable steps as the other women in her family, destined to live out her days in Brimrock under isolation and mistreatment. She would never find love. She would never find adventure. Happiness wasn't in the cards.

Aiden was more proof of that.

"You okay?" Noelle asked when several seconds went by in silence. The only sound in the coffeeshop came from the bathroom; Aunt Bibi flushed the toilet for what was the fourth time.

Selene brushed a hand over her face, fingers digging into her curls, and she nodded. "I'm fine. Just…just shocked."

"He didn't tell you?"

"No."

"That's shady as hell," Noelle said. "Why would he say he's a freelance writer? He's a YouTVer!"

"Because he wanted access."

Noelle wasn't tracking. "Access to the coffee shop?"

"Access to me. To *Luna*. He hosts a paranormal show, Noe. He's out for his next episode."

"What a dick," Noelle whispered under her breath. "Let me log on InstaPixel. We're gonna tag his ass in a post—"

"Stop. No social media."

Noelle's face was crestfallen. She exited the InstaPixel app and pocketed her phone. "Tell me you're not about to let him get away with being a creep."

"He's here for the holidays. He's not going anywhere. I'm going to get him off my trail," Selene said with a slow trickling determination. "And you're going to help me."

"Me? Selly, I don't mind dragging someone online, but you're taking it to a whole 'nother level."

"We're going to make him forget he was ever curious about Luna."

Noelle groaned. "Don't tell me how."

"There's a potion for it, isn't there? We can influence him to change his mind. It'll get him off our back."

"Why couldn't you stalk him online before the date like a normal person?"

"I didn't think he was lying about who he was, Noe."

"Selly, let's be real. You're the most un-millennial millennial I've ever met," said Noelle bluntly. She shuddered out a sigh, one hand on her waist and the other steeped in her cropped curls. "This is gonna be a shit show. I just know it."

"Are you going to help me or…?"

Noelle closed her eyes, resigning herself to her fate. "Girl, you know I'm ride or die."

Selene's smile was still spreading by the time the restroom door was yanked open and Aunt Bibi emerged. She looked relieved, the bulge in her belly significantly lighter, as she joined them midconversation. Her eyes shrunk, eying them both, wrinkle lines prominent around her mouth. Finally, she gave in and cackled out an amused witch's laugh.

"Alright, girls, go on. Tell Bibi. Those devilish lil' smirks don't fool me. Who're we hexing now?"

CHAPTER SEVEN

Nobody knew what happened to Peter Feinberg, but Aiden was determined to find out. Since the story had hit the town headlines, he was spending his free time reading up on the details. The more info the Brimrock PD released, the murkier the situation became. Peter Feinberg, able-bodied male of twenty-seven years, was attacked inside his apartment building on Monday night. Police estimated the attack happened between the hours of 8:00 and 10:00 p.m. The building's security camera coincidentally malfunctioned during that time block, failing to capture any visitors walking up to his apartment.

His injuries were even stranger. Peter showed no signs of bodily harm other than a bruise on his arm from what doctors speculated was his fall once he lost consciousness. He had no broken bones, no concussion or any other discernible physical injury. Yet he was comatose. He was severely dehydrated, skin pruned and shriveled up, and his vital signs were weak, as though the energy had been permanently drained from his body.

Doctors claimed it was a medical anomaly.

Aiden was new to town, but he knew better than to dismiss Peter's attack as a one-off. His research into Luna Blackstone and the town of Brimrock had turned up a number of odd occurrences over the years. Things like magical floating objects or the spontaneous combustion of a car. The people who bore witness always experienced a sudden memory dump after the fact. Even the ones who claimed to see the Blackstone women wandering the woods at night. Most damning of all was the peculiar fact that the men they loved either died or disappeared. No case more infamous than what happened to John Grisby.

The legend went that engaged John Grisby was having an illicit affair with Luna for months. One night on Halloween, a confrontation broke out between Luna, John, and his fiancée, Aurora. John was found the next morning permanently comatose. Both Luna and John's fiancée disappeared. Neither were heard from again, though many in town believed Luna's ghost *still* haunted the streets of Brimrock.

The Brimrock PD had released a statement assuring residents they had nothing to worry about. The investigation was underway and they would do their best to find Peter's attacker. Aiden saw the statement for what it was: the police department's attempt to placate the public. He wasn't one to be easily fooled, channeling his inner Hercule Poirot as he dived deeper.

His first choice would have been to interview Rory about Peter, but she was spending the days leading up to Christmas locked away sullenly in her room. The only time she came out was when Mrs. Myers begged for whatever latest Christmas activity she had scheduled. He gave up on Rory and traveled down other avenues.

Aiden surfed the web and read articles about the case. He logged onto social media and tracked local tags for Brimrock.

If anyone in town knew anything, wouldn't they post about it? His hunch proved correct when he came across the hashtag #SavePeter.

Given Brimrock's microscopic size compared to the rest of the country—even the rest of the state—it was only used 142 times. Aiden lurked on the hashtag scrolling through dozens of posts about the incident, winding up with little for the first one hundred. He discovered a potential lead when scrolling through endless posts with the hashtag.

LipstixAddict99 saved the day. She posted a selfie of herself pouting seductively at the camera. Beneath she used Peter's hashtag. He assumed it was another ploy for attention until he caught the comments the other users left. One in particular, a reply from LipstixAddict99, confirmed that her mother knew Peter's mother.

It was a well-known fact that Ms. Feinberg wasn't accepting questions from anyone. She had largely denied the news outlets when asked for comments about Peter's ordeal. She wanted as little fodder as possible, hoping to quell potential sensationalism. Aiden understood her reasoning, but when he read that LipstixAddict99's mother knew the family, a light bulb above his head flickered on.

He wasn't someone who direct messaged women on InstaPixel. He thought it was cheesy, no matter if famous male celebs were known to do it. Any messages he received from *Paranormal Hunters* fans he usually ignored. He preferred to use social media accounts for run-of-the-mill things, like keeping in touch with faraway friends and family. InstaPixel networking wasn't on his to-do list.

This time he made an exception. He messaged LipstixAddict99 in private and asked for more information. She recognized him from YouTV and suggested coffee. His knee-jerk response was to say yes, thinking of it as a logical meetup.

Then he remembered the social element. How would that look to Noelle, Selene's best friend, if he were meeting another woman for coffee?

They decided on the diner on the outskirts of town. He escaped Mrs. Myers's clutch another morning, thankful he had gotten Ghost back from the auto shop, as pristine as a decades-old Dodge Caravan could be after so many decades. LipstixAddict99, whose real name was Isabelle Halsey, showed up sixteen minutes late. He hid his agitation behind an even-keeled gaze as she strutted up and plopped down at their booth.

"Thanks for coming," he said stiffly. He couldn't resist adding, "A few minutes late, but I appreciate you showing up."

"I have things to do. Like a nail appointment in thirty. Make it fast." Isabelle made no attempt at hiding her disdain for him, rolling her eyes and checking her nails. She did need them done. Two were broken and the glittery gold had started to fade off.

Aiden muted his penchant for noticing small details and got straight to the point. "We already discussed who I am and the show I host, but I'm in town for an investigation—"

"No shit," she interrupted, mocking him with a scrunched face. "What do you want? Am I gonna get to be on camera?"

"Uh, no."

"*Then*?"

Baffled by the exchange, he said, "I wanted to ask you about Peter Feinberg."

Her tight features softened. "Peter. What d'you wanna know?"

"Your family knows his, correct? I was hoping to find out more about his attack."

"I don't know Peter. Don't know his family. Except his

mom is a snooze. She barely leaves her house. Not that my mom is so exciting. Guess that's why they're friends."

"Has your mom spoken to her about it?"

"She called her on the phone and they talked. Can't tell you about what. Look, ask her."

Relief loosened the rigid tension gathered in Aiden's neck and shoulders. He would much prefer to talk to her—anyone but Isabelle. "I'd love to ask her about it. Is it alright if we set up a meeting?"

"Call her yourself. This is her number." Isabelle held up her phone with the contact info brought up on the screen: Gerri Halsey (350) 671-9811

Isabelle was gone before Aiden could even thank her for the meeting. More than fine with her abrupt exit, he saved Gerri Halsey's contact info in his phone, a small and victorious grin pulling at his mouth. He might not have known how the pieces to the puzzle fit together, but he was one step closer to finding out.

————

"You missed our gingerbread contest!" Mrs. Myers shrieked.

Aiden had gotten back from his meeting with Isabelle, padding toward the staircase with fingers crossed he wouldn't be seen. He froze on the bottom stair and reluctantly hazarded a glance down the hall. Mrs. Myers's brown eyes were bulging, her hands on her thick hips.

"I wasn't aware there was a contest," Aiden said flatly.

"It's one of our musts every Christmas!"

He swallowed what he really wanted to say. It was several days until Christmas. Even if it were Christmas Day, decorating gingerbread seemed tedious. The spiced cookie was delicious, but what was the point in decorating it when it was meant to be eaten?

Staring at Mrs. Myers's expectant face, he searched for a sensitive reply. "I'm sorry. I lost track of time. I'm sure the competition was, uh, tough."

"Jake and Camilla won like they do every year. Eddie is the worst baking partner," she said with a shake of her head. "Anyway, you can still join us for our trip to the mall."

"The *mall*?" He hoped he hid his distaste behind his blank expression.

"Last-minute Christmas shopping. We're leaving in twenty. Be down at the car."

Aiden wanted to mention he had no intention of going to the Brimrock shopping mall. Particularly any time around Christmas.

Upstairs in his room, Aiden shut the door and hoped if he stayed as mouse quiet as possible, no one would notice his absence. His attempt proved futile the moment Eddie knocked on his door and poked his head in.

"We're leaving in five."

"You guys go without me. I'll stay behind."

"You know my aunt's going to have a meltdown, right?"

"If I skip out?"

Eddie nodded, leaning his stocky build against the door frame. "She already thinks you're miserable here. If you skip out on another family event, she's gonna lose it. If you hated it here, you'd tell me, right?"

"I never said I hate it here…"

"Where've you been all this time? You keep taking Ghost out for drives," said Eddie. "There's not enough to see in Brimrock that warrants more than a ten-minute drive."

Aiden's stomach wrenched, forcing him to think fast. "I…I've been doing everything I told you. It took the mechanics hours to fix Ghost yesterday and today I was at Balford's."

"Again? You went when we got here."

"Do you know who you're talking to?" Aiden grabbed his stack of books off the nightstand and held them up. "You're the one always telling me I read too much."

His defense seemed to work, throwing Eddie off his trail. Eddie nodded and crossed his muscular arms over his broad chest. "What's one trip to the mall? We humor my aunt for like five minutes and then split off on our own."

"Shopping's not really—"

"We've known each other since college. When have you seen me at a mall?"

Aiden couldn't refute Eddie's point. He sighed, fingers pinching the bridge of his nose. In another fifteen minutes, he sat in the Myerses' van in the same pose. His nails dug into the skin on his nose and he clenched his eyes shut. Mr. and Mrs. Myers cracked lighthearted jokes from the front seats of the van, supplied by occasional laughter from Eddie and Camilla. Rory sat glaring out the window.

He couldn't stop thinking about his first opportunity to bail. The mall was crowded and loud like every other mall in the country, and he supposed the strung lights and towering Christmas tree were meant to be festive delights. Other shoppers ogled them while he strolled bored out of his mind. The Myerses each had an idea of the stores they wanted to visit. He partnered up with Eddie.

"Are you really shopping?"

"Perfume for Auntie Priscilla," Eddie answered, shrugging. "I waited 'til the last second."

"Fair enough."

"What'd you get your mom? Cash and a card?"

Eddie's question was a joke, but it was also the truth.

Aiden had mailed his mom a card with cash. He had done so every year since he'd been out from under his parents' roof. He wasn't big on gift-giving and neither were his parents. They appreciated the sentiments, normally mailing him a card of their own. The bland O'Hare tradition juxtaposed the Myerses in every way, but he wasn't sure he would opt to change. His family was what it was, for better or worse.

"Okay, perfume first stop," said Aiden as they approached a mega department store. "Then after that can we do something worthwhile?"

"Easy guess. Worthwhile as in the food court?"

"Ed, you know me better than I know myself," he replied in his deepest sarcastic tone.

The two friends hit up the department store perfume section, which was full of plenty of flowery scents that conjured coughs out of them. A saleswoman helped Eddie choose a perfume Mrs. Myers would love, and Aiden thanked his lucky stars on their walk out. His throat had started to close up from the overly feminine, chemicalized smells.

His mind jumped back to the other night. Selene's light scent was heavenly in comparison to the overdone perfumes in the store. Hers was sweet and floral but fleeting. The tease of it had him intoxicated in the back of the URide they shared. Even during their date at the Magic Bean, he had inhaled an accidental whiff and realized he was drunk. What was her secret?

The food court was a mishmash of shoppers. No matter the cuisine, the line stretched long. Aiden and Eddie glanced at each other as they searched for the shortest. They decided on the pizza spot, shuffling to the back of the line.

"Any news with Margot? You two talked awhile at the party," said Aiden.

Eddie grinned. "We might be meeting up."

"Might as in you're definitely going to meet up."

"You're one to talk," replied Eddie as the line shortened. "Aunt Priscilla told me you're seeing someone. She thinks that's where you've been going whenever you disappear."

Aiden wasn't ready to explain. He stayed vague. "Tell your aunt I'm a big boy. I don't need a curfew." Aiden was busy basking in his smart-alecky retort, failing to spot the two women who sidled up on their left. He noticed only as Eddie grinned and guffawed. His heart thwacked against his chest out of surprise. At his side stood Selene and her friend Noelle. He stared wide-eyed at them, his tongue a lost artifact.

Selene spoke first. "I didn't know you liked shopping."

"I...I don't," he said dumbly. He swallowed against his shock. "Here with a friend."

Eddie waved. "Hello, ladies."

Noelle rolled her eyes while Selene raised a brow and smirked. If Aiden had to guess, Selene had suggested coming over much to Noelle's chagrin. But he wasn't focused on whose idea it was so much as he secretly reveled in the chance to see Selene again. His pulse increased and he recognized how dopey his mood became whenever around her, like he could smile for no reason.

Was this what it was like to have a crush on a woman? For him it had been years...

Selene ignored Noelle and Eddie and fixed Aiden with a rapt stare. Even her glasses couldn't hide the soft curl of her lashes and warm dreaminess in her brown eyes. He might have had a thing for her cute librarian glasses, but his fingers yearned to reach up and slowly pull them away. For a chance to stare openly back into her eyes and study the teeny, tiny flecks of gold in them.

"I had a good time on our coffee date," said Selene in a

tone he hadn't heard out of her. Soft and sultry, the tone paired well with the flirtatious smirk on her full, wine-red lips. Something was different about her today, like she was acting on a dare. "I was wondering if you wanted to do dinner."

"Dinner with me?" he asked, mind uncharacteristically blank.

Selene snickered. "Yes, you. I definitely didn't mean the neighborhood mailman. I figured it would be nice to sit down for a real date."

Aiden stared, gobsmacked. He struggled to overcome the initial roadblock that was shock. Thankfully it passed before it was too late. He dug his hands into his pockets and gave what was probably a much too enthusiastic nod. "Sure! Dinner sounds great. How about the Mulberry?"

"Tomorrow night?"

"I'll be there with bells on." He sprinkled in sarcasm in hopes he sounded less overzealous fanboy and more dry and mundane like a true O'Hare.

Selene's smirk spread slightly, its own goodbye, and then she was off. Her friend Noelle followed, but only after a pointed, head-to-toe stink eye. Aiden stood on the spot unable to process what had happened. He forgot about Eddie at his side or the line they were in to get pizza. All he could think about was Selene and how she had asked him for another date. *She* had asked *him*! Did that mean she was as interested in him as he was in her?

Eddie waved a hand in front of his face. "Careful or you'll swallow your tongue. You there?"

"Of course I am," said Aiden, smoothing a hand over the front of his V-neck sweater. "Why wouldn't I be?"

"You and Selene Blackstone went on a coffee date? Why am I just now hearing about this?"

"It's…it's not important. It was a few minutes."

Eddie stared at him long and hard. "You like her, don't you? Selene Blackstone?"

"You don't have to keep repeating her name."

"Yeah, I sorta do. Because I don't think you get who she is," said Eddie. He beckoned Aiden out of the long, winding line for the pizza stand and stepped off to the side. "You do know what you're doing, right? Getting involved with a woman like Selene?"

Aiden laughed at the ridiculous, heavy-browed expression on Eddie's face. "Why do you sound like you're speaking about the bogeyman?"

"Bro, that's because every man the Blackstone women get involved with…something happens to them," Eddie said, dropping his voice a level. He glanced around as if paranoid Selene might somehow overhear. "Research their family history. It's been going on since Luna. The guys either disappear or die."

"Am I supposed to be afraid of Selene? Eddie, she comes up to my elbow."

"Aiden," Eddie said over him, "you can't bring it up around my family—Rory's still upset about the whole thing —but the blind date Selene was on the other night? You know when you went over to her table at the Mulberry?"

"What's your point?"

"That date," said Eddie with a gulp of a swallow, "was with Peter Feinberg."

CHAPTER EIGHT

"We probably need a code name," said Noelle over her bowl of chili. She scooped up a spoonful and blew against the wisps of heat to cool it off. "How about Operation Fuckboy?"

Selene almost choked on her mouthful of hearty, beefy bean and cheese goodness. "Wait, are you saying Aiden is a...?"

"What else do you call a guy who visits town undercover as a freelance writer, takes you out to coffee, and tries to win you over *all* so he can film an episode for his YouTV show?" Noelle presented her counter questions as an attorney would during a trial. Even her expression read as so, finely penciled brows high and fuchsia lips still pursed from blowing on her spoon. "Let's hope this plan works so you asking him out doesn't backfire. Back to this code name. I vote Operation Fuckboy, but I also like Project Trifling Male too."

"Aiden is a paranormal investigator. Can we really blame him for doing his job?"

"Yes."

Selene rolled her eyes and laughed at Noelle's unapologetic bluntness. She couldn't fault her best friend for it. At the core of Noelle's abrasive opinions on Aiden was her concern. Noelle protected Selene like a sister and Selene returned the favor whenever necessary. They had grown up side by side, thick as thieves from the time they were small girls, and she wouldn't have it any other way.

Noelle walked to the fridge for another Dr. Pepper. "I don't get what you see in him."

"He's cute. Smart. Bookish. What's not to like?"

"Um, he's out to expose you, Luna, your whole existence as a witch?"

Selene pushed away her bowl of chili. At her feet beneath the table, Yukie waited in vain hope for a lick of her spoon or torn scrap of bread. "That's just it, Noe. I don't think Aiden thinks I'm a witch. I watched a couple episodes of their show last night and Aiden's always out to prove the paranormal *doesn't* exist. Eddie is the one who believes it does."

"Girl, stop rationalizing his deceit. He's still out to exploit you."

Noelle spoke the truth and deep down Selene knew it. Even if it was difficult hearing. She fell silent and broke off a piece of bread, holding it below for Yukie to nibble on. Since discovering Aiden's true identity, she had struggled deciding what to do. At any given moment, she ranged from anger that he had the audacity to lie to her to flat out hurt that he would. Then there were the brief moments where she bargained with herself and tried to rationalize the situation.

Maybe Aiden wasn't out to exploit her. Maybe he was really just visiting town for Christmas. Maybe he lied about being a freelance writer so not to alarm her. Was it possible he didn't know about Luna, the urban legend surrounding her, and its stigmatic effects on Selene? Could it be coincidence?

"Back to the plan," said Noelle, popping the tab on her

can of Dr. Pepper. She slid into her seat across from Selene at the kitchen table. "You and him tomorrow night at the Mulberry."

Selene nodded. "I flirt with him. Distract him a little."

"*And*?"

"You know what I'm about to say," said Selene. She fed Yukie the last small tear of bread and then sat up straighter, folding her hands businesslike. "Do you think Shayla will be able to help us feed Aiden a persuasion potion? She's head chef at the Mulberry. It's perfect."

"Shayla and I don't talk like that anymore."

"Because you broke her heart," Selene muttered.

Noelle scoffed between slurps of her Dr. Pepper. "I didn't break her heart. We were never exclusive. Something I made clear from the get-go. It's not my fault she caught feelings. Besides, it was kind of a rebound thing. I was getting over Angelique. I wanted to still be friends. *She* cut me off."

"I liked you two together. That's all I'm saying."

"I can't hit up Shayla out of the blue and ask for a favor. Too much tension."

"She would help. Plus she would love to hear from you," Selene pointed out. "The last time she came by the library, she asked about you."

"I'll think about it. We have to be careful. Let's focus on brewing the potion first. Bibi should be here any minute."

Selene magicked the table clear, emptying bowls into the trash and twisting on the faucet to rinse them off in the sink. The fridge door sprang open and the pot of chili whizzed inside. She was dusting her hands off, impressed by her own magical doing, when the doorbell's deep tone trilled through the three-story house. Her eyes snapped to Noelle and Noelle's onto her. They shared in a tiny smirk.

"Speak of the devil."

———

"I love our little mini coven," said Noelle half an hour later. "Imagine if we had numbers. We'd be so fly."

"What are you on about? I'm already fly," rasped Bibi, winking at her niece. She had arrived to Selene's in her thick oversized overcoat, house slippers, and kit of magical herbs in tow.

The three gathered around the coffee table in the living room and unpacked their supplies. Selene blew dust off her cast-iron cauldron and centered it on the table. Noelle thumbed through her encyclopedia-sized book entitled *Magickal Brews and Potions*. Aunt Bibi dimmed the lights and lit the dragon's blood incense, holding the burning sticks above her head and pacing the room, ridding it of any unwanted spirits. Yukie lounged on the tufted velvet armchair nearby, watching the three witches at work with a lazy wag of her tail.

Selene was an amateur potion maker. Mom hadn't taught her about her own lunar power growing up, let alone allowed her to receive any instruction on other magic forms. She had begged for years for the chance to receive instruction from the likes of Bibi, but the answer was always a hard no. In the years since Mom's passing, Selene had dabbled, though her attempts were amateur. Potion brewing and other herbal magic just didn't come naturally to her like it did green witches like Noelle and Bibi.

"What next, O great herbology gods?" Selene smiled, crisscross folding her legs.

"I think you meant that singular. Everybody knows Auntie is the true OG." Noelle glanced across the room at Bibi as she rounded another corner of the room, the smoking incenses high, its floral scent sweetening up the air. Returning to her potions book, Noelle read the page titles aloud as she flipped through. "Herbal divination. Botanicals and beauty. Natural charms for love. No, no, and *hell* no. Here we are: practical potions for everyday use."

"Is there one there you think will work?" Selene leaned over for a peek at the pages.

"No need to make things complicated, girls," said Bibi. She placed the incense sticks in a miniature pot to finish burning and joined them at the coffee table. "What am I always telling you—my favorite motto in the world?"

Selene and Noelle recited together, "Work smarter, not harder."

Bibi's lips curled, bracketed by soft wrinkles. "That's right. We don't need anything fancy for Fudgeboy. A basic persuasion potion'll do."

Selene did a double take, gaping at Bibi with confusion. "Fudgeboy?"

"Bibi's on a new no-cusswords kick," said Noelle. "It's her yearly resolution for Yule. The *F* word is now fudge. The *S* word is now poopoo. I forget what the new *B* word is."

"I like to think son of a witch is pretty dang funny," cackled Bibi. She cut her laugh off with an abrupt cough and then cleared her throat. "Anywho, there should be a good one in there—probably around page fifty-six."

"Page sixty-five," said Noelle, flipping over.

"Close enough." Bibi laughed again and gestured to the row of herbal ingredients she had handpicked from her garden. "I've brought you all the goodies. Time to get to work."

Selene's mouth fell open. "You're not helping us?"

"I'm the OG, ain't I? I supervise. If I see anything too off track, I'll take pity and steer you back."

"We got this," said Noelle with confidence that squared

her shoulders. She elbowed Selene. "This is the perfect chance for you to bring out your inner green witch."

"We've all got a lil' of each other in us," preached Bibi wisely. "That's the true test of a powerful witch—if she can master all magical elements. You girls ain't ready for that truth bomb yet, though, so let me sit back and sip my tea."

Selene and Noelle accepted the challenge from their witchy elder. Noelle splayed open the potions book for them to reference, listing off the steps in order.

"First things first, basil leaves."

"Basil leaves check," said Selene. She grabbed a handful and placed them down at the base of the cauldron, spreading them evenly into a bed.

"We need a quart of the spring water. Then we boil that."

With Bibi's watchful eyes on her, a wave of determination flooded Selene. She prodded her glasses up her nose and focused on the pitcher of water on the coffee table. It obeyed her will, tipping over to pour into the measuring cup below. She leaned close, eying the red line as the water rose toward it. In years past, as a growing teenage girl with fledging control over her telekinetic ability, she would've lost the connection or overflowed the cup. But this go-around, years older, more experienced and on a beat of confidence, she stopped exactly on the red line.

She smirked. Though she didn't glance at either of them, both Noelle and Bibi exchanged impressed nods in her peripheral vision. Pressing on as though alone, she set the pitcher straight again and let the measuring cup float off the table and over the empty cauldron. That she emptied inside, creating a small pool of basil leaves and cold spring water.

"I'll light it—" Noelle started to get up.

Selene shook her head and held her hands out in front of the cauldron. She rose onto her feet, her hands also rising, and the cauldron along with her, hovering above the table. It was heavier than most everyday objects she levitated thanks to not only the water but the pot's authentic cast-iron. She guided it toward the fireplace, hanging it carefully onto the waiting hook.

Now to light the fire. She could feel her magic waning in her veins. Exhaustion sunk in, making her slower and less precise. She refused to give up, still determined to spearhead the potion brewing. Holding out her hand, she summoned the pile of newspapers from the end table across the room and the matches needed for lighting the fire. In the next minute, after lighting the newspaper and magicking it flush against the firewood, she stood back and admired her handiwork. The cauldron dangled inches above the flames. The basil leaves and spring water would warm in no time.

"Next step," she said, ignoring the drain on her energy. She fixed her glasses and knelt beside the coffee table. "We need to prep the rest of the ingredients. Do you want to grind the tarragon? I'll handle the oils and supervise the cauldron."

"Operation Fuckboy is underway," Noelle joked, picking up the pestle and mortar off the table. She realized her error a split second too late and threw a cautious glance over her shoulder at Bibi. "Sorry, Auntie. I *meant* to say Operation Fudgeboy."

"Dang right you did." Bibi pursed her lips from over the rim of her teacup.

For the next half hour Selene and Noelle toiled away at brewing the persuasion potion. Noelle crushed the necessary herbs like tarragon and fennel into a lumpy powder. Selene collected the glass vials she needed and mixed the oils into a small bowl, adding droplets of lemon oil and bergamot. They both chopped the remaining ingredients from Bibi's magic garden, sliding the chunks of horseradish and ginger into the brewing cauldron.

The cauldron hissed and sputtered the more ingredients they added. The magical properties melted together as the potion thickened up, coloring a sickly grayish green. Selene wiped her brow on her sweater sleeve, the heat flushing her skin.

Bibi sat up from her cushion on the sofa, squinting behind her wire glasses. "Is that Luna's?"

At first Selene didn't understand the question, then she flinched and her hand clapped over the crystal pendant around her neck. Sometimes she forgot she was wearing it. She hadn't thought about it in days, sleeping and showering with the sterling silver necklace as though she'd always worn it. She had meant to call—or at least email—Uncle Zee back and thank him for the gift. She made another mental note to do it tomorrow.

"My uncle Zee sent it," she replied. She glanced down at the crystal pendant in her hand and noticed its bright diamond-like white glow. "It used to be Luna's favorite."

Bibi eyed the necklace with a vague expression, bushy gray brows scrunched up. "Yeah, I remember. You sure Zee gave that to you? How'd he get his hands on that?"

"He said he found it in an old box of Luna's things…"

"Hmm…" Bibi trailed off.

Selene glanced at Noelle, who shrugged and returned to stirring the cauldron. "What does that 'hmm' mean, Bibi?"

"Nothing but a hmm…for now. Just surprised is all. I haven't seen it in many years."

"Maybe you should take it off," said Noelle. She waved an arm over the cauldron as thick smoke wafted into the air. "Is this persuasion potion supposed to be this smoky? We're about to set off the fire alarm."

"You wouldn't be doing it right otherwise," said Bibi.

"Why do you think I should take it off?" Selene asked at Noelle's side.

Again, Noelle shrugged midstir. "I don't know. If it was Luna's, it might draw suspicion. We still don't know if the cops are keeping an eye out on you."

The room fell silent. It was an unaddressed possibility up until that point. Selene hadn't let herself consider it, knowing she would be the first one suspected when Peter was found in his comatose state. But it had been days and Officer Gustin, or any other cop on the Brimrock police force, hadn't turned up on her doorstep for questioning—*yet*.

"I didn't do anything," said Selene finally.

"Oh, chile, *we* know that," said Bibi.

"But everybody else in town?" Noelle shook her head and stared into the smoking, bubbling cauldron. "Not so much. You know how they act about us, *especially* you and your family. That's why I'm still not convinced we need to involve Shayla in this. For all we know, they're watching."

"There's nothing to watch. We're not doing anything illegal," said Selene defiantly.

Noelle snorted. "Except brew a magical persuasion potion to influence Fudgeboy into leaving you the fudge alone? *Totally* legal."

Selene nudged Noelle aside so that she could take over stirring the potion. "We've been over this, Noe. There's no crime if there are no witnesses."

———

It was half past eleven by the time Noelle and Aunt Bibi packed up and went home. Selene's body ached and her eyes itched, begging for sleep. Yukie had curled up in her dog bed in Selene's bedroom and dozed off. The giant three-story house was quiet enough to hear a mouse scuttle by, the darkness engulfing its corners overbearing.

Only the scant flame from the dozen odd tea light candles lit up her bedroom. She slipped into her soft cotton nightgown and warm, wooly socks and wandered to the window. The half-moon winked down at her, silvery and bright. She sat on the ledge and unlatched the lock on the window, lifting the glass and welcoming in the winter chill.

But it wasn't the cold she cared about as a frigid wind swept into the room. Her gaze was still on the moon, transfixed by its ethereal pull. The fatigue plaguing her body lifted and a jolt of lunar energy rushed through her veins. It wasn't as reenergizing as her usual lunar rituals, where she wandered into the woodland behind her house and reconnected with the moon spirit like other lunar witches before her.

Selene's eyes closed and she drew her legs up to her chest. She could sit right here like this for the rest of the night and feel at peace. No matter the cold or wind gusting into the room, so long as she was under the moon's silvery beams of light. Finally, the day's worries melted away, her mind opened up, and she drifted off…

Her leg dangled freely off the ledge, Yukie nudging it with the tip of her nose. Selene jerked awake, disoriented for the first few passing seconds. She squinted and shivered and realized she was sitting on her window ledge. The morning cold invaded her bedroom and made it colder than any icebox. She glanced down at Yukie also shaking on the spot.

"I'm so sorry, Yukes. I must've fallen asleep with the window open. C'mere."

Selene spent the better half of the next thirty minutes cuddling the trembling terrier and feeding her her favorite snack in hopes of making amends. Yukie quickly forgave her, trotting in her wake when Selene moved onto morning errands. Thankfully she was off Fridays, which gave her the entire day to prepare for the night's date at the Mulberry.

After finishing the persuasion potion, Selene and Noelle had carefully sealed the concoction in the kind of canister normally used for coffee on the go. She brought the stainless steel coffee cup with her when meeting up with Shayla. The plan was for Shayla to mix the potion with whatever Aiden ordered as his main course. The three were meeting up at the Magic Bean, where they could talk in private.

Or so Selene had hoped.

On her stroll from 1221 Gifford to the Magic Bean, she was being followed. She might've been a frequent daydreamer, always with her head in the clouds, thinking about whatever book she was reading, or wondering things like what it'd be like to step foot outside of Brimrock, but even *she* noticed Officer Gustin's patrol car. How could she not? As she turned off Gifford Lane, the car trailed half a block away. When she moved onto Watson, again he was in the distance, coasting at a snail's pace so that each light caught him, or that stop signs prolonged his drive.

Selene had half a mind to cut between some trees and cross through the town park, shake him off her trail. But she decided against it. That would only rouse more suspicions and clearly she was on Brimrock PD's radar. So she tugged on her scarf, tucked her chin inside, plugged her hands in her peacoat pockets, and kicked through the snow as though on a merry journey about town.

Today the sun said hello, even if weakly, more light than warmth. She pulled the glass door to the Magic Bean open and snuck a peek over her shoulder. Officer Gustin had parked his patrol vehicle and gotten out. What he didn't foresee was that Mr. Higgley, the town mailman, would stop him short and engage him in lengthy conversation. She snorted out a small laugh and disappeared inside the eccentric coffee shop.

Aunt Bibi's latest hire, Isabelle Halsey, was behind the counter. She was on her third shift and already on the brink of quitting. When Selene stepped up to the counter, Bibi was scolding the nineteen-year-old about being on her phone when at the register. Isabelle huffed out a sigh and openly rolled her eyes.

"Fine," she muttered.

"There's a customer," said Bibi expectantly. Her wire glasses slipped low onto her nose and her brows jumped high. Both warning signs of her impending temper.

"Morning. I'll just take a small soy latte," said Selene.

Bibi put her left and right hands on her hips. "Did you hear her order? Punch it in!"

Noelle was seated in the back, her apron swathed over her chair. "You see the training going on over there? Isabelle is about to have Bibi giving up her no cuss resolution before Yule is over. She'll be cussing up a storm any sec now."

"I noticed. Isabelle doesn't seem to care."

"You know how teenagers are. This is apparently her first job."

"If she's anything like her mother, good luck," said Selene. "Gerri is basically real-life Cruella De Vil."

"Miriam's Voldemort. Gerri's Cruella De Vil. Who are *you* exactly?"

"Now you already know."

"You are *not* Jo March from *Little Women*."

"I think Selene is a lot like Jo," came a third female voice from behind.

Noelle locked up in her chair, her once lackadaisical body stiffening. She didn't need to turn around to know who it was.

Neither did Selene, who smiled wide and motioned for Shayla to grab a seat. Noelle seemed to blink away her shock and snap back to her senses.

"And…and who am I?"

"You're Amy," said Shayla with a tinge of teasing to her voice. She was as stylish as ever in a silk blouse and fitted cigarette pants, her honey-colored coils dusting her shoulders. "Spoiled, loud, always up to no good. Sounds like you, Noelle."

Selene sat back and observed the two exes tread water between light flirtation and feelings left unsaid. One thing was clear: the two women still cared for each other. Noelle's tell was how dopey her expression became, her brown eyes soft and wistful. She leaned closer, elbow on the table, ears perked up to catch Shayla's every word.

"Of course I'll help," said Shayla when they explained the situation. She shared in an affectionate smile with Noelle, her light brown eyes sparking. "I'm pretty sure I owe you a favor."

Selene didn't want to know. Her heart warmed at the rekindled connection between the two. She scooted her chair back and excused herself, figuring some alone time was needed. Besides, if she was going to distract Aiden tonight, she needed time to *really* fix herself up.

———

The Mulberry saw a full house every night of the week. No night, though, was busier than Friday. Selene arrived to the steakhouse dressed unlike herself. Noelle had allowed her to dig around in her closet for a dressier outfit than what was her usual style. She shuffled up to the door feeling like a baby calf, wobbly on her five-inch heels.

Noelle had pressed her coiled hair bone straight and tied it up into a topknot on her head. Her face wasn't hers either, layers of makeup like foundation, highlighter, and something Noelle called contour slathered onto her skin. Contacts replaced her thick-framed glasses and Noelle glued fakes to her lash lines. The end result produced a gasp when Selene looked in the mirror. She looked like a pampered princess. She felt like one too until she started moving and fumbled within five steps.

Still, entering the Mulberry, she earned several long stares. One man in particular did a double take as she passed him by. It didn't occur to her why he was staring, but when he winked at her, she put two and two together. He was looking because he found her attractive. She wasn't used to men noticing her as anything more than a bookish wallflower, with her frumpy sweaters and fleshy thighs. She hid behind her bold-framed glasses and the covers of her books.

Except for tonight.

Tonight she was a bombshell who had to flirt and distract Aiden O'Hare.

The hostess was the same from Monday night. She regarded Selene with even more disdain now that she had her makeover. Sighing and spinning on her heel, the hostess told her to follow her to her table. Selene rolled her shoulders back, standing up with proper straight posture, and tried her best at a basic sexy strut. She caught her reflection in the glass of a decorative wine bottle on display and she flinched.

No glasses. No big hair. No baggy sweater or naked face. She really did look like a new woman.

Her temporary break in concentration caused her to forget she was walking in five-inch heels. She stumbled, her ankles bending like rubber as she yelped and tried to regain balance. The hostess stopped and stared at her with irritation spelled out on her birdlike features. Recovering at the last possible second, Selene breathed in relief and motioned for the hostess to continue.

"My table, please," she said with a false haughty air. Some payback for the hostess's attitude.

Selene almost tripped a second time in minutes when the hostess led her to the reserved table. Sudden, jittery nerves exploded in Selene's stomach and her mouth dropped open from the shock. It shouldn't have surprised her that Aiden was there already. She was fifteen minutes early. Was he twenty minutes early again?

Aiden grinned, his hazel eyes dark green in the ambient lighting. She grinned back, acutely aware of the secrets they hid from each other. The only difference being that she knew his. He had no clue what the night had in store for him.

CHAPTER NINE

Selene Blackstone rendered Aiden speechless. A man with a greater vocabulary than most, known for his sardonic humor and dry delivery on *Paranormal Hunters*, he wasn't at a loss for words often. It was a lot more common for him to have the opposite problem: too many words that were unfiltered and perhaps a little too honest. But sitting at the table for two at the Mulberry, every last word eluded him. He was grinning before he knew what hit him, brainless and bewitched in his chair.

Selene looked like a Hollywood starlet on the red carpet. The dress she wore showed off a figure her woolly sweaters usually hid. Curves that distracted the male, caveman part of his brain—even he had one. Her face was done up. He had zero knowledge of makeup, but her brown skin glowed under the restaurant lights and her cheekbones were more pronounced than usual, highlighted with a soft sheen. Her lips were a berry shade, playing up their already natural pouty appeal.

For as gorgeous as she was, though, he couldn't help

missing the things that stood out most about her. He missed her headful of a thousand tiny curls. Tonight her hair was sleek, straight, and slicked back into a bun. He missed her thick, bold-framed glasses. Tonight she ditched them for contacts. He missed the Selene he had met over the past few days, more concerned with her books than looking in the mirror. Had she dressed to the nines to impress him?

He had worn a V-neck sweater and jeans. Granted he had sprayed on his best cologne—the one he used for special occasions—but that was all. The sudden flicker of doubt passed through him as he wondered if he had underestimated the evening. Maybe he should've worn something more formal. Bought her flowers? Chocolates? Did women expect those on first dates?

It had been over six years since his last one. His one serious relationship had started freshman year of college and ended a year and a half post-graduation when he and Delilah realized they had become two incompatible people. He hadn't made an effort with his love life since then beyond the occasional dead-end coffee date. His travels and investigations for *Paranormal Hunters* required too much time and energy. His love life fell by the wayside.

The thought struck him at the last second to get up and pull out her chair. Aiden clambered out of his seat and pulled back hers. She smiled and thanked him, dropping down into the chair as he pushed her in.

"You…you look nice," he stammered. The muscles in his cheeks twitched. Had he come up with no better compliment than *nice*?

Selene's right brow rose. "Uh, thanks. You look nice too."

He settled back into his chair and searched the crevices of his brain for a topic of discussion. Any topic would do. He combed over the selection—everything from the weather to the crowd at the restaurant. His eyes were on hers, glazed over from his overanalytical deep dive into his own head. Finally, he decided on…

"I had no idea you wore contacts," he blurted. Then he wanted to kick himself for sounding vain.

Selene's slender fingers automatically reached up as if to readjust her glasses out of habit, but she caught herself midway and stopped. "I forgot I don't have them on. I'm so used to them I don't even feel them anymore."

"But I'm betting you do feel the burn in your eyes." Spotting the confused twist of her mouth, he elaborated. "I wear contacts too. Clear. The hazel's mine."

"The hazel's currently dark green. And I didn't peg you for a four-eyes."

"I was *the* four-eyes growing up. That term of endearment was invented with me in mind."

"Oh, really? Twelve-year-old me with lenses as thick as plexiglass disagrees."

"I'll raise your plexiglass for a set of blue metallic braces."

Selene's eyes narrowed and she leaned closer. "Pink metallic braces."

His chuckle was throaty and unfettered. "Touché. But were you a ginger with freckles?"

"The childhood trump card of all trump cards. You win this round."

The waitress popped up and interrupted their banter. They ordered a bottle of merlot to start off with, to which the waitress nodded her approval.

"Good choice," she said, setting down two glasses. The burgundy liquid flowed into the glasses as a waterfall of wine.

Aiden noticed Selene's smile. His earlier doubt sprouted

into a bean of pride, growing by the second. If he could continue showing Selene a good time…

He scratched that thought. While he wanted her to enjoy herself—would pride himself on that without question—he had to keep his head. His investigation was about unearthing the truth. The speculation going around town was wrong. Peter was not attacked by some paranormal entity. The real perpetrator behind his attack was still out there and required solving. In order to do so, he needed to make some progress soon. Tomorrow he would meet with Gerri Halsey and interview her about Peter.

Tonight he needed to charm Selene.

By the glint in her eye, he was succeeding. Eddie would shirk with worry that he sat alone with her, but Aiden found it laughable to think of Selene as dangerous. The only danger she posed was making him forget his motive. She had the ability to distract him as his head filled with thoughts of how amazing she was.

When the waitress finished pouring their wine, Aiden raised his glass for a toast. "What should we toast to? Being four-eyes or brace faces?"

Selene giggled. The first real giggle he had ever heard out of her. It was spry and youthful sounding. He enjoyed it so much he wanted more. Holding her glass to chink his, she said, "Four-eyed brace faces has a decent ring to it, don't you think?"

Their chatter continued over menu appraisals. They consulted with each other over what appetizers and entrees seemed like good picks. Aiden was enthused to discover Selene was a foodie just like him. She considered it a hobby, as did he. One of his only others outside his enthusiasm for books and outdoorsy stuff.

He hated the idea that there was a perfect woman out there for him, but Selene....

Eddie would joke that he had accomplished the impossible. He had finally found a woman who was actually compatible with him. It would be his luck that the woman would also be the subject of his latest paranormal investigation.

"Finish *Jurassic Park* yet?" Selene asked.

"I did, actually. Last night just in case."

"Of what?"

He fought the amused smile forming and said, "I was worried we would run out of things to talk about. It was going to be a backup topic. I'm an overpreparer."

"Terrible habit, isn't it?"

"You're telling me? When I'm preparing for an invest—" He dropped off midsentence, catching himself before he used the *I* word. As far as Selene knew, he was a freelance writer. *Not* a paranormal investigator. He played off his almost flub with a cough and started again. "Whenever I'm preparing for an article, I do so much research—too much research. I'm the research guy."

Selene nursed her wine, seemingly tempted to laugh. "You'll have to send me some of your articles. I'd love to read them."

A cold sweat passed over him, though he forced an enthusiastic nod. "Of course. I'll send you some links. Just give me your email."

No, no, no! Why was he volunteering to send her links to nonexistent articles? He wanted to smack a hand to his forehead and cuss his poor lying skills.

What he needed was a change of subject. Anything, like...

"So, why are you single?" he blurted out like the numbskull he was. As soon as he said it, regret crashed onto him like an avalanche on Mount Everest. He held his breath and stared in horror across the table at Selene, whose neatly shaped brows knitted together. "Don't answer that. I have no idea why I asked you that—it was stupid. I…I guess I'm nervous and clearly not the best at charming women. It's a personality flaw for sure. Probably why my best friend, Eddie, is usually the one with a contact list full of women's numbers and mine has all the numbers to local bookshops."

"That doesn't surprise me," she said. A short pause lingered before her smile returned. Almost as though she was endeared. "I'll answer, but *only* if you answer first. Why are you single?"

"I'm always putting my career first. It's hard for me to connect with people. I've always been fine with that, but lately, I guess I'm starting to, uh, want something more." He surprised himself with his candor, every last word the truth even despite his other lies and hidden motive. Selene had opened up that possibility for him, though the likelihood it would be a reality was slim to none. With a firm clearing of his throat, he said, "I'm not usually this reflective. You're bringing it out in me."

"Isn't that a good thing?" Selene teased, sipping from her wineglass. Her lip color was infallible, leaving no smudges on the glass and still as berry-colored as ever on her lips—the definition of kissable. "I'm single because most guys in Brimrock aren't interested in some nerdy librarian who lives in the town's most haunted house. I'm sure you've heard about the stories."

"Stories? What stories?" He feigned a confused frown.

"About my grandmother, Luna. There's this crazy story that she was a witch and now she haunts the town."

"Oh, right. I might have heard a thing or two about that."

Selene smirked. "You don't have to pretend like you haven't. I'm at the point where it doesn't offend me. People are going to believe what they want. It is what it is."

"But," he said, unable to help himself and his investigative instinct, "if the town thinks your grandmother is a witch, then doesn't that also mean they think you…?"

"Like I said, it's *crazy*." She laughed dismissively. "Don't you think?"

"Pure insanity. Unless you have a flying broomstick waiting out back."

"Would I have needed that URide the other night if I did?"

Aiden joined her laughter. Of course she wouldn't have. Witches weren't real and neither were ghost witches who haunted small towns. The spooky fables about Luna were all incorrect, blown out of proportion like other paranormal mysteries he had investigated. He fully intended to prove so, as well as uncover the truth behind Peter's attack. He only needed time and Selene's trust.

The two moved onto other conversation. They traded barbs oozing with sarcasm until the waitress brought them their entrees. Selene had ordered a steak beefier than his, her slab of medium rare meat covering half her plate. He nodded, impressed by his fellow foodie. They dug into the mouthwatering sirloin, loaded mashed potatoes, and roast veggies. The first bite was heavenly. The second one too. By the third, a funny feeling hit him.

The dizzying heat made him pause. He couldn't explain it, but he assumed it had to do with Selene. Something was different about her tonight. It was in how she looked at him. The shine in her eyes differed from before, contrasting the dark brown of her irises. The spark was coquettish, burning brighter than the table's candlelit flames. Before tonight he would've never pegged Selene as an overly flirtatious woman. She was proving otherwise. She stared at him with a teasing humor—borderline *entrancing* in a way. He had no clue what to make of it. She must have been as into him as he was into her.

Then his mouth tingled and he smacked a hand to his jaw to scratch it away. He tried to wash it away with wine, but the fiery tingle was too strong. His breathing shortened not for the reason it normally would on an intimate candlelit dinner date with a woman. He had thought wrong. The funny feeling wasn't due to Selene. It was something else; something like...

"Basil," he croaked. His eyes widened, surveying his plate. "There's basil in this food."

The coy smirk dropped off Selene's face. Her eyes doubled to match his in size. "You're allergic to basil?"

He was only capable of a nod as his breathing devolved into sharp gasps. His throat was closing up. His mouth was burning and his tongue swelling. His brain started fogging up as he blinked through the sudden onslaught of side effects. Others at the surrounding tables craned their necks for a look at him, some half rising out of their chairs.

Selene knocked over her own dashing around the table to check on him. She was at his side in a flash of panic, pulling him back off the table. He had slumped without realizing it, unable to make sense of the strange reactions crippling his body. Another was on his other side—possibly their waitress —and someone in the background shouted they were calling 911.

Aiden flopped to the ground. He must've been redder than a cherry tomato at this point. He could feel his skin breaking out in deep splotches. The fogginess made it near impossible to tell how much time was passing, but soon sirens wailed in the distance. The last thing he remembered was looking up at the restaurant ceiling. The Mulberry's delicate, crystalline, low-lit chandeliers must have cost a fortune. Probably *thousands*.

And then they all went black as if snuffed like the flame of a candle.

CHAPTER TEN

Selene had screwed up. What she thought was a harmless persuasion potion turned into an evening at Brimrock Hospital's emergency room. Her eyes bulged with worry as she chased after the paramedics wheeling Aiden on a gurney. They carted him through double doors leading into the emergency care stations and she rushed to follow, only to be turned away by a nurse on shift.

"Family only," she said in a pinched, nasal voice. "You can wait here in the waiting room."

"But—" Selene started.

The nurse interrupted. "Waiting room is for friends and nonimmediate family. We'll update you on your boyfriend as soon as we can."

Selene was in such horror it didn't occur to her until she plopped into one of the many empty chairs that the nurse thought she was Aiden's girlfriend. She sat shell-shocked by the night's turn of events. The evening had begun on such a high note. She had felt so sexy, confident, and self-assured about her dinner date with Aiden. She had him right where she wanted him as their chemistry exploded like a blast of fireworks into the night sky.

He drank and ate merrily without the slightest clue. The medium rare sirloin steak he ordered came drizzled in a sauce described as peppercorn butter on the menu. Shayla had slipped enough of the persuasion potion into the sauce so that it worked, but was also undetectable to the taste buds. He swallowed each bite none the wiser that any second it would kick in. Selene would then influence him to drop his investigation.

It puzzled her how it could go so wrong. The ingredients from the potion were herbs grown in Aunt Bibi's garden— green magic was the most natural on earth. They followed the instructions in *Magickal Brews and Potions* down to the letter. How could the potion possibly hurt Aiden?

Allergies. Selene's face dropped into her hands. It never occurred to her that Aiden would be allergic to one of the ingredients. The chances were slim to none. That was the risk she took dabbling in potion work. She had put Aiden's life in jeopardy because she couldn't handle the possibility he was investigating Luna.

Though she had felt justified at the time, now she felt more than ridiculous. She had devised an entire plan to lure Aiden like a black widow caught insects in her web. The night was about her using feminine wiles to distract him. For him to digest that potion so she could steer his investigative mind elsewhere.

The thing was, she had had a great time. Better than she expected. Their mini meetup for coffee at the Magic Bean was pleasant, but tonight was another level of sparks. It was a full-blown electrical charge. She was feeling him. Her intuition said he felt the same. Warmth radiated throughout her body as she had flirted throughout dinner.

And then disaster struck.

Selene groaned through her fingers. She didn't notice the ER nurse walk up until she cleared her throat. Hands still on her face, she looked up at the scrub-clad nurse from between her fingers.

"The doc says you can see Mr. O'Hare if you'd like."

The rest of the waiting room blurred as Selene hopped to her feet and clambered to follow. Aiden sat up on a hospital bed, his legs so long they reached the bed corners. The worrisome patches of red that had broken out on his skin had cleared. His once sweat-soaked hair was brushed sideways, giving a windswept quality that made him look even more handsome. He sat up straighter when the nurse pulled aside the curtains and Selene walked through.

"The doc will be back in a few minutes," the nurse announced. She strode up to Aiden's bed and collected the tray of empty paper cups and leftover meds. They waited for her to right the curtains around the station before they concentrated on each other.

Aiden made zero attempt hiding his intent study, like she was a book he was reading.

"Your hair. You took it down."

Selene reached up to her thick mane. Her silky press had only lasted for so long. The once pin-straight hair was reverting back to her stubborn curls. She grinned, feeling the defined, kinky waves under her fingertips, and gave a nod. "I guess I did. The bun was too tight."

"And your contacts. You're wearing your glasses again."

Another keen observation. Selene's grin spread. "My glasses are more comfortable."

"You look good like this. I…I mean…it's definitely practical." Aiden cleared his throat and hints of pink colored his cheeks.

Selene felt her own belly flutter as she recognized his slip of the tongue. "I'm glad you're okay. You scared me."

"You stuck around."

"I wanted to make sure you weren't on your deathbed."

"Check back in another fifty years…" The beginnings of a smile pulled at his lips, his eyes holding hers.

The connection was inexplicable. Even standing there at his bedside, she was drawn to him. If she had a shred of courage, she would throw her arms around him and squeeze him tight, apologizing profusely for the trouble she caused. She would confess she found out his identity and was trying to throw him off her trail. The truth would then be at his feet for him to decide how to move forward.

No potion. No persuasion. No cat and mouse games over bloody steaks and romantic candlelight.

But she didn't. She chickened out with a deep swallow and her gaze skirted to the tile beneath her heels. Like her topknot and contacts, she would've long ago ditched the heels if she had a choice. Walking barefoot wasn't exactly an appealing alternative.

Selene sighed and said, "You never mentioned you had a basil allergy."

"It's not usually a big topic of conversation. We all have strange allergies, don't we?"

"Try being allergic to the sun. It's not a good time when it gets too hot and a rash breaks out."

"I'll take the sun over basil right about now. I checked the ingredients on the menu. There wasn't basil in anything I ordered."

"Right." Tremors rocked her insides as she gauged where this was headed…

"It begs the question how basil wound up in my food."

"Are...are you sure it wasn't anything else you've eaten today—"

"It couldn't be."

"How can you be so sure?" She almost cringed at the crack in her voice.

"I could tell. I've had reactions before. It was every time I took a bite of that steak. It didn't register immediately because I thought...I thought..." He paused in between with hazel eyes deepening to an earthy-brown shade under the florescent light. "I thought it was me being caught up in our dinner."

Her brows pressed together. "You mean nerves? Like butterflies?"

He reached up to rub his reddening neck. "If that's what you call it. I told you I'm not a big dater. It's been a while since I've felt...since I've enjoyed myself like that."

"Me too," she whispered back. The guilt swung into her like a sledgehammer and she couldn't bear his presence another second. She needed a buffer. "I should call Noelle. Let her know everything's okay. I always call her after my dates. Considering how late it is, I know she's worried."

The excuse was a copout. Something fabricated in order to about-face and retreat. She sucked in the frigid night's air as soon as she escaped to the courtyard outside. Never mind that the plunging temperatures forced a shudder out of her or that her fingers tingled from the cold. None of that mattered so long as she had space from Aiden.

What had she done? She had almost gotten him killed!

She liked the guy, felt a chemistry with him she had never experienced with another man. She didn't know what to do with that, or what to make of it, but it was there, an invisible presence. In her heart and stomach it was palpitations and flutters. In her head it was a sudden reasoning why she and Aiden fit. They made sense on paper.

Until she started thinking about circumstance. He was a paranormal investigator. She was a witch—not just any witch —the granddaughter of Luna Blackstone, the evil witch many believed haunted Brimrock. These two details couldn't be swept under the rug no matter how drawn she was to Aiden both physically and mentally. So what now?

That was the question at the tip of her tongue when she called Noelle for the rescue. She needed the lifeline to help her sort out her jumbled thoughts. Briefly, after the ER nurse directed her to the waiting room, she had pulled out her phone and texted Noelle an update on Aiden and the potion.

Noelle answered on the first ring and shrieked, "Girl, what the fudge?"

"Fudge? Still?"

"Bibi's got me doing that Yuletide no-cuss resolution thing with her. Anyway, *what* happened?"

"I don't even know. I can barely speak right now!"

"Is Aiden okay? We didn't kill him, did we? I'm too bougie and cute for jail."

"Noe, stop. No jokes. Aiden's okay—we got him help in time—but I'm not. What do I do? What do I say? He knows it was the steak sauce!"

"First things first, breathe. We don't need you passing out 'cuz you're holding your breath. Second thing, girl, stop with the dramatics. Play it cool."

"Play it cool? Noe, are you serious? Aiden ended up in the ER!"

"I know that. And there's nothing you can do to change it right now. Why stress on it?"

Selene paced the length of the courtyard, phone pressed against her ear. "I like the guy, Noe. I like him—as in I want him to wrap his arms around me as I stare into his hazel eyes. And, yes, I know I sound like a Nicholas Sparks novel."

"Everybody loves *The Notebook* but *Dear John* is sooo slept on."

"Definitely not helping."

"Sorry," she apologized. "But do you hear yourself? This thing between you can't go anywhere. It's never going to work."

"The worst part is that I know you're right." She groaned and stopped pacing. For the next moment she focused on her breathing, calming the antsy nerves in her system. Breathing at a even cadence, she moved onto the chaos that had become her mind. "What do I tell him? How can I keep lying about the potion?"

"You tell him you don't know what caused his allergic reaction."

"But I do. I suck at lying."

"Not tonight you don't. Keep it simple. We'll figure something else out later. Promise me you're not going to spill? It's more than just you involved now—Shayla and I helped you."

Selene hung up from her conversation with Noelle more torn than when it began. She stuck her fingers in her curlier-by-the-minute mane and paused to mull over what to do next. Aiden was being released any minute now. She was going to have to see him. She was going to have to look him in the eye and bury the truth.

On her feet, Selene sighed, resolving to do what she had to in order to keep the truth hidden.

———

"You really don't have to wait on me," said Aiden.

"I probably should," replied Selene, shrugging.

They stood at the outpatient counter finalizing Aiden's release. He looked worse for wear compared to earlier that night. His V-neck sweater was wrinkled and his skin complexion was dull and pallid. His normally arrow-straight posture was slouched and drowsiness crept into his timbre. Selene imagined she looked little better.

"This is probably the time we call it a night," he said once outside in the snow. He held his cell phone in his large palm and pulled up the URide app. "I'll admit, Selene, you know how to make a night interesting. I can't say I've ever been to the ER on a date."

"Me? Don't you mean you? You're the allergic one!"

"To basil. Who would've guessed that would be my undoing?"

Selene dug the sharp point of her stiletto heel into the cracked pavement. His dry retort almost coaxed a laugh out of her, but she fended off the urge. Instead she stared at the crevices beneath her feet and marveled at how she related to the jagged fractures in the cement.

Part of her yearned to look up into Aiden's eyes, confess the truth, touch her lips to his, and revel in what a real romantic moment would be like after being denied love for years. The other, colder part of her insisted she stick to the plan—more than just her heart was at stake.

No matter how attracted she was to Aiden, he was just a man. He sought to uproot her life, expose her, Luna, and the rest of the Blackstone family. If anything, he was much worse than an unsuspecting man like Peter, who stood her up. Aiden actually posed a threat to her life as a witch in Brimrock.

He had to go.

She shut her eyes and struggled for another breath. Aiden

must've sensed she was upset because he moved to touch her arm. She shirked his touch, keeping her back to him.

"Are you alright?" he asked in his ever sturdy voice, calm despite his close call.

Her feelings continued warring inside of her. Her eyes clenched harder and she marveled how she cared so much about a man she had only met days ago. It should've been easy for her to walk away. So why was she breathless, unable to keep him at bay? Why did she want to spin around and jump into his arms?

Here Aiden stood, a man concerned for her despite his own troubles that night. Troubles *she* had caused him.

"I'm…I'm fine," she mumbled. Confident she could keep it together, she finally faced him again. "Just didn't expect tonight to end up like this."

"That makes two of us. But, hey, if you aren't feeling well, the ER's a footstep away. They're probably missing us already."

He meant it as a joke, but when Selene focused on him, the humor shifted to the back burner. She had drifted closer, neither noticing until that second, and she knew then what was to come. Her next breath froze in her lungs as deep yearning seized control. He bent toward her and she welcomed his soft kiss on her lips.

The guilt and tension zinging through her body vanished. She felt lighter in his arms, standing with him outside of the ER half past midnight. The snow fell as tiny icy flurries, but his cautious lips brushing hers were enough to warm her. The sweet kiss was over quickly, its lasting effects felt long after.

Aiden rubbed his jaw to hide his grin. Selene ran her tongue over her bottom lip as if savoring his taste. Before either could utter a word, the URide car pulled up to the curb. The driver rolled down the window with an impatient scowl.

"Ride's here," Aiden said. He opened the back passenger door and waited for her to get in.

Selene slid onto the far seat and thanked her lucky stars. The night needed to end. If she and Aiden stood on the curb and kissed a second longer, she was afraid of what she would do. After tonight, it was undeniable—a real problem she needed to figure out. She liked Aiden O'Hare, and she had no clue what the fudge she was going to do about it.

CHAPTER ELEVEN

"You hate it here," said Eddie. He wandered into the kitchen in his basketball shorts and baggy T-shirt from college. His sneakers were by the door. Mrs. Myers forbade shoes in the house.

Aiden was at the breakfast table with a bowl of sugary cereal. He had waited for the Myerses to leave before creeping downstairs. Today's festive holiday outing was a trip one town over to do more shopping. Apparently the mall in Cowbridge was better than the one in Brimrock—it had three levels and a bowling alley inside, after all.

Only Eddie and Rory stayed behind. Rory had left shortly after her parents, muttering something about market day. Eddie had slept in longer than Mrs. Myers preferred.

It was fine with Aiden. He had largely avoided Eddie. His best pal would call him out. He had already noticed Aiden's behavior and had stopped him with questions more than once. Last night's date with Selene and today's interview with Gerri Halsey wouldn't help matters.

As it turned out, Aiden was right. Eddie pulled up a chair at the breakfast table, twisting it around so he could sit backward. Arms folded on top of the chair, he stared expectantly as Aiden funneled another spoonful of sugary lumps into his mouth.

"You gonna tell me what's up?" Eddie asked after another second of silence. He grabbed the Sugar Rings cereal box and peered inside for the marshmallows. "You've been acting off ever since we got to Brimrock. The fam's a lot to handle—I get that—but it's gotta be something else."

"Why do you say that?"

Eddie shrugged and popped a marshmallow into his mouth. "You've been gone half the time. You've been hitting up Selene Blackstone of all people. You didn't get home 'til one last night."

"Do I have a curfew I didn't know about?"

"You must not know Aunt Priscilla. She notices everything."

"It sounds like you do too."

"Bro, I've tried to give you space, but you've gotta admit you've been weird."

"I've been myself. I've been doing a lot of thinking."

"Yeah, but about what? It can't be what I think it is."

"Eddie, don't you think you're overreacting—?"

"I should've picked up on it sooner," Eddie continued with a shake of his head.

Aiden gave up with a resigned sigh. Eddie rolled his eyes as if it were the most obvious fact in the world.

"The time of year. The dates with Selene. You're missing Delilah."

"You think I'm upset because of Delilah?"

"You broke up a year ago this month. Now all of a sudden you're rebounding with Selene."

"Selene is *not* a rebound."

"But there's no need to be all secretive. If you wanna talk about it, I'm here."

Aiden swallowed his latest spoonful of Sugar Rings. "Even if you do think I'm acting different, is it that big of a deal?"

"You're like a brother. If you're in a funk, I've gotta do something about it. You tried to move on with Selene but you can't stop thinking about Delilah. It sucks, but we've gotta snap you out of it. Enjoy the holiday break while we can. Once the New Year hits, it's back to filming."

"About that," said Aiden, "I've been doing some research. Haven't you noticed what happened to Peter is a lot like what's happened to others in the past?"

"Don't tell me *you're* now believing in the paranormal." Eddie bellowed out a loud laugh, smacking the table with his hand. "Who would've thought it'd take Brimrock to turn you into a believer!"

"I didn't say all that. I'm saying there's similarities. I'm sure there's a—"

"Reasonable explanation, yada yada yada. *Or* Luna Blackstone really is an evil witch and Brimrock really is haunted."

"That's impossible. There's no such thing as evil witches or hauntings. I'm going to prove it. I'm going to do what Brimrock PD hasn't been able to do in forty years—figure out what really happened to Peter Feinberg and John Grisby."

"Good luck," scoffed Eddie. "You do know the mayor's big brother was the first victim, right?"

"John Grisby?"

"Brother of John Grisby, *Marc* Grisby is mayor."

"I'm sure he's not a big fan of the Blackstones."

"The Grisbys hate the Blackstones. That's a given."

"I'd be interested to know what he really thinks about

Peter's attack," Aiden pondered aloud. "All of his statements to the press have been very neat and rehearsed."

"You won't get his real opinion 'til you hear it behind the scenes. Aunt Priscilla works at town hall and is always talking about how he goes off in meetings, but then it's all smiles when cameras are flashing," Eddie explained. He rose off his backward chair and clapped a hand to Aiden's back. "Anyway, if we play our cards right, this episode could really go viral. I'm taking Ghost to the gym for a few hours, but how about we do something tonight? Something not Christmas related. There's that bar I told you about—the Gin House. We should hit it up and let loose a little."

Aiden didn't protest. He was too busy processing what Eddie had told him. The pieces didn't yet seem to connect, but he wasn't even close to giving up. With the house now empty, he was free to ponder on everything to his brain's content. At least until his meeting at noon with Gerri Halsey.

———

"Who's ringing my bell?" Gerri screeched from inside her home.

Aiden was on the front stoop with a box of Earl Grey tea he picked up at the Magic Bean. The older woman on shift, Bibi, had suggested it to him. She said it was the finest brand they carried; the tea leaves themselves were imported from England.

The door swung open and fifty-six-year-old Gerri Halsey scowled at him. "I don't want to subscribe to your magazine or buy your chocolate bars or whatever else it is you're selling."

"Huh?" Aiden realized it was the box of tea in his hands. He shook his head so profusely he messed his neatly combed hair. A single reddish-brown tendril fell against his forehead. "Mrs. Halsey, I'm Aiden O'Hare, the investigative reporter who reached out to you. This is a thank-you gift for the interview."

"Oh. Right." Gerri begrudgingly snatched the box of Earl Grey from him and then beckoned him inside.

The chemical stench of cigarettes hit him at once and he sputtered out of surprise. He wasn't used to cigarettes, hated their pungent smell and the secondhand taste of them. The whole house reeked of it. She must've smoked a pack a day indoors, which meant it permeated every inch, embedded even within the fabric of the sofa cushions and the curtains in the window.

When Gerri turned a bugged eye onto him, he straightened up and held in his next cough. There was something distinctly intimidating about Gerri Halsey. She stood at five feet nothing and was rather bony, premature wrinkles creased on her pale skin, but it was in her face. The cock-eyed, thin-lipped scowls she doled out. The hunched but severe stance of hers didn't help; it was how she carried herself, like she could give a scolding tongue-lashing at any second.

"Well? What do you want? I've got things to do and sorry to break it to you, but speaking to you isn't at the top of the list."

"Right, uh, I was hoping I could ask you a couple of questions about Peter Feinberg. I've tried reaching out to his family and haven't heard back. Your daughter, Isabelle, told me you're a close family friend."

Gerri perked up—or as close to it as someone as disgruntled as she was could get. Her skeletal hand clamped onto his arm and she dragged him across the stinky hall. He cringed when she nudged him toward one of the sofas. He was wearing an expensive wool sweater with a ribbed collar and fine stitching. He hated exposing it to the cigarette smell.

"You sit here for a tick. I'm going to make us some of this tea. Then when I get back we can talk about Peter." She bustled out of the room like a fly chasing a hot plate of food.

Aiden groaned out his next sigh. He had hoped for the interview to be brief. He hadn't counted on Gerri wanting to sit and chat over freshly brewed tea. If he'd anticipated that, he wouldn't have brought the Earl Grey in the first place. Damn him and his misguided attempt at being a polite house-guest. Suddenly, that rude and dismissive meetup with Isabelle at the diner wasn't looking too bad…

He simply had to keep his best game face on. Hercule Poirot wouldn't lose focus or become distracted by bad smells. Neither would Sherlock Holmes. He couldn't afford to either.

"Back!" Gerri announced minutes later. The teacups rattled on their saucers as she scurried toward him.

The Earl Grey was the most pleasant scent in the Halsey home. Its mild citrusy notes soothed Aiden at a time where he was seconds away from turning blue in the face. He vaguely wondered if he'd set a new Guinness World Record for longest breath held. He definitely had to be in the top ten.

Gerri crossed one knobby knee over the other and held her teacup centimeters away from her lips. She seemed to be trying to mimic a posh type of woman seen in house decor magazines or in window displays at Neiman Marcus. She failed from the get-go, brittle auburn hair more rat's nest and wrinkled house clothes more bargain bin than anything upscale.

"It's a shame what happened," she said with a well-timed sniffle. The tonal change to her once prickly voice was obvi-ous. She used her soft inflection for Peter, playing up the sympathy angle. "I've known Peter since he was a boy—he's always been a good person. Cecile is so heartbroken."

"I'd like to ask more about that. Have you spoken with Cecile, his mother, since what happened?"

"We belong to the same book club. We meet Tuesdays and Thursdays. I left her a voice message expressing my condolences."

Aiden wished she would get to the point. His tea was untouched on the coffee table as he leaned forward, hands folded, elbows digging into his thighs. "Mrs. Halsey, did Mrs. Feinberg ever return your call?"

"Just yesterday. I'll tell you this—the devil never takes a vacation. He's ready 24/7/365. Best we stay ready ourselves," she rambled, sipping Earl Grey. "Cecile was a wreck. Kept crying and crying over the phone. Docs aren't sure when—or even if—Peter will wake up."

"How about who was in contact with Peter that night?" Old school even during an investigation, he withdrew a small notepad and flipped to the first blank page.

Gerri's scowl returned in full force. The smoker's lines in her face deepened and she spat, "Oh, I know who last talked to him alright. If only Brimrock PD took it seriously! He was with that girl."

Aiden was certain he knew who "that girl" was, but he pretended as though he were ignorant. He was supposed to be a clueless visitor to the New England town; it would make his investigative report easier if he had clear-cut answers, not postulations.

The rise in his brows and clueless stare clued Gerri in that she needed to explain. She set her teacup down and dusted off bony fingers, pruned lips pursing.

"Selene Blackstone." She said the name like a dirty word. "She's a weird girl—weirder than her mother—maybe as bad as that spooky grandmother of hers. I see her day in, day out at the library, and…and she's a *weird* girl."

"As in, what? She has peculiar tastes?" Aiden scribbled notes within the trim blue lines.

Gerri shook her head. "As in she's into the occult. Just like the rest of 'em. Those Blackstones are trouble. Mark my words."

"How do you know, Mrs. Halsey? Pardon my skepticism, but that's a serious accusation," said Aiden, fishing for deeper details. His pen hovered over the miniature legal notepad.

"How do I know she's a weird girl? Did you miss the part where I said I work with her? Strange things happen whenever she's around. Maybe a book cart crashing into the wall. A glass jar shattering out of nowhere. Lights go out and doors jam. You name it. It's happened."

"But what does that have to do with Peter Feinberg?"

"I *told* you. She was with him that night."

"The night he was attacked? So they did meet up?"

"Blind date," said Gerri. Her brows rose at the scandalous piece of gossip, scooping up her teacup for another sip. "I'm no conspiracy theorist, but you do the math. It doesn't take some genius to figure out two plus two is four. And you bet your bottom dollar those Blackstones are always part of the equation somewhere."

CHAPTER TWELVE

To clear her head and get some fresh air, Selene ventured to the town square on market day. The snow failed to slow down the shop owners, who set up their foldable tables and cloth awnings in rows up and down the block. Their merchandise, ranging from homemade jam and baked goods to Christmas trinkets and knitted scarves and mittens, was laid out for browsing.

Selene wandered by the candles booth manned by a half-attentive Mrs. Jorgensen. Yule started tomorrow and she hadn't bought a single gift. Though the annual, intimate celebration with Noelle and Bibi would be enjoyable without presents, gifting them something special was one of her favorite parts.

She picked up a coconut milk and honey candle, catching a whiff of its pleasantly sweet scent. Noelle *loved* coconut. She also had about forty different candles decorating her bedroom at any given time, but was there such a thing as having *too* many candles?

"Nope, definitely not," she whispered to no one. Only after did she notice her old school teacher, Mrs. Palmer, and her young daughter at the same candle display. Both gawked at her, brows quirked and disturbed frowns on their faces. She smiled at them as an experiment she vaguely knew the outcome of. Mrs. Palmer gave a stiff, formal nod and then herded her daughter off to the other side of the booth. The elementary school teacher never had been her biggest fan.

Then again, no one in town really was. That was the worst part about the curse on the Blackstone name. She was doomed to living within Brimrock's town borders for life while being a pariah.

"It wouldn't be a curse if it was pleasant," she reasoned aloud, sighing. She caught herself again and bit her tongue. People in town were going to think she was strange regardless, but being out and about talking to herself didn't help. She'd had the bad habit since childhood. With the coconut milk and honey candle in hand, she marched up to the register and presented it to Mrs. Jorgensen. "This one smells so good."

"Yes," said Mrs. Jorgensen, reluctantly exchanging the bagged candle for cash. "It's one of our best sellers."

"You used to make one that was black cherry. That one was my favorite."

Mrs. Jorgensen humored her with a lazy smile and then turned to fuss with the candle display.

Selene shook it off, moving on from the awkward encounter. If Noelle were around, she would throw loud and unmistakable shade about Mrs. Jorgensen and her candle booth. If Bibi were there, it'd be even more of a fit, with Bibi calling out the rude behavior front and center. The alternate scenarios eked a soft laugh out of Selene, this time any ounce of care as to who saw her falling by the wayside.

At the next shop table she stopped at, it was more of the same. At Miranda Letterman's jewelry and hair accessories table, she was shunned when asking a question about the price of a silver crescent moon hair pin. Her eyes shrunk into a narrow gaze and she raked her teeth over her bottom lip, watching as Miranda Letterman, former high school mean girl, ignored her for another customer.

Selene glanced at the space where the price tag should have been for the sterling silver crescent moon pin and then over to one of the other, cheaper hair clips made of plastic. The price tag in front of those said $5.99. She drifted to the other side, putting distance between herself and the hair accessories. With a subtle flick of her wrist, she lifted the $5.99 price tag, floating it over to the crescent moon pin. Miranda turned around none the wiser, finally ready to treat Selene to some face-to-face bad customer service.

"What do you want?"

Selene smiled sweetly. "I was going to ask if that crescent moon hair pin is really six bucks. It's beautiful."

Miranda's brow furrowed as she snatched it off the table along with the price tag. "That's weird. I didn't mark it down. How did that happen?"

"I don't know, but that's what the tag says. I'll take it."

Minutes later, wallet six dollars lighter but another paper bag in hand, Selene left Miranda Letterman's booth. The afternoon was shaping up to be a chilly but good one after all. Maybe Noelle was onto something. Retail therapy did help clear muddied thoughts. Over the course of her browsing different shop booths, she had thought about Aiden and their date last night—the *kiss* they'd shared.

In the pale, sobering light of winter day, she had realized last night could never happen again. Her short time with Aiden was fun while it lasted, but all logic pointed to disaster. If him winding up in the ER after the persuasion potion wasn't clue enough, the fast pitter-patter of her heartbeat should have been. It couldn't be a good sign that she abandoned reason when around him. Better cut her losses now than fall any deeper.

From here on out, she was avoiding Aiden. He could investigate Luna as much as he wanted. He wasn't getting anything out of her. She wasn't cooperating. She wasn't even going to speak to him again if she could help it. Things would be for the best that way.

On her stroll through the town square, Selene stopped paying attention and bumped into a woman headed in the opposite direction. She began an apology before spotting who it was. Rory Myers had seen better days. Her hair was ratty and she had heavy bags beneath her eyes from lack of sleep. She wore a tweed coat that looked to be from the men's department, swallowing up what was her slim frame. Though Selene had spoken few words to Rory in either of their lifetimes, she was aware of the awkward fact that Peter was her ex-boyfriend.

"Watch where you're going," Rory snarled. Her nostrils flared, brow pinched.

Selene said nothing, moving on without a word. Rory was in such a staunchly bad mood that it seemed like anything Selene said would touch a nerve. Her safest bet was to escape the splash zone before Rory truly flew off the handle. Besides, she had gotten the gifts she wanted for Noelle and Bibi and even a special treat for herself.

It was a good day.

———

The day was not so good when Selene made it to Gifford Lane. Staked out in a police cruiser against the curb was Officer Adam Gustin and his partner, Trevor Nunn. She should've known Gustin would track her down sooner or later. He had been following her on and off since Peter's attack. Rather than the edgy nerves she assumed would kick in, agitation heated her up even in the cold. The driver's-side door popped open and Gustin unfolded his long, Gumby-like legs.

"Hello, Selene. I'm sorry to disturb you."

"I'm sure you are," she replied with a tart air of sarcasm. "I'm guessing you want to speak with me about something?"

"If you have a free moment."

Yukie was stunned to have a new visitor. The furry terrier yipped and ran circles around Gustin. Selene shrugged off her coat, dropped off her bags in the hall, and led the charge into the living room. That late into the afternoon, the shadows had already started creeping into the large gothic home and its curtain-drawn, stained-glass windows. She flicked on only a single, solitary table lamp and gestured to the sofa.

"You can have a seat if you want."

When he plopped down, a plume of dust burst free. He held off a sneeze and she smirked in mock apology.

"Ignore the dust. I don't have too many visitors," she said. She'd be lying if she denied that she derived at least some pleasure from making Gustin miserable inside her home. Not necessarily because he was a bad person—he wasn't—but because of the obvious implication being she was on Brimrock PD's radar. "What are these questions?"

"Uh, right. I'm sure you've heard about what's been going on in town."

"You're going to have to be more specific than that, Officer."

"The attack on Peter Feinberg," he began but stopped again. Yukie climbed up his shin, wagging her tail, a chew toy between her teeth. He took the irresistibly cute bait, grabbing the soggy, squeezable stuffed toy and tossing it across the room. Yukie launched after the toy before it even touched the ground, furry legs a blur. Her antics entertained him, a slow smile spreading onto his face.

Selene cleared her throat. "Officer?"

"Uh, sorry. Your dog—she's just so playful," he confessed. He shook his head to force himself back on track, the Adam's apple in his lanky neck bobbing. "Anyway, like I was saying, the attack on Peter Feinberg. As you know, there's an ongoing investigation into the events that transpired that night."

"And?"

"And," said Gustin with a deep, focusing breath, "I'm wondering if you can tell me your whereabouts on the evening of December 17?"

"My whereabouts," she repeated.

Gustin frowned, waiting attentively. This time he wouldn't let Yukie's spastic energy distract him as she chased down the chew toy and brought it back for another throw.

Selene thought fast. "If you're asking if I saw Peter the night he was attacked, I didn't. We had dinner reservations at the Mulberry. He stood me up."

"Did he say why?"

"Never answered the phone. Never answered my texts. He ghosted me," said Selene. She crossed her arms and shot Gustin a cold stare. "You can check with the Mulberry. I was there during the timeframe Peter was allegedly attacked."

He caught onto what she was implying, sitting up straighter. "Selene, if you think I've come by to question you because—"

"I don't think. I know. That's exactly what happens when something unexplained goes down in this town. Check with the Blackstones. You're *wrong*. I had nothing to do with it," she snapped. She popped to her feet, ready to move on. "Are we done here?"

Gustin surveyed her one last time, half puzzled and half suspicious, but he gave up. At least at face value. He got up off the dusty sofa and let her shoo him toward the door. He paused only once past the threshold for another quick look at her. "Selene?"

"What?"

"Your blind date with Peter—how did it come about?"

"Mutual friend. He had just broken up with his girlfriend and it was set up from there."

"Your friend Noelle Banks and his ex-girlfriend Rory Myers. Correct?"

"That's right. Why?"

"Trying to iron out this timeline of events and everyone involved. You have a good evening."

Selene stood in the doorway and watched Officer Gustin walk down the front path and back toward the police cruiser, where Nunn waited. Something told her this wasn't the last she'd hear from him about this investigation.

———

"Open up, Selly!" Noelle shouted from the other side of the door. She beat her fist against the door some more.

Selene groaned from where she stood in the hall, waving her fingers as she sent sprigs of holly into the air and hung them up. It was about time she put out some festive Yule decorations around the dusty, isolated home, even if it was mostly for herself and Yukie. She had also hung a giant evergreen wreath in the living room and lit up her best tea light candles.

"Finally," Noelle breathed when she opened the door. She

shivered, rubbing her hands together. "It's nice and toasty in here."

"Thank the brass radiator—I've affectionally named him Ol' Reliable. He never lets me down."

"I can hear him wheezing now." Noelle glanced over as the radiator sputtered, coughing up more heat. "How's your day off been?"

"I found out I'm under police investigation," said Selene, wandering into the kitchen. "You know, the usual."

"Wait, what? Pump the brakes and shift gears into reverse. You're being investigated?"

"Noe, we pretty much knew this was going to happen. We called it, remember?"

"That was in a worst-case scenario type of thing—it's different when it's real. What did they say?"

Selene raised her arms like a maestro leading an orchestra, with expert hand motions directing a kettle onto the stove and twisting on the burner. Then she summoned two teacups and the box of chai. It soared across the room and landed on the kitchen table as she said, "He wanted to know what I was doing that night."

"And?"

"I told him the truth. I was busy being ghosted at the Mulberry."

"They have nothing on you." Though Noelle's smooth voice was full of her trademark confidence, it sounded shakier than usual. More like she was convincing herself. "I'm low-key over these nonwitches in town. They act like they run the place."

"That's because they do. We're outnumbered thirty thousand to three."

"You ever wonder what happened to all the other witch

families? I've looked through Bibi's old photo albums. There used to be a whole undercover coven in Brimrock."

"They probably moved on—or died out. I'm the last Blackstone female. Whenever I asked my mom about other family, she always shushed me. Part of the curse, I'm guessing."

Noelle wiggled spooky fingers and moaned like a ghost. "The mysterious curse! We'll see if we're ever able to figure out how to break it."

"I've accepted my fate. I'm stuck here. It's not exactly exciting, but at least I've got my books and Yukie."

"And *me*," Noelle added. She bent forward as Yukie trotted into the kitchen and scratched her behind her floppy, furry ears. "Which brings me to why I'm here. Tomorrow's Winter Solstice, the start of Yule. Which means we need to celebrate!"

"I thought we were? Our usual little celebration at your house?"

"That's tomorrow. I'm talking about tonight. Let's go out."

Selene gave a vehement shake of her head, jumping to her feet. She skipped out on using her powers to twist off the burner and instead grabbed the whistling kettle by hand. "Nope. Not interested. I don't need a night out."

"You definitely do. When was the last time we went out to the Gin House?"

"Probably the last time I puked my guts out. You know witches have a low alcohol tolerance—yourself included."

"One or two drinks. That's it," pleaded Noelle. "You go ahead upstairs and get yourself prettified. I'll hang out down here with my BFF. Right, Yukie?"

Yukie, like the adorable traitor that she was, yipped a clear and indisputable yes.

———

"Maybe this wasn't such a bad idea after all," said Selene once seated at a booth in the Gin House. The ruckus around them was harsh on the ears, but also oddly infectious at the same time. Anywhere she looked, patrons enjoyed themselves. Some tossed back shots of gin at the counter while others mingled on the bar floor with bright gleams in their eyes.

For their part, she and Noelle had ordered two tall gin fizzes and a large supreme nachos platter. They noshed on the stacks of chips topped in jalapeños and smothered in cheesy beef galore and chatted about whatever came to mind.

"Have you and bae made up yet?"

"I'm not even bothering to answer that," said Noelle between crunches. She washed the mouthful down with a double gulp of her gin fizz. "Shayla and I are just friends."

"You both are so cute together. If you could only get your head out of your ass."

Noelle snorted. "You're one to talk. Didn't you just get done telling me you're quitting Fudgeboy cold turkey?"

"It's for the best. Things…things between us are too complicated."

"He *is* sorta cute. In a sarcastic, nerdy, bookish Fudgeboy kinda way," said Noelle thoughtfully. "And he looks good in that navy blue sweater he's wearing tonight."

"I mean, he'll always be cute to—*WHAT*?" Selene choked on her nacho chip. She had been following every word Noelle said until she got to that last part. Her throat burned as the salty, cheesy nacho chip lodged itself halfway down her esophagus, and she had to gulp down several mouthfuls of water to clear the jam. Eyes glossy and voice now husky, she said, "Stop messing around, Noe. That's not funny."

"I'm not messing around. Aiden and his bestie, Eddie, are at the bar counter. You gonna go say hi?"

Whatever buzz Selene had going faded at once. "You're serious. He's really here?"

"Turn around and see for yourself."

Selene hesitated for a second longer, fixing her glasses as though their slight crookedness would interfere with seeing Aiden. She held her breath and very cautiously, very slowly, snuck a glance over her shoulder. Was it physically possible for her spleen to flip, flop, and then fall to the floor?

If it was, it was exactly what happened to her as she set sights on Aiden from across the dimly lit barroom.

And dammit did he look *good*. The light caught his hair and showed off its reddish tints. Stubble had grown thick on his cheeks in the last twenty-four hours since she had seen him, and he'd rightfully skipped on shaving, adding a surprising rugged twist to what she once called his coffee shop guy cute face. His profile itself was a delight, the bridge of his nose and jut of his chin defined. He looked scholarly in his navy blue sweater vest and white button down shirt underneath—Noelle was right about that. He had rolled the sleeves up to his elbows, showing off the sexiest, veiniest forearms Selene had ever seen. Could forearms even *be* sexy?

Selene forgot how to swallow, throat still burning. Her mind flashed back to last night. Them standing outside the emergency room. The red neon lights bright in the snowy night's darkness as they stood on the curb and inched toward each other. Their lips touched and shocks shot through Selene's body. She leaned into him, deeper into his kiss, and felt like she was a bundle of excitable, spastic nerves. A thousand little ones that danced and twirled in celebration kissing the man she thought was seriously injured mere minutes ago.

They had said good-night and dared not look at each other

again. He didn't call or text. Neither did she. It was a one-time indulgence, and yet…

"I'll be right back," she said suddenly, boldly. All the big talk she'd done about quitting him cold turkey was out the window in that split second. She slid out of the booth and finger combed her cloud of curls. An invisible force pushed her forward. Next thing she knew, her feet were moving. She was diving into the crowd, farther away from the safety of her booth with Noelle. She broke through on the other side at a moment of perfect timing, Aiden's eyes landing on her.

There was no turning back now. She pasted her best smile onto her face and waved hello. Aiden was in the middle of a conversation with Eddie, but his attention diverted to her. He seemed to be as smitten from across the room as she was, as his lips stretched into a slow, bright return smile.

Selene banished any overthinking. Though nights out at bars had never been her thing—socializing on a mass scale in general not her forte—she had read plenty of scenes like this in books. Many, many books. She'd seen it play out on TV screens and in the movies countless times. She was supposed to play it cute and coy, sidle up to Aiden and flirt over drinks.

It was now the gin doing the walking and talking. She went along with it, trusting in its intoxicating powers.

"Hey, Selene," said Eddie when she walked up. His tone was innocent, though the dart of his dark brown eyes told a different story. The look he gave Aiden spoke for itself. He hid his expression behind his beer bottle. "Forgot I was gonna take a leak. Be back in a few."

Selene and Aiden watched him march off with beer bottle in hand. Aiden's cheeks blushed a faint pink barely traceable under the dim bar lights. He smiled at her again as if out of apology and then confessed, "I didn't expect to see you here tonight."

"Is that a good unexpected or bad unexpected?"

"Good. *Always* good."

"And a good save," she quipped, looping a tight curl around her finger. Since when did she play with her hair when she talked to guys? She racked her brain for what book or movie she'd gotten this from.

"Your hands are empty. I'm no expert but I'm pretty sure bar etiquette requires me to get you a drink," Aiden said. The pink on his pale skin began to spread, first on his cheeks and then fanning out toward his ears. "What are you drinking tonight?"

"How about a beer? Then I can join the club."

Aiden's brow creased and he blurted, "What club?"

"It was a joke. Both you and Eddie are—never mind."

"Oh! Beer club. I'm drinking beer. Got it," said Aiden. His ears were officially red now. "I'm blaming the beer for making me slow on the uptake."

They were *hopeless*. It was more glaringly obvious than ever that they were two people lacking social grace. Selene couldn't put her finger on why. Was it the alcohol or possibly the lingering uncertainty after their kiss last night?

"Here you go," he said, handing her a cold one. "So, what brings you here tonight? Eddie dragged me out. He insisted on a guys' night."

"Noelle." Selene pointed her friend out in the barroom. "Today was my day off and she told me we should celebrate Yuletide early."

"Yuletide? You mean Christmas?"

"Right. I mean this whole winter period—holiday season."

Aiden's expression loosened into one of relief. "I've had enough of celebrating the holidays. I'd rather spend time in the ER again."

"That beer doesn't have any basil in it, does it? If it does, you just might."

This time, Aiden caught onto her joke. He laughed a lot louder than what she was used to hearing out of him. *Definitely* the alcohol.

"I've double, triple, quadruple checked, and nope. Basil-free."

"Good. Now you can actually enjoy yourself."

"More so now that you're here."

Her brows jumped high on her forehead. He realized his mistake a second too late and mumbled something indistinguishable into his beer bottle. The awkwardness marinated between them as neither knew what to say next. Aiden was pinker with each blink of the eye and she was stumped on how to respond. Then, in her gin and beer tipsiness, an idea materialized.

"We should make up for last night."

"What do you mean?"

"Our date got cut short. We should finish what we started."

Aiden grinned broadly, his nod enthusiastic. "That sounds great. Let's see if I can find us a booth."

Her smile was her answer, but she was vaguely aware in the back of her mind she had thrown caution to wind once more. So much for never again.

CHAPTER THIRTEEN

"I'm calling it a night," said Eddie, rising from the booth cushions. "You good, man?"

Aiden couldn't feel his face anymore and his brain was foggy, but he was in high spirits. Brows lifting, he smiled. "Why wouldn't I be? We're having a good time hanging out."

Eddie laughed and clapped a hand to his back. "You are definitely on the way to being shitfaced. Almost hate to miss it."

"I'm out too," said Noelle. She nudged Selene for her attention. "You ready?"

"Go ahead without me. I'll arrange a URide."

Aiden might have been halfway drunk, but even he didn't miss the amused glance between Eddie and Noelle. Both best friends made weak attempts to hide their smirks, though failed. They wished them good night and then in another blink, Aiden and Selene were alone.

His pale, sensitive Irish skin had reddened right up to the tips of his ears. He couldn't stop smiling at whatever was said. His usual filter was gone, freeing him up to say whatever floated to mind. He couldn't even remember the last time he had more than two drinks, yet here he was in a bar at midnight. He might not buy into the theory that Selene and her family were witches, but he definitely bought into the idea she brought out another side of him.

"Another round?" he asked as the last drop from his beer bottle landed on his tongue.

Selene sat back, a blithe expression on her face. "How about we switch it up?"

"Switch it up?" Aiden couldn't quell his instant curiosity. The slight curl to Selene's lips held his attention. Those full lips that were achingly soft when he kissed her. If he were sober, he would've felt like a Neanderthal listening to such baser wants, but the alcohol drowned out the judgment. He found himself smirking back. "What did you have in mind?"

Fast forward another five minutes, he and Selene were at the bar counter. They held up their shot glasses of gin and tossed them back, toasting to the night. Aiden beat a fist against his chest as the bitter taste slithered down his esophagus. Selene shuddered and pulled a face like she had sucked on a lemon. He barked out a laugh louder than his typical, subdued chuckle.

"Look at us, we're pathetic. Clearly not big drinkers."

Selene grabbed on to his arm and said, "That's the fun part. It's so unexpected from us."

"I'm glad Eddie's not here to break out his phone. We'd already be live on InstaPixel. What now?"

It seemed like a thousand different ideas crossed Selene's mind. She scanned the barroom as though judging among them. Her eye caught on a sight that roused the widest smile out of her yet. Aiden turned to follow her gaze and shook his head, laughing. He must've been misunderstanding…

"Where are we going?" he asked as Selene slipped her

arm in his. She steered them toward the door, leaving the beer-soaked bar behind. They stumbled into the dark and snowy December night, receiving rapt hellos from the cold. The wind blew mercilessly in their direction, earning deep shudders out of them. Aiden stopped short and hiked up the collar of his coat against his chin. He needed all of the protection he could get against this bitter weather.

Selene was braver. She let go of him and spun out of reach, twirling on the sidewalk as if it weren't frosted over by snow. He edged closer, prepping to be near enough to catch her just in case. It was a battle between his beer-gin goggles and the wintry reality literally smacking him in the face.

"Selene, what are you—?" he started.

Her answer was a careless laugh that traveled melodically through the midnight air. He normally hated drunk people, found them obnoxious with their slurred speech and staggering movements, but Selene? There was something... endearingly cute about her when she was tipsy. She spun with girlish abandon, breaths fast and giggly, hundreds of her tight curls flouncing along with her. He wanted to join her.

For a second, he almost did. He was grinning as he watched, probably less composed than he was when sober. But somebody had to be the responsible one; somebody had to make sure they both got home safely. No surprise that it was him; it was *always* him.

"Get over here!" she called. She dashed away from him, jumping the sidewalk and then crossing the empty road onto the other side.

His pulse rabbited as he rushed after her. He caught her just as they made it back onto the sidewalk, but she had no intention of staying still. She slipped out of his grasp like a masterful escape artist, the fluid move so impressive even a skeptic like him would've believed it was magic if you told him.

"Selene!" he yelled fruitlessly. His own echo played back to him in the quiet New England town. "Now you're being difficult on purpose."

She frolicked over a snow hill, challenging him to a cat and mouse chase. He sighed and cussed under his breath. She knew him all too well. *Of course* he would follow.

This time, though, he would beat her at her own game. He used his long legs and broader reach to his advantage. In what took her four strides to crest the hill, he took two. She yelped as he surprised her from behind, hooking an arm around her waist to grab ahold of her.

Aiden lost his balance, so she lost her balance. They came crashing down like two hopeless klutzes, tumbling down the snowy hill. He lost count of how many times they rolled, but locked in a clumsy embrace, they shrieked as clumps of raw snow smacked into them. The snow got everywhere, into his mouth, caked in his hair, coating his eyelashes, and invasively down his trousers.

By the time they slid to a halt they were gasping for breath, laughing so hard it was a full body experience. Tears formed in his eyes and he choked on air. At his side, Selene tipped her head backward into the snow and clutched her stomach as if it pained her. They looked a mess, covered in an avalanche of snow.

He wiped his eye with his thumb and sat up. "I can't believe you did that."

She sat up beside him and fixed her glasses. Her once-raven curls were snow white. "It was *your* fault."

"Mine? How does that work? I was trying to stop you."

"Exactly why it was your fault," she replied with another

airy laugh. And then she twisted and surprised him with a kiss full on the mouth.

His hands rose instinctively to cradle her face. She tasted like gin and…snow? The crisp taste was a strange delight. It was another reminder, along with the cold tips of their noses and flakes of snow in their lashes, of the unexpected moment between them. The second night in a row where he gladly felt Selene Blackstone's soft lips against his own.

"You taste like snow," Selene mumbled with a slow smile.

"It might have something to do with us being knee-deep in it."

His dry delivery earned another breathless giggle out of her. Neither made any attempt to get up, their bodies adjusting to the icy cold as they sat there in the snow. It was then that the neon glow from above seemed noticeably brighter. Their eyes flitted up to the red and green lights strung along the street lamps. Other holiday decorations hung too, depending on the post. Everything from wreaths to velvet bows to—

"Mistletoe," Aiden said aloud. He shared in a laugh with Selene before they kissed again.

As if enchanted, the dangling Christmas lights started blinking. The bright red and green looked like tiny, twinkling sparks out of the corner his eye, and as they broke apart for another fond look at each other, he couldn't help buying into the surreal element. He was the last man on earth to believe in silly notions like special inklings or cosmic signs, but yet here he was, experiencing just that with Selene.

It was the alcohol, he decided. He brushed an errant curl behind her ear and convinced himself it had to be the gin. And the beer and whatever else they had downed that night. There was no other explanation for the bizarre feelings being stirred up. A warmth lit up inside of him and radiated from limb to limb, leaving him flushed and light-headed.

Aiden had already learned Selene was a special woman, but tonight felt like something else entirely. He couldn't look away from her if he tried. Her eyes were like the dark side of the moon, dreamy and full with only a slight shine reflecting in them. If he didn't know any better, she was aware of the moment. The odd energy suddenly swirling in the air as he gave in to her bewitching trance.

The last thing he remembered was the corner of her lips curling into a smile as she leaned forward and distracted him with another kiss. Very special woman indeed.

———

Aiden woke up with a crooked grin on his face. It took a second or two, but he patched together last night. He and Selene had spent hours at the Gin House enjoying drinks and conversation. At some point, though he couldn't pinpoint exactly when, Eddie had called it. Noelle wasn't far behind. But he and Selene stayed put, finally able to spend uninterrupted time together.

Though the gin enveloped him in a tipsy haze, his impression rang true. He and Selene were so well matched it was hard to believe. He had never thought coming to a town like Brimrock for a nauseatingly cheerful Christmas with the Myers family would lead him to a woman like her. The first woman he could see himself with—*actually* look into the future and envision a solid relationship with.

Delilah had been the closest thing, but even that was fraught with complications and incompatibility. She was a people person; someone who loved spending large chunks of time in the presence of others. He was the polar opposite;

someone who preferred his own company, or the company of the select few in his inner circle. Whereas Delilah loved being smack-dab in the middle of a party, Aiden gravitated toward the edges of the room...

He swung his legs over the side of the bed and cracked his neck. His sweater vest from last night was in a wrinkled heap on the floor. His shoes knocked over onto their sides by the door. His wallet and watch dropped off carelessly on top of the dresser. Normally, a mess disturbed him, but considering he had gotten home in a drunken stupor, he gave himself a pass.

The closing moments were a little fuzzy, but he faintly remembered rolling in the snow with Selene. He definitely remembered the pillow-soft feel of her lips and the alluring shine in her eyes before he kissed said soft lips. It had been a good night. So good he could overlook a mess in his room just this once.

Besides, there were more important matters at hand, like Peter Feinberg's attack. The more days passed without the case being solved, the likelier it appeared it would go down in the town history books like many of its other anomalies. He was determined to get to the bottom of it. Find out the facts and prove Brimrock was like any other town—there was no such thing as evil witches named Luna attacking residents. He fully intended on proving so on the fiftieth episode.

Mrs. Myers sighed when he apologized and declined her breakfast offering. He was certain he would hear about it later, but he had his investigation to dive into. Guilt pricked the back of his neck as he hid the details from Eddie, but he rationalized it as sparing him from work on his holiday vacation. He would fill him in post–New Year's.

Ghost waited for him parked in the Myerses' driveway, the Dodge Caravan covered in snow. As soon as he scraped off the ice from the windshield and warmed up the engine, he was headed for Brimrock's town hall. Yesterday's conversation with Eddie had piqued his curiosity about Mayor Grisby and his brother's attack so many years ago. It might have been a long shot he would gather any intel, but the attempt couldn't hurt. Maybe he would get lucky and finagle his way into an interview with someone on city council.

Aiden wasn't sure what he expected of the town hall building, but he entered to polished ceramic floors and a domed ceiling made up of skylights. The lobby was empty but open, breaking off into a north and south wing.

As he stood there in his pullover sweater and jeans, he felt underdressed when a councilwoman suddenly strode past him in a tailored suit and heels. The resounding echo of her heels died out when she disappeared. He was alone again. Another reminder it would be Christmas in a few short days; most employees were likely home with their families.

That was perfect for him. The fewer people around, the better. He walked up to the brass directory posted on the far wall and skimmed the listings. The municipal court and chambers were on the first floor in the south wing. On the north wing was the armory and evidence storage. Second floor was where the mayor, the police chief, and many other departments like housing and community development were located. He rode the elevator to the second floor.

Like the first floor, it was largely vacant, with councilmen scarce no matter where he looked. He slunk down the hall that led to Mayor Grisby's office. If somebody happened to stop him along the way, he would lie on the spot and claim he was a newly staffed intern. He wasn't the most skilled liar— that talent belonging to Eddie in their partnership—but he would give it his best shot.

Mere footsteps outside of the office marked as Mayor

Grisby's, two voices rose out of the silence. Both male, one grizzly and the other higher pitched and Bostonian. Aiden hovered by the door's edges, his heart skipping a beat when he heard the last name Feinberg.

"We've gotten nowhere with this investigation," said the man with the Boston accent. "There's no leads. No suspects. Gustin already paid Blackstone a visit."

"And?"

"And nothing. She has an alibi. We double-checked with the Mulberry. She was there."

"What about before the Mulberry? What about after? An alibi isn't an automatic marker of innocence."

Aiden frowned and edged even closer. He had no clue Selene was under official investigation by the Brimrock Police Department. Could they really believe she was capable of hurting Peter? He had seen her that night at the Mulberry, sat down at the table with her as she was stood up. He had even arranged her a URide car home.

"We've been keeping tabs on her all week. She hasn't done anything suspicious. In fact, all she seems to do is go to work at the library, stay home, or hang around that friend of hers—Noelle Banks."

"Because the Bankses aren't known for their kooky shenanigans around town?" the grizzlier-voiced man asked. He must've sprung to his feet from a chair because his footsteps padded across the tile floor. He was pacing. "I don't trust anyone named Blackstone and I don't trust the Bankses either. Something strange happened to Peter Feinberg, and I don't believe it was anything like a routine crime."

"Sir, are you really suggesting...you can't possibly believe...?"

"Every time, Whitaker. Every last time we think we've got a Blackstone, something happens, and it all goes up in smoke. Months of hard work for naught. But not this time. Feinberg is a healthy, able-bodied twenty-seven-year-old. For him to collapse like nothing is an anomaly. He was found with his cell phone in hand texting her, for Christ's sake. I know what happened to Feinberg is exactly what happened to…" He cut himself off with a choked sob that went on for a few seconds. He must've swallowed it down when he next spoke. His tone was back to being harsh. "I'm never letting go what happened to John. I'm not about to let it happen again. Not in *my* town."

The men moved toward the door. Aiden fled faster than a shadow in the light. By the time Mayor Grisby and Police Chief Whitaker emerged in the corridor, Aiden was down another hall, lurking out of sight. He pressed deeper into the dark corners of his hiding space. The two men passed him by none the wiser. He waited minutes after they were gone before moving again.

All sorts of thoughts raced through his mind. He needed time to process what he had overheard. The town hall was no place to do so. He escaped the large building unseen, bolting into the snowy terrain outside. Once again, he thanked his luck the area was so empty. He wasn't sure where he was headed, but he knew that along the way, he would only be thinking of one thing: Selene and the role she potentially played in Peter Feinberg's attack.

———

Mrs. Myers's guilt trip began as soon as he set foot inside the Myers home. He entered to the five Myerses geared up with beanies, scarves and ice skates. Another annual tradition of theirs, they always went ice skating leading up to Christmas.

Aiden scanned their faces. Mr. Myers looked as merry and

clueless as ever, his primary concern trivial things like finding parking at the skating rink and what was for dessert later that night. Camilla was on her phone, texting her friends. Eddie stood on the sidelines, bulky arms across his chest, a lot like his uncle in the way he seemed casual and unconcerned. Rory sat on the bottom stair with a glum expression, bony elbows digging into her thighs. Rather than comb her hair, she had shoved a beanie over her head. And then there was Mrs. Myers.

She controlled the vibe in the house, clucking her tongue at Aiden and hurrying toward him for fussing. She picked any snowflakes out of his hair, dusting them off his coat. "You've been gone for hours. I was so worried. I'm beginning to take it personally."

"Uh, you shouldn't. I'm fine."

"Today has been such a rough day for our family. You were missing and that Officer Gustin came poking around to ask Rory questions about you-know-who."

"Peter?"

"I think it's best we don't use the *P* word!" Mrs. Myers looked scandalized, like he had uttered the most offensive curse word known to man. "We're trying to stay as positive as we can. It's the holidays and I won't let anything bring us down."

"That's good. I'm, uh, glad." Aiden kept it simple, though the crease of his brows betrayed him. Even growing up, his mother never paid him this much mind. Eddie's aunt was possibly one of the most dramatic people he had ever met in his life...

Mr. Myers chimed in, his tone a deep baritone. "Grab some skates, Aiden. It's going to be a good time at the rink."

"Actually," said Aiden, "I was thinking maybe I should—"

"Got a sec?" Eddie tossed an arm around him and steered him off down the hall. He double-checked to ensure they were out of earshot from the other four. His thick brows were high on his forehead as he stared at Aiden with distinct exasperation. "You've been MIA most of the time you've been here. Don't you think you can come out ice skating? Hang around for an hour and then dip. My aunt's probably going to burst into tears if you don't. She takes these family things very seriously."

He sighed and gave a nod. In another half hour, as night fell over Brimrock, he trailed behind the Myerses at the town skating rink. The others, with the exception of Rory, put their skates on without second thoughts. He hesitated before he followed suit. A good chunk of the town was there, skaters of all ages gliding across the ice.

At first he followed Eddie's advice. He stumbled through a couple trips around the rectangular-shaped rink and narrowly avoided colliding with other skaters. He was clumsier than most, by far one of the worst skaters out tonight. It seemed most in Brimrock were decent on ice.

Mr. and Mrs. Myers canoodled while they skated. Camilla met up with friends as teenage and standoffish as she was. Rory plopped down on a bench and moped. Eddie and he stuck together for the first couple of laps around the ice, but eventually, Eddie skated off to flirt with Margot. He had spotted her from across the rink.

The following half hour was spent with Aiden biding his time. He skated a couple rounds, feeling ridiculous among the celebratory families, groups of friends, and lovers. The last straw was when a teenager collided with him. They both tumbled onto the icy ground and the squeaky-voiced teenager barely apologized for his mistake. Aiden gave a curt nod, though he pushed himself up and swatted ice shavings from his clothes.

Eddie and Margot were cozier than ever. Camilla was still with her friends, the gang of high schoolers pretending they were too cool to skate too enthusiastically. He searched the rink for Mr. and Mrs. Myers but came up short. Rory also seemed to be nowhere to be found.

That was Aiden's perfect cue to exit stage left. He did so happily, cheeks rosy and his sigh of relief frosting in the air. Nobody would ever notice he was gone. He could sneak off and head back to the Myerses', spend the rest of the night as he preferred—in solitude with his books, his laptop, and his thoughts. He had plenty to think about. He had hardly scratched the surface after his eavesdropping earlier between Mayor Grisby and Police Chief Whitaker.

He slung his ice skates over his shoulder and started down the dark street. Soon the mash of chatter and laughter faded away and the distant blares of traffic and the howl of the wind replaced them. The background noises that were just right for him to concentrate on his thoughts and sort them out.

His strides were long and fast, his attention on the investigation and not where he was going. He played back the conversation from town hall. Mayor Grisby was convinced Selene was not simply involved in Peter's attack, but that she was the perpetrator. It had sounded personal, like he was determined to carry out his vendetta against the Blackstone family, whether or not Selene was actually guilty.

Aiden wasn't going to let that happen. His investigation might have started as research for the next *Paranormal Hunters* episode on Luna, transforming into connecting the dots with Peter's attack, but it had changed again. Now it was quickly becoming about protecting Selene and proving her innocence. She wasn't going to take the fall for something she didn't do—*not* on his watch.

It had begun to flurry as he waited on a street corner for the pedestrian signal to light up. Once it did, the little man glowing, he entered the crosswalk, hands burrowed in his coat pockets. He made it halfway before he sensed it. His head jerked up from its bowed, tucked into his chest position, and the tremor of extreme terror rocked him. Speeding toward him was a car, the driver behind the wheel noticing him last second and jerking to make a hard left.

But it was too late. The car skidded out of control on the icy road.

Aiden couldn't move. His brain and body froze, stuck in the middle of the crosswalk, hazel eyes wide. Funny that he had time to register his horror as the death-mobile barreled toward him, but still funnier was the fact that it was only a split second long. The time between him spotting the car and it colliding with him felt like forever, his twenty-eight years flashing before his eyes—

"NO!" screamed a woman out of nowhere. From the sidelines, her voice tore as she shrieked into the cold night.

Aiden wasn't sure what happened next, but he remembered flying—or as close to it as one could be. He was spinning, spinning, spinning through the air. His body was glowing, lit up in a strange silver color, as though encased in thousands of tiny sparks. Before he could gather what the hell was going on, he was no longer flying—no longer spinning—but rather falling, falling, falling.

He hit the snowy grass with a hard thud, half-pained but fully conscious. His face splattered into the sloshy snow and his gasp for air injected brutal cold into his lungs. He stayed like that for another second. He couldn't process what had happened. That he was presumably in one piece. That he was alive.

With shaking limbs, he pushed himself onto his knees. Sirens were already wailing in the dark night. The screeching tires from the car that was about to hit him had stopped, but he made out heavy footsteps of two people rushing toward him. They threw themselves onto the ground beside him, checking he was okay.

Aiden shrugged them off. "What in the hell—?"

"Come with me!" Selene said, grabbing his arm and pulling. She was trying to get him onto his feet; she wanted him to run off with her.

The damn sirens wouldn't stop. They just kept getting louder and louder, closer and closer. Aiden shook his head and clenched his teeth, so lost it wasn't funny. Selene tugged on him again.

"I said *c'mon*!"

"What's going on?"

"No time to explain. That car just crashed and the cops and paramedics are on their way. We've gotta go!"

The second person—his blurry eyes recognized her as Noelle—forced him to his feet and hauled him off toward the many nearby bushes and trees in the park area. He went along with it for the first few paces, though he began to resist as his mind only muddied further.

"I was almost killed," he said on another wave of shock. "I was about to be hit by that car and then I wasn't."

"That's because I saved you."

"You...saved...me?"

"Aiden, c'mon."

He stamped his feet down into the snow so that he was immovable despite Selene's and Noelle's efforts.

"How'd you do that?"

"We've. Got. To. Go," Selene growled. His expression must've been a dumb one because she rolled her eyes and blew a frustrated breath. She knew he wasn't going anywhere until he got the truth. "Fine, you really want to choose now to do this? I'm a witch. Are you happy?"

CHAPTER FOURTEEN

Winter Solstice was supposed to be a celebratory night kicking off Yule. In past years she celebrated with Noelle and Aunt Bibi at their house. That had been their plan again this year until Bibi was under the weather. Instead of a small party for three drinking spiced cider and snacking on baked goods, they had spent the evening feeding soup and medicine to a bedridden Bibi. By late evening she drifted off into a deep bout of nasally snores, so they figured they'd get out of the house and go do something.

They were en route to the town cinema when they crossed paths with Aiden. She hadn't meant to put herself in another situation with him let alone save his life, but what other choice did she have as a car bulleted toward him? She had acted out of impulse, surprising even herself with the strength of her powers. She had raced over and mustered every ounce of lunar magic in her body, shooting a silvery beam that ripped Aiden off the ground and sent him flying into the air. What was worse, and still more surprising, was that she'd outed herself to him not a minute later.

She was a witch.

"You're…you're a…*what*?!" he exclaimed, his voice cracking.

"No time. C'mon!"

"What about the driver?"

"He's alright. I healed him," said Noelle, dragging him by his left arm.

Selene pulled him onward by his right. Together the two women managed to haul him off into the park tree line despite his size advantage over them both. His body was a rigid board, his eyes blinking against the darkness with an otherwise slack-jawed expression on his face. He had gone dumb with shock.

They crossed through the brush, ducking under low-hanging branches and stumbling into shrubs, and emerged onto the other side. A full two streets later, the echo of sirens still ringing in the night, they were far enough that they could slow up for a breather.

"The Magic Bean!" Noelle exclaimed. "I've got the key on me. Don't tell Bibi or she'll kill me. She's hates opening up the shop after hours."

Noelle led the charge around the back of the coffee shop. Selene and Aiden filed inside and Noelle locked the door behind them. The lights were off and all of the chairs were stacked on tables, but they stumbled their way to the front. Noelle flicked on the switch. Aiden went to pull up chairs. Selene saved him the trouble with a wave of her hand. Three chairs sprang to life, flipping off the tabletops and setting themselves right side up on the ground. He stopped in his tracks, gawked at the chairs, and then dragged his bulging hazel eyes to Selene.

Under the light, he looked more shocked than Selene first thought. Any semblance of color had drained from his skin, leaving him ghostly white, a clammy sheen on his forehead. He didn't seem to care that his normally tidy red-brown hair was all out of whack, tousled by the commotion. She yearned to reach up and fix it for him—smooth her fingers against his scalp and put each strand back where it neatly belonged. She resisted by keeping her arms pressed firmly at her sides.

"Since it seems like we're winging things tonight, what now?" Noelle asked into the awkward silence. She leaned against the coffee counter, her mouth flattened into a line. "We left the scene of an accident, by the way."

"You made sure he was okay. There were no serious injuries," snapped Selene. "Besides, he probably should have been driving more carefully in the first place. He almost killed someone."

"That someone being *me*," said Aiden, still in a daze. He hadn't stopped gaping at Selene.

Noelle stood up straighter, her own temper triggered. "Don't snap at me. I'm not the one responsible for this shit show—poop show—you know what I mean!"

"Okay, okay, I'm sorry," said Selene. She hated when Noelle lost her cool and they bickered. It always felt like warring with a part of herself. Sighing, she pulled off her glasses and polished them on her sweater. Her head was pounding. "You're right, Noe. Everything that's happening is my fault. I keep messing up. I'm not thinking."

"I didn't mean for you to start beating yourself up, Selly. You're human. You make mistakes. Just…just go easy on the big ones, okay?"

Aiden ran a hand over his face, blinking slowly. His shock had gone nowhere. "How did you know where I was?"

"Don't flatter yourself," scoffed Noelle. "We were walking down the street and saw you."

"And how did you...how did you...do what you did?" he asked. He looked from Selene to Noelle and then back at Selene. "That car was about to hit me. It was going to mow me down. But then...then I was flying—or floating—and there was this silver light around me. That was you?"

Selene's gaze met Noelle's. Neither witch confirmed nor denied the allegation. Selene hadn't thought it through when she told him the truth, blurting out the first thing on her frustrated mind. Aiden was swimming in shock, so confused that if she and Noelle wanted, they could conjure a memory loss spell. She pushed that thought aside. She couldn't jinx Aiden even if she wanted to; she liked the guy too much.

But she also knew now more than ever, it could never work. This had to be the end. A bittersweet smile worked itself onto her lips.

"I guess this is what you wanted for your investigation, isn't it?"

Aiden was thrown by the question. "My investigation? What investigation?"

"I know who you are, Aiden," she replied half-heartedly. "Just like you know who I am—granddaughter of Luna Blackstone—*the* Luna Blackstone. You really thought you could film an episode for your show and I wouldn't know?"

"Selene—"

"I don't trust people for a reason. You've proven exactly why that is. I hope you enjoy using me as bait for your show." Selene was on her feet and hurrying for the door before Aiden or Noelle could protest. She didn't care at the moment what either had to say. She was done with all of it.

———

The walk home helped. The moon followed her wherever she went, like a watchful guardian angel, shining its magical silver light down on her. Only half of it was viewable, in its first quarter phase, but still she soaked up the lunar energy in the air. After a night of unexpected twists and turns, the lunar pick-me-up was needed.

Her fingers sought the crystal pendant dangling from her neck. It might've been her imagination, but like the moon up above, the necklace offered protection in its own peculiar way. It started glowing dully underneath her touch, making her feel safe despite her surroundings. Wandering down the dark street, basking in the light of the moon, she was aware of the complications to come tomorrow. Many of them, like what she was going to do about Aiden and his investigation, shrouded closer and closer over her and her life.

She could only toy with the necklace and remember that Luna had been through worse. Luna had been a fierce, powerful witch through it all—a strong woman who never backed down 'til her dying day. Though she knew none of the details, she sensed that was the case.

Now it was Selene's turn for trials and tribulations. She sighed and wished things could be as formulaic as in the books she read, with a guaranteed happy ending or resolution by the last page. Real life wasn't so giving. She had already accepted that she'd spend her life stuck in Brimrock, a cursed loner reading about adventures she'd never get to go on. What she had never considered was that the nonwitches in town would seek to destroy her the way they did Luna.

One of them kept an eye on her in that very moment.

Officer Gustin was parked a few houses down from 1221 Gifford Lane, clearly on a stakeout. She strolled past his police cruiser and gave him the dirtiest look possible, skin mottling from hot irritation. Why wouldn't they leave her alone? What did they want? To prove that she was a big, bad, evil witch?

Selene stopped halfway down the path leading up to her house. She had half a mind to confront him and ask, to lay everything out on the table once and for all.

———

In the days leading up to Christmas, Selene played the role of a recluse. The library closed early and she stayed home, holed up with books, fatty snacks, and Yukie. Her phone she buried under pillows or forgot in unused rooms on the third floor. Aiden called and texted, but she never answered. It was the first time she had ever ghosted someone.

"So this is what it feels like to be the ghoster, not the ghostee," she said as she relaxed on the ledge of the living room bay window and flipped to the next page of her book.

Hurting Aiden wasn't easy, but necessary evils never were. What he chose to do with the knowledge of her identity was up to him. She had let go of it. The matter was out of her hands.

On Christmas Day, Noelle convinced her to come over for Bibi's cooking. Tired of peanut butter banana sandwiches and sriracha-drizzled ramen noodles, Selene caved and gave in. She showed up bearing gifts, shoving the wrapped boxes into Noelle's arms.

"Happy Yule," she mumbled.

Noelle kicked the front door shut with her leg and unloaded the armful of presents on the console table by the closet. In the kitchen Bibi was toiling away at the stove, two of the four burners boiling giant steel pots. The oven glowed with what looked like a well-seasoned pot roast inside. Bibi was swaying along in her terry cloth robe and fuzzy slippers to the radio on the counter. The old boombox sounded as good as new, blasting a cassette tape of the Supremes singing "Silver Bells."

"Do you need any help, Bibi?" Selene asked.

Bibi waved her hand and stirred the pot on the back burner. "You girls go chat. Let Auntie Bibi handle all this."

Selene followed Noelle into her room, plopping down on the corner of her bed. Noelle moved onto her dresser and finger combed her short crop of curls. The uncomfortable silence weighed on Selene and she sighed. Since she'd been a homebody the past few days, she and Noelle had yet to hash out what happened the other night.

"You're not mad at me, are you?"

"Why would I be?"

"Cut the crap, Noe. You're pissed I told Aiden."

"I'm not."

"Yes, you are."

"No," said Noelle, fingers dug into her hair roots. She rumpled her curls some more. "If I were mad, I'd tell you."

"Then why's there this weird energy?"

"Probably because I'm disappointed."

Selene's face fell into her hands. There it was. The *D* word. It was actually worse than Noelle being angry. Anger she could handle, but Noelle being disappointed was a whole different beast. How could she possibly fix the situation when it was broken enough for Noelle to be disappointed?

"Go ahead," she said in a defeated tone, "lay into me. Tell me how I fudged up."

Noelle cut her a vague smile. "Bibi would be pleased you've joined the Yule Resolution Club. And, Selly, you already know *why* I'm disappointed. I've told you—this whole thing between you and Aiden is about more than just you now. You've involved me, Bibi, even Shayla. Have you forgotten I'm a witch too?"

"You're right. I'm so sorry. It wasn't my place to make that decision and out us to Aiden."

"On the bright side," said Noelle, inhaling a deep breath, "if this Fudgeboy is as amazing as you've made him out to be, he'll do the right thing. He'll keep our secret."

Selene looked up in time to spot Noelle's smile in the mirror. She smiled back and said, "You really are my ride or die BFF, Noe. Thanks."

"Eh, you return the favor often enough. Do you smell that coming from the kitchen? Time to grub."

———

Dusk was on the horizon when Selene waved goodbye to Noelle and Aunt Bibi. She prodded her glasses up her nose and took off down the frosty street, her mood contemplative. The afternoon celebrating their witchy blend of Yuletide with Christmas had been an enjoyable one, but in the back of her mind, she was thinking about Aiden.

Noelle had broken it down to the basics: if he was the guy she thought he was, he wouldn't tell a soul what she was. If she truly was cursed, he was just another guy from a long line of douchebags, and he would proceed to ruin her life. The latter seemed to fall in line with how her life usually played out.

At first, Selene was headed home, but she changed course on the street corner of Gifford Lane and Thompson. She had spent so long locked up at home that she craved different scenery. The one other place in Brimrock that made her feel safe and sane, even if it was frequently tainted by Lord Voldemort.

The library was pitch-black inside, the doors locked. Selene glanced left and then right, ensuring no one was around, and then wiggled her fingers. The metal bolt unclicked itself and the door sprang open. Being alone with thousands upon thousands of books brought an instant, indescribable sense of bliss to Selene as she breathed in the familiar scents of crisp paper, errant dust, and aged leather.

She collapsed onto the carpet, legs folded crisscross, and propped open *Song of Solomon*. She had read Toni Morrison's most celebrated novel probably a dozen times, but she believed there was no such thing as reading a good book too many times. She felt that way about many of her favorites.

The time ticked by without her checking the oversized clock on the far wall. The heavy statement piece was a purchase by Miriam from the library's annual budget, built with barn wood and featuring distinct black spade hands. They circled the giant Roman numerals in never-ending fashion, always tracking how many hours, minutes, seconds went by.

Her eyes fell back onto the page. She only made it two more sentences before a loud bang interrupted the stark silence. She jumped in place, startled and confused, her heart lurching against her rib cage. The bang came from the double glass doors in the front. Those she had ensured were still locked. She had also kept the lights in that section of the library off in case anyone passed by. But who could possibly be knocking on the door of a library that was clearly closed?

Selene should've known the answer before she rose on sleepy, tingly legs to go check. She approached the double glass doors with a curious frown and then stopped footsteps away when the man on the other side waved at her.

Of course it'd be Aiden. She couldn't bring herself to move a muscle. Except for the ones in her face required for her frown to deepen. Aiden didn't seem to care, knocking again, and mouthing through the glass.

"Selene! Will you open up? We need to talk!"

CHAPTER FIFTEEN

"The library's closed," said Selene through the narrow crack in the door. She didn't open it any further, the glass between them serving as a barrier.

"That's funny, because you're inside."

"I work here."

"On *Christmas*?"

"Goodbye, Aiden," she said, moving to pull shut the door.

He grabbed the handle on his end and provided resistance. "Selene, please. Can we sit down and talk? Just a few minutes is all I ask—straighten everything out."

From behind the lenses of her bold-framed glasses, Selene squeezed shut her eyes. He waited with bated breath, hope kindling despite his best efforts to squash it. She had been avoiding him for days now. Their issues weren't about to be solved easily, if at all.

"Five minutes." Selene pushed the door open and stepped aside.

They walked through the dark library, Aiden half a pace behind. Selene navigated the library in the dark like a pro, weaving between long study tables and rounding the world history display cases. She led him to the far back reading section, where cozy armchairs were arranged between end tables and potted plants. She dropped into one chair and he chose the other across from her.

"How have you been?" he asked. His palms were suddenly sweaty, nerves puddling in his stomach.

"Aiden, let's skip the basics. Say what you're here to say."

"I really *am* here to see how you've been," he said and then sighed. "I've been wanting to talk to you for days. It seems like a lot happened so fast we didn't get a chance to figure any of it out. I'm...I'm still lost on what I saw the other night. You saved me from that car."

She slumped in the armchair and closed her eyes. "We've been over this. I told you what happened."

"You did and it's still...a lot for me to process. I don't even know where to begin. I know what I saw. I know I was a millisecond away from being roadkill and then...then you showed up and I was flying through the air. I remember spinning, the silver light that surrounded me. I wasn't imagining those things. They actually happened," he said, swallowing against the golf ball in his throat. "But how? How was that possible?"

"I *told* you! I'm a you-know-what. Why are you dragging this out?"

Aiden shook his head, working through the fog in his brain. "I know you're a you-know-what—that's what I can't fathom. It makes no sense."

"Says who?"

"For starters, logic and reason. Scientific fact and reality."

Selene glared at him from across the lounge section, her once warm brown eyes hardened. Her chin was set, the muscles in her jaw pulled tight. He had no clue what to expect, having never seen such an expression on her face. Was she a lot more pissed with him than he had assumed?

The tense pause stretched on until Selene held out her hand and flicked her wrist. Aiden's brow creased and he started to ask what was going on, but the book whipping through the air cut him off. It rushed past him, so close its edges grazed the tip of his ear. She had done that on purpose, directing the book on a path that shot right by him. Her fingers clamped onto the front and back covers as the book landed neatly in hand. She smirked, one corner of her mouth lifting.

"Is that enough reality for you?"

"That book...you just...through the air..." he babbled. Glancing behind him and then back at her, he opened and closed his mouth, blanking on what to say.

A tremor of shock zapped a path down his spine. He was short-circuiting. Over the last four years, he had investigated some of the country's strangest phenomena. He had braved haunted houses and wandered dark forests. He had traveled abroad to investigate ancient tombs and ruins. He had always done so confident in realism. That there was an explanation for so-called paranormal activity. Everything was grounded in fact, *never* fiction.

Yet, he had witnessed Selene performing magic again with his own two eyes. The proof he always claimed he needed had almost quite literally hit him in the head. How could he possibly deny that?

His brain still rejected the notion with a dizzying shake of his head. "None of this is making any sense. How are you able to do that?"

"I don't know how. I just *do*—I was born this way."

"It's impossible."

"Is it?"

"Yes!" Aiden bounced to his feet, a sudden backlog of frenetic energy in his body. He had to burn it off. He started pacing the lounge area, face screwed up in denial. The only explanation left was that he was either dreaming or a cruel, albeit well-executed, prank was being played on him. "This is some sort of joke. Some sort of rigged—"

"Nothing's rigged."

"There have to be cables somewhere—"

"Aiden!" Selene shouted over him. She was on her feet too, all sixty-two inches of her, as she strode toward him. Though he had a foot on her, she was an undeniably formidable force, sweeping over to him and causing him to stumble a step back. He bumped against an end table as she jammed a pointy finger into his chest. "You're being ridiculous! You wanted to investigate Luna. You wanted to know about me since I'm her granddaughter. Well, you're getting what you wanted! Newsflash: your reality isn't the only one."

His brain was hurting. He struggled to understand, but his eyes riveted onto hers, and the truth shone in them. What he had seen was very real. She was right. He couldn't pretend otherwise any longer.

"I'm sorry," he whispered. His heart thumped harder by the second. "You've shared private information about yourself with me and I've…I've been a jerk about it. I don't know what else to say but I'm sorry, Selene."

She dropped her gaze to the floor, her glasses slipping down her nose. She pushed them back and said, "I get this is a huge shock to you. But you have to realize that just because science says something is impossible doesn't make it so. *I'm* living proof of that."

"I'm beginning to realize that," he said with a shocked laugh. He still felt like he was dreaming.

Selene seemed to sense this, because she smirked and

rolled her eyes, waving both hands. In the next second, more books zoomed across the lounge, barreling straight toward him. He had flashbacks to the other night and flinched, the memory of the car about to mow him down much too fresh. The books slammed on invisible brakes inches away from them, floating as if inviting him to snatch them out of midair.

"If you're going to accept that I'm a you-know-what—a *witch*," said Selene with another wave, sending the books flying back to where they came from, "then sometimes you're going to have to believe in the impossible with me."

Speechless and breathless but suddenly brave, Aiden kissed her. It might have been the shock permanently taking up real estate in his brain, or maybe it was the overwhelming fondness for her flooding in, but no other response seemed to do the moment justice. His large hands swept up her back, holding her flush against him, journeying across the length of her spine. She moaned and shifted, liquifying in his arms, her soft lips an addictively sweet taste.

The dreaded caveman part of his brain woke up and grunted his approval. Before Selene, it had been so long since the last time he kissed a woman, he had forgotten how good it could be. If it had ever been this good—he couldn't think of a time when kissing Delilah had him brainless and breathless, filled with an intense urge to make it unequivocally known how he felt. For once in his life, he chose heavy kisses to express himself, words themselves *not* enough.

They were floating when they broke apart, skin warm and pupils large. Selene backed away, retreating as though in need of space to compose herself. He could relate. His head reeled and hands ached to touch her again. He was unlike himself, thick in whatever it was he felt for Selene. He pushed his neatly combed strands backward, praying he'd cool off and logic would return.

Selene polished her glasses on her sweater, that delicious bottom lip of hers caught under her teeth. "I don't know why I find it so hard to stay away from you."

Truer words had never been spoken. He laughed and said, "Here I was thinking I was the only one who felt that way."

"What are we going to do?" Her glasses were back on her face, magnifying the worry in her dark brown eyes. She crumpled into an armchair and heaved a great sigh.

He sat down across from her on the coffee table, grabbing her hands. "How about we figure it out together? We...we can make sense of everything going on."

"Always looking for reason," she muttered.

"You know what I mean—we've been working separately. I've been investigating what happened to Peter Feinberg. I've been researching your grandmother. Doesn't it seem like we should be teaming up?"

"I'm *not* doing your show."

"I wasn't asking you to. I don't want you to. Your secret is safe with me. It's in the vault."

Her brows rose. "The what?"

"Locked away in the vault. It's not getting out anytime soon."

"Aiden, it's not that simple. I don't want to expose you to magic. I don't want to get you in trouble or put you in danger." Selene pulled her hands from his and clasped them together in her lap. Her gaze fixed onto them as though working up the courage to continue. He leaned in closer. "Do you remember the night we had dinner at the Mulberry?"

"That ended with me at the ER? How could I forget?"

"I had no clue you were allergic to basil."

"Why would you?" He stared at her, perplexed where this was headed.

"I needed you to stop your investigation," she said

quietly. She wouldn't look at him. "I brewed a persuasion potion and had it put into your food. It was supposed to help me convince you to drop the Luna investigation. But it had basil in it and, um, you know the rest…"

Aiden couldn't say he was completely surprised. He had been suspicious of his sudden allergic reaction since it happened. He had mulled over that dinner a dozen different times. He hadn't seen basil as a listed ingredient and had double-checked with the restaurant. The instant he started feeling funny, it was clear *something* was up. He just had no clue that something was magic related.

"I'm sorry," Selene apologized flatly. "I've felt awful about it since. I almost told you several times that night. I'm a terrible liar and it was supposed to be harmless."

"No wonder you were fussing over me. You should've seen you at the ER."

Selene only nodded, worrying at her bottom lip.

"Hey," said Aiden, grabbing her hands again, "You were trying to protect yourself and your family against some guy— that guy being me. I'm pretty sure this makes us even. I *was* lying to you about who I was. Remember those articles I said I wrote?"

"You know I could've Googled you."

"Thankfully you didn't. That would've blown my cover in 2.5 seconds. All this tells me is that we need to be honest with each other," he said with a squeeze of her hands. "You and I are better together than apart. We can solve this."

"You're being serious," she said, studying his face.

He nodded. "Of course I am. Eddie and I will figure something else out for our show. Maybe film an episode on the yeti. I've always wanted to go to the Himalayan Mountains."

"That sounds like a more interesting trip than Brimrock,"

she teased, traces of a smile on her lips. "Let's say we do try to figure out what's going on, then what?"

"We prove you're innocent. Don't ask me how I know, but Brimrock PD considers you a suspect—"

"I know. They've had Gustin keeping tabs on me since Peter's attack."

"Wait a second. You haven't heard the latest news?"

"About what?"

"Officer Gustin's missing," he said. His grip on her hands tightened, giving another quick squeeze. "The story just broke an hour or two ago. The night that car almost ran me down was the last time he was seen. He had the past few days off, but he was supposed to be on patrol today and he never showed up."

"I had no clue. I was over at Noelle's for Christmas and then came here."

"Selene, you get what this means, don't you?"

"I haven't done anything wrong."

"We both know that, but I don't trust Mayor Grisby or the Brimrock PD. That's why it's so important we get to the bottom of this."

"Why do you care so much?" she asked quietly. "How did you even find me?"

"I went by your house and you weren't there. I figured you'd probably be somewhere with books. And I care because…isn't it obvious I like you?"

Her smile was small and shy. "I like you too."

"That's the best Christmas gift I've received all day. Much better than the ugly Christmas sweater Mrs. Myers knitted me."

They laughed together and then ended with a quick, sweet kiss. Aiden slipped an arm around Selene as she rose from the armchair and they ventured toward the fiction aisles.

"It should be interesting working with a partner other than Eddie," he said. "We always joke that we're the paranormal Hardy Boys."

Selene paused for a sideways look up at him. "Does that make me Nancy Drew?"

———

"Oh, just awful what's happened," moaned Mrs. Myers that night at Christmas dinner. "I can't believe poor Adam Gustin is gone so young."

"Priscilla," scolded Mr. Myers over a forkful of honeyed ham, "Officer Gustin isn't gone. He's missing."

"What's the difference?" she cried derisively.

Eddie sided with Mr. Myers. "Aunt Priscilla, calm down. I'm sure it's all a misunderstanding. Maybe he went out of town."

Camilla snorted, though she didn't look up from her phone. Her plate of food was largely untouched. "Yeah, and didn't bother letting his supervisor know. Wicked Witch Luna strikes again. That guy's like Peter—he's totally a goner."

"Camilla!" Mr. and Mrs. Myers shrieked at the same time.

Everyone's eyes darted across the table at Rory, who sat sullenly picking morsels of food off her plate. Aiden glanced back at Mr. and Mrs. Myers. Both had lost their wits, stammering for words. Nobody wanted to address the giant elephant in the room, but the confrontation was inevitable once the subject arose. Rory slammed her fork down. The metal clanged against her plate as she scooted her chair back and rose to her feet. Before anyone else could try to convince her to stay, she stormed off.

Mr. Myers crumpled his cloth napkin and tossed it onto

his plate. "You've done it now, Camilla. Go upstairs and apologize to your sister."

"This whole thing has everybody on edge," said Eddie with a shake of his head. "I just saw Mrs. Feinberg sobbing on TV. She's demanding the police do something about what's going on."

"That's because a mother will always protect her children. She's right to be distraught. Her son was attacked by what has been a clearly evil presence in this town. The police have failed us," said Mrs. Myers. Her cheeks pinkened and she shuddered out a frustrated breath. "I'll go check on Rory. You stay put, Camilla. You've said enough for now."

The four remaining stared at each other. Aiden considered doing something he never did and excused himself from dinner before finishing. He didn't care to sit around and listen to family arguments. If he wanted a dose of family drama he would have visited his own dysfunctional family for the holidays. He preferred being upstairs in his guest bedroom, digging into more research or thinking back on earlier with Selene.

"I should probably call it," he said slowly.

Eddie's bushy brows meshed into a thick, solitary line. "It's only seven."

"I'm exhausted."

"It's Christmas."

"Again, exhausted."

"We always watch *A Christmas Story* after dinner."

Aiden shrugged, collecting his plate and glass to drop off in the kitchen. "I've had my fill on Christmas for the year."

Tomorrow he would deal with an agitated Eddie. Tonight he would regroup and organize his thoughts. He and Selene would be spending the rest of his time in Brimrock working together to find out what happened to Peter and Officer

Gustin. What came after that he wasn't sure. Too many vari-ables still hung in the air for him to say definitively, but what-ever it was, he secretly wished it could somehow include Selene.

On the second floor landing, Aiden padded down the hall for his room. Excitement jolted his bones as it seemed he would make it inside without running into anyone. The third door on the right sprang open and Mrs. Myers emerged, already speaking.

"If you need anything else, sweetie, let me know. You stop worrying and get some shut-eye," she cooed, drawing the door shut. She turned to go, but flinched and clutched her chest when she saw him. "Aiden! You snuck up on me. You're as quick and quiet as a mouse for being so tall."

"Sorry. I was headed to my room."

"Oh, so soon? No dessert?"

"I'm exhausted but thank you anyway."

Mrs. Myers pouted, her naturally plump cheeks rounding. "You wouldn't be so exhausted if you didn't chase after that girl day in and day out."

"That girl?" he asked, chuckling. "You don't mean—"

"That's exactly who I mean. She's bad juju. The whole town knows it. Look at what's happened to Peter," said Mrs. Myers with a sniffle. "I would hate for something to happen to you."

"Mrs.—*Aunt Priscilla*, we've been over this. I'm a big boy. I promise you I can handle myself."

"Get some rest then." She patted him on the shoulder, the touch light but motherly, and trudged down the hall, back downstairs.

A frown crawled onto Aiden's lips as he couldn't resist pondering everything that had happened about town as of late, and how it fit together.

———

A pebble tapped the bedroom window and woke Aiden in the middle of the night. He thrashed in the armchair he had fallen asleep in and knocked his laptop to the floor. He had been scrolling through endless news articles about Officer Gustin's disappearance when he had dozed off. He swore under his breath and promptly picked up his laptop.

Thankfully, it was still functioning and in one piece. Next time he would have to be more careful and keep to the desk only. Especially late at night. He shook his head to rid himself of grogginess and glanced at the clock on the nightstand. Though his dreams were a mystery to him, his stomach churned. Something was unsettling.

Then it happened again. Another pebble struck his bedroom window. So it hadn't been a dream. It was very much real, and whoever it was down below needed his attention. He paused to stare at the window in drowsy confusion and then moved to lift up the glass. The frost made it harder than usual, but he managed, sticking his head out.

Selene nursed a palm full of small pebbles, her neck craned upward. Her eyes lit up even in the dark when his head poked out the window. "Good, you're up!" she whispered just loud enough for him to hear. "Put on some pants and meet me down here."

"Selene, what in the world are you doing?"

"Shh! Just meet me. I want to show you something."

Aiden hung out the window and stared at her like the madwoman she was. He wasn't the guy who randomly got up at late hours of the night and went on adventures unless necessary when filming *Paranormal Hunters*. He was the one who stayed home, read books, dabbled in the occasional TV show binge watch, or scoured the internet for news. If he ever felt like he had too much pent-up energy, he allowed for a quick abdominal or strength-based workout. That was who he was.

But looking down at an excited Selene, it wasn't as if he could say no. She was too hard to turn down. He was too curious to find out more. His mind shifted back to nights ago when they had gotten drunk at the Gin House and lay in the snow, kissing. If that was the something she wanted to show him then...

He shook his head, deciding for once to be the spontaneous guy, and whispered back, "Alright, fine. Wait for me across the street so the Myerses don't see you. I'll be down in five."

CHAPTER SIXTEEN

Selene and Aiden held hands walking off into the dark. It was awkward at first, but that was probably because they were both a bit awkward themselves. She snuck a couple glances at him and barely bit back her laughs. He looked so puzzled, it was borderline adorable. His reddish-brown hair was ruffled, a far cry from its usual meticulously combed style, and he'd thrown on whatever sweater he found first. It was moss green and hand-knitted with white snowflakes patterned across the chest. Was that the sweater Mrs. Myers had knitted for him?

That thought finally did it; she released a sudden laugh. Aiden squeezed her hand and cut her a curious frown. He was already moody for being out in the cold so late at night, but now she was laughing at him. She rolled her eyes at his umbrage.

"Is that *the* Myers ugly Christmas sweater?"

"The one and only."

"It's not so bad."

"Not so bad," he repeated skeptically. "Which part is the

not so bad? The hideous puke green shade or the lopsided snowflakes?"

"Okay, so it *is* bad—but if it helps any, I'm wearing two different pairs of boots."

Aiden stopped for a look. His eyes dropped down to her mismatched snow boots. He looked back up at her and gave a shocked chuckle. "You *are* wearing different boots. Did you put them on in the dark?"

"I grabbed the first ones in my closet. That just so happened to be a polka-dot galosh and my brown fur boot."

"Selene, why are we out here? What is it you wanted to show me?"

Selene matched his long stare with a slow and mischievous smile. She hadn't been able to relax since their moment in the library. Noelle probably would say she was doing too much, but it excited her someone else—a nonwitch at that—finally seemed open to understanding her. Aiden wasn't like the fearful people in Brimrock. He wasn't like the jerks she'd dated in the past. Though they had only known each other for a short time, she trusted him.

Excitement pinged through her and she rocked on the balls of her feet. Instead of explaining, she grabbed his hand again. He'd find out soon enough.

The crystalline pavement gleamed in the cold night. Homes were dark and streets empty, occupied only by the occasional whines from the wind. Selene steered him down the dead end that was 1221 Gifford Lane and he seemed to think that was where they were headed. She wrapped her arm around his and guided him off path, disappearing into the forested land behind the gothic home on the block. They found the dirt trail she usually took when heading out for her midnight rituals.

Another quarter mile trek later, the clearing emerged

beyond the thick bramble. The moon looked twice its usual size, no town buildings or abstractions to obscure the giant silvery orb from their gazes. It lit them up, framing them in a silver halo. Selene finally stopped and rounded on him.

"I wanted to show you how it works."

"How what works? The moon?"

"My lunar rituals," she said. She gestured to the open clearing. "I come here every few weeks to pay tribute to the moon."

"Why?"

"Because I'm a lunar witch. I get my powers from the moon."

The doubt on Aiden's face was impossible to deny. For her sake, he shifted his features into a more neutral expression. "Right. Powers from the moon. You're a lunar witch. That is most definitely a thing I was already very aware of."

"Aiden, you don't have to pretend. I didn't bring you here so you could sugarcoat what I'm showing you," Selene said, rolling her eyes. She slid off her leather book bag and unbuckled the top flap. "I brought all of my supplies."

"Oh, you, uh, you have supplies."

"Of course I do. How else am I going to set up the ritual?"

"Question," he said, glancing up at the purplish-black sky. "If you get your powers from the moon, then how are you able to use them during daylight? Or indoors? What about on nights when the moon is hidden behind clouds or heavy snow?"

"I'm a lunar witch, but it doesn't mean I can only use my powers at nighttime. It means that's my energy source. Think about it like a battery—the moon charges me."

"So if you go too long without you would lose them?" He

posed the question as though speaking of a complex math equation.

Selene gave a sharp nod. "It's also why most lunar witches avoid the sun. We can go outside in daylight, but not for hours at a time, or anywhere that's too bright and sunny. It weakens our powers."

"You said you were allergic."

"Still true," she teased, lighting the slim white taper candle in her hand. "I really do get hives if I spend too much time in the sun."

"So I guess you ever coming to Arizona to visit me is off the table." Aiden was teasing her back. He was grinning at her, waiting for whatever clever reply she had for him. Tonight his ever-changing eyes were as dark as the forest green surrounding them.

It should've pleased her to hear him hint about visiting him, but if anything, it had the opposite effect on her. A sudden deep sadness poured over her as she turned her back to him and focused on sticking the taper candle in its holder. He didn't need to know why she was upset. She had already shared more than she ever had with anyone not named Noelle, Bibi, or Yukie. He didn't need to know about the curse too.

Especially because it was so depressing. She'd never get a chance to visit Aiden in Arizona even if she wanted to. She was doomed to stay in Brimrock until her dying day.

In tune with her, Aiden noticed her glum lack of response. The grin dropped from his face. "Did I say something wrong?"

"It's not what you said."

"Then what is it? Selene." Aiden moved closer, her back to him. He wasn't giving up easily.

Selene drew fresh air into her lungs and then puffed it out

with a soft sigh. Her fingers wrapped around Luna's pendant necklace and instinct instructed her to go ahead and tell him. "There's this curse on my family."

"A *curse*? You mean like seven years bad luck?"

"More like a lifetime. It's been going on for decades. All the way back when Luna was still alive. All female Blackstones—the witches in our family—are stuck in Brimrock. We can't leave."

"That can't be true, Selene," he said with a confused laugh. "You can leave whenever you want. How about we take Ghost into Cowbridge tomorrow? You haven't met Ghost yet. He's my slightly vintage Dodge Caravan. Very old but very stylish. At least Eddie and I think so."

"No, I mean, I really can't leave. Even if I make it past the town border, I'm brought back."

"How?"

"Magic," she said, shrugging. "I've tried. My mom tried. I'm…I'm told *Luna* tried."

Being the man of logic he was, Aiden eased her around to face him and said, "Then let's find a way to break the curse. There has to be some counter spell you can cast, isn't there? Some way for you to reverse Uno the curse?"

"*Reverse Uno*?" Her pang of sadness faded for a light tickle of humor. She shook her head and continued setting up for the ritual. They had no time to waste. It was already nearing four in the morning, which meant the moon would be on the descent. At least the full moon would come on the day before New Year's Eve. She always absorbed the most energy on full moons.

Aiden hung in the background as Selene finished prepping. She produced the charmed piece of chalk from her leather book bag and drew a big circle on the ground. Spotting the baffled, deer-in-the-headlights look on Aiden's face, she said, "It's for centering. It helps direct lunar energy to me."

"And what do you do?"

"Patience," she said. The candles she'd lit floated around the circle and she took her place in the center. The lunar energy in the air was ripe and frenetic, immediately soothing as its mystical properties touched her skin. She sat cross-legged and closed her eyes, focusing on the moon and how she felt under its ethereal glow.

Soon she surrendered to the moon's pull, its transportive, borderline dizzying spell enveloping her. The amazing, rejuvenating feeling spread across her skin and she was floating. She felt like she could fly among the stars or leap over mountaintops. Comforting warmth brushed against her as dozens of little sparks, dancing in the dark.

Selene lost track of time, the rest of the world quiet and empty. She basked in the lunar energy coursing through her veins and giving her the boost she sorely needed after a rough few days. An elated sigh escaped her lips as she opened her eyes feeling reborn. She had forgotten for once she wasn't alone.

Aiden had backed up toward the trees, his brow lined. "Err...what's going on?"

"What do you mean? I was showing you what I do during my moon meditations. Why do you look like you've seen Casper the Not-So-Friendly Ghost?"

"Selene, you're levitating. You're *glowing*," he said.

She held up her hands and smiled. The silver glow emanated off her brown skin like magical radiation. She was also seven feet in the air, legs still crossed and candles circling around her. She had never levitated so high up before. Another reason for her smile to widen. With a more complicated sweep of her arms than her usual motions, she set herself back down on the ground, sent the candles flying for her book bag, and blew dust to cover the chalk marks.

If Aiden looked like he'd seen Casper the Not-So-Friendly Ghost before, he looked like he'd seen the poltergeist now. She walked toward him. "Are you okay? I promise I'm not some evil witch. I didn't bring you here to kill you and cook you in a stew."

"It's just…a lot to digest," he said, swallowing with difficulty. "It made you look unreal, like some sparkly hologram."

"It's fading now." She glanced down at her arms; she was absorbing the last of it.

"Aren't you concerned the police will follow you and see what you do? You're out in the open."

"This clearing is where we do our rituals. It's got a bunch of protection charms placed on the area," she said. "Trust me, they've tried for decades to figure out where we go at night. It eats them up that they can't make anything stick on us. To the nonwitch eye, it appears like we disappear, which only confuses anyone following us."

"Then how come I'm here? I'm a nonwitch."

"You're with me. So long as you are, the protection charm works for you too."

"Then explain the howling."

"What howling?"

"You…you didn't hear it? In the distance?"

"No," said Selene and her tone softened. "Don't you think you're being a little paranoid? There's nothing spooky about what just happened."

Aiden relaxed a bit, breathing in with a deep rise of his chest. "You're right. I…I guess I'm just the last guy I ever expected to date a witch."

"I'm the last girl I'd ever expect to date a paranormal investigator from a YouTV show."

"Sounds like we're a match made in heaven."

Selene drifted closer, her body grazing his. Her eyes, big, brown, and dreamy, pinned his so that he couldn't look away. He was in a trance, drawn to her as much as she was drawn to him. She rose on the tips of her toes and he gripped her chin to drop a kiss on her lips.

———

"You can't resist these bagels!" Noelle screeched early the next morning.

Yukie barked. Selene rubbed her eyes. She tied her robe around her waist and dragged her feet toward the front door. Yukie at her heels trotted along, curious as to what was going on so early. Noelle held up the bag of bagels when Selene opened the door.

"Brought you plenty of cream cheese," she boasted.

Selene stepped aside with a wide-mouthed yawn. "Are you nuts? It's not even seven yet…"

"I needed to see you. I *know* what you've been up to."

"Am I in trouble, Mom?"

"If I were Bibi, I just might whack you over the head with a fuzzy slipper," joked Noelle. She barged down the hall, shooting for the kitchen. Today's eccentric style was a mustard-yellow turtleneck, acid-wash jean shorts, and matching mustard tights. She topped it off with the crescent-moon hairpin Selene had bought her for Yule. In the kitchen, she flicked on the light and clucked her tongue looking at the black-and-white diamond tile. "When was the last time you mopped? You know you can magic a mop and broom to go around the room and clean up for you, right?"

"I haven't had time since that whole suspected of

attempted murder thing started. Are you here to do a white glove inspection of my house or feed me bagels?"

"You ask that like I can't do both. Sit. I'll do the legwork."

Selene did as told, plucking a chair out from the table and plopping into it. "I'm guessing you know Aiden and I are back on speaking terms."

"Girl, you know I know the latest witch gossip. It's not exactly hard since there's only three of us in town."

"How did you find out?"

"The streets have eyes and ears. You know that."

"Noe," said Selene sternly.

Noelle rolled her eyes. "If you must know, I only suspected. You confirmed it as soon as I said it and you got that hand-caught-in-the-cookie-jar look on your face."

"Aiden's going to help me figure out what happened to Peter."

"Since when is that your goal?"

"Since the police started thinking I'm the one who put him in a coma. Officer Gustin suddenly disappearing hasn't helped."

"But do we need to involve Fudgeboy, though?" Noelle asked, carrying over two plates of bagels. "Want to do pros and cons? I'll start. Con: Fudgeboy is a nonwitch."

"Pro: he's a paranormal investigator, which means he's good at solving things."

"*Con*," said Noelle with a level of eagerness that revealed she had thought this out, "he's a paranormal investigator for a YouTV streaming show. He's out for clicks and views."

"Pro: Aiden doesn't give a damn about going viral."

"Con: how do you know? You've known the guy for, what, a week and a half? This could be all part of his master plan."

Selene rolled her eyes and slathered her bagel with cream cheese. "Just say you don't trust him and be done with it."

"I don't trust him. Now what?"

"I *do* trust him," said Selene. "It sounds dumb, but there's something about him. Besides, what happened to your thing about him being the guy I said he was?"

"That was before you agreed to collab with him. Selene, how are you dickmatized *before* the dick?"

Her jaw dropped midbite of her crisp bagel, cheeks heating up. "I'm *not* dickmatized!"

"Then what is it? What is it about him that makes him so worthy of your trust? Think about how wrong this could go."

"I have," Selene replied between bites. "What do you think I was doing those days I was holed up here? I thought through every possible scenario. I've talked about it with Aiden. We're going to work together and solve whatever it is that's going on. You might not think I'm making much sense, but it feels like the right thing to do."

Noelle wiped cream cheese off her chin with her thumb. "Alright, Selly, you're my ride or die so you already know I'm buckled in for the ride. I just wish you'd at least gotten some dick first. In case this all backfires and blows up in your face."

———

Late that morning at the library, Gerri wouldn't shut up about the Peter Feinberg and Officer Gustin investigation. "Scary things happening around these parts. It feels like evil is never done with this town."

Libby stirred artificial sweetener into her Earl Grey tea. "Ger, can I at least enjoy my tea? You've been yapping about that story all morning."

"It's the biggest tragedy that's happened in years," rasped Gerri in her smoker's drawl. She wheeled out from under her spot at the massive L-shaped front desk and grabbed documents off the printer. "You can stick your head in the sand and pretend you don't notice a thing, Lib, but I refuse. Cecile is hysterical with grief."

"I saw her crying on the news," said Miriam with a solemn head shake. "Isn't it gruesome what's happened to Peter?"

Selene held her breath sorting the book returns cart. She kept her back to the other three, afraid that if she turned around and looked at them eye to eye, her emotions would swing out of control again. Though she had gotten better at controlling her magic with age, whenever she was upset, it was harder to keep her lunar magic in check. Sometimes that worked in her favor, like when she rescued Aiden from that careless motorist. Other times it worked against her, like when Lord Voldemort and her two Death Eaters pushed the wrong buttons.

She wasn't risking it today. Not when she was already on Brimrock PD's radar and recently tardy to work. Her job at the library meant too much to her.

The ladies carried on with their gossip. Selene grabbed the last book in need of filing and then pushed the squeaky, wobbly cart from around the L-shaped desk. She didn't make it more than a couple feet before Miriam called after her.

"A word in private," said Miriam. Her stern, nasal pitch was worse than razor-sharp acrylic nails on a chalkboard. She moseyed over to Selene in her latest feathery sweater, horn-rimmed glasses dangling on beads around her neck. "I know what you did."

"Excuse me?"

"You were here on Christmas."

A bad liar, Selene begged the muscles in her face to stay still. Wearing a blank expression was her best bet. "Um, you mean here in the library on Christmas?"

"You know exactly what I mean."

"I'm sorry, but I don't, Miriam. I wasn't here on Christmas."

"You're lucky I don't have proof, but I need you to know, one more time," warned Miriam, coming closer. The cool mint smell from her morning tea lingered in the small space between them. "One more time, Selene."

Selene knitted her brows and frowned. "What does that mean?"

"I have my eye on you. One more time. You're done for, understand?"

CHAPTER SEVENTEEN

"We're doing something else," said Aiden flatly.

Eddie gaped at him. "You don't mean what I think you mean…right?"

"I mean exactly what you think I mean."

Aiden was cranky and sleep-deprived. He had been out for hours with Selene. Sleep deprivation slowed up his brain, making exact details hazy, but they had gone on a late-night stroll. Selene had shown him her lunar ritual and it had ended with some delicious kisses under moonlight. By the time he collapsed in bed, he was so exhausted he fell into a deep sleep. He didn't wake up until late afternoon.

Eddie buckled his seat belt and switched on Ghost's ignition. The van's engine protested with a whine. "Aiden, we're not changing the plan."

"The episode's not filmed yet. It hasn't even been investigated yet."

"What are you talking about? You've done nothing *but* investigate Luna since we've come to Brimrock." Eddie pulled the gear into reverse and backed out of the driveway. They were taking Ghost into town to iron out show details with their executive producer, Paulina. The rest of the Myers clan were spending the day in Cowbridge except Rory, who was still upset from last night's drama. "Anyway, since when does having some fun mean you get caught up? You weren't supposed to let the girl talk you out of the Luna episode."

"This isn't about Selene."

"Oh, c'mon, bro. It's definitely about Selene. You've got it bad if you're sneaking out at 3:00 a.m."

Aiden's stomach bottomed out. He was caught between shock and defensiveness. "You know about last night? Have you been following me?"

Eddie snorted. "Not my style. I heard Selene outside. She wasn't exactly discreet. Look, man, do what you want on your own time, but you should know better by now to mix business with pleasure. I get Selene's the pleasure and the business in this case—"

"It's not about Selene."

"Then why do you got a problem all of a sudden with the Luna stuff?"

"Considering everything going on in town, it's in bad taste."

Eddie hooked a right at the next street corner, shaking his head. "That's exactly why it's a gold mine. It's a hot topic right now. Peter Feinberg, all around good guy, in a coma. Officer Gustin, also a decent and obviously well-known guy about town, now disappeared. What's going on in Brimrock made the news in Boston. The case is gaining traction. Next national. Perfect setup for our ep to go viral."

"We're supposed to be investigating *Luna*, not what's going on with Feinberg and Gustin."

"Wake up. You know better than anyone what's going on with Feinberg and Gustin is investigating Luna. Nobody has a clue what happened to her. She disappeared—one day terrorizing the town, the next day poofing into thin air. You've already studied the background. Don't act like you don't get what Luna might have to do with this," Eddie ranted, braking as a light blinked to red. "People all over town have claimed to see Luna's specter wandering around. Not to mention all the weird stuff happening anytime they go near that house."

"As in 1221 Gifford Lane? The house Selene lives in?"

"You've had your fun, but it's time to cut the cord, bro. We're leaving town as soon as we're done filming next week. This is the perfect out for your breakup with her."

Aiden clenched his eyes shut and breathed hard enough to blow steam out of his nostrils. He hadn't been thinking about next week. He had been trying to avoid focusing on what came after New Year's. When he first arrived in Brimrock, he had been counting the days until he could leave, but many things had changed over the course of the holiday.

Now, he dreaded the idea of leaving, living without Selene when they had connected so well. He couldn't think of a simple solution and that only made leaving worse. He had real decisions to make.

———

"Getting down to business," said Paulina over the video call. She was seated in her home office, clutching a cold glass of kombucha.

Aiden and Eddie sipped from their coffee cups. They were at Hot Java, the other coffee shop in town. When Aiden asked Eddie why he had picked Hot Java over the Magic Bean, Eddie insisted they needed space away from listening ears. He meant Noelle, who inevitably would let Selene know anything she overheard.

Hot Java was the polar opposite of the Magic Bean right

down to the generic taste of their coffee. The coffeeshop was as small, but they made use of their limited space with sleek tables and chairs that felt paper thin enough to blow away in the wind. Pretentious, artsy black-and-white photography was framed on the walls and they played smooth jazz from the speakers overhead. Behind the counter was thousands of dollars of fancy coffee equipment, the chrome on the machines gleaming, their complicated buttons plentiful.

Aiden sipped from his large black coffee and sighed, missing the eccentric charm of the Magic Bean. He had made his disinterest clear the second he muttered a lukewarm hello to Paulina and skipped other pleasantries like asking about her Christmas. Eddie talked her up, as always building toward his pitch.

"What do you have for me?"

"Have you been keeping up with the attacks going on in Brimrock?" Eddie asked back.

Paulina choked trying to answer him. She cussed and wiped her mouth. "You think I've got time to follow what's going on over there? I can't even keep up with current events in real cities and you expect me to keep up with bumfuck Brimrock? I've got fifteen minutes for this collab before I'm moving onto the next video call with the guys from *Prank Wars*. They premiere a week after you. Get on with it."

"Sorry." Eddie cleared his throat and referenced the notes he had jotted down. It was irregular for him. He usually winged his pitches. Aiden was the neat and overly prepared one. "Anyway, so a guy named Peter Feinberg was attacked last week. He was found with no physical injuries except he's in a comatose state that doctors can't figure out. It's the exact case from 1976—John Grisby was found comatose in Luna Blackstone's bed. He later died."

"Okay, and you think there's a link to Luna Blackstone?"

Eddie nodded sharply. "Not think, know. Just a few nights ago, a Brimrock police officer by the name of Adam Gustin disappeared from his patrol shift. The same exact officer tasked with keeping tabs on Luna's granddaughter, Selene."

"I'm liking it. The connection between past and present is compelling."

"Grisby's brother just so happens to be mayor. My aunt works for him at town hall. The plan is, interview the Grisbys. Pretty sure she can hook us up with an interview with the police department too. We were going to visit the Blackstone home on our own. I've been researching historical experts, but couldn't find any local—luckily the head librarian Miriam Hofstetter volunteered to back us up on that front."

"Gets my stamp of approval. Dale should be flying out in a few days to film. Aiden, where are you at in all of this?"

Aiden glanced at the iPad for the first time. Paulina had gone back to sipping her kombucha. He made no attempt at hiding his pinched expression from the camera, looking straight into the lens and shaking his head side to side.

"I'm not doing the episode," he said.

Eddie's eyes bulged. Paulina choked a second time, cussing when the tea spilled down the front of her blouse.

"He's kidding," said Eddie quickly. He flashed a smile at the camera.

"No, I'm not. I'm being serious."

"Aiden, what are you talking about? What do you mean you're not doing the episode?"

He ignored Eddie's glare and said, "I don't believe it's right, so I won't be participating."

"You don't believe in anything—that's your role as the skeptic. You're the Scully to Eddie's Mulder. We've gone over this before."

"No, I mean I don't think it's right to cover this case for

the show. I can't go along with it. I'll excuse myself." Aiden pushed back his chair and grabbed his coat. He started to walk off, but paused for one last jab. "And you need to stop insinuating we're sleeping together," he warned Eddie. "I'll set the record straight. You're wrong. Good luck with the episode."

He left his coffee untouched on the table and didn't answer Eddie's call, storming out of the shop and into the chilly afternoon.

———

Aiden's only regret storming out of Hot Java was that he didn't swipe the keys to Ghost. He was left walking the twelve blocks between the coffeeshop and 1221 Gifford Lane. The long, slippery walk at least gave him time to reflect on what he had done. Eddie was going to be pissed. Paulina was going to be confused and then she would transition into being pissed alongside Eddie. He would have to deal with both when he made it back to the Myerses'. Paulina was already potentially blowing up his phone. He wouldn't know for sure until he powered it back on.

When he fled Hot Java, he hadn't given thought to why he headed for 1221 Gifford. His feet moved in that direction. The rest of his body complied. His brain failed to think up a single reason why he shouldn't. His heart palpitated at the prospect of seeing Selene that evening. Eddie was right about one thing—he had it bad. He cared about Selene more than he ever anticipated. If only there was a how-to instruction manual on falling for a cursed witch. He would buy a dozen copies...

Aiden inhaled a deep breath standing on the steps to 1221 Gifford. He wasn't sure why he was so nervous. The nerves swarmed his stomach on the attack, buzzing with no discernible pattern. Just chaos. He shook his shoulders to loosen himself up and then knocked.

On the other side of the door, Selene scrambled. Her feet thumped on the floor and what sounded like a small dog barked its best impersonation of a much bigger dog. The curtains in the front window rustled and he smirked at the face peeking through. The chain on the door clanked and the lock unclicked and she finally opened up.

"What are you doing here?"

For the umpteenth time since meeting her, he was reminded how irresistibly cute she was. She stood at the door in a chunky lavender knit sweater and charcoal leggings, fuzzy socks on her feet and curls half twisted back into a loose braid. One lone curl dangled on her forehead, straying from the others. Her glasses hung low on the bridge of her nose before she nudged them back up into place. Would it be a proper hello for him to reach for her and kiss her lips?

He chased away the urge by clearing his throat. "I wanted to come and see you. I figured we could start working on the Feinberg and Gustin case."

"Oh. Oh! I had no clue you wanted to start so soon."

"No better time than the present, right?"

Selene dug her left foot into the floorboard, gaze skirting downward. "I don't know. Just that I know your obligation is to your show. It's your job—don't you have to run it by your boss first?"

"Screw the show," he said. The surprise lit up her eyes and caused him to smile. "You heard me right the first time. I'm Team Selene in this whole debacle."

"Team Selene, huh? Team Everybody Else in Brimrock won't like that." She played off him well, only making his smile turn into a laugh.

"What can I say? Your kisses help."

"You know how to flatter a girl. Come in."

Aiden entered into darkness, like every gothic home he had studied in textbooks and seen on documentaries. The ceilings were high and vaulted and the walls were covered in an ugly pewter wallpaper, its pattern damask. Chandeliers dangled from above, made of brass and chain, holding melted candles. Dust floated thick in the air with a distinct musk that tickled the nostrils and stirred allergies. He hung his coat and scarf on the coatrack and fought off a sneeze.

From down the hall, a tiny, furry Yorkshire terrier scurried at him and barked hello.

"That's Yukie," said Selene. "She's a cuddle bug—loves whatever attention you'll give her."

"You like attention, huh, Yukie? Fortunately for you, I'm a big dog person. My French bulldog Ruby eats up attention too. You two have that in common."

"You have a dog?"

"Is that surprising?" Aiden welcomed Yukie with strategic scratches on her neck.

"A little bit. I never pegged you as a dog person. Where does Ruby stay when you're traveling for the show?"

"I'm fortunate enough to have a great neighbor who has three other dogs. Ruby fits right in."

"You'll have to show me pictures," said Selene, starting down the hall.

Aiden and Yukie followed, the small dog in a light trot beside him. They were already friends. That gave him a jolt of happiness; dog owners loved when you won over their canine companion. Selene might not have realized it, but he wanted to impress her. What she thought of him mattered.

"Bagel? Don't look at me like that. It's all I have. I haven't been shopping lately. Noelle brought these over this morning. They're still good—I could warm them up in the oven or something. There's plenty of cream cheese. I also have some really delicious hot chocolate! I'm guessing you're not a big tea guy."

He chuckled. "Sure. A bagel and hot cocoa for dinner is living life on the wild side for me."

"After seeing you drunk, I believe it."

"You mean that night at the Gin House? You're one to talk."

"I have an excuse," she pointed out, offended. Her brows drew closer. "Witches don't hold their liquor well—*everybody* knows that."

"Everybody? Something tells me that's a giant exaggeration."

Her nose scrunched, lips pursed to hold back a smile. "Aiden, shut up."

He laughed instead. He wanted to scoop her up and kiss her, carry her into another room and spend time lavishing her with affection.

"I never got a chance to ask you how your Christmas was." Selene dropped two bagels onto a baking sheet and pulled open the oven door. Even the kitchen appliances in the gothic home were antiquated. The oven looked right out of a Sears catalogue circa 1952. "What happened when you got home from the library but before our late-night walk?"

"You mean before you woke me up at 3:00 a.m. throwing a rock at my window," he corrected, bantering. "Last night we had a big Myers family Christmas feast. The food was good, but I'm not sure it was worth the family drama. There's enough of that at the O'Hare household to last a lifetime."

"Is everyone okay?"

"Everyone's fine. Eddie's cousin Camilla made a

comment about Peter and his other cousin Rory didn't like that too much. Then his aunt guilt-tripped us all. The usual."

Selene grimaced. "I'm not too surprised, though. I ran into Rory on market day and she wasn't too happy."

"No kidding."

"What kind of drama is at the O'Hare household?" Selene joined him at the table after setting a kettle to heat up.

"It's complicated," he said. "My family's the kind of family that never fits. It's like we're all Lego pieces from a different Lego box. Everybody's a smartass. Everybody's moody. Everybody would rather be somewhere else."

"Sorry for bringing it up. Family stuff always interests me. I guess mostly because I don't really have one."

Aiden glanced around the kitchen and then down the hall of the empty three-story house. "It's a lot of space for one person. Where are the other Blackstones?"

"What other Blackstones? I have a few distant relatives that I know of who live far away, but I'm the last one like me, the last witch."

"And you're stuck here," said Aiden, frowning. He covered her hand with his, running the pads of his fingers over her knuckles. "I wish there was a way for us to break that curse."

"Well, there isn't, so no use talking about it. I've accepted it's how it's supposed to be. It's not so bad thanks to Noelle and her aunt and Yukie too. The library has thousands of books."

Aiden didn't want to touch a nerve by mentioning that was beside the point. She shouldn't have had to adjust to a cursed life in the first place. He didn't want to overstep a boundary, though, so he dropped the subject and opted for something lighter.

"Why did you put the bagels in by hand? Why not use your magic?"

She sat up straighter, smiling, and tugged her hand from under his. "Watch this."

Aiden sat as flabbergasted as the first time he had seen her magic. Selene gestured toward the oven, fingers fluid and deft as they waved. The oven door popped open. The tray of toasted bagels floated off the rack and across the room. It landed neatly between them, served as if by a ghost butler. Last but not least was the piping-hot kettle and pair of mugs for their hot cocoa. He shouldn't have been shocked and yet he still was.

"Is that using my powers enough for you?" she teased.

"If I had the ability to levitate objects, I'd probably never get up again. Why would I? I can bring everything to me."

"It's kinda convenient sometimes. But I still like doing things the nonwitch way." She shrugged, reaching for a bagel.

He reached for one too. "Is that what we're called? Nonwitches?"

"Is that offensive?"

"I'm sure some would say so. I think it's hilarious. I'm fairly certain most 'nonwitches' would choose to be like you if we could."

"That's what you think. All my life I've been made to feel ashamed of my powers. Before she passed, my mom refused to use hers. She wanted to assimilate as much as possible with everyone in town. It's funny that she didn't realize they were never going to like her," said Selene. She shook her head and smeared cream cheese onto her bagel. "She wasted her whole life being afraid of her own magic. It's like what happened to Luna terrified her."

"And, err, what did happen to Luna?"

Selene paused. Her eyes snapped onto his face and her

expression was unreadable. He started to worry he had asked the wrong question before she answered. "Nobody knows. Even me. I'm pretty sure my mom knew—she was young when Luna disappeared, but she never told me about it. I think she wanted to forget so badly she pretended like she had. The look in her eyes always said differently."

"Can I ask you a question that's probably entirely too blunt and possible grounds for you to kick me out?"

She dropped the knife and bagel and subtly cringed. "Aiden, I'm almost afraid to say yes."

"I don't mean any harm. I'd just like to help and I...I need to know before we can get started figuring this out."

"Okay, fine. Shoot."

"Do you think—now that it's established witches and paranormal things are real—is it at all possible that Luna is behind these attacks?"

"Luna is dead, Aiden," she said without consideration. Her tone hardened and she picked up the knife for another slather of cream cheese. "She's been dead for over thirty years. All that's left of her are her old possessions. Spell books, family trinkets, scarves. That kind of stuff. I'm wearing one of her favorite necklaces now."

"Right," he trailed off. He wasn't hungry and stared blankly at the bagel on his plate.

"You're thinking something, so just say it."

"What's happened to Feinberg is a lot like what happened to Grisby."

"Are you suggesting my grandma is back from the dead? Because if you are, you can drop it now," she countered. "Bringing someone back from the dead is the darkest kind of magic there is. I don't care what anybody says about Luna— she was *not* a bad witch. She was a wrongly crucified witch, but what else is new? We've been vilified since the beginning of time. You see how I'm treated. What harm have I done anyone?"

"Then we're going to get to the bottom of it," said Aiden. He grabbed his mug of hot chocolate and paused before taking a sip. "I've been thinking and I've come up with a plan."

CHAPTER EIGHTEEN

"How do I look?" Aiden asked with a broad grin.

Selene face-palmed in answer. Aiden stood before her in sea-foam green hospital scrubs, the glint in his hazel eyes a proud one. A hundred different questions popped into her head and she sorted through them, searching for the best one to express her disbelief. She ended on, "Why are you traveling around with a pair of scrubs?"

Aiden shrugged. "Because they come in handy more often than not."

"Your investigations?"

"You'd be surprised."

"I'm learning not to be when it comes to you," replied Selene with a shake of her head. She turned away from him and headed for the staircase.

Aiden followed, Yukie at his heels in a peppy trot. They had spent hours discussing their plan last night, snacking on bagels and hot chocolate, mapping out finer points. Selene still wasn't convinced. Aiden insisted their plan would work. She agreed under the pretense she had gloating rights *when* it failcd. He accepted after mentioning how she'd never get the chance—they were going to pull it off.

At the bottom of the staircase, Aiden grabbed her arm and said, "If you're really having second thoughts about what we're going to do—"

"It's fine," Selene said, offering him a glimpse of a smile. Though small, it possessed faint mischief and humor wrapped into one. "If you think it's going to work, I'm all in. We have to find out what's going on with these attacks."

Aiden returned her smile twofold. His was more pronounced. It spread across his lips and touched his eyes. He even edged a little closer. Selene held her breath as the already small space between them shrank. She had forced herself not to pay mind to their alone time in her house, but how could she ignore the flip of her heartbeat every time he drew nearer?

The air was taut and tense, like an overstrung violin. She couldn't take a step back, couldn't walk away, or even look away. The energy coursing between them was too strong, its pull too trance-inducing. They stayed like that for a while, drawn together so closely his body heat left her breathless. Hers left him flushed, his ears betraying him by going red.

She wanted him to grab her and kiss her—like he had the night they rolled in the snow. The words needed for that ask escaped her. Brain useless and out of order, she did the only thing she could do, and kept her eyes fixed onto him. His handsome face was like the faces of countless heroes she'd imagined. The ones she read about in fiction books stacked shelf to shelf in the town library. Some even hoarded in her bedroom, cluttering her desk or hidden under her bed.

Aiden O'Hare might not have realized it about himself, but he was like the hero in storybooks. He was tall and dashing. He was there to whisk her away from the cursed existence she had lived in Brimrock, seeking to solve her problems by any means necessary. Instead of a coat of armor, he wore hospital scrubs, and instead of a sword, he wielded the power of his unfailing intellect.

Selene hated thinking of him in this way, but how could she not? She'd lived her entire life in books, spending years embarking on fantastical journeys and adventures that weren't her own, but if she pretended they were, it was good enough. He was simply a part of that. Only he was real in the flesh—a real game changer.

"We better get going then," said Aiden with a clearing of his throat. He tore his eyes away from her and checked his watch. "If I miss another dinner at the Myerses', they're going to sic the hounds after me."

She snort-laughed. "They don't have any hounds. Wait...*do* they?"

"Maybe not hounds," said Aiden in consideration, fingers stroking his chin. "How about a flock of peckish birds? I feel like that's more Mrs. Myers's style."

Selene couldn't contain her second laugh. She clapped a hand to her mouth and giggled freely at the joke. From the time she was a child, Mrs. Myers—and the other Myerses—hadn't been the nicest people in town to her. In fact, like her boss, Miriam, Priscilla Myers often led the charge when it came to spreading rumors about Selene and the Blackstone family.

"Eddie let you borrow Ghost?" Selene asked as they buckled into the van.

"*Technically*, we both own Ghost. It's just that he acts like it's more his than mine."

She twisted in the front passenger seat and glanced at the back. The second row of seats had been removed, leaving nothing but the flat carpet flooring and two rolled-up sleeping bags. The area seemed dauntingly underutilized given the amount of space. Like its dull beige exterior with a wooden stripe down the sides, the interior was nothing special.

"Do you guys sleep in here when you're filming for your show?"

"Sometimes. It depends on if it's in the budget for us to stay at a hotel. We took out the back seating to make room for the sleeping bags."

"Why not just remodel it and install a bed? And a table wouldn't hurt either. There's space for it."

"That was our plan when we first bought Ghost. Eddie thinks it's a waste of money. The sleeping bags and carpet floor are good enough."

"You two are like night and day. It's funny you're best friends."

"We were college roommates. I liked when he went out to parties and left me the dorm to study in. He liked when I went to the library and left him the dorm for some alone time with girls. We balanced each other out."

"And what about you?" she found herself asking, unplanned and unprompted. "Did you ever need the dorm for some alone time with girls?"

Humor sprinkled into Aiden's hazel-eyed gaze. "I dated two girls in college. One was a disaster. The other was slightly less of a disaster."

"'Slightly' less of a disaster, huh? What a flattering way to describe an ex."

"We dated for six years. There's a couple more less than flattering things I can say."

Selene smirked, developing a snarky tone. "She broke your heart."

"Define breaking someone's heart," said Aiden. He rivaled her snark with a scholarly air of importance.

"You know exactly what it means, Aiden."

He huffed out a sigh and admitted defeat as he braked for a red light. "Alright, if I'm honest, she broke up with me."

"She—who's she?"

"Her name was Delilah. She was…she was different."

"Different how?"

"She was outgoing. She was off-the-wall—believed in UFOs, which was ridiculous," he said. "But she was also very caring and thoughtful. It was an opposites kind of relationship. She liked chocolate, I liked vanilla type of thing."

"Nobody likes vanilla," teased Selene.

Aiden cut her a sideways glance. "Oh? Are you sure? Because I thought it was one of the most popular flavors."

"Vanilla with sprinkles. Vanilla with strawberries. Vanilla with chocolate syrup."

He chuckled and nodded along. "You might have a point. It's for the best we broke up. We were wasting each other's time. We're both happier apart."

Selene fell silent as she stared out of Ghost's window. Teasing Aiden was fun, but they were on the way to the hospital to execute their plan. Maybe it was time she got serious. They drove past a quaint home with children playing in the heaps of snow on the front lawn. They were giggling and sliding down the mound in what looked like a makeshift sled. It was round and silver and resembled a flying saucer more than anything. Their freckled faces bright with laughter brought another smile to her face. She couldn't resist just one more tease.

"I believe in UFOs, you know," she said, raising her brows at him.

Aiden gave in to her. He smiled too, trading glancing between her and the road. "I figured you do. I suppose that means I have a type, doesn't it?"

Baker Street came up and they hooked a left. The Brimrock Hospital was on the right. Aiden parked in the back. The walk might've been farther, but it was better for keeping a low profile. In a town as nosy as Brimrock, anyone could be watching at any time. Aiden and Selene unbuckled their seat belts and turned to look at each other.

"I'll go in first," said Selene.

"I'll wait about five minutes before I head in."

"And you'll be waiting outside the men's restroom on the ground floor—the one right next to the water fountains and stairwell?"

"That's the one."

Selene grabbed the door handle and winked at him. "See you there, Doctor."

———

"How may I help you?" the male nurse behind the nurse's desk asked. He hadn't looked up from the clipboard in his hands, but when he did, his eyes doubled to twice their size and shock flashed in them. He was expecting any ol' regular visitor. Instead he got Selene Blackstone.

Selene offered a polite smile and folded her arms on the desk counter. It was a lot like the one at the library except it was C-shaped rather than a giant L. "Hello, sir. I was hoping you can help me. I'm here to visit my friend who is in the ICU."

"Your friend," he repeated. He set down the clipboard and lifted a dubious brow.

"Yes, Peter Feinberg. Can you direct me to his room?"

"Mr. Feinberg is under close surveillance right now. Only visitors on the authorized list can see him," replied the nurse.

The badge clipped to the chest of his scrubs said his name was Neil. "I'm sorry but you're not on that list."

Selene leaned more onto the desk, as if about to crane her neck and look at the computer monitor in front of him. "Are you positive? Can you maybe…check just to be sure?"

Neil started to roll his eyes before thinking better of it. He gave a tight nod and then typed fast on his keyboard. Selene watched him with great interest, smiling wider at him whenever he glanced up at her.

"I've double-checked. You're not on the list," he said.

She turned her smile upside down for a pouty frown. "That's so weird. Peter and I are very close."

"Ms. Blackstone, you're not on the list. Please step away from the desk."

"It's just…we're good friends," she continued with dramatic flair. She threw her arms up and collapsed half onto the desk, bursting into a muffled cry. "I'm so, so worried about him."

Neil jumped out of his chair, features arranged in horror. He was living every man's nightmare—a woman bursting into spontaneous tears right in front of him. He grabbed a tissue box off the desk and presented it to her. "Ms. Blackstone, please calm down. You're getting hysterical. If you continue to cause a scene, I'll have to call hospital security to remove you."

Selene only sobbed harder, holding his absolute attention. He was too focused on her face tucked into the crook of her arm and the loud wail now drawing looks from passersby. He missed how her other arm was propped on the counter too—how she gave a slight flick of her wrist.

The stacks of folders on the shelf behind him flew off and tumbled to the ground. The tissue box fell out of Neil's grasp. He forgot about Selene and turned to gape at the sudden mess. Dozens of folders and sheets of paper scattered everywhere. His earlier horror from Selene's tears was nothing compared to the sheer frustration and shock that seized hold of him. His jaw dropped and he cussed, kneeling low to start collecting the fallen papers.

Selene cried for a second longer, peeking through half-closed lids. He was too busy dealing with the mess to notice she had snatched his badge with another flick of her wrist. It whipped through the air and into her waiting hand. She slipped it into her jean pocket and sniffled, slowing down on the tears.

"Well, I guess I'll have to get over it," she said loudly. She stood up straighter and backed away from the nurse's station now in shambles. "But thank you for your help. Good luck with those folders!"

As she scurried away, she passed a couple visitors on their way to the elevator and a nurse or two en route somewhere. She ignored their curious stares and walked faster, turning down the corridor that led to the restrooms. No one was waiting for her. She stumbled to a halt and her stomach dropped. Where was Aiden?

"Pssst. In here."

Selene turned her head and breathed quick relief. The door to the men's restroom was cracked open, waiting for her to slip inside.

CHAPTER NINETEEN

"Did you get the badge?" Aiden asked.

Selene's smirk spoke for itself. She dug into her jean pocket and produced Neil Barrymore's badge. Funnily enough, he and Neil didn't look much different. Neil's nose was slightly crooked and his overall face shape was gaunter, but it was sellable if one saw the badge at only a glance. They both were as pale as ghosts. Both of them had reddish-brown hair. So long as nobody took a long, hard look at the badge, he could pass.

Aiden stood back and let Selene pin it onto him. Her warm brown eyes met his and he pretended he didn't almost choke on his next breath. For the second time that day they were close enough that their bodies almost grazed; she was close enough for him to reach right for her and plant an impassioned kiss on those pouty lips.

The primitive, less evolved part of him was like Tarzan; it thought about Selene's mouth and the curves of her body, and spoke in nothing but unintelligible, deep-throated grunts.

Grunt. Me Tarzan. You Jane. Grunt. Grunt.

He swallowed as the heat crept up his neck and dispersed

across his skin. Selene's lips parted, a slight curl to them. He touched his hand to her cheek, filling up his large palm with the curve of her soft skin. He moved closer, though slowly, giving another second for her to pull away if that was what she wanted.

Selene leaned into him. She sucked in a breath and she warmed up under his palm. He smiled, inching even closer 'til finally his lips were on hers. Instant gratification lit a fuse inside of him and exploded in a thousand tiny sparks. They blazed a tingly trail up his spine and numbed his brain, paving the way for his body to take the lead and revel in their kiss.

The dreamy soft feel of her lips. The muscle in her cheek that worked under his palm as he held her face in his hand. The little sigh she breathed into him, so light it was almost mute. The taste of her, sweet yet indescribable and addictive all at once.

He wrapped an arm around her waist and brought her back against the wall. She flowed with him, pulling him into her, balling fists into his scrubs, and opening her mouth wider —*begging* for his tongue to wander inside.

Any thoughts about their mission at the hospital escaped their minds. They were shoved aside in order to answer the deeper primal urge taking hold.

Selene was light in his arms. She rose on tiptoe and he snatched her up, hoisting her off the ground so that her short legs banded around him, fleshy thighs notched about his waist. He was in heaven, groaning into her mouth as a hand fell to the gloriously plush skin. Even through her jeans, her full thighs tantalized him. He held her up and kissed her harder, eventually snaking around for a feel of her even-fuller backside.

She slipped her glasses up her face and atop her head,

returning her fists to his shirt to goad him on for more. His mind was too blank to think on what they were doing or how it had interrupted their plans to investigate the attacks, blood pumping hot and fast as it surged through him and set him on fire.

He wanted Selene Blackstone and that was the only thing he knew. The caveman grunted his approval and he listened, losing himself to the moment. His lower half stirred like a bear out of hibernation and his eyelids fluttered as Selene's thighs brushed against his overly sensitive hard-on.

They kept going, kissing more, hands roving. Hers slipped under his shirt and his mouth landed on her neck. He happily sucked the skin there, fueled by caveman lust, when footsteps padded from outside the door to the men's restroom. He and Selene reacted a second later than they usually would've, but both froze as they were, against the tiled wall.

They waited with bated breath. The footsteps passed by the men's restroom and continued down the hall. Whoever it was was headed toward the women's restroom or the elevator —or anywhere else but the men's room, to their great sighs of relief.

Selene dropped her legs from around his waist. His mouth left her throat and he backed off enough for a direct look at her. If he looked anything like her, he was disheveled. Her lips were still parted, moist and kiss-swollen, a dizziness in her eyes. Her tight curls bundled atop her head were wild and she tugged on the hem of her sweater to set it straight. He did the same to his hospital scrubs and his own rumpled hair fell onto his forehead.

"That…that was not part of the plan," Selene breathed.

He shook his head. "No, it wasn't."

"Um, maybe we should press pause on that. Finish what we came here to do."

"Right. Of course. The plan."

"The plan," she repeated with an eagerness.

Her shining pink lips called to him again even at a quick glance, but he resisted. He diverted his gaze to one of the sink mirrors and stepped forward to fix his hair.

"Are you sure you'll be able to hack into the system?"

"I'm pretty sure—not one hundred percent, but close to it," he answered, arranging his strands as he liked them, neatly combed and parted. "I just need a few minutes and I should be able to break into the hospital system and download the Feinberg and Grisby files."

Selene lowered her glasses back onto her face. "I guess I'll wait in Ghost."

"Here's the keys. If anything happens, you drive away."

"Aiden—"

"Selene," he interrupted with a stern expression, "you drive away. I'll figure out a way to get back to your house. But you don't need to be caught here. We already know Brimrock PD is suspicious."

The corner of her mouth twitched. She shook her head in a hesitant nod. "Fine. But I don't want to leave you behind."

"I've been in worse situations—trust me. Fifty episodes into paranormal investigations, you become immune to strange phenomena."

"I like kissing you," Selene blabbed, biting her bottom lip. "I don't know where any of this is going, but it's nice."

Aiden's heart jumped and he smiled so quickly he had no time to censor himself. "I like kissing you too. Maybe we should talk about that—what exactly we're doing."

She smiled, teeth still on her bottom lip. "Go ahead. I'll wait for you. Good luck."

———

It took him longer than expected, but Aiden rode an elevator to the third floor. He marched down the corridors, passing nurses and doctors alike with polite nods of his head, and searched for the first room available. Any room with a computer and a lockable door would suffice.

He stumbled on an administrative room that was empty except for another woman in scrubs. Her badge identified her as a registered nurse named Kathy. She put hands on hips and watched him enter the room.

"I don't think we've met," she said with unmistakable suspicion.

Aiden ignored her, passing her up for the computer desk. He sat down and muttered an answer from over his shoulder. "I'm the newest hire. Today's my first day."

"I didn't realize we had a new RN. I'm Kathy."

"Neil."

She squinted. "Funny. We already have a Neil."

"Well, Neil is a pretty common name." Aiden stuck Barrymore's badge into the keyboard's card reader slot and waited for the prompt to pop up. He typed in his first code to bypass the log in request, but was denied. He paused and hoped Kathy noticed nothing. He had a couple more to try. Luckily for him, Kathy seemed fixated on firing off questions.

"How do you like it so far?"

"I like it fine enough." He typed in another combination and then a third. The second failed. The third was a success, logging him in as though he were Neil Barrymore. He inhaled a quiet breath of respite and pretended like he was unsurprised by the development. If he were Neil Barrymore, of course he would be able to log on using his own access badge.

Kathy wasn't done with him. "Where'd you earn your license?"

Aiden almost pulled an exasperated face, but resisted. Kathy the registered nurse obviously didn't trust him—she suspected something was up, hence the game of twenty-one questions. He only wished she had saved her interrogation for *after* he hacked the system. He couldn't exactly work his magic with her gawking at him.

"Oh, you know, the usual," he answered vaguely, waiting on the home screen to load.

Kathy frowned. "The usual—as in University of Mass-achusetts?"

"Sure."

"What doc are you under?"

The door opened and another woman poked her head inside. "Oh, there you are! Doc Dhar is looking for you."

"Can it wait? I'm asking the new—"

"It can't," replied the other nurse. "He says it's very important. It's about Iverson in room 323."

Kathy huffed out a sigh of displeasure but listened. She threw one more nasty glare in Aiden's direction and then followed instruction. The door clicked shut after her and Aiden grinned at finally being alone.

His fingers worked fast. He brought up the hospital records. The system wasn't difficult to sort out once he clicked around a bit. He discovered the search engine and typed in Peter Fein-berg's name. That was after he inserted a miniature flash drive. He clicked download and waited for the flash drive to save the files. He finished up with what Brimrock Hospital had on John Grisby—which wasn't much given the year of the attack.

Still, something was better than nothing. Aiden pocketed the flash drive and logged off the computer. He had to get out of the hospital as soon as possible. The longer he was there, the riskier it got. The real Neil Barrymore must've noticed his badge was missing by now. Kathy would sooner than later figure out there was no new RN.

And then there was Selene, who waited for him in the parking lot. He couldn't risk her being associated with his undercover plan. He was a visitor in Brimrock. She lived here; she was the one under investigation by Brimrock PD. He had to protect her reputation at all costs.

Aiden checked left and right as he reentered the corridor. He headed down the long stretch of hallway, largely ignored by the other staff and visitors passing him. At the elevator, he smashed a finger against the down arrow button and inhaled a self-congratulatory breath.

"Excuse me," sobbed a woman from behind. "I'm hoping you can help me."

His self-congratulatory breath choked him. He held back a cough and beat a fist to his chest. "Oh, uh, I'm sorry, I'm actually on lunch—"

"I'm looking to speak with someone about my son," said the sniveling woman, her blonde hair a stringy, unwashed mess. "His regular doctor isn't here today. Can you help?"

"Your son."

"Peter Feinberg," she said, clutching a tissue.

The elevator doors sprang open and he stepped inside. Mrs. Feinberg followed him. His top row of teeth ground against his bottom row, showing as a tense grimace rather than a smile. He racked his brain for an answer.

"Have you tried the nurse's desk?"

Mrs. Feinberg rolled her eyes. "The nurses in the ICU aren't any help. I've been trying to find out what's going on with my son for days now—they only give me the runaround.

The doctors too. I'm sick and tired of this hospital. It makes me miss Boston."

Aiden pressed the button for the ground floor. "Err, well, Mrs. Feinberg, I wish I could help you more. But…but I'm a new hire."

The hope fell off her face. "Oh. I figured you'd be able to help."

The guilt bit at him, a large chunk felt at once. He weighed his options and said, "I don't know much about what's going on with your son, ma'am, but have you looked into John Grisby?"

"John Grisby," she repeated slowly.

"The library has old papers from 1976 on what happened to him. That…that might shed some light."

The elevator reached the ground floor and its doors rolled open. Aiden offered a goodbye smile and then hurried across the lobby. He already had his badge off and head bowed as he reached the automatic sliding doors. The winter air greeted him with its usual frozen chill and he wouldn't have it any other way crossing the parking lot toward Ghost parked in the back.

He was home free.

CHAPTER TWENTY

Aiden parked two blocks away from 1221 Gifford Lane. Selene walked back first. He followed fifteen minutes later. She cracked the door open and he slunk inside. It might've been dark out already, but they wanted to take no risks in case prying eyes were on them.

"Are you sure you don't have to go back to the Myerses'?"

"I probably should, but Eddie and I aren't on the best terms right now."

"The whole pitch meeting at Hot Java?"

Aiden slipped off his shoes and hung up his coat next to Selene's. "Paulina, our executive producer, is calling it creative differences, but really it's me refusing to bend to their will."

"They want to do the Luna Blackstone episode," said Selene. Her voice shrunk as she wandered down the hall. The rest of the house was dark, the shadows haunting every corner of the home. She had it memorized even with her eyes closed, but Aiden bumped his knee against a table. She flipped on the first light switch she crossed and entered the kitchen. "I've already told you, Aiden, if your job on YouTV is on the line —go ahead and do the episode."

Aiden was rubbing his knee as he limped into the room. "That's not an option. I refuse to film the episode on Luna. I've given you my word."

"I hate causing trouble for you." Selene crossed her arms, her hands on the opposite elbow. She was cold, hungry, and tired from their long day. Not to mention paranoia was trickling in drop by drop after their stunt at the hospital. What if this blew up in their faces in the worst way?

"I like a little trouble. I wouldn't be a paranormal investigator if I didn't."

She directed a faint sideways smirk at him. "You don't even believe in the paranormal."

"I do now that I'm dating a witch," he replied. His usual tightly wound masculine features relaxed and he sported half a grin, his growing stubble more red than brown under the shoddy kitchen lighting. How she had ever labeled him *just* coffee shop guy cute was beyond her...

Aiden was smart and handsome, his humor sarcastic and at times self-depreciating, which made him infinitely sexier. Today was the first time they'd spent the entire day together, and everything about him had started to awaken desire. Even his scent, a vague fresh but woodsy pine smell, drew flustered heat out of her.

Maybe Noelle was right. Maybe she was already dickmatized. Before the actual *dicking*.

Her cheeks heated up at that last thought and she turned toward the cabinets. "Do you want something to drink?"

"Got any soda?" Aiden reached into the pocket of his scrubs and held up the flash drive. "We should probably see what's on this bad boy."

The perfect distraction. Something other than the growing lustful throbs of her body. Her nod was quick and eager. "My laptop's upstairs."

———

"Patient is suffering from undiagnosed coma, no sign of traumatic brain injury or underlying illness," read Selene aloud. Her face glowed with the whitish blue light from her laptop screen. Aiden hovered above her shoulder, looking on. His woodsy Alpine cologne permeated the small space between them, pure sabotage in how it muddied her brain, but she fought off its effects and kept reading. "CAT scans reveal no bleeding, loss of oxygen, or increased pressure to the brain. The patient is simply unresponsive."

"Well, so much for the authorities hiding something in his medical record," he said, sighing.

"It seems like they haven't made any progress since Peter's been found. They're just letting him lay comatose. Just like Grisby all those years ago."

"Open Grisby's file anyway. We can look over that."

Selene clicked out of Peter's record and then dragged the mouse toward the folder marked Grisby. She double-clicked on it, but a pop-up window requested further authorization. The text read:

Two-Step Authentication required. Please enter access code below.

She glanced at Aiden. "Access code? What access code?"

"Try Neil's password—it's 13985."

"Nope," said Selene, typing in the numbers. The pop-up window shook on screen as it buzzed its denial. "Apparently even Neil Barrymore doesn't have access to John Grisby's file."

"Do you mind if I try?"

Selene quirked a brow at him. "I forgot I was with the hacker of our generation."

"I appreciate the vote of confidence, but I told you already I only dabble. I'll take a crack at it."

"By all means." Selene swapped places with Aiden. She scooped up Yukie and cradled the furry pooch in her arms as Aiden settled into her desk chair. His fast fingers flew over her keyboard. He had to type a hundred words a minute, if not more.

For a long moment, the heavy tapping from his fingers filled the room. The occasional whine from the old brass radiator joined him, its knocks and cracks a hard, labored effort as it kicked out more heat. Selene walked Yukie over to the radiator and spent a couple seconds bathing in its warmth, giving Aiden time to solve the riddle.

He punched in a bunch of different alpha-numeric combinations. None of them worked. When he exhausted all of his tricks, he leaned back into the desk chair and stroked his chin, stumped.

"No luck?"

"Whoever set the parameters for this authentication knew what they were doing," he answered. He glanced at her. "How about you use your superpowers and unlock the folder that way?"

"I hate to break it to you, but my magic doesn't work like that. I can't magic a digital folder open."

"It looks like we're at an impasse then."

They both stared at the computer screen, silently racking

their brains for any other options. Neither came up with anything. In the newfound quiet, Aiden's stomach grumbled. Selene turned Yukie free and snickered at his stomach's honesty.

"Hungry?"

"It is about to be seven. I haven't eaten anything since lunch."

Now that he mentioned it, she hadn't either. They'd spent most of the day executing the hospital plan. Her stomach must've had ears, because it seemed to speak to Aiden's with an agreeable gurgle. She was starving too. This time they both laughed.

"How about we break for dinner? I *think* I have food in the kitchen."

Aiden rose out of the desk chair and let his sarcasm run free. "I always thought most people stored their food in the bathroom."

———

"Nothing reminds you how hungry you are like pepperoni pizza," said Selene between bites. She was on her second slice with no signs of slowing down. She and Aiden sat on the floor in the living room, the coffee table between them. The pizza box lay open beside two cans of Dr. Pepper and a stack of already greasy napkins.

They had gone downstairs into the kitchen and searched the cabinets. Selene forgot she still hadn't gone grocery shopping. The best she had were ingredients to slap together a peanut butter banana sandwich or a bowl of white rice and pinto beans. Her eyes fastened onto Aiden's face and his brows rose and they both grinned at each other with the same thought running through their minds. In another second they were dialing up the local pizza parlor and ordering a large pie with extra cheese and pepperoni.

Selene giggled as Aiden stretched his long legs underneath the coffee table. "I don't know how you function being so tall."

"How do you function being so short?"

"That's where magic—*and* footstools—come in handy."

Aiden swallowed the last bite of his slice and chuckled. "I duck my head a lot."

"I noticed earlier. You almost hit it when getting into the van."

"It wouldn't be the first time. I've lost several brain cells thanks to Ghost."

"Don't worry, it seems like you still have plenty left," said Selene, wiping her greasy fingers on her napkin. "What's the plan moving forward if we can't unlock the Grisby file?"

"I was thinking that over. We have two options."

"You say that like neither are good ones."

"Neither are what we were hoping for. First option, we can find a hacker who can get into this flash drive for us," said Aiden, holding up the small USB key. He pocketed it again and chugged the rest of his Dr. Pepper. "The other option is we try and finagle our way into an interview with someone from the Grisbys."

"Did you forget the Grisbys hate me?"

"Well, not *you*. More so we as in me. Eddie's aunt works for Mayor Grisby and is close with the family. I can probably sweet-talk her into getting me an interview."

"The same Eddie you're not really speaking to right now? His aunt?" Selene's eyebrows emphasized her point by arching higher. She hated being pessimistic, but somebody had to keep Aiden tethered to the possibility their investigation wouldn't pan out. He seemed confident he could solve what was going on, whereas she erred more on the cautious side.

"Eddie and I have disagreements all the time. This isn't the first and won't be the last. We're opposites so it happens."

"We'll do what you think is best. You're the professional."

"I don't know I'd go that far. The show was an accident. Who would've thought there was a market for two guys filming low-budget videos of themselves wandering around haunted mansions? It wasn't exactly part of my post-graduation plan when I left college," he said.

"I'm surprised you went along with it. You seem like the type of guy to always stick to the plan."

Aiden shrugged. "Even I like some surprises. As crazy as it sounds, I enjoy the investigations. I might not believe in what we're investigating, but it keeps me on my toes. Besides, if I'm honest, I think a part of me always wondered if maybe one day I'd be proven wrong."

"And then you met me." Selene wasn't sure why she said it, but when she did, a mellifluous giggle escaped her. All day she had been fending off her attraction, ignoring the tremor in her belly when his gaze met hers. It required an effort that had since waned. After hours of fighting the good fight, she was ready to stop overthinking and let loose.

For his part, Aiden laughed too. His timbre was throatier than usual and his hazel eyes had a knowing spark in them. "And then I met you, and it's been nothing but trouble since."

Selene gasped in outrage and used her magic to her advantage. She gave a quick flick of her hand and the pizza crust flew off her plate. It whizzed across the coffee table and whacked Aiden on the forehead. She scooted back, preparing for retaliation of some sort. Instead Aiden, being the foodie that he was, popped the thrown pizza crust into his mouth, chewing the buttery bread.

"Feel free to keep 'em coming," he mumbled with a mouthful of crust.

"You're impossible."

"A week ago, I would've said the same thing about you," he said and the spark in his eyes evolved. It became something intense, electrically charged that sent a shock through her body. "But I'm learning I kind of like the impossible —*and* the irresistible."

Heat engulfed her like a scalding-hot blast from the radiator. Her mind spun as she sat suddenly flustered, unable to remember how to speak much less remember her name. The same tantalizing quakes from earlier started up again in her belly, only now deeper.

Aiden O'Hare really *was* impossible—the effect he had on her was something Selene thought would never happen.

The small handful of guys she had slept with weren't anything serious, more so out of a curiosity for what she was possibly missing. It turned out she wasn't missing much. Most of her sexual experiences could be sorted into two categories: pathetic and pitiful. If they weren't one-minute men, they were clumsy and heavy-handed, pawing at her like they hadn't the faintest clue about female anatomy. After her first few attempts, she'd given up altogether, accepting that like other Blackstone women, she was simply cursed when it came to love and sex.

But she had an inkling things could be different with Aiden. If their chemistry was explosive with only kisses— even at times without touching—that had to mean something.

Selene nibbled on her bottom lip and fixed her stare onto her empty plate. It was more hopeful thinking. The constant swell of hope in her chest that maybe she wasn't so cursed after all. She could somehow break the bind keeping her in Brimrock; she could finally have a *real* relationship with a man. No other man made it feel remotely possible like Aiden did, but she tamped down on that thought. It was wishful thinking. Nothing more.

"I can't sit here and pretend like I'm not thinking what I'm thinking," said Aiden in a burst of candor. He brushed aside the empty pizza box and his can of Dr. Pepper and sat up straighter, all seventy-five inches of him. "Selene"—he paused to tighten his jaw and let his darkening hazel eyes bore into hers—"I want to kiss you. I've been thinking about it all day. Since the hospital."

Selene smiled. Aiden wasn't what Noelle would call a guy with swag. He didn't have that usual cool, almost cocky vibe most guys their age tried to pull off. Quite the opposite, he was fine being the rigid, sarcastic, bookish man that he was. And Selene was more than fine with that too—she wasn't the most conventional woman herself.

Teeth still on her bottom lip, her smile stretched slow but far. She rose onto her knees and then slid backward onto the sofa. Her invitation was clear with the two empty sofa spaces next to her. Aiden was on her in another second, eagerly claiming her mouth with his own. She lay back against the cushions and curled fingers into his hair, matching his kisses with equal fervor.

They broke apart slightly for brief giggles when her thick glasses got in the way. Aiden's once-hazel eyes were a chestnut brown, darkened by unmistakable lust, as he reached up for her glasses.

"Mind if I—?"

She shook her head and let him remove her second pair of eyes from her face. He folded them carefully, using the long stretch of his arm to set them onto the coffee table. Their kisses resumed without skipping a beat, mouths slanted and tongues mingling. The earlier heat flaming over her burned hotter. It transformed into slick heat between her thighs as a fever broke onto her skin.

With flushed breathlessness taking over, she couldn't resist feeling like she was living in some Harlequin romance, a duchess waiting for the duke to rip her bodice off. Only she would think of books as she kissed Aiden thoroughly, earning a small smile out of her, lips pressed against his.

A moan freely escaped from her throat and she watched in real time as it drove Aiden wild. He buried his face into her neck, gifting the smooth skin a dozen fervent kisses. Her hands rode up his arms, holding on to him, tracing the protruding veins in his skin like a map.

He kissed his way to her chest after a suckling detour on her collarbone and she squirmed, overly sensitive to his hot mouth. His fingers slid under the hem of her sweater and danced across her stomach. The wool fabric rode up, but she found she didn't care, too immersed in kissing and rocking against each other.

Aiden pulled away a second time for a breathless, dizzied look at her. His skin was splotched the reddest shade she'd ever seen it go, and thanks to her, his hair was a disheveled mess. He breathed long and hard, his breath tickling her skin. "In case the sarcasm thing was still a question, I was being serious when I said I wanted you."

She half rolled her eyes. "I know, Aiden."

"Then I'm pretty sure you feel how…*happy*…I am this is happening."

How could Selene not notice the hard bulge lodged between her thighs? It was large and rock-solid, poking against her supple flesh as an insistent reminder of how much Aiden wanted her. She wanted him the same, answering him with hands on the leather band of his belt. In the middle of more kisses, she coaxed him on.

"You might not be able to tell, but I'm *just as* happy."

They shuffled against the sofa cushions, struggling to tug off articles of clothing. She helped Aiden remove his shirt and he returned the favor, lifting her wool sweater. The cool air hit her flesh as she lay beneath him in her bra and jeans. Already on a sensitive high, the air rushing against her skin only turned her on further. She moaned again as they unbuttoned each other's jeans.

"Um, about protection…" She trailed off.

"No need to worry," he said. He held himself up like he was doing a one-armed pushup and used his other to dig into his back pocket for his wallet. "I try to always carry some with me."

"*You*…carry around condoms?"

His cheeks grew rosier. "Thanks for the vote of confidence. I like to be prepared for every situation. Even if it's a rare one."

Selene giggled and helped him out of his jeans. The denim fell to the floor soon followed by hers. She wiggled her curvy hips as together they pulled them off. Aiden sat back and fought the crinkling foil condom wrapper.

"Need some help?" she teased, holding out her hand.

The wrapper split open and the thin latex sheath fell into Aiden's open palm. He raised his brows at her, smirking with a shake of his head, but he slipped it on anyway. Her eyes shot down his pelvis, watching the rubber rolling onto his length—and *damn* was it lengthy.

Selene could only lie still and stare. Aiden sensed her shock and kissed his way back up her neck. He drifted onto her jawline over time and then her mouth.

"We can go slow," he said, resting his forehead into hers. "You tell me what you want."

Selene kissed him back and rocked her hips against his. "I'm not sure if you're aware of this or not, Aiden O'Hare, but you're, um, packing. It might take a minute, but I'm up for the challenge."

Aiden grinned before planting another long kiss on her. Arms wound around his neck, Selene focused on his hot mouth, anticipation rising for that initial feel of him slipping inside. Slowly, enough time for several heartbeats to thump by, his fat mushroom tip pushed its way in, causing her to tense up and gasp. He stopped there, holding himself still and kissing her harder.

"Is this okay?" he breathed against her lips.

She nodded. "Mmm, keep going."

Her eyelids dropped close, feeling herself stretch to accommodate him. It was a snug fit, but a good, full feeling that had her moaning into his mouth. Her hand swept down his back, his lean muscles corded knots beneath her fingers, holding her breath for his first real stroke. He did not disappoint, his thrust slow but deeper, the intense, pulsating feeling exploding inside of her. She wanted more, needed him to keep going as the thousands of nerve endings in her core tingled their approval.

Aiden buried his face into her neck, drawing back slightly for another thrust, but never getting there. His girthy member twitched once, then twice, and finally, a third time enveloped by her warmth. Her eyes flicked to his face in time for the orgasm to unfold on his features. His brow creased and his mouth hung open and he grunted out his pleasure. He hadn't been able to hold on a second longer—halfway inside of her, he'd given in, and came.

The disappointment was immediate, zapping away any

lustful feelings in her body, leaving her speechless. Aiden pulled out of her and sat back onto his knees, his entire face lit up a neon red. He launched into explanation.

"It's been a long time," he said on a frantic wave. "It's been a year—I...I didn't realize I'd finish so fast—I can do better."

Selene pushed herself up against the sofa cushions. "Um, it's...okay."

"Selene, I'm being serious. No sarcasm in sight."

"I know..." she drifted off. She pressed together her knees and stared at the pool of their clothes on the floor. "Um, it's getting late."

Aiden leaned closer, his hand on her kneecap. "No, really, Selene...I pride myself at being proficient. That...that includes my performance with women. Give me another shot. It'll be better."

"It's really fine. And it is late. You should get going."

"I can do better! I...I *have* done better."

Any drip of desire was long gone, exhaustion settling in its place. Selene shook her head and moved to separate the pile of clothes. "It's probably better if you go."

The next few minutes were some of the most awkward ones of their lives. Selene knew with certainty for herself. She sensed the same for Aiden. In silence they sorted their clothes and got dressed. Aiden snuck her glances that she ignored. She walked him to the door, gnawing on her bottom lip as he wished her good night.

"I'll call you tomorrow," he said. The redness had yet to fade.

She shrugged. "Sure. Tomorrow."

"Selene..."

"Aiden, it's okay," she said, chancing a look up at him. "It's to be expected at this point."

The look on his face was one of unabashed insult when she shut the door, but what he didn't realize was that it wasn't about him. It was about her more than anything. The curse sabotaging her mere existence so that even the simplest sexual encounter was disappointing. She should've known better than to expect differently, even with Aiden.

Selene was a Blackstone, cursed for the rest of her life— matters of the heart included.

CHAPTER TWENTY-ONE

I n Aiden's twenty-eight years, he had never been so
embarrassed. In his twenty-eight years, he had never
failed to…perform. He might not have bedded a score
of women like Eddie and other guys his age, but he had
always made an effort to please. Delilah had never had any
complaints.

Or had she?

Maybe she had been too sympathetic, deciding to cushion
his male ego. Selene seemed to be willing to, judging how
she let him down easy with her exhaustion excuse. The paranoia seeped into his brain and wound up churning his stomach. He almost forgot where he was going.

He parked Ghost in the Myerses' driveway and sat there
with the engine off. He didn't care for the idea of waltzing
through the Myers home for some post-Christmas cheer. In
their household it was still the holiday season. The limbo
between Christmas and New Year's was worth its own mini
celebration. If he had any luck at all, he would get to run up
to his room unnoticed, where he could spend the rest of the
night wallowing in his failure.

His fifth groan in the last hour convulsed in his throat. He wasn't going to forget about this anytime soon. The first real woman he was compatible with in a long time, and he had to blow his shot. He clenched his teeth as the literal meaning to that phrase wasn't lost on him. He *had* blown his shot in more ways than one.

It was just that it had been so long for him. She had felt so good. The anticipation had piled up so unbelievably high that he had buckled under the pressure and let go sooner than he thought he would. Right as they were getting started. The moment between them had been one crackling with their electric chemistry and yet he had ruined everything. Would Selene be able to give him another chance?

Her melancholic tone and glum expression hinted at probably not...

Aiden dragged his feet on his walk up the front path to the Myerses'. The other homes on the block were as pristine, lawns preened to perfection as if for a residential beauty pageant. Cars were filed in the driveways of each home with the window shutters open and inviting passersby to witness their brightly lit, festive evening. The Myerses most of all, their massive Christmas tree on display in their den window.

Warmth enveloped him as he set foot inside. He shook off the snow clinging to his coat and hair, tossing the keys to Ghost on the console table. Mr. Myers had his Christmas jazz album playing again. The harmonic tunes spread cheer throughout the house much to Aiden's dismay. He didn't care to celebrate the holidays for the fiftieth time in a week and a half.

Mr. Myers poked his head into the hall and boomed, "Well, a stranger just walked in! Priscilla, you can stop the tears now."

Aiden winced as he was sighted. He would never escape

now. Mrs. Myers bustled out of the kitchen with her apron still tied about her thick waist and a wooden rolling pin in hand. For the vaguest second, she reminded him of Mom. Her cheeks were rosy, her wispy hair flew free from its bun, and he was transported back to evenings in their cramped two-bedroom apartment. She always lurked in the kitchen for a chance to scold him when he got home late from wasting time anywhere but home.

It finally hit him. That was what he resented about the Myers home. Even in its over-the-top Hallmark corniness, it still reminded him of home. Mrs. Myers was his scolding mother. Mr. Myers was his aloof, clueless father. Camila and Rory were his sister, Cara, all rolled into one, constantly on their own plane of existence, for better or worse. And Eddie —he was different. He had never had anyone like Eddie to rely on growing up.

His realization worsened his already bad mood. He rotated to the direction of the staircase. Mrs. Myers called out to him.

"I thought you'd gotten lost!"

When he said nothing, she sucked in a hissing breath.

"It's still the holiday. We're drinking spiked eggnog!"

"No thanks, I should probably head—"

"You only have a few more days left in town—don't you want to spend them with the family who has taken you into their home?"

Aiden held back, one foot on the bottom stair. "I appreciate your hospitality, Mrs. Myers, but I've mentioned I'm not really big on the holidays."

"It's a courtesy thing! Here I am slaving away for you, cooking big meals and baking tasty treats, and you're... you're gone half the time!" she exploded, a whistle coming out her button nose like steam from a hot kettle. "You come and go whenever you please—usually at odd hours of the night and day—you barely say a word to any of us except for Eddie! I'm supposed to bite my tongue and pretend it's all roses!"

"Mrs. Myers, I'm sorry..." Aiden stepped off the bottom stair and faced her, searching for a proper apology.

Mr. Myers wandered into the hall from the den, a mug of what looked like spiked eggnog in his clutches. "What's all this shouting for?"

"I've had enough!" Mrs. Myers shrieked.

"Priscilla, what are you—?"

Mrs. Myers ignored her husband and stomped closer to Aiden. "All I ask for is a happy Christmas! Is that too much?"

"I haven't meant to upset you," said Aiden carefully. He wasn't sure what about the moment made him feel like he had been confronted by a mountain lion, now needing to ease its carnivorous appetite.

Mrs. Myers only stalked closer. Her eyes thinned into narrow slits. "You say that, but you continue to disregard everyone but that girl!"

"And what girl would that be?" Aiden said. He pinched the bridge of his nose.

"You know exactly who!"

"I don't, actually."

"Selene Blackstone! You've spent so much time with her, going on midnight walks and secret meetups on Christmas—it's gotten out of hand."

"I happen to *like* Selene."

"She's not right that girl! Peter is laying comatose in a hospital bed because of her. Now Officer Gustin is missing after he patrolled her!" Mrs. Myers argued. "How could you involve yourself with her after what she's done? Do you know what Rory has been going through?"

Aiden didn't know where to begin. Mrs. Myers had fired off a number of falsehoods. He wished to debunk each one, but confusion twisted him up, his tongue uncooperative. He settled on a curt, blunt solution that would cut short any more feuding.

"I should probably stay in a hotel," he said. "I'll go pack my things."

"Priscilla!" Mr. Myers exclaimed. "See what you've done!"

"Aiden, that's not what I was suggesting at all." Mrs. Myers's anger vanished for sniffling tears.

But Aiden was already torpedoing up the stairs. He shot into his room, the door banging against the wall, and heaved his suitcase onto his bed. He was a methodical packer through and through, preferring to carefully fold and fit each item into the suitcase like a live game of Tetris. His pulse beating fast, throbbing in the side of his neck, he skipped out on meticulousness and stuffed whatever he got his hands on. The result was a crumpled mishmash of his possessions.

It didn't matter. He would leave Ghost behind for Eddie and take a URide to the town square to find a local hotel. Hopefully one would have a room available on short notice.

Aiden crammed his size-eleven Oxford shoes into the last available space and then forced the zipper around the suitcase's perimeter. He would unpack and reorder everything once he got to his hotel. In his own room paid for on his own card, he could finally have the privacy and seclusion he had yearned for since arriving in Brimrock.

Eddie rapped his knuckles on the bedroom door. Aiden ignored him and pressed on, rounding the corner of his bed to grab his laptop case. Eddie refused to be shunned, calling out to him.

"Bro! What the fuck?"

"What the fuck is right," Aiden snapped, in no mood for ribbing. He placed his MacBook inside his laptop case and zipped that up too. "I think it was probably a mistake for me to stay here, Eddie."

"Everybody needs to chill."

"I'm chill. Very chill. Always chill."

"You are the opposite of chill," said Eddie against the door frame. "So is Aunt Priscilla. I'll talk to her."

"I'm done feeling uncomfortable, Eddie."

"So you haven't been liking it here. I thought so. Why didn't you just tell me?"

"Because it was bearable before your aunt decided to throw Selene in my face!" Aiden slung his laptop case onto his shoulder, his long-legged strides crossing the room in half the steps of an average person. "It's not on you. It's not your fault. And I appreciate the invite, but I've had enough of the guilt trips over how I spend my time."

"Look, I get it. Aunt Priscilla is a lot to digest. But all she's asking is a little time with the family—"

"It's not my family!" he retorted. He wasn't at a shout, but his dry tone packed more punch. He was tired of the interrogation, sick of the Myerses making him feel like an anomaly. He already knew he was an anomaly—an anti-holiday, cheerless, studious prick who most people did not like. *Except* Selene. "I've made up my mind. It's better that I leave."

"And what about me? Your best friend?"

Aiden paused, his hand wrapped around the handle of his rolling suitcase. "I'm not following."

"You're gonna leave me hanging for some girl you've known for a week?"

"It's been longer than a week."

"By a couple days! Wake up, bro, you don't even know the girl. You realize you're ruining our show?"

"Eddie, if me not filming one episode ruins the show, then maybe it was time for it to end," said Aiden. He wheeled his suitcase toward the door, bypassing Eddie on his exit. "I'll text you which hotel I end up at. See you later."

Down the second floor hall, Camilla on the phone gossiping with her friend penetrated the walls of her bedroom. He rolled his suitcase along, headed for the staircase, walking by Mr. and Mrs. Myers's bedroom and Eddie's. The last he passed was Rory's, the sound of muffled tears distinct. He gave a somber shake of his head thinking about her grief over Peter's condition and carried on toward the stairs.

Outside, the night was a blinding wall of wind and snow. He blinked against the icy flakes falling sideways, catching in his hair and sticking in his eyes, and awaited the URide to pull up. More than once the door to the Myerses' opened and somebody called out to him. More than once he ignored them, back turned, as he braved the frost and cold, standing on a dark plane highlighted only by the streetlamp above.

Finally, a maroon Honda Accord slowed up beside the curb, the URide logo slapped onto the side. Aiden dropped his luggage off in the trunk and hopped in, relieved when the car rode away and the flurrying snow wiped the Myers home from view.

CHAPTER TWENTY-TWO

"**C**an I say it yet?"

Selene hung her head, her granola bar limp in her grasp. It was the morning after last night's disaster and she had decided to pay Noelle an early visit before work. "You can't possibly be this petty."

"Selly, you've known me for how many years and you're still asking that question? I'm that petty—the pettiest of the petty to ever petty," said Noelle plainly. She blew on her freshly coated nails. The grape purple shade paired magnificently with her medium brown skin. "Anyway, here it goes: I told you so."

"You did not," argued Selene as a small child would. Her bottom lip even poked out in a pout.

"I did so. I told you to leave Fudgeboy alone."

"But it's hard. We vibe so well, Noe. I enjoy myself around him. It's the first time I've felt that way."

Noelle screwed on the cap to her bottle of nail polish and took pity on Selene with a dragged-out sigh. "You guys *are* kinda cute together. I noticed it the night of Winter Solstice."

"When Aiden almost got run over? What was cute about that?"

"After you left, you know when you had your little tantrum and stormed out of the coffee shop, Aiden was worried about you," said Noelle. "Really worried. He wanted to go after you, but I had to tell him to give you your space. You're the type when you mad, you mad."

"I had no clue."

"I give him hell, but I do think the guy really cares. Either that or he's one hell of an actor."

Selene's teeth tore off a major chunk from her granola bar, the oats and apple bits a lump in her cheek. Her slow, pitiful chewing caught Noelle's eye and she cocked her left hip out, a hand on top.

"I finally admitted Fudgeboy's not so bad. Now what's the problem?"

"Did you miss the part where the sex was a disaster? He was mortified. I was mortified. Everything else had been going great the whole day. We were like this Bonnie and Clyde, Hardy Boy and Nancy Drew combination. It was exciting."

Noelle erupted into a laugh. "Bonnie and Clyde? Hardy Boy and Nancy Drew? Those are two combinations I never thought I'd hear."

"You know what I mean," Selene groaned.

"So your first attempt was…underwhelming. You're both obviously attracted to each other. You both obviously like each other. This isn't the movies—*or* the books you read. Next time will be better." Noelle crossed the room and sat on the edge of the bed beside Selene. "I already know you and how in your head you are. This isn't your fault. It's not because of the curse."

"Aiden said it's never happened to him before."

"That's kinda flattering in a way. He was that excited."

The subtlest smile broke out on Selene's face. "But he leaves soon."

"Girl, we live in the twenty-first century. Long-distance relationships have never been easier with camming and instant messaging. He can always come visit when he's not filming. That curse stuff has always been in your head. Probably made up by your mom to keep you in line."

"You mean like when we were in high school and wanted to sneak out to go to a house party?"

"Exactly."

Selene inhaled a breath, the air filling up her lungs. When she exhaled, she felt lighter. Noelle made sense. She and Aiden could work through what happened last night. They could move on to some type of long-distance relationship when he left. If he was still interested. Her heart fluttered at the prospect.

Noelle moved to get up, but Selene grabbed her arm to hold her back. Another thought had occurred to her. This time not Aiden related. "How are things with you and Shayla?"

"How did I not see that coming?"

"You haven't updated me! Bibi told me she's come by the coffee shop twice since the persuasion potion disaster."

"My own aunt diming me out." Noelle shook her head, popping to her feet. She returned to the dresser mirror in her room and got started on her makeup, filling in her brows. "Shayla and I are friends. We're back on speaking terms, but that's it. Nothing more."

"Uh-huh. We'll see," Selene teased.

The unmistakable scratch of slippers padded down the hall outside Noelle's room. Both Selene and Noelle held still, going silent, listening to her fuzzy slippers scrape against the floorboards. Bibi appeared at last in the doorway with her terry cloth robe and lavender-gray curls in a stylish scarf tied around her head. In her hand she clutched a mug with wisps of steam drifting into the air. Its pleasant citrusy notes clued Selene into it being Earl Grey.

"Did I hear my name?"

"No, Auntie. Go back to sipping your tea."

"Are you talking about that boy from the internet show again?"

"It's all settled."

"You mean you're not sending him to the emergency room again?" Bibi cackled over a small sip from her mug.

Noelle joined her laughter as Selene cried out, "It was a mistake! I never wanted that to happen."

"We know, we know. We're pulling your leg," said Bibi, dark eyes twinkling. "But don't you forget, if you ever need to whip up another potion, I've got a garden full of magical herbs. The possibilities are endless."

———

In the sluggish days after Christmas but before New Year's, the last place anyone wanted to be was the library. For the bulk of the day, the computer lab collected dust. The dozens of book aisles were empty and unoccupied. Only a handful of patrons visited, coming in for pit stops like a quick print or copy, a book return, or even a restroom break, bolting after the toilet use.

It hadn't stopped snowing since last night, though now it was more so flurries. The forecast called for more snow the rest of the week with little to no sun and lots of central heating. The latter being a joke the town weatherman cracked to lighten the mood.

For Selene, the one bright spot was tonight's full moon; she could finally perform another lunar ritual.

She pushed her bold-framed glasses up her nose and glanced around the deserted library. Miriam and Gerri were in the back office doing what they did every afternoon: gossiping over tea and cookies. Elsewhere in the big and barren library, few visitors remained. The later it got, the sky darker and angrier by the hour, the more it seemed like everyone in town must've been at home already.

She sighed and considered a little cheat from her magic to finish her work. A few days after the New Year, the library was launching a brand-new children's literacy program, which meant advertising said program. Since Miriam thought that task was beneath her and Gerri, it was a given it would be Selene's job to print flyers, hand out pamphlets, and hang banners wherever possible.

Nobody was looking. Nobody would have to know. Would anybody notice if she wiggled her fingers and posted the last few with her lunar magic?

At the last second she chickened out. Her hand hovered over the rolled-up banners when two unsuspecting college students passed by whispering among themselves. She jumped and almost fell off her step stool. That was all it took for her to decide to do it the nonwitch way.

For the rest of the afternoon, Selene manned the checkout counter, slumped at the desk with her face propped up by her fist. Beneath the L-shaped desk, she had her portable heater going, spitting out waves of heat to combat the general chill permeating the air. Goosebumps still sprang up on her skin here and there, but at least it kept her feet warm.

It was afternoons like this, dreary and gray ones, that made her second-guess her job at the library. She loved the books, loved helping patrons discover them, and occasionally watching children's faces light up when in love with a book, but the slow, wintry afternoons felt like a thousand years rolled into one.

She started drifting off, her lids too heavy, thoughts on the full moon tonight and her lunar ritual. The quiet flip of a page woke her up. She jerked in her chair and stared across the study area in the vicinity, its long tables and chairs arranged like separate pieces to a puzzle. A lone patron sat at a table flipping through his book, the sound indistinguishable on most days, even in a library, but on an afternoon as quiet and dead as today, startlingly loud.

Selene tossed another cautious glance over her shoulder. Miriam and Gerri were still yakking away in the back office over their milky tea. Her hand inched toward her leather book bag and she snuck out her cell phone. Rarely did she use her phone while at work. She reasoned it was okay this once because Miriam was breaking the rules. She hadn't gotten any real work done since her shift began. Why couldn't she use her phone for five minutes?

Her notifications were the usual. Spam emails from companies she didn't remember giving her address to. News notifications about current events in the country, including localized ones regarding Peter's attack and Officer Gustin's disappearance. A random text or two from Noelle venting about rude customers at the Magic Bean.

The last notification lit her face up with a surprised smile. She had a text from Aiden. In typical Aiden O'Hare fashion, he addressed last night's flub head-on:

If you haven't completely written me off as pathetic, nonboyfriend material, I'd love a second chance to prove myself. Do-over?

Selene giggled rereading the message two and then three times. She stole another look over her shoulder to double-check nobody was watching, then set to work crafting a careful response. She almost wished Noelle was around to assist. In the end, she decided on:

I'm willing to blame the entire large, double cheese pepperoni pizza we consumed if you are? Is being drunk off grease a thing?

She thought it would've taken minutes for Aiden to answer, being the analytical overthinker he was, but his response came through straightaway:

If it wasn't, we definitely invented it. Dinner tonight? I'm free whenever you are.

Joy burst free as a rush of endorphins hit her, a floaty sensation picking her up and making her feel like she was flying high. She shook her shoulders to rid herself of the overabundant feeling and focus on a cool, casual response.

How about 6? You can pick me up from my house.

Aiden's answer was a thumbs-up. She deposited her phone back into her book bag and breathed in a shuddery breath, still high on their exchange. Though it was only earlier that day, she couldn't believe she had worried about what would happen between them. Aiden had proven time and time again he wasn't like any of the guys she had dated before.

No curse was going to keep her from him.

Selene rode the optimistic wave all the way to its end. Eventually, as another hour snailed by and the sky darkened into steel gray, she figured it would be a good idea to patrol the library. They tried to do regular walk-throughs to ensure books were in their proper place, no litter was in the aisles, and other hijinks weren't happening on the massive property.

But like the rest of the day, her walk-through proved uneventful. She tucked in a few chairs into tables and logged off computers, picking up books left in the lounge and filing them back. She was rounding another corner when she paused to look out the oblong window, much of the glass frosted over from the cold.

At first it was a throwaway glance, fleeting and unsuspecting, but she fumbled and stopped again. The flurries were fast and dizzying, hailing down like tiny crystalline bullets, piling onto the heaps of preexisting snow, but through the white haze, a man crawled.

Selene's stomach dropped. She forgot how to breathe. She couldn't look away as the man's body writhed in the snow, his limbs out of sync with each other. He used his arms to propel himself forward, winding them up and clawing at the tufts of snow, pulling himself a couple inches each time. His face was tucked into his chest, his hair dusted by the snow, but as if he sensed her prying eyes, he paused. His body lay flush against the hill and he lifted his chin, his face rising, his sunken eyes on the window.

Officer Gustin.

She jumped back and gasped. The shock of it paralyzed her, gluing her to the spot so that her feet wouldn't move and she could do nothing except gape out the library window. If another second went by or another minute, she had no clue.

The crawling man in the snow—*Officer Gustin*—dragged himself another foot, the effort taking its toll on him as he slowed up, his Gumby legs sprawled out as squiggly noodles lagging behind.

Her body finally thawed from its frozen state and she spun around to go grab her phone. She needed to call 911 and go outside to make sure he was okay. She ran into what first felt like an immovable wall but what turned out to be nothing but Miriam's stocky, feathery sweater–clad build. She stumbled back.

"What are you doing?" Miriam asked, her tone as nasal and pinched as ever.

Selene's brows squashed into one and she said, "I was going for help! Did you look outside? The man crawling in the snow—"

"I don't see anyone," said Miriam dismissively. "What man in the snow?"

"Right *there*!" Selene growled as she pointed a stiff, irritated finger at the window. The tip of her index finger bumped against the cold glass and she gasped as her eyes surveyed the landscape a second time.

Officer Gustin was gone. He was nowhere to be found, like he'd never been there at all. She blinked, mouth agape.

"I don't see anything but snow."

"He…he was there…a second ago…" she trailed off. "Officer Gustin."

"Joking about Officer Gustin's disappearance is a vile thing to do, Selene," scolded Miriam, straightening her horn-rimmed glasses. Her face was twisted up in a distasteful scowl, thin lips bunched. "It's in extremely bad taste and I won't have an employee doing it."

"But…but…he was."

"You're on lockup," said Miriam, skipping over her objection. "Gerri has something last-minute that came up, so it's on you."

"I can't tonight."

"There's nobody else available. It's on you," she repeated.

Selene spent the next second trying to digest her shock. She blinked away from Miriam and turned for another look out the window. More snow. More steely-gray sky. No sign of Officer Gustin. Was she imagining things?

"Don't forget," said Miriam with unfiltered venom, "I'm watching you."

The wind outside whistled its next powerful gust, banging window shutters and knocking over trash bins. At the library front entrance, the glass door slipped beyond a patron's grasp and flew open, the wind blowing off his beanie and shoving him back a step with its force. The bitter cold wasted no time invading the library, traveling into the aisle where Selene stood with Miriam and conjuring a shiver out of her.

Selene glanced back at Miriam. "I made plans after work—"

"For lockup." Miriam pushed the keys into Selene's hand.

Without another word, she shambled off, leaving Selene standing dumbfounded and speechless.

The afternoon faded into a heavy, cumbersome dusk. The last patron wandered past the exit with an armful of books she'd checked out on anthropology. Gerri clocked out. Miriam followed minutes after. The place was dead, no living being except for Selene.

No one would know if she locked up early. She could rush through the closing checklist in under fifteen minutes and make it out in time for her date with Aiden. She popped to her feet from behind the L-shaped desk and got started performing the checklist. She powered off computers and printers in the lab and filed any last book returns.

The massive wall clock, wooden framing surrounding black spade hands, ticked and ticked in the silence. She checked the time it read and then hurried to finish her last walk-through. She only dragged her feet by the window where she was certain she had seen Officer Gustin crawling in the snow.

She even paused and stared long and hard out the now-dark window.

But nothing was out of the ordinary. Nothing met her gaze but a blanket of velvety purple sky kissing steep, powdery snow hills. If Gustin had ever been out there—and by the second she doubting herself more and more—he was long gone. He had gone *somewhere.*

Selene swallowed and moved on, wending down the next stretch of aisles. She passed each one without incident until a loud thump behind her made her stop in her tracks. She whirled around to pinpoint the noise, again seeing nothing out of the ordinary. Innate curiosity urged her to retrace her steps, back up toward the aisles she'd already passed, and double-check them.

Nothing, nothing, nothing—

Something. Selene braked when she came across an aisle with a random fallen book on the floor. She had passed this aisle seconds ago and no book had been out of place. Her stomach quaked, innards knotting.

"Hello?"

Her single, solitary word echoed into the quiet, empty library.

Only silence answered her. She licked her lips and fixed her glasses and then edged forward to pick up the book. She filed it back where it belonged when the lights above cut off. She paused, her heart now a runaway string of heavy beats.

Ears now trained for any sound, she picked up on the pad of footsteps. She gulped and her knees knocked as a cold tremor traveled down her spine.

She wasn't alone anymore.

CHAPTER TWENTY-THREE

The Brimrock Inn was like paradise after a week-and-a-half stay at the Myerses'. Aiden woke to the snow blowing outside of his hotel window and the day's newspaper slipped under his door. He stretched his long arms above his head, a relaxed grin on his face. He hadn't left the Myerses to be malicious, though he had been in a foul mood last night, but he was now sure he made the right decision.

The space was for the best. Hopefully Eddie and his family would understand.

He showered, skipped shaving, and threw on a hoodie, his dark reddish-brown hair still wet as he went downstairs for the free continental breakfast. He parked himself at a table by the large lobby window, sipped from his coffee, savored a buttery danish, and browsed the *Brimrock Tribune* front to back.

After a full night's sleep, the mishap with Selene didn't feel as debilitating. They were both mature. They both liked each other and enjoyed spending time together. It stood to reason that Selene would be willing to see him again…right?

He pondered what to text her with his gaze on the lobby window. The snow wasn't coming down as incessantly as last night, but it showed no signs of stopping altogether either. Warmth lit him from within when he thought back fondly to the night he and Selene had left the Gin House. They had rolled in the snow, laughing at the absurdity and kissing underneath mistletoe.

Yearning gripped him, a deep pull on his heart. He wanted more of that—more of *her*. As insane as it sounded, he couldn't imagine leaving Brimrock without Selene in his life in some capacity.

Several times he typed up a message and then deleted it. He caught the eye of the front desk receptionist and his cheeks blushed pink. The pitying look she gave him said enough; she might not have known his exact situation, but she understood his sitting at the table studying his phone had to do with a woman. She mouthed "good luck" to him and he gave a grateful nod.

In his room, he had more luck. He figured he would lean into his dry, self-depreciating humor and sent her a text he hoped would at least draw a smile out of her. Selene responded within minutes and he breathed in light-headed relief like a man denied air.

They agreed to meet later tonight for dinner. He couldn't stop whistling after that, though he couldn't remember starting. He had never been a whistler, which made it a happy surprise. Another bright sign of how goofy a straight-laced, even-keeled man like him became thanks to Selene.

But it was only morning. The afternoon was a blank space of time he needed to fill. He powered on his laptop and considered looking into that interview with Mayor Grisby or Police Chief Whitaker. Both were a long shot at this point.

Eddie called him. In their years of friendship, it was probably the fourth or fifth time. Eddie hated talking on the phone and Aiden wasn't a big fan either. When it came to communication, they were the typical guys their age. They preferred short texts and the occasional thumbs-up emoji.

"I survived the night," said Aiden upon answering. "No need to send the search party to rescue me."

"No kidding. I bet you're laid up at the Brimrock Inn with your laptop and some coffee."

One thing about Eddie, for all his faults, he knew Aiden well. Better than most. Aiden glanced around his hotel room and then at his laptop in front of him.

"I finished my coffee."

"I feel like a piece of shit."

"That seems like it should be my line," said Aiden, half joking. The other half of him was entirely serious. "I'm the one who had your aunt near tears."

"Yeah, but I'm the one who dragged you out here in the first place. Clearly Brimrock wasn't for you. I thought, yeah, maybe the Christmas cheer stuff would annoy you, but you'd at least like all the food."

"I *did* like all of the food."

"Just hated everything else."

"I didn't hate everything else." Aiden ended his sentence there as he dug through his memory for examples of things he didn't dislike about his time with the Myerses. He came up short. Better to change the subject. "We should probably talk about what we're doing for the fiftieth episode."

Eddie's sigh was audible. "You're really dead set against the Luna thing, huh?"

"Completely."

"She really has you whipped."

"Eddie," said Aiden firmly, "don't talk about Selene like that."

"Alright, sorry. I didn't mean to be disrespectful. It…it was a joke is all. I thought it was a fling, but it seems like you've fallen hard for her."

"Things have gotten complicated fast."

"Is that Aiden speak for you've already sealed the deal? I *knew* it!"

"You can calm down. I, uh, I kind of messed up. It's been a while."

Eddie paused for half a second, comprehension dawning, and then he asked, "Wait, how long's it been since you got laid?"

"I broke up with Delilah a year ago."

"A *year*? Nobody in between? No wonder you're sprung over Selene—I had no idea."

"I usually like to keep it that way. No offense."

"I mean…bro, TMI I know, but don't you at least…you know, play tug of war with Cyclops?"

"I'm human, Eddie. Not an android. But I think we can both agree it's not the same as the real thing," he said with an awkward clear of his throat. He wanted off this subject now. "We're still seeing each other. That's enough details on what's going on."

"Kinda seems obvious that you don't want to do the episode because of Selene. Obviously that's your call and I'm not changing your mind. Just sucks we're on different pages about stuff."

Aiden's jaw hardened and his brow creased. "Eddie, it's a difference of opinion is all. How about we take another day and then regroup about the episode?"

"Yeah, alright. Guess I'll talk to you later."

The delight Aiden had been feeling before the phone call evaporated. He couldn't place his finger on it, but something felt different about their friendship, like it was evolving—or rather *devolving*. A pang of sadness hit him at that prospect.

He and Eddie might have been opposites, but he treasured their friendship. It had worked for years, from the time they were freshmen dorm mates in college to now, hosting their YouTV show as paranormal investigative partners. It saddened him to think they could be growing apart. He didn't exactly have a brother, and the rest of his family wasn't the warmest.

Aiden sighed and decided he needed some air. A trip to the town square would clear his head.

———

The after Christmas sales were in full effect. He stopped by Balford's Books for a gander at their discount section and left carrying a paper bag loaded with buys. He had no clue how he was going to squeeze the books into his suitcase, but he would find a way. Perhaps Selene could use her magic to jam them inside. He had no clue if that were possible. The thought brought him a private smile anyway.

Strolling by the Magic Bean, he caught Noelle's eye. She nodded hello at him and he nodded back, pleased to be on friendly terms with Selene's best friend. Just like Eddie was an unofficial brother type to him, Noelle was important to Selene. It mattered what Noelle thought of him. Besides, though he didn't know her well, he liked how brash she was, holding back no punches.

As he stopped by the town electronics store Gigabyte, his mind turned to the Peter Feinberg case and Officer Gustin's disappearance. On the many flatscreen TV displays, the local news aired a press conference with Mayor Grisby. He spoke

from his executive-sized oak desk with hands clasped, glaring
into the camera—and the viewer at home—with conviction.

"We are working tirelessly to put an end to these heinous
acts around town. I refuse to rest until the culprit is in
custody," he said in his grizzly tone. "Believe me when I say
I do not take these attacks lightly. The tragedy in my family
history doesn't allow me to. Your safety is my top priority."

Even through the TV screen, Aiden sensed the vengeful
vibe coming from Grisby. He had no qualms about making it
known this was a personal matter for him. He wanted revenge
for what happened to his brother. If he believed Luna had
been responsible, then he likely still believed Selene was too.

Aiden left the electronics store, combing over the
evidence in the case. It made no sense to him to suspect
Selene, but what he hypothesized didn't matter to the mayor,
nor did it matter to Brimrock PD. Turning the corner from
Spencer Street onto Pine, he picked out a familiar face
through the floating flurries.

Rory navigated the snow hills like a pro. Either that or she
didn't notice them, too immersed in her head to register the
wintry surroundings. Her scruffy appearance was no surprise,
chestnut hair shoved into her beanie and her face pink and
moist not from the cold but from tears. She tugged on her
tweed coat and trudged on, headed for what was the opposite
direction of home.

Normally, Aiden hated comforting people in distress. He
never knew what to say. His sarcasm got him into trouble and
cliché condolences always felt insincere and awkward. The
person tended to walk away more upset after his attempts, so
he stopped altogether.

But Rory was Eddie's cousin, which automatically indoc-
trinated her into Aiden's short list of people to care about. He

couldn't leave without at least checking up on her. Even if he wasn't her favorite person.

"Out for an afternoon stroll? There's a lot of good sales today." He came up on her left at a crosswalk.

Rory fell several steps back as though he had knocked into her. Her pale face contorted into an emotion Aiden couldn't place, but it wasn't a positive one. It was a mix of what felt like outrage and resentment, like she couldn't believe he would come up to her and start a conversation.

"I'm sorry," he apologized straightaway. "I...I just wanted to make sure you were—"

"I need alone time. Away from you—away from my mother—away from everyone! What's so hard to understand about that?"

Before he could get another word in edgewise, she was gone. She scurried off into the crosswalk and snow flurries. He remained where he was, digesting yet another odd interaction with Rory.

Then the gears in his brain squeaked to life, suddenly oiled enough to crank up and start turning. He jumped back to his first night in Brimrock, meeting the Myerses at the Mulberry. He had met Selene that evening, their infamous URide debacle still worthy of a laugh. At the steakhouse, he had spent half his time silent at the Myerses' table and the other half at Selene's, trying to inexplicably brighten her mood after being stood up.

Rory had been there. She had left early. It meant nothing, of course, but next his thoughts drifted to the night he discovered Selene was a witch. He had been coerced into the Myerses' annual skating fun. The festive family had enjoyed themselves. Except for Rory. She was on the sidelines almost the entire time.

Now that he thought about it, he couldn't remember if she

was still around when he left the rink. Officer Gustin had disappeared that night. But why would Rory be distraught if she were the one who attacked Peter?

"Guilt," Aiden mumbled to himself. The December wind smacked him in the face and he took the hint it was time to get off the street.

The circumstances surrounding how Peter was found *were* strange. He had been discovered inside his apartment, the door wide open as though the perpetrator fled shortly after. There were no signs of a break in, which meant Peter likely let whoever it was in by choice. He knew the person.

But how would Rory have harmed him? He was discovered comatose, suffering from extreme dehydration, his body shriveled-up. Rory was a normal twenty something woman—or was she?

He had thought Selene was your average woman before she saved him from being mowed down by an out-of-control car. She was a witch.

"Can't be," he muttered a block away from the Brimrock Inn.

Yet, his thoughts continued to ramble. He combed over every interaction he had had with Rory over the past two weeks, trying to shake the suspicion filling him up to the brim, but finding it harder and harder.

———

The streetlights twinkled on, the sky a vast purple sea, when Aiden headed out for his date with Selene. She had asked him to meet her at her house at six o'clock. Being an early man, he planned to show a quarter to the hour. He couldn't land a reservation at the Mulberry on such short notice, but he had found a kitsch little sushi spot called the Slippery Mermaid he hoped Selene would like.

His watch confirmed it was 5:43 p.m. as the URide pulled up outside 1221 Gifford Lane. The towering three-story gothic home looked ominous with all of the lights off, but Aiden figured Selene had a couple candles going. She had mentioned she preferred keeping things dim. He knocked and waited and then waited some more. He knocked a second time, standing back with his hands in his coat pockets, glancing up at the second-story window he knew to be Selene's.

The window was blacked out. From inside Yukie yipped her tiny little bark, but no pad of Selene's feet as she approached the door. Could she still be at work?

Aiden sent a text, ducking further under the porch covering to escape the errant flurries. Selene was a punctual person herself. It seemed like she would be the type to text him if she were running late. When she didn't answer after five minutes, he pulled up her number on his contact list and called her. No answer, straight to voice mail.

Worry congealed in his stomach, heavy and thick. He swallowed uncertainly and then took another look around at the ghost quiet, pitch dark home. He wasn't a guy who operated off of gut feelings often, preferring sound reason and facts, but something felt wrong about the situation. *Something* he couldn't articulate if he tried.

Aiden gave up on scoping out her house, waiting on the porch for her to answer. She wasn't home. He knew that now, but it only led to the mystery of where else she could be. A numbing chill rippled through his body as he walked back onto the sidewalk and weighed his options. He had to find out if Selene was okay. He couldn't stand by and passively wait it out.

"The library," he whispered and then he set off into the dark snow, pulling up his URide app on a hope and a prayer he could land another car. He might have been overreacting, but he had to know either way. If there was even a sliver of a chance Selene needed him, he would be there.

CHAPTER TWENTY-FOUR

"**A**nyone there?" Selene asked into the silence.

Only the silence answered her. She blinked and straightened her glasses, unsure what else to do standing in the middle of the deserted aisle. The knocked-down book lay at her feet, ironically it was a deluxe edition of *Grimm's Fairy Tales*. It was impossible to feel like she wasn't in some twisted sort of tale alone in a dark and abandoned library, hearing noises and picking up mysterious books.

Selene bent down and plucked the copy off the carpet floor. The hefty book weighed enough to be a weapon on its own, bound by rich bloodred leather and embossed by gold detailing. She returned it to its original spot, sliding the thick book back onto the shelf. The padding started up again. It couldn't have been more than two or three aisles away.

She considered running for it. If she pelted down the aisles toward the front, snatched her things up and made it to the door, she could regroup outside. Whatever it was wandering the barren halls of the library, it wasn't friendly. He or she—*or it*—didn't want to say hello and have a chat. The individual was clearly trying to spook her…

Unlike the other times, the padding didn't slow down. The soft footfalls continued, growing closer, passing another aisle, coming up on hers. Selene couldn't describe what washed over her standing there listening to the mystery figure draw nearer, but she didn't run away. She turned around and faced the end the footsteps were coming from and stared at the blank space where they'd eventually appear.

The strange feeling was rooted in intuition. She sensed that whoever this was and whatever they wanted was inevitable. She couldn't flee them. She was supposed to stand her ground and confront them. Her fingers enclosed around Luna's necklace as they had a dozen and one times since she began wearing it, the crystal pendant smooth and warm under her touch. Just like the other times she had grabbed it out of habit or nervous tic, it soothed her. It almost felt like a protective layer, like somehow it would see her through whatever was about to happen.

"I can hear you," said Selene.

In the vast emptiness of the Brimrock library, her voice echoed. The footsteps stopped. Selene's temper snapped and she marched forward to round the corner herself. If the person didn't want to come over and reveal themself—

A stream of red light flew by her right ear, narrowly missing her by less than a centimeter, but still so close and hot that the tip was singed. The scalding red light soared past her from behind and blasted a hole in the wall where she would've been in the next second. Selene tossed herself toward the ground, landing sideways with a thump, the tip of her ear tingling. What the hell was that?

Selene rolled onto her back in time to notice the figure's shadow expanding on the carpet. The padded steps returned, slow and unhurried, like a lazy stroll through the park. Her eyes stayed on the shadow, watching it lengthen, gathering her wits after what had just happened.

Someone had shot *something* at her. It was a blast of powerful heat. It punctured a hole into the wall, smoke sizzling out of the giant crater. The only thing that popped into her head was molten hot magma, but that was absurd. Then again, she said herself nothing was impossible.

No longer feeling bold and confrontational, Selene scrambled to her feet and took off running. The mystery figure must've anticipated this, because the ghost-quiet library filled with the sound of laughter. The shrieks were hideous and bone-chilling, the deep cackle reminding her of the Wicked Witch of the West.

That made her Dorothy—or maybe Glinda?

Selene had no time to ponder such literary quandaries as her legs pumped faster. The witchlike laughter had started off as a lone cackle, but had grown into an all-encompassing, inescapable sound that invaded every corner of the library, occupying its dark spaces. It was difficult to tell where it was coming from, if it was an aisle away or five.

She swung around the corner into the next aisle, narrowly missing what was a second blast. The sparkling red light streaked through the air and blew chunks off the wooden shelf it struck. She paused only for a split second with bulging eyes as the wooden shelf splintered open, swaying unsteadily due to its injury and the weight of books it carried.

Her heart raced and her mind reeled, horror encapsulating her head to toe. Who, or what, could burn holes through walls and blow chunks off of wood? She could only levitate a book or two on most days...

In a few more quick strides, Selene reached the end of the aisle and cut across the lounge area. Without the lights on, shadows swept over the furniture, making it that much more difficult to navigate in a frenzy. Twice she bumped into an armchair or knocked over an end table. The third time she tripped over a large area rug Miriam had insisted buying with last year's annual budget.

She crashed face-first, her chin hitting the ground hard. Her glasses slipped off, but she snatched them up and shoved them back on. The evil cackling laughter followed her, looming in the dark. The outline of the mystery woman emerged through the shadows, now a definitive presence mere feet away. She crawled behind the armchair on her left for cover.

The second Selene got up and ran, the mystery woman was going to send another hot blast in her direction. She'd burn a hole right through her if she had the chance. Sweaty, shaky, and out of breath, Selene willed herself to calm down enough to concentrate.

Maybe a taste of her own medicine was what the mystery woman needed.

She duck-walked to the next armchair as soundlessly as possible, staying low, and then poked her head around. Though still half shrouded in shadows, the mystery woman was in better view. At least her back was. She wore a heavy navy overcoat, dusted by snowflakes, and she had long white hair.

Sparing no time to ponder her identity, Selene held up her hands and motioned at the end table the woman had passed by. It wobbled side to side before listening and floating off the ground. Into the air the table climbed and with another aggressive gesture from Selene's hands, it went flying toward her. The woman sensed its presence and spun around. She blasted the table in half, shooting the sparkly red light from her palms, her pale and flushed face finally in view.

Selene gasped and fell backward. She questioned what

she was seeing. If she was smack-dab in the middle of a nightmare that felt too real.

Priscilla Myers grinned watching the end table crack into two. Only she didn't look like the Priscilla Myers Selene was used to seeing out and about in Brimrock. She had aged by at least fifty years, giving her the appearance of a woman double her age. Her eyes were mad and ringed with dark circles, the rest of her face haggard. Her once plump cheeks were gone, hollowed out by age, and when she grinned, she showed off decaying teeth and gray gums. The streak of long white hair Selene had seen from behind was actually stringy and threadbare, so thin her scalp peeked out from underneath. She was hideous.

Her cold gaze lingered on Selene. "Did you think you could stop me with a little table? Is that your best effort, Selene?"

"I...I don't understand," Selene said in a hushed tone. Nothing made sense. Again, she questioned if she were dreaming.

"What don't you understand, you stupid girl?"

Selene scooted back. Mrs. Myers drifted forward. Her body, even though cloaked by her overcoat, was shrunken too. Rather than the chubbier build she usually had, she looked almost frail, like the coat was a disguise to hide her true size. Her hands hung at her sides, pointy claws with liver spots and varicose veins.

"Who are you?"

"You know exactly who I am. You know exactly what I am."

"I have no clue." Selene pushed herself onto her feet, feeling unsteady and dizzy.

Two lounge chairs and another table lamp separated them. It didn't feel like much.

Mrs. Myers shrieked another ugly laugh. It rang through the silent library. "You mean to tell me your mother never told you? I knew she was weak, but to not even tell her own daughter—*pathetic*!"

"Tell me what?" Selene snapped. "What's going on?"

"Did you really think you and your green witch gal pal are the only ones in Brimrock who can whip up some magic?" Mrs. Myers mocked, clapping her gnarled clawlike hands together. "What if I told you I'm stronger than you both? I'm stronger than your weak mother. I'm stronger than your traitorous grandmother, Luna."

"You're…a witch?"

Mrs. Myers tossed her head back for a wild shriek of laughter, the blue-green veins in her neck thick. "No, you stupid girl, I'm no regular witch. I'm much more than that. I don't levitate a little book or two and call that magic. I have abilities you could never even come close to possessing yourself. I have the power to end life—to suck the life force from living beings like it's nothing."

"Like a succubus?" Selene blurted out the word without thinking. Mrs. Myers hissed in offense and she jumped another wide step back. "You're the one who attacked Peter —you drained his energy and now he's in a coma. You've basically killed him!"

"Am I supposed to feel bad? After what he's done to Rory? You might not realize this because yours was pathetic, but a mother will do anything to protect her child."

Selene backed away some more, putting another leather armchair between them. She snuck a subtle glance beyond Mrs. Myers, to the other end of the library where the front exit was. Even from where she stood, she could see the double glass doors and the mounds of snow against the inky night's backdrop. She needed to keep her talking, distract her, and then run like hell.

"You attacked Peter because he broke up with Rory? Are you trying to frame me too?"

"*You* were the last straw," snarled Mrs. Myers. Loathing darkened her tone and shone in her eyes as a fanatical gleam. "It had to be you. He had to choose you of all the women in town. But I shouldn't say I'm surprised—you are Luna's granddaughter, after all."

"What does Luna have to do with all of this? You keep mentioning her. Clearly you have it out for Blackstones. I've never done anything to you. Is this beef from the past?"

"Luna is a conniving, evil, traitorous bitch who got what she deserved!"

"You call my grandma an evil bitch, but you're the one attacking people in town. How many of the men who've disappeared over the years are because of you? You killed them and then you let everyone think it was Luna and the rest of my family!" Selene shouted back, fingers bunching into fists. Her fear disappeared as her temper roared in. She was still dizzy, still shaky and unsteady on her feet, but now hot and irrational. She was *tired* of the bullshit.

Mrs. Myers flocked toward her like a vulture descending on its prey. Though gaunt and frail, she was frightening, her haggard face twisted up and claw hands raised. "Don't you dare speak to me like that, stupid girl! Who do you think you are? I've let you live—I let your coward of a mother live for years after what Luna did to me! After what she took!"

"This can't be about a man," Selene argued. "You're mad because Luna stole a guy from you?"

"She stole my life!" Mrs. Myers screeched. The blue-green veins in her neck protruded so far out they looked fit to burst. "She stole my happy ending, so I stole hers—and the rest of yours too!"

For a strange reason Selene couldn't pinpoint, that admission garnered the instant prick of tears in her eyes. Angry tears that glistened from behind her bold-framed glasses. Her entire life she'd lived with the mysterious curse hanging over her head, denied any explanation from Mom, shushed whenever she asked, living day in and day out knowing she would never truly be happy.

She could never leave Brimrock, never seek adventure, never fall in love. It was all because of Priscilla Myers, a haggard succubus who hated her guts from before she was even born.

"So," said Selene, swallowing down emotion, "what do you want now that you've taken everything? Are you here to kill me? Why now? Why not kill me any other day?"

"Because it was so much sweeter watching you suffer every day of your life."

"And now?"

"Things have gotten all messy," replied Mrs. Myers with a gray, gummy smile. "It started off good, with you being the prime suspect for Peter's attack, but then it got complicated. Gustin was sniffing around Rory a little too much. I couldn't have him suspecting her."

"What did you do to him?" The muscles in Selene's stomach contracted as she tensed up, almost afraid to hear the answer.

"I did what I always do. I sucked him dry—or tried to, but he got away. That's when I knew I had to do something. I had to clean up this mess before Marc started poking around even more."

"And, what, find out that it was *you* who killed his brother?"

"Obviously!"

Selene backed up again with a couple more steps. She had surveyed the area while talking to Mrs. Myers and had decided that the heavy brass table lamp was her best bet. If she could lull the evil hag into a false, superior sense of security, then she could use her lunar magic and strike.

"I still don't understand," said Selene in feigned confusion, "if you've survived off of draining the energy from others for so long, how has no one noticed? How do you even change your appearance?"

"That hasn't been an issue. Not when I'm married to a man I can feed off of whenever I like—just enough to keep me going."

"And the other men in town who've disappeared or died of mysterious causes?"

"Sometimes I like a big snack," she joked darkly. Her pointy fingers brushed straggly white strands over her shoulder as she advanced some more. "This is my true form. It's what I become when I feed. It might not be pretty, but being as old as I am can't all be perks."

Selene forced her features to remain blank, giving nothing away. Her temper coursed adrenaline through her veins and the pulse in her neck throbbed nonstop. She couldn't quiet how her heart pounded in her ears, but for the time being, she learned to ignore it and pay attention to the powerful succubus in front of her.

"Luna and I dueled that night. We both disappeared as far as the police and media were concerned. I was no longer Aurora," she explained bitterly, "not after what she did to me. I was on the brink of death. It took years for me to nurse myself back. You'd be amazed to discover what healing work and beauty spells can do for you. I returned to Brimrock knowing I deserved a second chance. I came back as Priscilla, the sweet woman I knew the town would love. I met a nice man in Jake—the kind of nice man I thought John was—and he married me. We adopted two beautiful little girls and lived the life I've always deserved. I've been happy."

Selene held Mrs. Myers's cold gaze, standing still as she gave a quick flick of her wrist. The brass lamp on a table rose up and jetted toward Mrs. Myers from behind. It rammed into her spine with brute force and knocked her over. Selene didn't waste another second. She bolted across the library, sprinting past study tables and the computer lab.

The large L-shaped desk curved into view as she dashed for the exit. She outstretched her arm to untwist the locks on the double glass doors, but only managed one lock before a major crash reverberated through the library. It sounded like a window breaking, though she couldn't be sure what caused the glass smashing. She dove behind the L-shaped desk as a precaution.

Mrs. Myers was screaming somewhere in the dark. Her witchy cackle had gone nowhere. "Was that you making all that big, bad noise? Come out, you stupid girl, and let's settle this face to face!"

CHAPTER TWENTY-FIVE

N o URide was available. Aiden ran as fast as he could in the snow, which turned out to be more of a light jog. The evening had turned dark, a rolling canvas of white meets black. The snow twinkled like diamonds. The sky blanketed over him like lush velvet. He came up to the next street corner and smashed a finger into the cross button, his breathing off rhythm.

Every half a block he had checked his phone for an update from either Selene or the URide app. Neither came. Selene had yet to return his texts or calls. The URide still showed a wait time, which had now increased from thirty minutes to forty.

The little digital man blinked, alerting him to his time to go. He entered traffic, trotting into the crosswalk. He was halfway to the other side when out of nowhere, a car horn trumpeted and nearly startled him off his feet. Involuntary flashbacks to the night he had almost gotten run over rocked him, but it passed as soon as his eyes fell on the car that had honked at him.

Or rather, *van*.

Eddie braked at the red light and slammed his palm into the horn on his steering wheel. Ghost listened, blaring his horn at Aiden, capturing his wide-eyed attention. Eddie stuck his head out the window and shouted, "Bro, what the hell? What are you doing running around town at night in the snow? Get in! I'll drop you off at your hotel."

Aiden's deep, relieved exhale deflated him. He didn't need to think about it. He jogged up to the passenger side of the van and hopped in. For a fleeting second, things between him and Eddie felt like old times. They were filming an episode for their show, riding off to dive headfirst into an investigation. The good ol' days.

"You've been off since we got to Brimrock," said Eddie with a shake of his head. The light flashed green and he pressed the gas. "First the Selene stuff. Then that blowup you had with my aunt. Now I find you going for a run in twenty-degree weather."

"This is more Selene stuff," Aiden interrupted. He slicked back his once neatly combed hair and caught his breath. "I need you to drive me to the library."

"The library? What—?"

"Don't ask. I can't explain. I'm looking for Selene."

"How many times do I have to tell you—you know what, never mind. I'm gonna stop judging. You like Selene. That's a thing now, so I'll have to learn to accept it."

Aiden half listened as Eddie rambled. For as insensitive and crass as he could be, Eddie hated when there was conflict. He usually buckled and tried to bridge whatever gap existed. It was to be expected he would attempt to smooth over anything he had said about Selene in order to keep the peace, but Aiden was more interested in staring out the passenger-side window.

They drove by the Magic Bean among other shops.

Inside, Noelle and what looked like Isabelle Halsey cleaned up post-closing.

"Stop the van!"

"For what?" Eddie tightened his clutch on the steering wheel.

"Just stop for a second!"

Aiden flew from the curb into the eccentric coffee shop. The door sprang open and both Noelle and Isabelle looked up with question marks on their faces.

"Have you seen Selene?" he asked Noelle.

"Not since this morning. Why are you so sweaty?"

"She was supposed to meet me for a dinner date. That was over an hour ago," he said. He checked his phone for the umpteenth time, finding no new notifications. "She hasn't shown up. No calls. No texts."

"Did you go by her house?"

"That was where I was picking her up from."

"That's not like Selene," said Noelle. Her gaze skirted up to the black cat wall clock. "She's usually off work at five, but maybe she's still at the library."

"I was headed there now. Want to come along?"

Noelle's meticulously filled-in brows rose.

Aiden elaborated. "I...I can't explain why, but I have a bad feeling. I'm the last guy to say something like that, but I do. It'd be nice to have some...assistance."

Noelle seemed to understand what he was implying. She yanked off her apron and passed her mop to Isabelle, who rolled her eyes.

As they piled inside the van, Noelle mumbled to him, "I hope you know the best I can do as a green witch is whip somebody up a remedy for their cold."

"Any little bit helps," said Aiden. He slid shut the van door and they were off.

From the outside the library looked deserted. The parking lot was empty and the windows were oblong black glass. Eddie shifted gears into park and turned for a look at the other two.

"This place is dead. Are you sure—?"

"Let's get out and take a closer look," said Aiden, unclicking his seat belt.

Noelle joined him without hesitation. Only Eddie hung back and huffed out a reluctant sigh. He sped up toward them from the rear as they crossed the front lawn frozen over with snow. Aiden leapt up the stacked stone steps two at a time, Noelle second.

"The door's locked." Aiden pulled on the handles twice and then cupped a hand against the glass to peer inside.

"There's a back entrance," said Noelle. "Let's try that one. I usually go in through there whenever I've snuck in. The lock's easier to pick."

Aiden wanted to ask why Noelle was sneaking into the library in the first place, but reserved the question for another time. Noelle led them to the back of the library, where there was a lone door that looked like an emergency exit.

"The alarm doesn't set off on this door. Miriam hasn't gotten it fixed yet," she said. She reached up to her short crop of hair and withdrew a silver crescent moon pin. "It looks like this Yule gift from Selene will come in handy. Give me a second, I've done it before, but it takes a while."

Both Aiden and Eddie gave Noelle the space she needed to work the lock. She slipped the pin's fine tip into the door's keyhole and twisted it in varying patterns. The lock clicked and clicked, the handle jerking and jiggling, but it wouldn't budge.

"We need to call the cops," said Eddie. "Officer Nunn can come check out the premises for us."

"No cops." Aiden didn't bother elaborating further. Any police involvement would spell disaster for Selene and her secret identity as a witch.

In the otherwise still evening air, a huge crash resounded from inside followed by shrieks. Aiden's pulse spiked, a ball of panic exploding in his chest. He ran over to the trash bin and lifted it above his head, yelling, "Get out of the way! I'm going to break this glass!"

He charged at the oblong window off to the left and threw the trash bin with a throaty grunt. The bin launched at the glass, shattering it into a thousand pieces. He carefully kicked out the remaining shards in the window and then climbed through. Eddie and Noelle hesitated for half a second before following. Shadows engulfed the library without any ceiling lights. Except at the far opposite end, where the lighting near the front L-shaped desk was still on. Was that where Selene was?

Any aftermath of the crash went unheard as he listened for any other sounds. As a string of three wanderers, he, Eddie, and Noelle crept along a line of bookshelves. Once at the edge, Aiden poked his head out to survey what he could of the library.

He choked on his own intake of breath.

An older woman floated through the matrix of long study tables and headed in his direction. Her face was sunken in to the point it looked like a skull with sparse white hair as its frame. Her nasty grin ate up half her face, teeth rotten and clenched. But it was when his eyes met hers that he recognized who she was.

He tottered backward and bumped into Eddie and Noelle. Eddie grabbed him by the shoulders to steady him, though the shock was too much, jolting him to the core. He whirled around and twisted hands into the lapel of Eddie's coat, struggling to describe what he had seen, but knowing it was urgent for him to explain before Eddie saw it for himself.

"Your aunt. She's…she's here."

"Aunt Priscilla? That makes no sense—"

"Something's wrong with her."

"Is she hurt?"

"Who's there?" screeched the old woman from the rows of study tables. She navigated through them, cutting the space from her to them down by a fourth. "You smashed a window, which tells me you want to see me. Go on and come over. I'd love to say hello."

The most grotesque sound Aiden had ever heard rang through the library halls, Mrs. Myers's laugh an ugly, witchy cackle. The hairs on the back of Aiden's neck shot up stiff from root to end. He found he couldn't move listening to the foreboding sound, horrified to his core as his brain malfunctioned trying to make sense of everything.

Why was Mrs. Myers in the library? What had happened to her face? Where was Selene?

"I know it's you, Aiden!" Mrs. Myers cried out. "I can sense your presence—come out now. Tell Auntie Priscilla what's wrong." She cackled all over again, louder and uglier than before.

Eddie pushed Aiden's hands off him and brushed past him for a look. Aiden tried to stop him, but it was too late. Eddie got a glimpse of his aunt from around the corner of the book aisle just like Aiden had. His body locked up as rigid as a wooden plank and the color drained from his tan complexion. Slowly, he shook his head side to side.

"No…no…no…" he repeated.

"We have to find somewhere to hide."

Aiden snatched Eddie by the collar of his coat and dragged him back the way they had come. Noelle chanced a peek for herself, clapped hands over her mouth to subdue a squeal, and then scurried in Aiden and Eddie's wake. They crouched beneath a Sixteenth Century World History display they crossed.

"No…" Eddie whispered, his shock flattening his features. "No…that can't be…"

"She looks like a hag," whispered Noelle and then she added, "Sorry, Eddie. No offense."

"What is she? A witch too?"

That snapped Eddie out of his trance. "Too? Who's the first? Luna? Selene? Is this why you've been—"

"Shhhhh," Noelle hushed. She pressed a finger to her lips and fished into the front pouch of her overalls with her other hand. "I might have some magic chalk—it's charmed so that we can use it for rituals or casting spells. We might be able to do a protection spell."

"A protection, *what*?" Eddie stared at them dumbly.

"No time to explain." Aiden peeked over the rim of the glass display case for a look at where Mrs. Myers was. She was nowhere in the vicinity and she had gone quiet. Somehow that was spookier. "We have to find Selene."

"I'm right here," came a fourth voice.

Noelle tipped over out of her squat position. Eddie's mouth hung open wider, brows squished. Aiden had no discernible reaction on the outside, but on the inside, his stomach dropped. The bottom caved in and the nervous emptiness had him second-guessing if he were seeing things. He surveyed her as though she were a hologram.

There she was, crouching beside them. She had crawled up from the rear and joined them without any of them noticing. She had seen better days. Her curls had fallen out of a loose braid and she had scrapes on her cheek and chin, glasses themselves cracked.

What had Mrs. Myers done to her? He wanted to reach for her, envelop her in his embrace, but he resisted, remembering where they were.

"Selene," breathed Noelle. "What the fudge is going on?"

"Mrs. Myers attacked Peter," answered Selene in a low, cautious tone. "She's behind what happened to Gustin too. She's been behind everything—all the way back to Grisby."

"No way," Eddie disagreed with a fervent shake of his head. "This has to be some kinda joke."

"What is she?" Noelle asked.

"She's…she's some kind of enchantress, like a succubus. I'll explain more later, but she shoots this red light from her hands and it burns through walls. I'm just happy to still have all of my limbs."

"We can make a break for the window," Noelle said.

"No, she's expecting that. She's probably by the broken window." Being the tallest, Aiden used his height for a look beyond the display case. She had disappeared, lurking somewhere in the many shadows. "We should go for the front exit."

"I already tried that. She almost blasted my arm off," said Selene.

"We have to do something," said Noelle in an impatient whisper. "The longer we stay here arguing about it, the more time she has to find us."

Eddie rubbed hands over his face. "This is batshit crazy."

"Shhhh," Noelle shushed.

"I'll go first," said Selene. "Lure her toward the front. You guys get out by the back."

"What sense does that make? We're here to rescue you," Noelle argued back.

"We all make a break for it or none of us do," said Aiden sternly.

Another bout of menacing cackles cut their back and forth short. Their eyes traveled between each other's faces as the cold, callous cackling played on a seeming continuous loop. Then, among the taunting laughter, came the gradual footsteps, one after the other, closer and closer…

"We don't have a choice," said Selene in exasperation. "We have to run for it. Again."

"Which way?"

"The broken window." Selene's fingers curled around her necklace out of nervous habit and she closed her eyes as if to prepare herself.

It was then Aiden noticed the faint silver glow under her fingers. He opened his mouth to say something, but Noelle whispered "Go!" and they were off. Eddie lagged behind, but Aiden fisted the front of his coat and dragged him along.

They sprinted through the maze of historical display cases with eyes set on the distant broken window. The four made it to the halfway point before a fiery red light jetted toward them and blew a huge hole in the ground, knocking them backward, off their feet.

The display cases shattered and rained glass on them. Aiden shielded himself with one arm over his head and crawled over to the others. Eddie had rammed straight into a display case, the glass smashed in. Blood trickled down the side of his face and he shook his head in clear disorientation. Selene and Noelle were luckier, shoved down onto their knees, though scraped up by flying shards.

From around the corner, Mrs. Myers strolled into view. Her haggard features were so twisted up that she gave new meaning to the term "shell of your former self." She stopped in front of them and put veiny, pointy hands on her hips.

"Are you ready to stop playing games?" she asked in a sickening version of her usual sweet simper. "Eddie, get out of here. You shouldn't be here for this."

"Aunt Priscilla," Eddie panted. His dizziness hadn't worn off from his nasty tumble, but he pushed himself to his feet anyway. "What's happened to you?"

"Sweetie, it's none of your concern. Now go."

"But—"

"I said *GO!*" she shrieked and they each flinched.

Confusion clouded in Aiden's brain as he watched Eddie's fighting spirit evaporate into nothing. He nodded, tossing a throwaway glance at the other three, and then he slunk off. *He left them.*

Aiden didn't understand. He and Eddie had been friends since they were eighteen. They had lived together, worked together, and spent countless hours together bonding. They had braved some of the country's spookiest haunted mansions and deserted wastelands and not once had they left the other. They always had each other's back, but now…

Eddie disappeared into the shadows. The hope among Aiden and the other two sank as they turned their attention back onto Mrs. Myers. She was grinning nastily, the shine in her gaze one of a mad person.

"I've never had three people to feed off of," she snickered. She paused and unscrewed her jaw like a snake before devouring a rat, revealing a long and revolting tongue she must have used to suck energy. "What a treat for me this will be."

"If you think you're feeding off anyone, you're as crazy as you are ugly." Noelle held her chin aloft despite the fact that the rest of her body trembled.

"It sounds like you want to be first, which is fine with me. I've never liked the Bankses. Your aunt is incompetent and your mother was too. None of you are talented witches, which is why you hide behind being weird," said Mrs. Myers. She held her hands out, palm side up, and they glowed red as if heating up. "I can't say I feel too bad about finishing you off. It's what you deserve."

A double dose of fiery red light formed, ready to blast their way, but as she raised her hands higher for a shot, Eddie sprang from the darkness and dropped a hard elbow into Mrs. Myers's hollow jaw. She wailed and half twisted to redirect her aim. One hand blasted the floor by mistake and the other sent a streak of red light right at—

"EDDIE!" Aiden howled, scrambling to his feet.

But he was too late.

The burst of red light struck Eddie across his chest and he flew back, colliding with a display case and then toppling over.

Selene and Noelle sprang into action beside Aiden. The three rushed to Eddie's side while Mrs. Myers hung back. For once the cruelty had slipped off her face and her hideous features untwisted themselves. She hadn't meant to strike Eddie.

"He…he caught me off guard. I'd never hurt my nephew," she sobbed. The shock did nothing to make her voice any less shrewd and harsh on the ears. "I didn't mean to hurt him. He should've left like I asked him to!"

Aiden turned Eddie over onto his back and cringed at the charred crater on his shoulder, wisps of heat emanating from the wound. She had burned a hole right through his skin. His head rolled from side to side and a gurgled groan of pain left his lips.

"Stay still," Aiden urged. "Noelle, do you think you can heal him?"

"I can try. But I need some light."

"I'll lift him—we can bring him outside."

"Nobody goes anywhere!" shrieked Mrs. Myers.

Aiden clenched his teeth. "Your nephew—"

"Shouldn't have tried to play the hero!" she snapped, her guilt subsiding. Her cold rage had returned, as though she had insanely convinced herself what she did was justified. "He chose his fate. Now it's time you all meet yours."

Selene, who had largely been quiet, rose up to her feet. She pushed her glasses back onto her face and narrowed her eyes into a challenging glare.

"This is between *our* families. Leave the others out of this."

"You stupid girl, you don't tell me what to do."

"Shut up!" Selene yelled. "I'm sick of your threats!"

Mrs. Myers's top lip curved. "Then what are you going to do about it?"

The sinking sensation known as dread filled Aiden's stomach. "Selene, what are you—?"

But it seemed like Selene didn't hear him. Her focus was solely on the hag threatening their lives. Though her body was trembling, when she spoke she did so with a determined bravado. "The only thing that's left to do. It's time to end this now."

CHAPTER TWENTY-SIX

Every hair on Selene's body snapped upright, shooting up on their ends. Her heart slammed against her ribcage, each harsh beat an echo in her ears. She swallowed so thickly it was an audible gulp, but thankfully, Mrs. Myers's horrid cackle drowned out the sound. On the outside, she might've looked stoic, standing her ground against some unspeakably powerful succubus type witch.

But on the inside? She redefined what it meant to be a hot mess.

She would've fainted if Aiden, Noelle, and Eddie's lives weren't on the line. The thing was, despite the fear and uncertainty which threatened to cripple her, she had to be strong. It was up to her to defeat Mrs. Myers. Whatever the truth was about the past, it boiled down to bad blood between Luna and Mrs. Myers, which made it Selene's problem too.

Now if she could only figure out how to defeat a powerful succubus on a fiery, energy-sucking rampage...

"So," said Mrs. Myers in a sickening sweet hiss, "why

don't you do it then? End me here and now—that's if you're stupid enough to think you can."

"First things first, you let the other three go."

Mrs. Myers interpreted the request as a joke. She laughed and said, "You have some gall making demands. Tonight is your undoing and your idiot friends won't be spared."

"They have nothing to do with this! They go free."

"I'll tell you what? Compromise. We'll lock them away for safe keeping." The fanatical glint in her gaze flashed brighter, accompanied by an even crazier grin. She lifted her wizened hands and pointed one clawlike finger toward the back office behind the L-shaped desk. "Winners keepers. Losers weepers."

"What does that mean?"

"Winner decides what to do with them. GET UP!"

Aiden and Noelle winced at Mrs. Myers's sudden screech. She kicked the side of a shattered display case for emphasis. Neither said a word or made a move to get up as directed. They remained crouched around a half-conscious and groaning Eddie. Selene took another step between them and Mrs. Myers.

Her first reaction was to once again insist they go free, but then another possibility floated to mind. If Aiden, Noelle, and Eddie were locked in the back office, they would be safe. They would be out of harm's way. It would open the ground floor for Selene to find out how to beat Mrs. Myers at her own game. She might not have been as all-powerful as Mrs. Myers, but she had an advantage in her disadvantage. For as weak as she was in comparison, she was also underestimated. Was there a way to use that against Mrs. Myers?

"Fine," she bit out, teeth gritted. "They get locked in the office. Then it's me and you."

"Stupid girl." Mrs. Myers cackled at Selene's perceived

foolishness, letting her shrill tone ring in the quiet library. She loved rubbing in her superiority, basking in how inferior Selene and the others were. She demonstrated it again a second later as she shot a stream of red light at an empty space five feet away from where Aiden and Noelle knelt beside Eddie.

"Stop!" screamed Selene.

"Get going! Toward the back office—NOW!"

Her flaming hot threat was enough to get them moving. Aiden hooked an arm around Eddie and hoisted him upward into a slump against his side. Noelle glared at Mrs. Myers before she joined Eddie's other side and started for the back office with the kind of stilted movements of someone being held at gunpoint.

Selene's chin trembled watching her friends go. She felt helpless and afraid. She felt angry and uncertain. But probably most of all, she felt determined. She refused to give up. Failure was not an option.

Mrs. Myers blasted more warning shots every few footsteps, hurrying Aiden and the others along. She laughed each time as if their fear was her entertainment. When they reached the back office, Mrs. Myers turned to Selene. Her hollowed out cheeks sharpened with her wide grin, black-rimmed eyes popping from her sockets.

"Well? Be useful and barricade them inside!"

Selene swallowed against the lump in her throat and held out her hands. Her concentration was off, brain much too cluttered to harness her full lunar ability. The cabinet next to the door teetered left and then right as though rocked by an earthquake and not her influence.

From the sidelines, Mrs. Myers gave a pompous snort. The curl of her grin broadened and she tapped an impatient foot. Her mockery didn't help Selene and that was probably her intent —to get into her head and make her feel even more inferior than she already did.

Selene's expression tightened as she inhaled a deeper breath. She urged herself to shut out any distractions, ignoring her surroundings and focusing only on the heavy metal filing cabinet. For its part, the filing cabinet swayed side to side. At one point it almost tipped over before finally it lifted half a foot off the ground and dropped down in front of the door.

No longer supporting its weight, Selene's posture sagged and her breath hitched. Aside from Aiden, the filing cabinet was the heaviest object she had ever levitated. It might not have seemed like much facing a deadly adversary like Mrs. Myers, but it sent an encouraging beat through her veins.

Mrs. Myers hadn't stopped observing her. With feigned sympathy, she asked, "Are you winded? Did that take a lot out of you? Poor, poor thing."

Just as it seemed Mrs. Myers was about to revel in more cruel taunts, the haggish witch chose the element of surprise. She cut herself off midtaunt, conjuring a hot ball of red light and firing it in Selene's direction. The sizzling ball crashed inches away from Selene, torching a hole in the L-shaped librarians' desk.

Selene was on the move before the burning wood could even sizzle. She took off in the opposite direction, rounding the other end of the large desk as Mrs. Myers sent another scorching blast. If she could lead Mrs. Myers *away* from the front of the library, farther out from the back office with the others locked inside, and instead toward the darker half of the building, she could gain some leverage.

The deep shadows ate her up. She only ran faster, senses heightened. Her ears and sense of touch became her eyes. Luckily, she knew the layout of the library like the back of her hand. Though she stumbled in the dark once or twice, it was nothing compared to the bumps and thuds of Mrs. Myers's attempt. The evil witch shrieked out her frustration when colliding into what sounded like a study table. A second later that same table was blasted in half.

"I thought we were done with the cat and mouse! You really think a little couple of shadows will stop me?" Mrs. Myers lit up another ball of red light in the palm of her hands and carried it forward like its own magical flashlight.

While it may have helped her see better, it also gave Selene a clue to her whereabouts. Already hidden out of sight near the computer lab, Selene crouched low and let Mrs. Myers pass her by. Mrs. Myers wandered deeper into the library's darkness, clueless to the fact that she had overlooked Selene's hiding spot.

Before Mrs. Meyers could realize her error, Selene had to throw more obstacles into the mix. Selene crawled out from under a table, flicking her wrist at a bookcase in the distance. A hardcover copy of Agatha Christie's *Murder on the Orient Express* flew off the shelf and thumped onto the ground, mimicking a footstep. Mrs. Myers stopped in her tracks and scanned the area with her palmful of fiery light.

"I heard you!" she called. Though her shrill voice maintained a menacing tone, there was also a growing note of uncertainty. She had no clue *where* Selene was. "You know, Luna at least fought me face to face. But her own granddaughter hides like a coward. I see you take after your mother."

Selene wasn't letting any taunts dig under her skin. That was exactly what Mrs. Myers wanted. Instead she focused on formulating an impromptu game plan. Her gaze fell on the faraway broken window. Aiden had shattered it earlier in his haste to find her.

It was then that the soft glow from Luna's necklace drew her attention. She had noticed it earlier, the crystalline pendant blinking on and off. Though it might've seemed like a placebo effect, the necklace was a form of indescribable protection.

Selene connected the dots between the glowing crystal pendant and the open, broken window waiting for her. Tonight was the full moon. She needed to lure Mrs. Myers outside…

For another second, Selene stayed put and collected herself, breathing in and out and shoving down jittery nerves. Then she ran. Mrs. Myers was still stumbling around in the dark in search of her. By the time she caught onto the thud of fast footfalls, Selene had whizzed down another section of the library.

Adrenaline exploded like a bomb inside of Selene and propelled her faster. She sprinted down the last aisle leading up to the broken window, barely pausing before she jumped through. She landed in a tumble on the other side, rolling onto the chilling snow.

Mrs. Myers shrieked and conjured a flaming-hot double dose of her dark magic. The sparkling red light jetted through the broken window and smashed into a snow hill, sending flakes flying everywhere. Some of it fell onto Selene, but that didn't slow her down. She was back on her feet, slogging across the snowy courtyard.

The night air smacked into her and the full moon high-lighted her in its silvery cast. Both were immediate shots of energy to her system. She could feel the lunar magic flowing in her veins, giving her that familiar high normally felt during her rituals.

"You think a little cold is going to stop me?" Mrs. Myers had managed to get over the window ledge, though not without some difficulty her haggish build brought her. She panted and staggered, for the first real time her intimidating facade slipping. She carried on as if she wasn't struggling in the snow, sinking knee deep. "Guess what? I have enough dark magic to burn through every flake of snow here!"

Mrs. Myers melted the snow entrapping her legs and then charged forward. Her next hot blast rushed toward Selene. There was no time to think. No time for fear. No time to do anything but follow instinct much like she had the night she saved Aiden from the out of control car. Selene reacted with her own sweeping arm motions, harnessing more power than she was aware of ever possessing.

A silvery current of light erupted from her fingertips, forming a massive force field of sorts. Mrs. Myers's bloodred sparks bounced off of Selene's silver light and boomeranged back the way it had come.

"*ARGHHH*!" Mrs. Myers screeched. The heat streaked across her chest and sent her floundering off balance. She flopped into the snow, her shrunken body twitching.

Selene hesitated, only half lowering her arms. "It's over. Give it up now and we can call the cops—or *someone* to come arrest you."

Mrs. Myers wheezed, pushing herself up on shaky limbs. The dark night and her dark attire made it difficult to tell for certain, but smoke sizzled from what looked like a gaping wound on her chest. Her arrogance was gone, replaced by a clammy bitterness. Her jowls quivered and the varicose veins in her skin were more twisted and swollen than ever. She hobbled closer, refusing to give up. "It's not over 'til I make you pay like I made your backstabbing grandmother pay!"

The duel between them became a dizzying dance in the snow. Flashes of sparkly red and silver light colored the air as Mrs. Myers swept toward Selene and Selene parried her advances. Once Selene was too slow on the uptake and Mrs. Myers landed a grazing shot on her side. Selene fell back, the singe a throb on her skin, but nowhere enough for her to lose focus. She countered Mrs. Myers's follow-up blast with one of her own. The force of her lunar magic knocked the haggish witch off her feet for a second time.

Out of breath and fueled by adrenaline, Selene tore off her necklace and clutched the crystalline pendant tightly in hand. It had shone like a perfect diamond under the full moon. She hadn't the faintest clue what spurred her on or how she trusted the crystal. Everything simply clicked into place and something inside of her just knew.

This was *it*. Luna's pendant would help her defeat Mrs. Myers once and for all.

Mrs. Myers could hardly stand. She staggered left and right, swaying on her weak legs. Her frail body contrasted the mad gleam still present in her eyes. The slow curl forming on her lips. She wasn't going to stop until one of them was dead. Raising her arms and whipping up two more globes of red light, she let them grow in size in the palm of her hands.

Selene shut out the whine of fear and doubt and embraced the courage washing over her. She had nothing left to fear. She had no room for second guessing. She was going to put up one hell of a fight as she believed Luna would.

As Mrs. Myers flocked toward her for a head-on collision, Selene stood her ground, holding up the glowing crystal. The lunar magic surged through her body, using it as a vessel, lighting up the crystal brighter and brighter until it was blinding. Mrs. Myers fired more red blasts, but it was no match for Selene's lunar magic.

The blinding light engulfed Mrs. Myers's blast like it was nothing, shining brighter still. Mrs. Myers's eyes bulged and she grimaced, her decayed teeth and gray gums a hideous sight. She doubled back, shooting more desperate streaks of red light, but that too was eaten up by Selene's blinding crystal.

"Get that thing away from me!"

Selene only advanced. The light only shone brighter. Streams of lunar energy illuminated the library courtyard, soon enveloping everything in its cast. As it touched Selene, she felt hope swell in her heart and the tightness in her chest loosened. The opposite was true for Mrs. Myers. She let out a bloodcurdling scream as the blinding light raked over her.

"No, stop," she shrieked. "I SAID NOOO!"

For a moment of indeterminable length, the bright light consumed everything. Selene's eyes watered trying to stay open. Eventually, she caved and closed them for fear of going blind. The air warmed up, not in the scalding way from Mrs. Myers's dark magic, but rather in a soothing warmth that signaled safety. The entire library grounds was being cleansed of Mrs. Myers's evil presence, the light chasing away all shadows.

And then, in another blink, it was gone. The blinding crystal lost its massive, magnificent luster, powering off and slipping from Selene's grasp to the snow at her feet. She was in a daze as she followed its lead and dropped to her knees, exhausted and confused, but also overwhelmed by great relief.

Mrs. Myers was no more, a small pile of grainy dust beside the now dull crystal pendant.

"Selene!"

Aiden howled as he climbed through the broken window. He sprinted across the courtyard with Noelle not far behind. Only as he slid onto his knees beside her did Selene finally pick up on distant sirens. Brimrock's first responders were on the way.

"We rammed through the door and made it outside as that bright light was shining," said Aiden, putting his arms around her, checking she was okay. "I couldn't see a thing—it was so bright. But Mrs. Myers is gone?"

Noelle kicked the crystal and eyed the pile of dust as though paranoid either would reactivate the evil witch. "Has she been blasted into ash?"

Selene couldn't find the energy to move let alone speak. Her tone was soft and uncertain as she basked in the warmth of Aiden's embrace and muttered, "I…I don't know."

CHAPTER TWENTY-SEVEN

The sun crested over the distant snow-capped tree line for the last time that year. Now early morning on New Year's Eve, Aiden stood at the sink in front of the kitchen window and rinsed out the coffee pot. The aromatic and bitter notes of freshly brewed coffee filled the room, roaming elsewhere throughout the three-story gothic home that was 1221 Gifford Lane.

He was in good spirits, though his body and brain called for more rest. The small catnap he had squeezed in between police reports, hospital visits, and the general shock of last night wasn't enough. The Brimrock Police Department had kept them on the scene for a good two hours, jotting down statements and investigating the destruction done to the library.

For an uncertain moment, Aiden worried the police would take them into custody. With Mrs. Myers gone and their story sounding like any other loony paranormal encounter, it was headed in that direction. Officer Gustin turning up was their saving grace. He was found collapsed in a shriveled-up heap in the snow, having crawled his way from the surrounding woodland. His partner Officer Nunn couldn't believe his story when asked.

"Priscilla Myers," he had croaked, his skin blue and pruned. "She…she's some sort of creature. She…she did this to me."

The disbelief unfolded on the officers' faces as they tried their damnedest to find another explanation. Nothing else would stick. There was no physical evidence against Selene. No trace of Mrs. Myers anywhere. And five witnesses who all said the same thing, including one of their own from Brimrock PD. Officer Nunn was on the brink of accepting their version, but then Chief Whitaker and Mayor Grisby showed up.

Both agitated, wearing overcoats and scowls, they invaded the crime scene and shut everything down. They turned away reporters from the *Brimrock Tribune* and sent Eddie and Officer Gustin in ambulances to the hospital. Aiden watched firsthand as Chief Whitaker ordered his men to cordon off the library, stop searching for evidence and collecting statements about what happened. Mayor Grisby toured the library as though assessing how much it would cost to fix and fast. He was seen off by himself on his cell phone more than once, placing several unknown calls.

"This isn't the first time they've covered something like this up," Noelle had mumbled with a shake of her head. "They don't want the public finding out."

As much as the situation provoked Aiden's investigative mind, calling for him to launch into action, his relief for Selene was far greater. They were letting her go, allowing her to walk away from a situation that could have been disastrous for her. In their eyes, it was easier to sweep the paranormal under the rug than deal with the hysteria the truth would bring.

Aiden was just glad Selene was okay. That she, Eddie, and Noelle had survived. It might not have been how the past prickly paranormal investigator Aiden O'Hare would have felt about the situation, but over the past two weeks, he had learned there were more important things than his investigations. His friends being one of those things. His evolving feelings for Selene being the other. Even if no one else in Brimrock knew, it was enough for him that he knew the truth.

Like him, Selene was pensive. She sat perched in the largest bay window of 1221 Gifford and watched the sun rise among the hopeful, bright colors of dawn. The flurries had stopped, the street outside blanketed by snow hills. Aiden paused in the arched doorway for a few reverent seconds, clutching two piping-hot mugs of coffee. She dragged her gaze from the frosted glass and looked over at him, her smile warm and affectionate.

His was too. He crossed the living room and handed over her mug. "Well? What's the verdict?"

Selene cradled the mug in both hands and inhaled the freshly brewed coffee. After two sips, she said, "It's good. A little heavy-handed on the creamer, but good."

He leaned against the sofa's armrest. "You're quite the critic."

"I compare everyone's coffee to the Magic Bean."

"The Magic Bean does roast one hell of a cup of coffee. I'll take the comparison as a compliment."

Selene scooted over on the bay window ledge and patted the empty space next to her. "Come sit with me."

"Fresh coffee and quality time with Selene," said Aiden. "Could this morning get any better?"

"Probably with more sleep. Sleep sounds amazing right now."

"It's winter. Perfect time for hibernation."

"I mean, I have time now that I have no job," said Selene.

Aiden slid an arm around her shoulders and gave a squeeze. "Is that confirmed? The police seem to be trying to frame everything as a random break-in vandal situation."

"Miriam doesn't care. I'm still being blamed. She called me twenty minutes ago screaming."

"Ouch."

"I'll get over it eventually." Selene sighed and cupped the ceramic mug tighter. "How's Eddie?"

"He's knocked out on painkillers right now. He won't be coherent for hours. His nurse advised I go home and get some shut-eye."

"I'm sorry about what happened to him."

"You mean you're sorry his crazy succubus aunt cornered you in a library and then accidentally burned a hole through her nephew's shoulder? Yeah, that sounds like it's all *your* fault."

"Apparently, it's my grandmother's…"

"I wouldn't put too much stock in what a loon hag says. She could've been lying."

Selene reached up to fiddle with her necklace but found nothing but her naked throat. Aiden could see the windmills in her mind spinning fast as she mulled over last night for the twentieth time. If he knew her as well as he felt like he did, she was thinking about Luna and the crystal pendant she had used against Mrs. Myers. He wanted to take her mind off things. At least for the time being. They needed to take things easy and get some rest.

But first—

"What are you feeling for breakfast?"

Selene's brows quirked and uncertain humor flittered across her features. "Have you seen my food pantry? I have pinto beans, peanut butter, and garlic salt. I *still* haven't gone grocery shopping."

"So we need to get a little creative," he joked, pulling her up with him. "I think we've proven we're both pretty good at that, don't you think?"

————

Later that day, Aiden returned to the hospital to see Eddie. Before he even arrived, he decided Eddie needed someone to lean on. His best friend had been through a lot in the last twenty-four hours. He had discovered his favorite aunt was some type of evil witch. That same witchy aunt had burned a hole into his shoulder and caused irreparable damage to his nerve endings. The doctors said he would be able to use his right arm again after intensive physical therapy, but his movements would always be limited. Though Eddie hadn't discussed how he felt, if Aiden knew his best friend like he thought he did, Eddie was devastated.

In a bid to keep his spirits high, Aiden picked up takeout from Eddie's favorite fast food restaurant and delivered it to his hospital bedside.

"Your favorite. Double cheeseburger with bacon and tomatoes. Large fries and Diet Coke."

"Sounds like I'm about to be in a food coma," said Eddie, propped up by pillows in his hospital bed. His right shoulder and arm were bandaged in a thick sling. "It's a lot better than hospital food."

"That bad?"

"That bad. The chicken noodle soup is more noodle than chicken."

"Noodle's not so bad," said Aiden. He claimed the seat

along the wall, positioned at an angle so that the mounted flat screen was still in view.

"It's all about balance," said Eddie. "You need an equal noodle, chicken, veggie ratio."

Aiden smirked at his best friend as he eagerly bit into his double cheeseburger and satisfaction unfolded on his face. It felt good to see Eddie in an even moderately good mood after what he had been through last night.

"How are you feeling?" Aiden asked. The threads of humor disappeared from his timbre and concern creased his brow.

Eddie shrugged, cheeks plump from a mouthful of hamburger meat. "I dunno how I'm supposed to feel. It's all…it's all still kinda what the fuck, if that makes sense?"

"Believe it or not, it makes a whole lot of sense all things considered."

"I've known Aunt Priscilla all my life," Eddie said, swallowing. He forgot about the rest of his burger and fries, pushing aside his food tray with his left arm. "She was there for me growing up. When my parents were too busy with their careers, it was Aunt Pricilla who had my back. To…to learn she's some sort of…creature is like some living nightmare."

"I can't pretend I know what that's like." Aiden sighed heavily, wishing he had something more profound to offer, but like usual, he blanked on how to console him.

Eddie glanced at the door to his hospital room, checking the coast was clear. "If Aunt Priscilla was some sort of… witch, then that means the paranormal—all the stuff we've investigated—is real."

"Yeah…I guess it does, doesn't it?"

"I know I'm the believer of our partnership, but…" Eddie trailed off as if reality was too much to digest. He blew out a breath and then scrubbed a hand over his face. His thick brows were a single, squiggly line on his forehead. "But damn, bro, it's real? It really *is* true. Even I second-guessed myself during the past few years."

"You have?"

That was news to Aiden. Since the beginning of their show, Eddie had been resolute in his belief of ghosts, ghouls, werewolves, vampires, and every other paranormal creature under the sun. He believed in all of the famous urban legends from the yeti to Bloody Mary and the Men in Black. Not once in the filming of four seasons and forty-nine episodes had he ever indicated a doubt in his beliefs. It had been Aiden who was staunchly skeptical through and through.

"Of course. I just never said anything to you because I knew it'd be some big 'I told you so' kinda thing," said Eddie. "But to know it's all been real. And you've known about it and didn't tell me."

"Eddie—"

"You *knew* Selene was a witch," he continued. The accusation came through in how his jaw clenched and eyes thinned. "You've known since we've been in Brimrock and you never told me."

"I didn't know the whole time. I found out by accident. It's a long story, Eddie."

"We've always kept each other in the loop. What makes now so different? Selene?"

Aiden hadn't expected an argument. He had hoped for some casual ribbing and light talk about things like movies and the nurse with the 1980s helmet hair. But one look at Eddie and the hurt was spelled out as clear as the sky on any bright and sunny spring day. He averted his gaze to the hospital window overlooking the parking garage. Though it hadn't snowed since yesterday, clumps still remained, soggy and mishappen in sporadic heaps.

"Eddie, I've already told you, you need to stop bringing up Selene like she's the enemy."

"You expect me to ignore how she's changed things?" Eddie gaped at him like he were a madman with a bomb strapped to his chest. Then a sound of disgust gurgled in his throat and he threw up his left arm in frustration. "I thought we came to Brimrock as partners. I thought we were going to figure out the Luna thing together. *You* went out of your way to shut me out of whatever you were doing. *You* fell for Selene and decided that was more important than keeping me in the loop. *You* let me drive you straight to the library to find out my aunt was some freaky energy zapper witch like I didn't matter! You realize my life's never gonna be the same now? All to protect your little girlfriend?"

"I didn't know about your aunt! That was a surprise to me."

"But you suspected something was up!" Eddie raged unforgivingly. "You and Selene were looking into what was going on. Don't play dumb."

Frustration hardened in Aiden's stomach and he jerked to a stand. "It wasn't intentional, Ed. I wasn't leaving you out to be malicious. When I found out the truth about Selene, it all unraveled unexpectedly. None of it was planned. I couldn't tell Selene's secret."

"I'm your partner. I'm your best friend." Eddie shook his head and said nothing else, allowing his heavy words to sink down with gravity. "My life is changed forever now. My arm is never gonna be the same. My family is never gonna be the same. But, hey, congrats—you and Selene are solid."

"Eddie, I never wanted for any of this to happen this way—"

"Bro, just go," said Eddie. He was shutting down, closing himself off to anything Aiden had to say. He picked up the TV remote and began flipping through channels. "Thanks for the meal. You don't have to come back."

That was Aiden's cue to exit. He hovered another second, on the rare chance Eddie would give him another sign that said to stay. It never came and Aiden pushed his reddish-brown hair back along his scalp with both hands. Eddie pretended to watch the TV on his walk out, the future of their friendship left unsaid.

CHAPTER TWENTY-EIGHT

Selene spent the bulk of New Year's Eve at the Magic Bean. Isabelle Halsey had quit on short notice after being stuck alone closing last night. Selene readily backfilled, brewing coffee and whipping up lattes. She wiped down tables and decorated the main window. New Year's Eve called for some glitter and sparkle, even if the coffee shop would be closed at midnight.

Anything to keep busy and avoid being home alone. Within the walls of 1221 Gifford, she would be stuck with her own thoughts, replaying last night. She wasn't sure she was ready to dissect everything that had happened. Her brain was operating like an old PC, lurching along with basic thoughts of relief rather than focusing on more nuanced aspects like Priscilla Myers and the revenge she sought. She was simply happy to have survived, grateful for how Luna's pendant had given her protection during her darkest hour…

Eventually, business slowed around the Magic Bean. Noelle ripped off her apron and slumped at the counter. "That was rough. I thought Mr. Higgley was never going to shut up."

"He likes to hear himself talk."

"Okay! I figured that out the time he trapped me on Bibi's porch, had me nodding and smiling for twenty minutes," Noelle regaled. She observed Selene as she pasted sparkling gold stars to the window. "Girl, give it a rest. We all know we're about to be snoring in bed once midnight hits. After last night, we deserve it."

"I'm running on thirty-one hours without sleep," said Selene. She stuck another gold star to the glass and admired her handiwork. "I need to keep myself busy or I'll pass out right here."

"We need to talk about what's going on with you and Fudgeboy."

"What's there to say?"

"The man who knows you're a witch, saw some weird succubus lady attack you, and then saw you use a magic crystal to defend yourself. It's not the normal start to a relationship."

"Aiden was over at the house this morning. He's got my back."

"And his friend, the bushy-browed one whose aunt was a psycho killer?"

"Um," said Selene, pausing, "that's still up in the air. He's recovering."

"*I'm* still recovering." Noelle shook her head and checked her nails. She had broken two last night in the library fray. "I still don't get what happened. Your grandma and Mrs. Myers were beefing over John Grisby?"

Selene forgot about the rest of the gold stars and took a break, pulling up a chair at an empty table. "Apparently. I don't know too many details. Just that Grisby wound up in a coma and my grandma and Mrs. Myers had some epic magic duel."

"For all these years anything strange in town has been blamed on Luna—or the rest of you Blackstones. It's crazy to think it was Priscilla Myers all along."

"Who knows what it was? I'm learning more and more to expect the unexpected out of this town."

Noelle leaned on the counter, elbows digging into its smooth surface. "Bibi has always said there used to be a lot more magic way back when than there is now."

"Who said that?" Aunt Bibi emerged from the flapping kitchen doors. She carried a tray of freshly baked pastries shaped like cats, the center a mysterious green jelly. "What would you know about way back when?"

"Only what you've told me." Noelle stole a pastry off the baking tray and bit off the cat's flaky head. The jelly exploded in her mouth and trickled onto her lips.

"I'm not surprised about Priscilla," said Bibi. Her expression was mild, but behind her wire-framed glasses, her dark brown eyes flashed with knowing. "I've suspected something was up for a while. She's always been a little too sweet for Bibi's tastes."

"Bibi, did you know my necklace was magical?" Selene asked.

"I suspected. That crystal looked a lot like it was from Luna's collection. When I saw it glowing, I as good as knew what it was."

Selene frowned, pushing her brows together. "What was it?"

"That mother of yours really didn't teach you a dang thing, did she? How are you a lunar witch and you don't know a lunar crystal when you see it?"

"*That* was a lunar crystal?"

"Now, what did I just say? Yes, it was a lunar crystal! A rare find. Very pure, very powerful."

"No wonder it was Luna's favorite necklace…" Selene sat gobsmacked, staring around the small coffee shop.

"Lunar crystals are usually used for protection against dark forces—makes sense why Luna would wear it."

"And maybe why it was sent to you," added Noelle. "Did your uncle Zee say why he sent it when he did?"

Selene answered with a shake of her head. "I thought it was a fashion accessory. I didn't know all this time it was a magical crystal protecting me. It makes sense why I felt different when wearing it."

"Different how?"

"I don't know, safer somehow. The night we saved Aiden and I walked home, I felt a lot of bad energy in the air. But then I held Luna's necklace and it seemed like everything was okay," said Selene. "Even if danger was lurking, *I* was going to be fine. That was the night Gustin went missing."

"Danger probably *was* lurking," said Bibi bluntly. She loaded the green-jellied pastries into the glass case and then tucked the baking tray under her armpit. "We know ol' Priscilla attacked him that night. Stands to reason if he was following you, she was following you both."

An icy shiver trembled its way down Selene's spine and she avoided thinking on that point. "Bibi, how did I know what to do? Something came over me and I just knew—I knew I needed to use the crystal on my necklace."

"Magic is a mystery," said Bibi, shrugging. "Folks say death is life's great mystery, but magic is up there in the top three. I've been on this earth for over six decades and I still don't know everything there is to know. Sometimes, we just *know*. It's in our blood, our hearts, our souls. We *are* magic."

Selene and Noelle met each other's gaze and shared the faintest of smiles. Bibi caught onto them and her laugh was crackly and warm, reminiscent of a campfire.

"You girls are so young. I remember when I was like you," she said fondly. "Soak it up. Enjoy it now. You've got so many years ahead of you to master your powers. Don't you worry about the nobodies in town. You girls are the real magic—one of the best kept secrets."

Once alone, Noelle said, "It's easy to forget. But last night makes me grateful."

"Me too." Selene moved toward the coffee shop window and stared out at the street, observing the shoppers pass them by and the snow flitter in the wind. "I already know the Brimrock PD are going to rule Mrs. Myers an unsolvable missing persons case. I already know they're going to sweep what happened at the library under the rug. And the town's going to play along and it's going to be back to business, like everything's normal."

"It's a blessing and a curse."

Noelle was spot on. The willful ignorance of those in town was both a positive and a negative. It meant that any sticky magical situations could be kept under wraps so long as they were smart about it. However, it also meant a denial of reality. That didn't sit well with her, upsetting her stomach with a twist of her innards.

"I guess we'll have to wait and see," said Selene, sighing. "That's the only way we're going to know how everything turns out."

———

That night, Selene and Aiden spent two hours collaborating on dinner. Due to the holiday, tables at the Mulberry were taken and no other place in town felt worthy of their special occasion. They decided a joint effort of cooking dinner was more fitting. As it turned out, neither of them was the best cook, but shockingly enough, it made their effort that much more fun.

Yukie parked herself on the floor of the kitchen and curiously tilted her head watching their attempts. Selene burnt the dinner rolls and Aiden oversalted the pasta. They *both* screwed up on the chicken breast but counted the salad as a success. Selene giggled as Aiden volunteered to set the table, but she snapped her fingers and silverware and cutlery burst from the cabinets and zoomed across the room, setting themselves up better than any waitstaff.

Aiden's ivory skin tinged a vague pink. "I forgot I'm dealing with a witch."

"You should probably get used to it," she teased. She waved her hand and the bottle of zinfandel obeyed her request. Together with the wine opener, it uncorked itself and poured two glasses.

They sat down to their meals of creamy Alfredo chicken and pasta and toasted to each other. Selene swallowed a generous mouthful and within a second, the jammy, peppery flavors hit her taste buds. She felt the difference almost instantly, more sensitive to any alcohol consumption than the average person. Her lips spread into a smile that roused Aiden's curiosity.

"What's that smile for?"

She set down her wineglass and shrugged. "I'm in a good mood."

"That's a relief to hear. You deserve it."

"But what about you? How's Eddie doing?"

"Long story I'd rather forget about tonight. I want to focus on ringing in the New Year with you," he said. His eyes had darkened into a brown, ever-changing from their natural hazel shade. It matched the mood as he grinned at her and her stomach flipped. "I was worried about you last night. When I showed up for our date and you didn't answer…"

"I'm sorry. My phone was in my book bag. Mistake number one when a succubus is chasing you."

Aiden tugged at his shirt collar. The rest of his dinner was forgotten. His shoulders squared and his chest rose and fell, his handsome face shadowed with doubt. He reached up halfway to slide his fingers through his neat hair, but then thought better of it. His eyes braved hers after another cautious second, where he seemed to work up his nerve.

"I really care about you, Selene. And…and I don't want to lose you. There's a lot of roadblocks in the way, but what do you think about us being together?" he asked. He seemed to gain courage the more he talked. His timbre deepened. "What do you think about being my girlfriend?"

Selene smiled and said, "That depends. What do you think about being my boyfriend?"

His smile matched hers. "It would be the best thing to happen out of this trip to Brimrock."

"You mean your vote *doesn't* go to the evil hag who attacked us last night?"

"It was a close race," he played along. "But you won out."

"I feel honored."

They stuffed themselves with the food they created. The pasta might have been too salty and the dinner rolls rock hard, but by the meal's end, it became one of the best they had enjoyed in recent memory. The company being the reason. The wine loosened their tongues and encouraged flirtatiousness, their usual mild manners abandoned.

In the living room sprawled on the floor in front of the cracking flames of the fireplace, they finished a whole bottle by themselves. Selene's cheeks ached from smiling hard and her belly was sore from the constant laughter. Both side effects she wasn't aware could be positives until she spent the evening alone with Aiden.

"I bet it was difficult," said Aiden over another glass of wine. "I know me as a kid and if I had to keep that a secret, it probably wouldn't have happened."

"My mom helped scare the crap out of me. She made me fear my powers."

"I remember you said she wanted to fit in with the rest of town. But do you think she knew about Luna and Mrs. Myers and she was trying to protect you from that?"

"I'm not sure. She grew up knowing firsthand about Luna's disappearance—how it happened. Maybe she did figure it would be easier if she didn't address it."

"It seems like one of those situations where you're stuck between a rock and a hard place."

Selene considered his point, her head tipped onto her left shoulder. "You can say that. But I think my mom's aversion to magic and telling me the truth did more harm than good in the long run. Now she's gone and I know nothing. Everything I do know, I've taught myself."

"That's impressive."

"It's simple stuff. You've seen the extent of what I can do."

"You tell me this after last night, where I witnessed you singlehandedly take out some crazy old witch lady shooting fireballs at us and trying to suck out our souls."

It must've been the wine that opened the gates for Selene to laugh. She downed the last of her glass and stared at Aiden with sparkling eyes. "I don't know how I did what I did. I just knew Luna's necklace would protect me. I knew it the more it glowed. It was like a lifeline."

"That's a very accurate comparison."

"It worked out."

Aiden nodded and then carefully placed his glass on the coffee table. The flames danced in his hazel eyes as the expression on his face took on a more heated look. He had scooted closer and she caught him glancing at her lips. His hand covered hers and when she looked at him again, he was waiting for her like an open book.

"Selene," he said slowly, "about the other night—I'm embarrassed. It's important to me to make you feel good. Including the moments we're physical. I failed at that. I…I, uh, I couldn't control myself and I let you down. But I want you to know, I can do better. I want you to feel special."

"I already feel special. Our time together has meant a lot. You should know what happened wasn't your fault, though."

"What do you mean?"

Selene pushed herself to her feet and left him sitting by the fireplace. She crossed the room to the first window and distracted herself by peering at the snow hills beyond the glass. Aiden was slower to follow, as though he wondered if he'd be crowding her. He joined her at the window on a note of patience. He was willing to wait for her answer.

She sighed. "Aiden, I've told you many times how I'm cursed."

"Selene, that has nothing to do with us."

"It has everything to do with us," she said. She turned to face him. "I'm unlucky in love. It never works out for me. Even when it seems like it will. It always goes wrong. *Always*. The other night was more proof of that. What happened happened because I'm not supposed to be in a good relationship. Maybe us being together isn't a good idea after all."

Aiden couldn't keep his hands to himself. He closed the small space between them and slid a hand to her cheek, his presence undeniably warm. "Selene, that's not it at all. The more you say that, the more I want to prove to you it's just not true."

"I want it not to be," she whispered. Her heart had started pounding. Her eyes on his, she couldn't look away, caught up in the quiet moment laced with inexplicable intimacy. She rose up and kissed him, using the affection as its own language. Her lips brushed his and she heard his sharp intake of breath as it got caught in his throat. She hung her arms around his neck and kissed him again. Soft, fleeting kisses that were cruel teases. Against his lips, she muttered, "Show me."

———

It was minutes before midnight and they were mixed up in each other. They ventured upstairs to Selene's bedroom, the many tea light candles providing a warm glow among the shadows, their mouths and hands eager and searching. They paused only long enough to strip one article off before returning for more enthusiastic kisses.

Selene's sweater dress pulled over her head and discarded on the floor.

Kiss.

Aiden's belt unbuckled, the metal clinking, cool under her fingertips.

Kiss.

Stumble to the bed in a joint effort to unhook her bra. Once accomplished, his large palms filling with her soft mounds of flesh.

More kisses *and* breathy moans.

Selene's head tipped back, body shuddering against him as his thumbs flicked over her pebbly nipples. Paired with his kneading palms, the attentive massage was everything she didn't know she needed in life. She was melting on the spot, slickness between her legs and a tremor in her heart.

A dreamy feeling fell over her, like floating into a fantasy. Some alternate universe where it was just her and Aiden and nothing mattered but the pleasure they sought in each other. Their candlelit shadows fell against the wall, reenacting their affectionate movements, a darker, lustier mirror to themselves.

They dropped onto the bed with limbs entangled. Selene reveled in the weight of Aiden on top of her, pinning him between her fleshy thighs, kissing him harder. He pulled back on his knees a disheveled, dazed, chest-heaving mess, but a sexy one that produced a small giggle out of her. He grinned back and moved in again, holding himself above her like he were executing a pushup.

"What's that laugh for?" His breath tickled the side of her face as he planted a kiss there and then started his way to her throat.

"Your hair's all messed up."

"Is that a bad thing?"

"It's a sexy thing," she purred playfully. "You're always so composed."

It made it feel that much more special when she realized she was probably one of the select few who got to see Aiden O'Hare like this.

He resumed his ministrations and she squirmed from under him. His tongue worked its magic on her throat and his hands slid down her body. She curled her fingers into his hair to mess it up further and ground against him. Her hips to his hips, she wanted nothing more than for him to crash into her.

But Aiden seemed determine to take his time. He lavished her with kisses and caresses, as though making up for what was cut short the other night. His touch slow and appreciative, his large hands mapping out the curves to her body.

With any other man she had slept with, she would've halfway flinched. Never a fan of the jiggle in her thighs or the small, untoned pouch of her belly, she would've pushed his hands away so they could hurry up and finish what was always a disappointing encounter. Things were different with Aiden.

He made her feel sexy. He made her feel *good*. His hands felt like fire on her skin, burning her up, making her sweat. She writhed as he teased, his fingers drifting low, dipping between her legs. He pressed his thumb to her clit and she gasped. She rocked into his touch. The hypersensitive, swollen button set off a frenzy of delight through the rest of her body.

His name fell from her lips in a whimper and he answered her with a rumbled groan, sounding distinctly like a caveman. He doubled down on his teasing. His thumb already strumming her, he slipped two fingers inside her slick heat, and her body arched on its own, no longer listening to her brain. Just as she teetered on the precipice of surrendering to the zings and pings of pleasure, he stopped altogether. His fingers left her swollen nub without a proper goodbye and her core throbbed in protest.

Her eyes found his face as he sat up and licked his fingers. He knew what he was doing because his gaze was waiting for her. Her breath hitched and more heat flushed over her skin. He serenaded her with more kisses, dropping them on her lips and cheeks and neck, muttering against her skin.

"I want to make this good for you. Tell me what you want."

She moaned her answer, unintelligible but honest. It

spoke for itself and his lips spread into a grin as he kissed her one more time. He seemed to decide his teasing was enough as she lay back and bit her lip, watching him roll the latex condom on his girth. His mouth was on hers when he pushed inside her in a solitary, breath-catching thrust.

Another moment passed where they reveled in the newfound ecstasy of each other, and then they began to move, developing their own dance. Selene banded her legs around his waist and he switched up his angle, allowing for her to take more of him in.

Their tongues swirled, kissing and rocking, creating a delicious friction that would be their undoing. The mind-numbing pleasure kindled inside of Selene. She panted and raised her hips to meet his, always searching to feel more of him. Her hands gripped his shoulders, their gazes pinned onto each other, and they rode the rhythm of Aiden's strokes. The heels of her feet pressed insistently against his backside, digging into his flesh to urge him deeper, and he listened. The further he slipped, the more she unraveled. His length reached her sweetest spot and her mouth hung open.

Now at the point of no return, she clung to him, so para-lyzed by the mounting pleasure she could do nothing else. She felt it before her brain registered what was happening. A thousand tiny tingles exploded and radiated from her core to the rest of her body. She cried out as it hit her, thighs shaky, legs like jelly. Delirious from her orgasm, she did the only thing she could think of, tightening her grip on Aiden. The heels of her feet left imprints on his backside. Her arms looped around his neck. Her walls pulsed and clenched and he grunted out a groan.

Aiden's hazel eyes shone in the low light of the tea candles, intense and heavy-lidded, fixed on her face as he held back no longer. His ivory skin reddened all over, his teeth gritted, his length buried deep inside. He twitched and then released and collapsed half on top of her. They lay smushed together breathing and elated, in a way never wanting the moment to end.

Selene glanced to the clock on her bedside table and smiled. "Midnight."

Aiden rolled off of her but couldn't keep from touching her. He pulled her into him and said, "Happy New Year, Selene."

She kissed him softly, exhausted and spent, ready for sleep. But not before she wished it back. Entangled in the sheets and surrounded by a dozen different flickering tea lights, she whispered, "Happy New Year, Aiden."

CHAPTER TWENTY-NINE

"Okay," said Selene, clapping shut her book. "What's wrong?"

Aiden reclined on the sofa opposite Selene's armchair, his own book in hand. The couple were spending a quiet evening at 1221 Gifford enjoying some light reading and the warmth from the living room fireplace. It had been a week since Mrs. Myers wreaked havoc on their lives and though Brimrock had returned to normal, his life was still out of sync.

He and Selene were in the honeymoon phase of their new relationship, spending as much time together while he was in Brimrock. His friendship with Eddie was fractured to the point every day when he showed up to the hospital, Eddie turned him away. The show's future hung in the air and his time left in Brimrock dwindled.

None of this was part of the plan when he first arrived in town. The plan had been to spend his couple of weeks investigating Luna Blackstone for the fiftieth episode of *Paranormal Hunters* and then leaving once filming wrapped. He hadn't expected to fall for Selene, fall out with Eddie and fall into deep confusion about his future. For a man of routine like him, it was disconcerting, though he hesitated bringing it up to Selene. She had enough on her plate.

But she wasn't letting him avoid the subject any longer. He tried to keep reading his book to no avail. She stretched a short leg across the coffee table and kicked him in the thigh, forcing his attention.

"Tell me."

"Tell you what?"

"You're upset. The tips of your ears are red."

"They are?"

"They only get red in three scenarios." Selene lifted her fingers to count down the different examples. "One, if you're upset or angry about something. Two, if you're nervous. Three, if you're horny. Considering me and you know each other pretty well at this point, and we just got done—*ahem*—having some fun a little while ago, I'd guess it's number one."

"You sound so convinced."

"That's because I am. I know it's about Eddie."

Aiden took off his glasses and rubbed his eyes. He had taken out his contacts earlier and opted for the comfort of his glasses when reading. With a sigh, he said, "Eddie and I had a fight. It was a few days ago, but I haven't told you about it."

"Why not?"

"Because…the fight was about you—and everything that happened with Mrs. Myers at the library."

"Oh." Selene nibbled on her bottom lip, crossing her legs beneath her on the armchair. Her book slipped from her lap and onto the floor, but she made no attempt to pick it up. Tonight's read was a James Patterson novel.

He smoothed his fingers over his own book, the sequel to *Jurassic Park* titled *The Lost World*. He had officially become a fan of the franchise. Thinking on how to explain the fight, he sorted out what to say. "The thing is, Eddie was kind of right. I did keep things from him. I did shut him out of what I was doing. He's paid the price for it. Everything that happened has directly affected his life."

"You didn't mean for it to," said Selene softly. "And I made you promise not to tell anyone about my secret life as a witch."

"I don't regret that. It's your prerogative who you want to know."

The corners of her lips lowered into a frown. "I've already told you I don't want to come between you and your friendship with Eddie."

"None of it is your fault. You can't help some crazy succubus lady hated your family. It just so happened that succubus lady was Eddie's aunt."

"It really does sound crazy when you say it aloud, doesn't it?"

"I've investigated paranormal activity for four years, and it's definitely on the top five of crazy list—if not top three."

They fell silent again for a companionable pause. Both thinkers relished in the moment to lie back and ruminate on what was already said and what they next wanted to say. Aiden loved that about Selene, how she assessed situations and pinpointed the frankness in them. It seemed to be a natural talent of hers.

"You can't change what's happened," she said. "But maybe you need to both try and see the other's perspective. He's going through a lot of different emotions. I think we all are. I know I am. But shutting each other out isn't helping."

"He's being discharged from the hospital tomorrow. I don't even know if I should show."

Selene left her armchair for a spot on the sofa and he

welcomed her into his lap. "I think you should. Your support shouldn't end just because he's not speaking to you right now. You're best friends."

"You're amazing," Aiden said, kissing the apple of her cheek. It wasn't until after as he pulled back and noticed the tightness working in her throat that he frowned again. "You're worried about me, but what about you? Eddie's not the only one who went through a lot that night. You haven't talked about it much…"

"I'm still sorting through everything. Just thinking about where to go from here. A lot's changed over the past three weeks. It's hard to imagine what comes next now that I know more about Luna and my family," explained Selene. She snuggled closer, resting her head on his shoulder and a palm on his chest. "I don't even have my job at the library anymore. It sounds pathetic, but that job brought me a lot of comfort. The books were like friends. I got to spend all day with them, and now…now I don't. It's like a part of my identity is gone."

"Selene…"

"Hmm?"

"Have you wondered if maybe the curse is broken? If Mrs. Myers was the one who cast it, and now she's gone…"

She laughed. "My life doesn't work that way, Aiden. I'm still cursed."

Aiden wanted to grill her for more, ponder how she knew for sure that was the case. Even offer a suggestion that they test out his theory, but he also didn't want to push her. She had resigned herself to that belief—at least for tonight—and he had enough to think over.

For the time being, sitting curled up with Selene, listening to the crackling fire was enough.

———

Aiden showed up the next day to pick Eddie up from the hospital. The disgruntlement wasn't hidden when Eddie saw him. He scowled and struggled to carry his bag of possessions, stubbornly refusing to ask for any assistance from Aiden. Aiden rushed to help him anyway, grabbing his duffel bag and tossing it over his shoulder.

"Where's my uncle?" Eddie asked. "He said he'd be here."

"I hope you don't mind I told him I'd pick you up. Ghost's waiting in the parking lot."

"I do mind. I said my piece last week."

"Eddie, you have every right to be pissed."

"I know I do. But thanks for admitting the obvious."

"A lot of things have gone wrong."

"Again, the obvious."

"I can't fix them," Aiden admitted. Eddie glanced at him, thrown off by the candor. "I wish I could but I can't. What's happened has happened and it would be naive to pretend like we can magically erase that. I just want you to know I'm still your best friend. You're always going to be mine."

They were halfway across the parking lot when Eddie stopped. "Since when are you touchy-feely?"

"I'm not. I'm just…I wanted you to know that."

"Selene *has* done a number on you."

The best friends hopped into Ghost and pulled out of the hospital parking lot in tense silence. Eddie had made no other mention of what Aiden had said, so Aiden dropped the subject. They drove through town ignoring each other, pretending like the melting snow and the street banners advertising post-holiday sales were more interesting.

When they reached the Myers residence, Aiden parked and waited for Eddie to decide what next.

"You're not coming in?"

"I think it's for the best I don't. I don't want to traumatize anyone."

Eddie sighed and stared out the window at the Cape Cod home. "Rory's still in bad shape."

"I can't say I blame her."

"My uncle is holding out hope Aunt Priscilla's still alive," he said. He gave off an ironic laugh. "Crazy I know all the answers, but I can't tell anybody, huh? Just more weird, unconfirmed rumors surrounding Brimrock."

"Eddie, it's your choice what you want to do with the info about your aunt."

"I can't tell them the truth. They love her. They'd be devastated. It might sound messed up, but I…I think I have to keep it a secret to protect them—to preserve the Aunt Priscilla we all loved." Eddie unbuckled his seat belt and then gripped the door handle, but he didn't pull on it to exit. "I spent a long time thinking about things last night."

"What sort of things?"

"Where to go from here," said Eddie. "I think it's probably for the best if I stay in Brimrock for a while."

Aiden's brows jumped on his forehead. "As in for how long?"

"I dunno. Maybe indefinitely. I gotta be here for my family. It's too much to leave them hanging. Aunt Priscilla's not coming back. Things are going to be rough for a while and I should be here for that."

"Oh. Alright. That makes sense." Aiden's response was clinical. He didn't want to give away his true feelings on the matter for fear it would offend Eddie. While he understood his reasoning, another part of him was disappointed. The end of an era evoked an empty sensation in the pit of his stomach that he didn't like at all.

Eddie seemed to pick up on his sadness anyway. "Bro, you'll be fine. We'll still keep in touch. You'll still go about your business and do investigations. The show'll live on without me."

"I wasn't thinking about the show—"

"I am," said Eddie. A hint of a bittersweet smile flickered on his face. "We worked so hard for years investigating the paranormal. We shouldn't give it up now."

"But I can't do it alone. I don't want to do it alone."

Pushing open the door, Eddie paused long enough for parting words. "I think you get what I'm implying. You want to make amends for what happened? You keep the show alive."

Aiden sat in driver's seat of Ghost for minutes after Eddie went inside the Myers home. He had pulled out his phone and scrolled through his contacts list three times. He hovered on different names, but ultimately knew in his heart who he needed to reach out to. With a rueful shake of his head and a conflicted frown, he selected their executive producer, Paulina, and pressed call.

CHAPTER THIRTY

I f there was one characteristic Brimrock championed more than any other, it was normalcy. For a town known for strange phenomena and unexplained happenings, the residents preferred to pretend like everything was peaches and cream. Into January the town came to the unspoken consensus that it was time to return to normal— normal being anything other than acknowledging the mysterious events during the holiday season.

Officer Gustin surely but slowly made a recovery. Mrs. Myers's attempt to suck the energy from his body left him with a host of immune system issues, which in return resulted in an indefinite leave of absence from the Brimrock police force. He didn't seem to mind, though, spotted around town with crutches and healing bruises.

Peter was much of the same except his recovery plodded along at a snail's pace. The *Brimrock Tribune* reported when he woke from his coma, slapping the breaking news on the front page. By the second week of the month, he was relegated to a small patch on the corner of page six.

Despite a lack of evidence, Selene suspected it was

Mayor Grisby's behind-the-scenes doing. He gave one press conference following the library incident and Mrs. Myers's disappearance. Though his speech covered the gamut of recent current events, it somehow still managed to be full of dry, rehearsed circular talk. No answers were provided. No details given. No truth bombs dropped. Just vague mentions of police investigations and prayers for the families involved.

She couldn't say she was surprised. Mayor Grisby would rather keep up the charade of normalcy than confront the possibility of the paranormal in his town. She would've cared if she wasn't so busy soaking up her time with Aiden. As his days in Brimrock counted down to zero, she wanted to enjoy the time they had together. Who knew when the next time she would see him would be?

"I never thought I'd meet someone who is a bigger foodie than I am," said Aiden on one of their date nights about town. He slumped in his chair and patted his stomach. "But, Selene Blackstone, you just may be the greatest foodie there is."

Selene dabbed at her mouth with a napkin and smug air of confidence. "You're not going to finish your dessert?"

"I could try, but then risk exploding. The question is, would it be worth it?"

Both of their gazes lowered to the half-eaten Boston cream pie on the table between them and they burst into laughter.

"Who am I kidding? *Of course* it's worth it," finished Aiden. He cut off another bite with his fork and hummed in decadence when the sweet mouthful melted on his tongue. "I never saw the appeal of New England, but I do have to admit, the food is delicious."

"We know how to stuff our faces." Selene winked as she scooped up her last bite and then tossed her crinkled napkin onto her plate.

"New Yorkers know how to stuff our faces too. Pizzas. Ballpark franks. Cheesecake. We're professional foodies by nature."

"I've always wanted to try New York–style pizza. It's on that bucket list I probably won't accomplish." A note of wistfulness embellished in her tone. She shook it away, deciding it was better to change the subject than to harp on things she would never get the chance to do. "I'm glad we came out for a night on the town. Considering it's one of your last."

"It won't be for long."

"That's true, you can always come visit. If...if that's what you want."

The couple had wandered onto the street, leaving the small eatery behind. Aiden's arm slunk over her shoulders and she walked curled into his side, their pace lazy. The evening glittered with life in the town square as others cruised into different shops or savored a nice dinner in a restaurant. The gas lamps flickered, providing light against the otherwise starless sky. Forecast called for stormy weather tomorrow. The moon itself was a silver crescent that still kept an eye on her no matter how far away.

Aiden paused in the middle of the sidewalk and released a short, quizzical laugh. "If I want to come visit isn't up for debate. Where else will I get my witty, smart, funny witch fix?"

"Shhhh," she hushed with a finger to his lips. "We can't have *them* hearing you say that."

"At this point, they're so stuck in their own bubbles even if they heard me, they would act like they didn't."

"That's scarily accurate."

They ventured into Balford's Books, perusing the aisles and trading bookish banter. It occurred to them both only they would visit a bookstore on a Saturday night. The cramped indie bookshop was overloaded wall to wall with hundreds if not thousands of books. The aisles were narrow enough for only one adult to walk down at any given time, which made for interesting human Tetris whenever encountering another shopper in the same section.

Mr. Balford sat on a stool behind the register with a copy of *Atlas Shrugged* concealing his face. Selene shushed Aiden as they meandered into the nonfiction aisle and his zealous fingers teased the ticklish skin on her sides. She shirked out of his grasp and glared at him in warning, the humor from his tickling efforts still in her eyes despite attempts otherwise. Aiden didn't give up there. He walked her backward against a bookshelf and gripped her chin, dropping a fervent kiss on her lips.

Selene responded in kind with a playful flick of her tongue, an invitation for a light game of cat and mouse. Her hands were balls on his chest and she leaned into him. He kissed her harder, slicking her tongue with his, flattening his hand against her lower back. They forgot where they were as they indulged in their passionate kiss, growing hot and breathless. Her soft purr was for his ears only.

They were enveloped enough in each other that the thud of footsteps didn't register with either of them. Aiden pulled away from her mouth at the last second and looked up to meet Miriam Hofstetter's horrified face. She looked like she had witnessed bloody murder and shrieked accordingly, dropping the books she hugged to her chest and scurrying away.

For a solitary second, Aiden and Selene stood still in mild shock, but once that expired they went with what felt true to the moment. They erupted in laughter. Mr. Balford didn't appreciate their shenanigans once discovered and asked them to leave, which they gladly did. They stumbled onto the street outside holding hands and indifferent to the perturbed glances they received.

"How did you work for her?" Aiden asked.

Shaking her head, Selene held on to his hands and said, "The books definitely helped a lot. The best—and probably only—perk of the job."

"Selene."

In an instant, his entire vibe changed. They went from engulfed with carefree laughter to Aiden's expression straightening into something more serious. He didn't let go of her hands and he wouldn't look away, his hazel eyes alive and riveted to hers. She hadn't seen him look this serious since the night Mrs. Myers attacked them in the library and the danger felt too real. She frowned and waited for him to go on, her heartbeat steadily gaining speed.

"I've been thinking all night how to ask you, but I've realized there's no easy way," he said and then inhaled a nervous, quivery breath. "What do you think about coming with me?"

Selene laughed. She thought it a joke and giggled as though the idea was preposterous. Aiden's grip on her hands tightened and he eased even closer, seemingly indifferent that they blocked half the sidewalk.

"You're laughing, but I'm serious. What if you came with me?"

"Come with you where? Aiden, what are you talking about?"

"I'm leaving Brimrock. I'm starting the next season of investigations."

"You and Eddie have always done that. That's the premise of your show."

"Eddie's staying," he said. His eyes searched hers, hope flickering feebly in them. "I spoke with my executive producer and she's on board with a new partner in his absence."

She laughed again and forced her hands from his. "Quit playing around. You already know I can't."

"Why?"

"I've told you. You *know* why." Now her humor was gone as she regarded him severely. He knew all about the curse…

"What if it doesn't matter anymore? It's probably all undone."

"And what makes you say that? Suddenly you're an expert?"

"We haven't even *tried*, Selene," he pointed out. He moved forward and captured her hands in his again, the hope growing. "Think about it. She's gone. You said you were unlucky in love, but here we are, still together, smooth sailing. What if you're able to leave? Come with me, have the adventures you've always read about."

Tears sprang in her eyes as a wave of emotion rushed her. She gasped trying to inhale another breath and then shook her head side to side, fighting the prospect that she could leave. The possibility she could travel the country with Aiden, embarking on some exciting quest where they investigated the unknown and fell deeper in love with each day. It was everything she had always wanted and everything she had never been able to have.

Her lungs burned as the tears slipped down her cheeks. She hated how skeptical she was. Her immediate reaction was that it was cruel to tease her in such a way when it could never happen for her. She was doomed to staying in Brimrock, living alone at 1221 Gifford with her massive imagination of what-ifs. Aiden wrapped his arms around her in a hug. He held her tightly against him and let her soak his neatly ironed button-down shirt with her tears.

"Let's try," he whispered into her ear. "Have you forgotten what you taught me? Believe in the impossible."

She tossed her arms around his neck, rose on absolute tiptoe, and smashed her lips against his in wet, teary, salty glory. He welcomed her tears *and* salt, encircling his arms around her waist and lifting her off her feet as he kissed her with burgeoning affection. The others on the street simply had to walk around them. For that moment, the space was theirs as they kissed and kissed some more, and then broke apart for air.

"Aiden," she said with an uncertain shake of her head. "I want to. You have no idea how much I'd like that, but I don't know. I...I need time to think. I can't just leave at the drop of a hat."

"Why not?"

The simple question was one she couldn't answer. It had always been the curse which kept her in Brimrock, but what if it really *were* broken? What if she really could leave and experience life as she had always dreamed? What if there was no longer anything holding her back and she was finally free? Could she be so lucky?

"But you told him no, right?" asked Noelle the next morning. Now that the snow had dissolved into mush and the sun peeked out from scattered clouds, they had braved the porch of 1221 Gifford. Yukie was sprawled in Noelle's lap, in pure heaven from all of the neck scratches and belly rubs. Noelle dragged her nails across the spot behind Yukie's ear and Yukie writhed appreciatively in her arms.

"I didn't say no. I said I needed time to think about it."

"But it is a no, *right*?"

Selene shrugged from her spot beside Noelle on the porch swing. The chains were still frozen over with ice, which made any rocking unnatural and stiff. She folded up her legs criss-cross style and frowned as she stared out onto the prim and proper residential street she had called home her entire life. "It's funny because I've dreamed of leaving Brimrock for twenty-six years. And now I might actually have the chance and I'm stuck on what to do."

"Girl, you can leave Brimrock without *leaving* Brimrock. You don't need to go on some paranormal expedition around the country to get some traveling in," pointed out Noelle.

"Yeah, but why not? It sounds like fun—the kind of thing I've always read about. Maybe everything that's happened these past few weeks is a sign."

Noelle snorted, her bias clear. "Girl, a sign of what?"

"I'm supposed to go. Me meeting Aiden. Me fighting Mrs. Myers. Me getting fired from the library. Even the neck-lace from Luna."

The best friends fell into contemplative silence. For what must have been the dozenth time since the library incident, she reached up to grasp Luna's crystal pendant necklace before remembering it was gone. It had felt like a very real lifeline to her grandmother. Now that it was gone, it was as if her one tangible tie to Luna had been severed. The house was full of old portraits and knickknacks like figurines and vases, but was she going to live her life in an empty home full of ancient family memories or go out and make her own?

"Well…" Noelle sighed with audible lament. "What's going to make you happy?"

Selene searched her heart in the seconds it took her to answer and then a small smile curved her mouth. "Something new."

"You can start your own YouTV streaming show!"

Noelle's big brown eyes lit up as she raked her nails over Yukie's furry back. "Call it *The Brimrock Paranormal Files*. Give your boyfriend some competition."

"That's not exactly what I had in mind. I'll tell you what —I'll get started on that as soon as you and Shayla work things out."

"And that's my cue to exit," said Noelle, clutching Yukie to her chest as she rose off the swing. "Sorry, Yukes, but we'll have to finish those belly rubs some other time."

Selene called after Noelle, but her best friend merely tossed up the peace sign and mentioned calling her later tonight. She should've known Noelle would book it as soon as she brought up Shayla. The prospect of asking her out again had Noelle running scared. With a shake of her head, Selene abandoned the swing and retired inside, Yukie trotting at her heels.

The timing seemed preordained because seconds after she shut the front door and wandered down the hall, her cell phone rang. She answered it assuming it was Noelle calling to tell her she had forgotten something inside the house, or even Aiden to remind her about dinner tonight. She was wrong on both accounts as a cool, easy breezy voice she hadn't heard in years greeted her hello.

"How is my delightful niece doing today?" asked Uncle Zee as though he were a regular caller.

Selene almost swallowed her tongue in shock. Her wits trickled back in and she said, "Uncle Zee, I didn't expect to hear from you."

"Aren't those the best calls?" He tittered at his own question before clearing his throat and realizing he was the only one laughing. "I wanted to reach out and check on how you're doing. Was your Yule as festive and fruitful as I hope?"

"No, it wasn't—not really. A lot's been happening in Brimrock. Uncle Zee, a woman who had a grudge against Grandma Luna was going around town attacking people. She was some sort of enchantress, like a succubus that drained people's energy."

"That sounds extra eventful," he patronized. His tone never wavered from its sunny nature. "And what about that gem of a necklace I sent you? Did you get plenty of wear out of it?"

"I did," said Selene, frowning. "But it turns out it was magical. You remember Bibi Banks? She says it was a lunar crystal. I used it against the succubus and she evaporated into dust."

"It's a great piece. One of a kind. It's no wonder why it's been precious to Luna."

"Uncle Zee, do you understand what I'm saying?"

"Of course I do, Selene. I'm calling to check up on you, aren't I?" His second chuckle played like a lighthearted song from over the phone.

But Selene was far from amused. Her mouth flattened as she sucked in her lips and her brow pinched into a deep line. The cold from outside no longer chilled her skin, warmed up by hot irritation. After a lifetime spent being told not to ask questions, never to speak about family history, and denied any pertinent information about even something as crucial as her magical powers, she was over the empty conversation. She was done with being left in the dark.

"Why does everything in our family have to be some big secret?" she shouted out of pent-up frustration. "Why can't we talk like normal people?"

"I don't think our family has ever cared much about being normal."

"You know exactly what I mean! I've spent years in the

dark about what's going on—shushed whenever I asked my mom any questions about Luna or the family or even about my powers."

"Your mother was a sensitive soul. She didn't like questions."

A breath caught in Selene's throat and turned into a cough. She was so agitated she had forgotten how to breathe. She coughed and started pacing the hall, the many family portraits on the wall strangely watchful. Ranting to Uncle Zee was useless. No matter how upset she became, he was going to keep up his casual, head-in-the-clouds demeanor. She had never seen him act any other way…

"Never mind," she mumbled. "I should go. Thanks anyway for calling."

"Selene," he said before she could hang up, "I am *very* glad you're alright and that everything has worked itself out."

Among the many portraits, Luna's stood out most. It hung in the center of the hall in a heavy gilded frame, bigger than the others along the line. Luna's twinkling, dark-side-of-the-moon eyes followed Selene no matter which direction she went. Her face itself was soft but regal, a subtle confidence in her smirking expression. She was glamorous in every sense of the word, tight afro curls blooming like a crown, the precious crystal pendant shining around her neck. The corners of Selene's lips quirked, mirroring Luna regardless of how many years separated them, and her frustration melted away.

"It'll work itself out," she whispered more to herself than anyone.

Uncle Zee heard and reaffirmed, "It always does in the end. Don't you forget the family is here for you. One way or another. Luna included."

"Right," she drifted off, suddenly pensive. "Luna helped me when I needed it."

"And she always will. Have a good evening, Selene."

Selene stayed put leaning against the wall even after the cryptic phone call with Uncle Zee ended. She was no closer to having any answers about what was going on with her family, what had happened to Luna, or what she was going to do about Aiden's proposal, but she had a slight inkling.

As she admired Luna's portrait and thought back on the last few weeks, something told her the answers were out there. She simply had to go out and seek them.

––––––––

Selene frowned as Noelle gave her the cold shoulder. She pushed open the screen door, accepted Yukie by her leash and slipped her supply bag over her shoulder. No hello. No good morning. Definitely not any interest in how Selene was doing that day.

Yukie, as guileless and enthusiastic as she was by nature, dashed into Bibi's house and disappeared down the hall.

Selene straightened her glasses and said, "You're mad at me for going."

"You're damn right I am," confirmed Noelle. "What do you think I'd be doing? Celebrating?"

"Noe—"

"Selly, you're leaving. On some whim. How am I supposed to feel?"

"Sad," said Selene. Her frown deepened. "Because that's how I feel. I'm going to miss you. So much. *So much*."

"So much you're leaving."

"I have to. It's time, Noe. I've spent my whole life in this town. I've never even been to Cowbridge. *Cowbridge*, the town next door! It might feel sudden, but I've wondered my whole life what it'd be like to leave, go somewhere else for a while," explained Selene. Her frown transformed, flipping upside down into a small, optimistic smile. "Now, if I'm able to leave, I'm going to travel the country and explore like I've always wanted to. Not in books or in movies, but in person. It's corny to say, but it's a dream come true."

Noelle cut her gaze to the floor, staring at their boots. "I don't like Fudgeboy."

"Why?"

"He's…he's taking away my best friend."

A sisterly warmth filled Selene's heart as she put her arms around Noelle and pulled her into an embrace. They clung to each other for a while, in a strange way celebrating but also mourning their friendship—what had passed and what was to come. When they separated, Noelle rolled her eyes and bent her arms across her chest.

"I guess he's okay. So long as he treats you right. Take care of yourself out there. You better text me at least once a day. Calls too."

Selene smiled. "I will. And I'm going to be back. It's temporary."

"You don't have to worry about Yukie. Bibi and I got her. She'll be well-fed and spoiled with nightly belly rubs."

"Thanks, Noe."

"Did I hear my name?"

The scratch of Bibi's slippers increased in volume as she shuffled down the hall. She finally appeared at Noelle's side in the doorway, her wire-framed glasses on the tip of her nose. Crinkles bracketed her mouth as she smiled at Selene.

"You off to go globetrotting?"

Selene laughed softly. "Something like that."

"You take care of yourself. And you remember you're a witch. The little world out there? It's your oyster. You magic the hell out of it."

Both Selene and Noelle gaped at the older woman, star-tled by her expletive. Bibi dismissed them with an impatient hand.

"I made it three weeks. That's damn impressive."

Selene finished hugging Noelle and Bibi and even Yukie, and then started off toward her future. Aiden waited in Ghost as the vintage Dodge Caravan idled along the curb. She stuck her arm in the air for another wave at Noelle and Bibi and then slid onto the front passenger seat. In the back of the van was everything they would need for the next few months, luggage stuffed with personal belongings, and other supplies for a life spent traveling cross-country.

They hit the road and headed for the town border. Selene's stomach knotted as nerves leading up to the big moment had her second-guessing what they were about to do. What if they reached the border and she encountered the usual invisible magical force that held her back, preventing her from leaving? She'd be devastated.

"You alright?" Aiden asked as they turned onto the final road leading out of town.

Selene nodded, though she nibbled her bottom lip. "I'm excited."

"Me too. This is going to be an interesting six months."

Aiden slowed up as they reached the town border, glancing sideways at her. Selene didn't realize she was holding her breath until seconds in. Her knees were bouncing as she tapped her feet to expend some of the nervous energy jumbled up inside of her. She inhaled a shuddering breath and then exhaled it, giving a nod for the go-ahead. He nodded too, pressing on the gas.

Ghost roamed forward, shooting down the road as the town border came and went. She had clenched her eyes shut and grit her teeth, her glasses fogging up from the gravity of the moment. Aiden slowed up once half a mile outside of the Brimrock town border and he laughed. She opened her eyes, gaped at him like he'd performed a type of magic of his own, and she joined him, surrendering to a delirious brand of laughter.

"We did it!" she gasped. "I'm out of Brimrock. We crossed the border. The curse is broken."

"Another point for Team Impossible," Aiden teased.

She giggled and twisted in her seat, glancing backward at the road behind them. Brimrock shrunk more and more the farther down the road they traveled, once her entire world, now nothing but a pocket-sized blip in the distance. Her heart soared as, for the first time in her life, tomorrow seemed like an unknown. She couldn't wait to find out what it held, the possibilities endless, and her adventures only just beginning.

TO BE CONTINUED...

Thank you for reading *Black Witch Magic*, episode 1 in my new *Paranormal Hunters* series! This book has been a constant on my mind for about two years now, so I am beyond ecstatic to be able to share it with you! Selene and Aiden have been a pleasure to write, and I hope they've been a pleasure to read as well. :)

If you have a free second, please log onto Amazon and Goodreads to leave a review.

Also feel free to visit www.milanickswrites.com for more info on upcoming books as well as story extras.

ALSO BY MILA NICKS

STAND ALONES:

Love's Recipe

Happily Ever Afters

North Star Angel (Coming Dec 2020)

SERIES:

Paranormal Hunters

Black Witch Magic

Black Moon Rising (Coming April 2021)

Wild Horse Ranch

Chasing Wild Horses

Taming Wild Horses (Coming Jan 2021)

Wild Horses Coming Home (Coming Summer 2021)

Made in the USA
Monee, IL
05 November 2020

46788550R00215